THEY CLAIM THAT I WAS DEAD

FLORIAN FRERICHS

Encyclopocalypse Publications
www.encyclopocalypse.com

Cover art by Valeryia Losikava aka Fabifa
Illustrations by Stephan Warnatsch
Interior Formatting by Christian Francis and Sean Duregger

First Edition
ISBN: 978-1-960721-13-6

Dedicated to all outsiders.

"Satire may do anything!"

CONTENTS

JESUS IS HERE!

Spotify Playlist 1

1. CRUCIFIXION

DENSE AND RANDOM CLOUD FORMATIONS OBSCURED THE SUNLIGHT over an undulating expanse of land. The wind sighed, ushering in sheets of light drizzle. On a distant hilltop, a group of people had gathered in an apparent state of excitement. Some threw stones and churned up the sand with their feet. All were clad in archaic garb. On either side of the group, two wooden crosses had been rammed into the ground. A person had been nailed to each cross —one black woman, and one white. Both women were dead. Between their crosses gaped a third hole in the ground.

A murmur swept through the crowd, as six men in SS-uniforms approached, pushing a seventh man out in front. It was Nico Pacinsky, dressed in nothing but a tattered loin cloth and bleeding from several wounds on his body. Behind, six Japanese soldiers in the Tenno army uniform with silver heatproof Zetex gloves carried a red-hot, glowing crucifix. The drizzle was fast developing into fat raindrops that dissipated with a hiss as they hit the cross. Behind them, six Italian Blackshirts played a military march on their drums. At the sight of the two crucified women up ahead, as well as the hole in the ground between them, a listless and exhausted Nico registered the imminent end of the path. He began to mutter under his breath:

"Wanted: Jesus Christ. Accused of seduction, anarchic tendencies, conspiring against the state. Distinguishing feature: scars on the hands and feet."

As though following some ghastly choreography, the Japanese soldiers set the cross down as the Blackshirts and SS-men formed a precise circle.

"Alleged profession: Laborer. Nationality: Unknown. Alias: Son of Man, Bringer of Peace, Light of the World—Redeemer. The wanted person is of no fixed abode."

Two of the SS-men pushed Nico onto the cross. He was too weak to put up any kind of resistance. As he was lowered onto the red-hot steel, it burned into the flesh of his back like a slab of steak on a barbecue.

"He has no wealthy friends and mostly resides in poor areas."

The Blackshirts approached, brandishing cordless rivet guns. With a scream of metal-on-metal, they drove thick bolts through Nico's wrists and into the steel cross. As well as looking pretty mean in their matt red-and-black color scheme, the big selling point of these devices was that the batteries could be interchanged between different pieces of equipment. The glowing red cross with Nico bolted to it was pulled upright and secured in the hole with boulders.

"His milieu is made up of blasphemers, stateless persons, gypsies, prostitutes, orphans, criminals, revolutionaries, anti-social individuals, the jobless, the homeless, the condemned, the imprisoned, the hunted, the abused, the angry, conscientious objectors, the desperate, screaming mothers in Vietnam, hippies, deadbeats, junkies, outcasts and those sentenced to death."

The SS-men grinned spitefully at the crucified man and began to clap in ironic appreciation of his monologue. The Blackshirts and the Japanese soldiers followed suit, triggering exaggeratedly frenetic ovations from bystanders at pains to please their sinister overlords. But then Nico fell silent, his eyes rolled back and his face crumpled in a grimace. KABOOM! A bolt of lightning cracked the sky, drenching the entire scene in white-hot light.

———

Nico started up from a hospital bed, his head in a fog. He was enveloped in darkness. Nothing but a whisper of moonlight through the window grille. His head was bound; his left wrist bandaged. His right arm was linked up to a drip; a dull cry of pain escaped as he came to. This roused the man in the next bed, who had already introduced himself as retired philosophy professor Atze Schotenhauer (think Jordan Peterson at age eighty-five). For a brief moment, Nico thought it was his dead grandfather lying there. Then he watched as the old man turned away, cursing the world and humanity for not leaving him in peace.

Slowly, Nico began to realize where he was. He carefully lowered his aching head back onto the pillow. He noticed his girlfriend Claudia sitting at the other end of the room. She had obviously fallen asleep on the chair. As though sensing Nico's gaze on her, she woke up with a start and hurried over to his bedside. She didn't notice her phone falling from her lap onto the floor and skimming under Nico's bed. Grumbling at the noise, the old man pressed a button on the side of his bed. Another shot of morphine flowed through his veins and he began snoring softly.

"Nico! Are you OK?" whispered Claudia.

"What happened?" stammered Nico.

She grabbed his hand. "You had a car accident." Nico touched his head gingerly.

"What? How long was I out?"

"Just a few hours," his girlfriend reassured him. "You've got severe concussion, but otherwise everything's ok."

"Wow...all I can really remember...is a Mercedes in front," Nico murmured. "And then...there was a crashing noise."

Claudia slipped into the narrow bed beside him and pressed herself up against Nico's body. "Move over a bit.—The police said you totally lost it."

Nico paused to consider this. He vaguely remembered, as though from a dream, a vast inner rage vented not long before. "Hmmm...yeah, could be right."

Suddenly, Claudia twisted her mouth into a strangely seductive smile.

"The guys from the other car are suing for libel and disorder."

"Ah, fuck," Nico sighed. But he knew that actually, he gave less of a fuck than the day before. Something indeterminable was taking hold, stirring up a new emotional intensity within him.

Claudia had been snuggling up closer to him all the while and declared:

"Well...to be honest, it really turns me on."

Flashing him a mischievous grin, she removed her skin-tight top. Braless underneath, she pressed her pert C-cups against Nico's face. The bed squeaked; she tried and failed to stifle a giggle. With a serpent-like movement, she slid down beneath the covers, positioned herself on Nico's hips and sat up straight. Removing her panties with an expert flick of the wrist, she catapulted them into the air and onto the bed of the old professor.

Nico smiled; he was unsettled.

"Er, I...I've got a bit of a headache."

But there was no stopping Claudia now. He submitted to his fate. Her moist sheath enclosed his sword. She rode him slowly and carefully at first, but built up the pace before long. While at her Catholic girls' boarding school, Claudia learned—with a single simultaneous movement backwards and downwards in the cowgirl position—how to simultaneously stimulate both G-spot and clitoris. Nico didn't have a clue about any of this of course.

Actually, he barely knew what was happening to him. His throbbing, traumatized head was jolted about until the stars came. But Claudia couldn't hold back. She was overcome by a sudden surge of desire for her boyfriend. The tough guy story was a total turn-on. Maybe he wasn't such a loser after all.

Her whimpers roused old Schotenhauer from his morphine-induced sleep. He thought he must be hallucinating and rubbed his eyes in disbelief. But then he spotted the red G-string dangling off the end of his bed. As Claudia neared her climax and threw him a glance, he smiled and gave her the thumbs-up with one hand, while fumbling beneath his blanket with the other. Claudia laid it on extra thick especially for him, her body shuddering with the contractions of a gushing, squirting orgasm, leaving Nico on the edge of consciousness.

2. IT'S HIM

IN A HUGE CONCRETE BUNKER, SOMEWHERE DEEP DOWN BELOW THE earth, was a wall bristling with monitors. Facing that wall was an immense leather armchair, a "Dragons" by the Irish interior designer Eileen Gray. Demonic grimaces had only recently been roughly scratched into its wooden frame with a bread knife. A rare Ashera cat sat on the arm of the chair. A hand was stroking the cat, slowly, its owner deep in malicious thoughts. The hand was attached to the arm of the inscrutable Verne Zog. A being that transgressed the boundaries of regular human existence. In its entirety, his person was more than just physical or metaphysical power. Verne Zog had fingers in many pies—some earthly, some spiritual. His activities were all managed and monitored by his manservant and loyal flunky Magnus Max, a man of stunted growth.

At that moment Magnus entered the room through a hydropneumatic sliding door that opened with a hiss. He was nattily dressed as usual, in a bullet and waterproof tailored suit studded with 881 diamonds by the Swiss company Suitart, shrunk to Magnus' size in a boil wash.

"Noble Master Zog!" He greeted his boss with a nod.

"Yes, Magnus, dear friend and compliant servant. Proclaim thy message! I hope you've good news from the casting front?" Zog was impatient to know.

"Master, something's come in from Berlin," the three feet tall Magnus reported excitedly.

For a brief moment, Zog appeared electrified.

"From the capital? Have you finally found a suitable actor to withstand my exorbitant megalomania?"

Magnus skirted the question somewhat: "Well yes… my local police contact sent me a video."

The master recoiled: "No more casting tapes, please! If I have to watch any more of that amateurish crap in vertical format I'll get exanthema on my retinas."

"No, my good sir, noble master Zog. I think…he's back.—It's him."

Zog stopped stroking the cat from one second to the next. It jumped off the chair and ran away.

"Who? Who do you mean? Not…Klaus?"

Magnus Max stepped up close to his master and whispered: "My venerable master Zog, I think our search may at last be at an end!"

Zog was speechless for the first time in his life. Eventually, he said: "Go on then, play the video."

"Of course, master." Magnus replied with a bow.

He took a remote control out of his suit pocket and pointed it at the wall of the bunker. Surveillance camera footage began playing on all screens simultaneously. The clip showed two cars at a stoplight; a Smart car rammed into the back of an S-Class AMG Mercedes with blue undercar lighting.

"A car accident," Zog commented laconically. "The wonderful world of Newton's laws. Where unchecked forces prevail without purpose. There are thousands of videos like this on YouTube and the like, I don't see the value of playing it here now!"

"If you will just be patient for a moment, noble master," said Magnus and pointed at the monitor. Seconds later, our hero Nico Pacinsky is seen jumping out of the Smart and giving the guys in the Mercedes a dressing down, gesticulating wildly as he does so. They fled back into the sanctuary of their beat-up car and sped away.

Verne Zog was far from impressed. "Hmmm—does the video have any sound?"

Magnus shook his head.

"The material comes from a surveillance camera. But my contact said the interaction was savagely preternatural. With monstrous expletives, threats and apoplexy. Just like...Klaus."

"Well the video doesn't prove anything," Verne Zog was dismissive.

Magnus rewound the footage to the moment when the two men from the Mercedes made off. "Just look: These guys are built like brick shithouses. See how desperate they are to get away from the manic guy! We can't simply ignore that."

"What do we know about the person who caused the accident? Where exactly does he live? What's his job?" asked Zog.

"I'll find all that out, Master. The only verifiable piece of information at present is that he's in hospital."

Zog considered this for a moment. Then he spoke: "Very well, Magnus. Take the helicopter and go to the capital. But when you're conducting your investigations, please bear in mind that the dramatic action of my screenplay for *'They will claim that I was dead...'* comes much closer to a true understanding of the existence of the universe than any other philosophical or religious theory that humanity has thus far produced. That's why we must finally make this movie. And if we should actually get Klaus for the leading role, I'll direct him for the last time in order that we might die together in the apocalyptic finale of the shoot—and posthumously win the silver medal for misunderstood artists at the Telluride Film Festival in Colorado!"

"That again?!" Magnus rolled his eyes wearily.

Zog showed him the door with a barely perceptible hand movement: "Now go on your way and find out a bit more about this..."

"His name is Pacinsky. Nico Pacinsky."

3. BERLIN, HUH?

JUST TWENTY-FOUR HOURS BEFORE THE ACCIDENT, NICO HAD BEEN wandering aimlessly through the leafy Berlin district of Charlottenburg. Although he'd just been invited to audition at the Ballhaus-Ost Theater the next day, he was an emotional wreck. Wallowing in his inadequacies, he could see no way out of his existential misery. Nothing was ever gonna change. Despite that, he couldn't be bothered to commit suicide. He liked watching movies too much—and he wouldn't be able to do that if he killed himself. And once a quarter, there was sex with his girlfriend Claudia.

Nico's clothing belied his mental turmoil. The white shirt and dark blue pants were freshly washed and ironed. Taking stock of his own future, he ambled languidly and with a touch of melancholy through the neighborhood around Savigny Platz, past the celeb magnets run by Albanians doing a pretty good imitation of Italians. He peered at the many sleek luxury motors double parked all over the place—many of them with tickets tucked under the wipers. And so what? Small change for people with this kinda cash. And for anyone else as well.

Nico was plugged into his white Apple headphones, listening to a song by the Berlin hip hop punk band K.I.Z. The song was about a man who boxed through windows in passing. Nico would've liked to be able to do that. But he just wasn't the type. He noticed an AMG S Class with lowered chassis, blue undercar lighting and 612 HP leaving its parking spot on the bike lane. As the car's ESP engaged, the roar of the engine drowned out the song. Fifty-fifty annoyed and envious, Nico stopped in his tracks and watched the Benz go. Reaching into his pocket, he pulled out his ancient iPhone 6s with its cracked screen, hit the volume button and decided to switch from hip hop to classical. The device played a piece by Paganini. Nico imagined the virtuoso carrying out a frenzied and merciless attack on his violin, while the women in the audience creamed their panties.

At that moment he was jostled from behind and roused from his daydreams. A man wearing a Hertha Berlin soccer shirt had tripped and catapulted a scoop of ice-cream onto his shirt. The man looked up at him and Nico was ready to dismiss his apology with a fixed smile. But he then realized that the soccer fan was pissed at him! Nico had been in his way. And he was not about to apologize for anything.

"Hey, I'm the one walking here, y'know?!" He snarled at Nico. The man then looked in disgust at his squashed ice-cream cone and held it directly under Nico's nose. He didn't give a monkeys about Nico's white shirt. "How the fuck am I supposed to eat this now? Un-fucking-believable."

Affronted, at first Nico had no clue how to react. But then a sardonic smile spread across his face. He reached for the holster underneath his shirt and in a single fluid motion pulled out an old Walther pistol, released the safety catch, cocked it and fired it three times with ice-cold indifference into the man's back, shattering his spine. A few passersby leaving a kindergarten found themselves spattered with a rain of blood and bone marrow, but instead of falling to the ground, the Hertha fan turned around to face Nico, completely unharmed, and spat, "Fuck you!"

Striding off in a rage, he hurled the mashed up ice-cream cone against the wall of a house, where it left a large stain. That blended in nicely with all the wedges of torn-off posters and graffiti. Nico thought he'd better quickly dispose of his gun in one of the orange bins by a traffic light, but then he realized two things: that he'd never owned a pistol or fired a shot from one. Grimacing, he inspected the ice-cream smudge on his otherwise snow-white shirt. There were still a few raisins stuck to it.

"Rum raisin. Yuck!"

Pushing on through streets teeming with tourists and West Berlin movers 'n' shakers, Nico eventually reached a row of 1960s buildings on a side street. Unbeknownst to him, two women were looking down from a top floor balcony. As soon as they saw him, they rushed back into the apartment. Nico crossed the street where a man was gathering up small change from the ground. As he fumbled in his pocket for his key, the door of the house was opened from inside and an enormous white hare jumped out onto the pavement sidewalk. The outsized buck threw him a friendly nod. From the undulating shape of the body in the costume, Nico reckoned it must have been a woman, but he couldn't be sure. He watched the hare as it went on its way, until the door shut on his nose.

He entered the hallway and dragged himself up the ninety-six steps to the top floor. As he reached it, puffed out and his ears still ringing with the music of the demonic fiddler Paganini, he ran into a second, lightly perspiring but extremely attractive woman. She had clearly just closed the door of his apartment behind her and was hastily buttoning up her blouse. Without paying him any further attention, she pushed past him, removed her damp wig, loosened her padded bra and took off her high heels with a sigh.

Was the woman a transvestite? A cross dresser? A drag queen? And why was the gorgeous creature exiting his place? Before he could say anything, she was already a few floors down and in any case, Nico wouldn't have had the nerve to speak to her. Opting to ignore rather than wonder any longer about these curious sightings, he entered his apartment deep in thought. Once in the hallway, he removed his shoes, placing them neatly in their assigned slot on the shoe stand, and hung his key on a board above. The walls were adorned with several framed and evidently valuable painted posters advertising films from the 1970s starring Klaus Kinski (if you don't know who Klaus Kinski was, google some of his videos. He was a German-Polish blend of Jack Nicholson, Nic Cage and Dennis Hopper—with a twist of common slavo-germanic megalomania). Scraps of an argument in Romanian escaped from the living room. Nico shuddered at the realization that his girlfriend Claudia's mother was still installed as a long-term guest in his home. At some point he would find the courage to eject her.

He hesitantly entered the living room. It was stuffed to the gills with movie devotionalia, his sacred shrine. In a glass case next to the television was the filthy old white floppy hat worn by Klaus Kinski during the filming of *Fitzcarraldo;* several display cases on the right-hand wall contained all sorts of odds and ends: Kinski's vampire teeth from *Nosferatu*, signed cards, soundtrack CDs, a few used condoms and even the shrunken head of an extra who'd triggered the crazed main protagonist during the filming of *Cobra Verde*. The extra hadn't injected sufficient pathos into his portrayal of a corpse and was beheaded for it. The living room walls were also adorned with neatly framed posters, pictures and vinyl discs bearing the image of Nico's idol.

On the sofa sat Erna Rosetzki, Claudia's mother. There was something alluring about her. She was buttoning up her pants, her skin glistening with a thin film of perspiration. As for Claudia, she was wearing nothing but a hastily-thrown-on Smiths T-shirt (with the slogan: *Barbarism Begins at Home*) and a G-String with an image of Morrissey on the front triangle. As soon as Nico walked into the room, the two women stopped their Romanian argument and looked at him indignantly.

"Nico! I thought you weren't coming back until eight," said Claudia.

"Er, no." Nico thought for a moment. "I thought I said eighteen hundred hours."

Claudia pointed to the radio-controlled clock on the wall: "But it's only five."

Nico hated it when Erna and Claudia excluded him from their conversations by chattering away to each other in Romanian. Not that they cared! He could only make out fragments of the dialogue that followed:

"He must have seen Bunny and Pedro in the hall!" said Erna.

Nico could understand two words at least:

"Bunny?! Pedro?!"

"No... She said...er...bani," said Claudia. "That's the plural of the subunit of the Romanian currency the Leu. And then she said...pedestru. That's Romanian for pedestrian."

Erna nodded and gestured towards the window: "Yes, that's right. There was a pedestrian on the street...who...was picking up a few coins. Really!"

She turned her eyes to Claudia, who in turn looked at Nico, who for his part tried to avoid the gaze of both women. After a few seconds' silence he said: "Weren't you planning to leave today, Erna?"

"She's my mama. And she can stay as long as she wants!" Claudia hissed at him, slipping into a pair of skinny jeans.

Nico sighed and pulled on a pair of white velvet gloves, taking a book out of the display case. It was a signed first edition of Klaus

Kinski's autobiography '*All I Need is Love: A Memoir*'. The pages were already fragile and stained yellow with age. He sat down on the sofa and started to read. He needed a distraction from the unwanted house guests. Erna and Claudia continued their discussion in Romanian:

"When are you going to finally get rid of this loser?" Erna asked her daughter.

Hearing the English word loser, Nico looked up involuntarily, but then quickly forced his eyes back down to the pages of the first German gonzo manifesto.

"Yeah, mama. I know. But he pays the rent," said Claudia.

Her mother started on her usual rant: "A girl with a body like yours should marry a banker or a doctor. Or a pimp for all I care! But not a good-for-nothing like this one here, papering the walls with the demonic image of a madman!" She gestured at the many Kinski posters in the room.

"You're right, mama. As soon as I've sold it all off, I'll split with him. Promise."

Claudia tugged her phone out of her back pocket and launched the app of an online auction house. She checked the status of a listing titled *Large Klaus Kinski Collection*. She yelped with excitement: "€4325—and just thirty-seven hours until the end of the auction. That should be enough for a fresh start."

Nodding in confirmation but without an ounce of sympathy, Erna replied: "It'll break his heart…"

"The poor thing…"

Both women looked over at Nico, who sensed their gaze and lost his focus for a moment—but quickly crept back behind his paper shield.

Seconds later, a sulphurous smell and an intense heat rising up towards his face interrupted him yet again. Looking up from his book, he could hardly believe his eyes: the entire apartment was lit up in blue-green flames behind Claudia and her mother! They had turned into rabid, cackling succubi hovering in the middle of the room with their leathery wings. Fixing a sinister gaze on her partner, the demonic Claudia lunged at him with her cat o' nine tails, which ripped a deep groove in his face with a loud crack.

4. A NEW MORNING

WITH AN IRRITATINGLY REPETITIVE, ELECTRONIC SOUND ALTERNATING between audio frequencies of 200Hz and 400Hz, the old Braun alarm clock on the bedside table fulfilled its duty and roused Nico from his sleep. He immediately put his hand up to his cheek, to feel for the wound inflicted by Claudia's whip. But there was nothing there. His gaze fell on the clock's flip-number display: 7:00 am. Hitting a worn-out button on the top of the device he turned off the alarm and rubbed his eyes. Then he discovered Claudia stretching out next to him. But instead of waking up, she pulled the covers over her head. Nico wanted to give her a kiss, but decided against it for fear of waking her up and somehow pissing her off. Instead, he whispered in her ear, barely audibly: "I'm going to have a shower. Then I'm off to an audition. Wish me luck!"

Claudia made a noise. Had she said something? It could've been her tummy rumbling. Nico couldn't tell. He sighed, waited for a couple of seconds and then got up. He walked over to the wardrobe and took out clean socks, crisp light-blue underpants, a white shirt and a dark blue suit. His next stop was the bathroom.

Under the shower, he allowed the powerful jet of water to crash over his body as though trying to sluice away layers of encrusted dirt. A small waterproof radio was fixed to the glass shower cubicle with a suction pad. He switched it on and skipped through the programs. A classical music station was playing the overture to Richard Wagner's *Lohengrin* and this stopped Nico in his tracks. The piece had always had a strange effect on him, catapulting him into a state of temporary rapture every time he heard it. For a moment, he bathed in the musical river conjured up by the poet-composer and recalled the Nietzsche quote—that "without music, life would be a mistake." Like others might have sung under the shower, Nico recited—inspired by the music and just like Klaus Kinski once did—passages by the philosopher as he washed his hair:

"You are hurt by every fetter, restless, unfree spirit, always triumphant and still bound, more and more nauseated, destroyed, until you drink the poison from every balm—Woe! You too kneel at the cross, you too! You too—Conqueror! Always I stand before this spectacle, breathing prison, sorrow, resentment and tomb, between consecrated clouds and church smells, strange to me, sad and frightening to me. I danced, throwing the fool's cap into the air, then I jumped away!"

Claudia banged hard on the door with her fist. "Nico, who are you talking to in there?—Let me in, I need to go!"

Nico rinsed the soap off his face and leant out of the shower to unlock the door. Claudia quickly tugged down her panties as she came in and headed straight for the toilet.

"Why do you lock the door? I know what you look like down there..."

"Force of habit," Nico said dismissively.

The sound could be heard of a viscous fluid hitting the side of the toilet bowl. From the shower cubicle, Nico looked at his girlfriend crouched on the toilet. Despite her lovely body, it somehow wasn't a good look.

"Stop staring, you weirdo!" She chided him and he turned away. "I've got my period," she added by way of explanation.

Vaguely repelled, Nico took a deep breath and climbed out of the shower. He collided with Claudia who was getting up from the toilet and pressing an adhesive pantyliner into her briefs.

"And who were you talking to just now? Yourself again?"

"What?—No, no. That was something on the radio."

"Aha."

As he dried himself off, Claudia left the bathroom without another word. Nico watched as a trickle of blood ran down the inside of her right thigh.

———

A short time later, he was hurrying past the brick arches underneath the S-Bahn tracks on Savigny Platz. As he nipped into the station and up the steps onto the platform, he was just in time to see the train pulling away. Breathing hard, he looked up at the LED display. The next train was due in nine minutes.

"Fuckin' marvelous!"

He pulled his old iPhone out of his pocket, shoved the earphones into his ears, scrolled through the menu, selected the album '*Kinski reads Villon*' and clicked on the track '*Worshipped and Spat On*'. Against the backdrop of the initially gentle, but then gradually more frenzied voice of his idol, Nico observed the billowing mass of humans emerging from another platform and spreading out around him to wait for their connection. Despite the large number of people there was a curious stillness in the air; no one was talking to each other. Most commuters stared at their smartphones to pass the time and deflect unwanted attention.

Nico's observational gaze betrayed neither disgust nor antipathy. With open curiosity, he trained his attention on those intent on standing out from the crowd. That crowd was, for the most part, just an unobtrusive grey mass that feared nothing more than a deviation from the daily routine. But now and again he'd spot an individualist—after all, Berlin is well-known for people claiming that title. Right at the front stood a young lesbian couple whose offensive stance was intended to show everyone that they were proud of their probably very recent coming-out. Alongside them was the Green Party deputy and former Red Army Faction attorney Hans Christian Ströbele (think Bernie Sanders on steroids). He always took an old bike with him onto the S-Bahn to make it clear that despite having had cancer and access to a parliamentary limo service, he chose to travel sustainably. His beloved beat-up bike might have blocked a row of three seats, but that wasn't his fault. So many other cyclists followed his good example, that there was never enough space in the designated bike carriage.

On the other platform, Nico could See the former US Ambassador and Commander of the American Sector, John Kornblum. He was waiting for someone to mistake him for Henry Kissinger, and to then correct their mistake with a smugly-formulated phrase. To his left, a group of migrants tried to draw attention to themselves by being generally loud and leery as well as by playing German hip-hop on their Bose soundbars. It wasn't working. These Berliners were hard nuts to crack. For sure, the four boys from Russia, Turkey and Croatia would've loved to have been like 2Pac or Biggie, but didn't take it any further than aping the look. After all, they had their futures to think about. The upcoming apprenticeship. A potential professional life! A Schöneberg latex and leather gay guy in skin-tight black leather trousers, barely concealing his impressive coil pierced with a bullring, showed off his full, plaited Viking beard as he rebuffed a few clean-cuts with a rightswipe on GrinDr A rugged bear such as he was didn't want anything to do with smooth-shaven yuppies. He was searching for his next otter.

All around and in between were crammed the worst excesses of T-shirt and full-beard-sporting hipsters. They basically had no place in Charlottenburg; they were heading to their Mitte girls armed with jute bag and kombucha bottle, to create the next Internet commercial for PayPal or an as yet unknown off-the-wall startup brand in the cafés around Torstraße. In Nico's ears, Kinski as Villon was just working up to a furious tirade that triggered the same from Nico. Suddenly, he cried out at the top of his voice: "Who are you?!"

No one appeared to notice him in the slightest, so he yelled even louder: "Who the fuck are you?!"

A few normies looked at him briefly before quickly disappearing back into the indeterminable grey mass. In desperation, he whispered once more to himself: "Who am I?!"

This time, a deathly silence descended and each and every person at the station stared at him. The gaze of his fellow humans was neither sympathetic nor judgmental, but it was precisely this that hurt his heart. Was he really so insignificant? At that moment the S-Bahn came rushing into the station and ground to a halt. One half of the crowd jostled past him into the pale-red carriages of the Berlin-Brandenburg transport association, while the other half continued to wait for the train on the other platform. Nico squeezed himself onto the train as the doors closed on a signal that could have been straight off Star Trek.

———

He exited the train at Schönhauser Allee and hurried up the stairs in the direction of Greifenhagener Straße. He ran past rows of shops, all of them still shut, and fought his way through the mass of bleary-eyed techno tourists and 'locals' drawling in their Swabian dialect, people who've controlled the territory of Prenzl'Berg since anno 1996 and since their migration claim that jokes about Swabians in Prenzlauer Berg stopped being funny a long time ago. But of course those jokes *were* still hilarious. And they'll remain so throughout eternity.

5. BALLHAUS-OST

Nico arrived at the Ballhaus-Ost sweaty and out of breath. He paused for a moment to collect himself. As he did so, he noticed a poster in a display case advertising the next theater production: *The Quick and the Enraged*. Nico gathered up his courage and strode through the main entrance into the foyer, where there was no one to be seen at first.

"Hello?—Is anyone there?"

A gorgeous suicide girl with dark skin, nose ring, colorfully tattooed arms and long blue hair shaved at the sides entered the foyer from a side door. She threw Nico a friendly nod—he responded in German with a shy smile.

"Good morning. My name is Nico Pacinsky, and I have an appointment with the Director...Christoph Gräve."

But the suicide girl just beamed at him in effusive openness:

"Oh, I'm terribly sorry—but...isch spresche nischt wirklisch deutsch." She had a sexy British accent.

"Oh, okay. No problem at all. English is fine for me," Nico answered honestly.

"Great. Thank you! By the way, I am Gwyneth. I know I should learn the *deutsche* language. But Berlin makes it too easy for me. Everybody speaks English around here!"

"Well, I can switch back into German?" answered Nico with a smugness that shocked even him.

But Gwyneth just laughed: "Oh, please don't!"

"Well...I'm actually already pretty late for my appointment with Mr Gräve, so..."

"Oh, of course. Follow me, please," said Gwyneth, heading off down the corridor.

———

She took Nico to the office of theater director Christoph Gräve. He was instantly recognizable as a genius—judging by his outward appearance at least: He was smoking an e-pipe with nicotine-cherry-vanilla flavor, wearing a white velvet scarf and leafing through the pages of a script that was clearly giving him a headache. He massaged his forehead as he read, striking passages of dialogue through with a red marker, muttering as he did so. His spacious office was rather chaotic: with papers, theater posters, old books and manuscripts all over the place, although there did appear to be some kind of order that only its creator could decode.

There was a knock at the door, and Gräve appeared relieved at the distraction. "Come in!"

The portal to the theater's creative power centre opened and Gwyneth entered. Nico followed rather timidly behind.

"Christoph, this is Nico Pacinsky, your nine o'clock," she said.

"You're eight-and-a-half minutes late!" Gräve always spoke quickly and with great precision. As he did so, he always chose the ductus of his words in such a way that left the final interpretation of his statements to his interlocutor. This meant that Nico couldn't quite guess whether the director was joking or whether a tardiness of just under nine minutes really did go against the grain.

"Yes, I missed my train. Please accept my apologies."

Gwyneth nodded once more at Gräve and left his office through a side door. Gräve offered Nico a chair: "Very well. Please sit down."

Nico did as he was told. But because Gräve didn't have an appointment calendar and didn't initially know the identity of his guest, there followed a few seconds of awkward silence. Until the director seized the initiative. "Well, tell me: What can I do for you?"

"Yes, er...I applied to your job advertisement in Tip magazine, and you called me in for an interview."

"Ah yes, that's right, correct. Er...right now I don't know, where..." Gräve scrabbled around in his papers, but couldn't find Nico's application anywhere in the chaos.

"No worries!" Nico interrupted the rustling. "I can sum it up for you now: I've just ended my twelve-year career with the German army and I want to reinvent myself. I love theater, films, musicals...acting. I would really love to be on stage myself one day. Then I saw your ad for a permanent position as theater extra. And I thought..."

Gräve couldn't help but smile at Nico's lofty ambitions: "And you thought: Great! That's my ticket to Hollywood?"

Nico felt bulldozed. "Yes, well...no—not directly..."

Gräve jumped up from his chair and walked towards another side door. "Follow me. I'll show you something! And if you still want to join our team afterwards, the job's yours."

He was gone within seconds, leaving Nico speechless for a moment. He only knew artist types like Gräve from books and television. The Director was an extrovert and anarchic person, as well as being a total showoff. The complete opposite to Nico. He moved along the corridor at such speed that Nico had trouble keeping up with him—and then the director started talking to himself as he walked, "*As a former German Chancellor once said: if I had visions, I'd go to the doctor.*" He stopped abruptly and grabbed Nico's shoulders: "Nico!—That was your name, wasn't it?"

"Er, yes. Nico Pacinsky."

Gräve's eyes were pulled wide open, and he nodded almost ominously but with zeal and anticipation. "Nico! I *have* visions!"

The director immediately loosened his grip and continued quickly on his way. After a few meters they reached an unassuming grey metal door. Opening it dramatically, Gräve gestured to Nico to go in first. Nico stepped through the door with some hesitation and found himself on the theater stage. From here, he could look out into the auditorium, which was totally empty apart from a few tripods and lights. He noticed several metal cables hanging in the center of the room. Attached to them were what looked like art objects—but Nico couldn't make them out properly in the dark. Gräve grinned happily as he looked at Nico's fascinated face and asked: "What do you see, my friend?"

Nico replied cautiously; he thought it was a trick question: "An auditorium and a stage—a very beautiful auditorium."

"You see a stage!—But what do I see?"

Gräve left a pregnant pause, but Nico was intelligent enough to understand where the manic theater type was going with this: "Maybe you see a play?"

Gräve uttered a half-crazed laugh; he was enjoying his guest's quick-witted perception. "A play! Yes! Exactly!—I see *my* next play!"

Nico knew instinctively what his next question had to be: "And what's it about?"

Gräve was pleased by Nico's curiosity and began to talk, pacing up and down the stage as he delivered the following monologue. He presented his ideas in pantomime style.

"Undercover police officer Brian gains access to the illegal road racing scene and hopes to be able to find out the perpetrators of several truck raids. Despite losing a race, he wins the respect of Dominic, who's clearly mixed up in the raids. Brian finds himself in a dilemma, because on the one hand his boss wants to see results, but on the other there's a friendship developing between the two men. The situation is further complicated by the fact that Brian falls in love with Mia, Dominic's sister. Then there's a clash between Brian and Vince, one of Dominic's loyal followers. To Mia's annoyance, Brian confesses his intentions and eventually discovers the location of the next raid. While Brian prevents it from going ahead, Dominic and Mia manage to get away. After a race opponent attempts to kill Dominic's side-kick Jesse, Brian is able to arrest Dominic but at the last minute, helps him to escape —Ultrafast races! Megahot babes and boys! Thrilling action!— and I'm calling it: '*The Quick and the Enraged!*'"

Nico's mouth was wide open—and not necessarily because he was impressed. While Gräve proudly waited for applause, Nico was speechless.

"I'm speechless."

"Of course you are!" Gräve erupted. "Because this is the kind of great thinking that only a few people can put into words!"

"Well, I reckon Klaus Kinski would now say the following..." Without any kind of warning, Nico yelled at the top of his voice, gesticulating wildly as though possessed: "Who's ever heard such drivel! It's so dull and stupid your subsidized ass should be shot to the moon...or to Holland!"

He then immediately reverted to the cool and calm Nico Pacinsky: "But I personally find the idea pretty good."

He took a step back and as he did so, trod on a mechanism concealed in the floor that released the steel cable construction on the ceiling: the cables tightened in an instant and the art object, which the stage lighting now revealed to be an oversized pink papier maché cock, came hurtling directly towards Nico and

FLORIAN FRERICHS

Gräve like a phallic missile. Nico instinctively stepped out of its path at the last moment, but Gräve was hit straight between the legs. He collapsed with guttural cries of pain.

"Oh, shit! Are you OK?" exclaimed Nico.

Gräve could hardly breathe: "You'd better leave now! We'll be in touch…"

Nico wanted to respond somehow, but then exited the room with his head bowed low, while Gräve writhed in agony.

———

In the foyer he met Gwyneth, who gave him a friendly wave.

"Leaving already? How did it go?"

"Just perfect. I think Christoph will call me very soon."

"Great!"

"Sorry, but I'm in a hurry," Nico lied, just to get out of the building as quickly as possible.

"Sure.—Have a nice day.—Would love to work with you…see you soon."

"Yes…same here…Thank you!"

And so he left the theater the same loser as he had been before. What he didn't realize however; Gwyneth's parting remark concealed something akin to an amorous invitation.

6. DETRACTORS

Still reeling from his disastrous job interview, Nico dug out his iPhone and launched a car-sharing app. For the journey home, he didn't want to put himself through another trip on the oh-so-cool-and-hip Berlin city transport system. The display showed an electric Smart close by and he booked the car with a swipe. He then started walking towards the vehicle's location. On a one-way street leading to Helmholtzplatz, Nico rounded the corner and watched as a BMW 5 station wagon, model E39, parked forwards in a disabled parking bay. The driver made such a ham-fist of it that the rear of the vehicle blocked the narrow one-way road preventing any cars from passing. But instead of properly maneuvering his vehicle into the parking space, the clearly not-disabled BMW driver just got out of his car and walked away. The beamer was blocking the path of an old Audi 80 with a classic car registration plate, model B2. The guy behind the wheel of the Audi wound down his window and yelled after the BMW driver—who was heading for a nearby house: "I geddit, even though you're not disabled, at least you park as though you are, huh?"

The BMW driver flipped out straightaway, ran towards the Audi and reached through the open window to grab the driver's sun glasses off his nose. In the flurry of ripe language that ensued, as the two men locked horns in their territorial battle, Nico carried on towards the point indicated on the app. Finally approaching the Smart, he fumbled for his Car2Go membership card and held it against the card reader. There was no initial response from the vehicle. So he presented the plastic card again, holding it against the windscreen at precisely the same moment that the car opened...and immediately locked itself again! Now the display showed that the vehicle was occupied. Nico checked the cracked display of his iPhone. In annoyance, he saw from the car-sharing app that the rental period had already started. This meant his credit card was already being charged, but he still didn't have any wheels. And of course, he could only end the rental from inside the Smart. He pulled emphatically at the door handle but it remained firmly shut. With a groan, he looked for an emergency telephone number on the app, found it and clicked on a button to establish the connection. It rang. It rang again. Nico started getting jittery by the sixth ring, but then came redemption: "Good morning, Mr Pacinsky, what can I do for you?"

"How do you know my name?"

At that moment, the Smart's warning light blinked briefly and with a loud clack, the doors announced they were ready to be opened. Dumbstruck, Nico hesitated for a second and pulled the handle once again. The door really was unlocked.

"We've unlocked the vehicle for you. Can I help you with anything else? For example, can we offer you a discounted minutes package for €19.99?"

Nico was bowled over by the efficient service and also rather overawed, so much so that he hung up without another word and returned the phone to his back pocket. Then he got into the car and closed the door behind him. On the large steering console display in the middle he read *Welcome to Car2Go, Nico Pacinsky!*

and heard the German dubbing voice of Kevin Spacey greet him: "Welcome to Car2Go."

Nico removed the car key from the glove compartment, started the electric engine with the press of a button and adjusted the seat and mirrors. Just before putting the vehicle into reverse to exit the parking space, he had the idea of connecting his iPhone to the car via the radio's bluetooth interface. The playback started straightaway on Spotify, and on the display in the car appeared an album cover showing the image of Klaus Kinski. From the loudspeakers rasped the jarring voice of the actor, who was now reciting the poem *Detractors* by Francois Villon.

During the journey, which took Nico first along Schönhauser Allee to Bornholmer Straße, the humbled young man battled his way listlessly though the dense morning traffic, always viewed by the Berliners as a welcome continuation of the war by other means—a struggle that regularly spilled over into skirmishes and battles with fatal results. Focused more intently on the poem recital than on the traffic, Nico listened to the crazed yowling coming out of the speakers and in his mind's eye, he saw himself in Kinski's place standing on the stage at the Ballhaus-Ost. He performed the poem with Kinski's gestures and impetus, liberated from all consideration of the reception of others.

"In lime, still unslaked, in iron pulp, in salt, salpetre, phosphor blazes, in urine of female donkeys in heat, in snake poison and in hag's spittle, in dogshit and water from the bathtubs, in wolf's milk, oxen's bile and latrine flood: In this juice detractors shall be stewed. In the brain of a tomcat which does not fish anymore, in the drivel, spouting from the teeth of the rabid dogs, mixed with monkey's piss, in quills, pulled out from a hedgehog, in the rain barrel, already floating with worms, croaked rats and the green slime from mushrooms, glowing like fire in the night, in horses' snot and also in hot glue: In this juice detractors shall be stewed. In the vessel where everything ends up which a physician extracts from the festering bowel, speaking of pus and polluted secretion, in ointments they salve into their slits, the whoring tarts, to keep themselves cold, in all the sludge which remains in the laces and the crevices: In this juice detractors shall be stewed. My lords, pack all the clean things into your trousers, to fill up the keg, also add the smell of a pig's arse, and when this has fermented for four weeks: In this juice your blaspheming tongues shall be stewed."

KRABOOM! Immersed in himself and Kinski, Nico had rammed the Smart straight into the back of a Mercedes S63AMG with blue undercar lighting. Nico didn't have a seatbelt which meant despite the airbag, which gave him a resounding punch on the ear, his head hit the steering wheel hard. As he reeled from the impact, trickles of blood began to run into his eyes from a number of wounds forming a wreath shape on his forehead. Trying desperately to collect himself, he watched through the cracked windshield as two tattooed superjocks in Ed Hardy T-shirts got out of the Benz to inspect the damage. There was barely a scratch on the Mercedes dreadnought, but the Smart was pretty mashed up and the two beefcakes stoked each others' anger towards Nico. Kevin Spacey's dubbing voice cut through the tension: "The rental has now finished. Thanks very much!"

Paule, one of the two gym freaks, approached the Smart with Nico inside it: "Yo! No eyes in your head, dude?"

His buddy Murat, on the other hand, was thinking more along administrative lines: "Phewwee! I'll call the fuzz. I hope you've got good insurance, sunshine!"

"Man, man, man! That's gonna be expensive, broski!"

"Check out the lower rear fender: We only just did that last week, homie!"

"Come out, bro!"

The two muscleheads stood right in front of the driver's door of the Smart. They had a good view of the messed up Nico staring back at them through eyes fogged up with blood. For a brief moment, Murat seemed almost concerned: "Wallah, are you hurt, Habibi?"

"Just wait till I'm done with him, fam." Paule smirked.

At that moment, Nico's eyes stretched wide as though suddenly roused from a long slumber. He threw open the dented door, climbed out and for the first time yelled back! He was overcome by a fit of lunacy, roaring and gesticulating like a wild animal. Spit sprayed from his mouth and in all directions. His language was completely inarticulate and he could only emit scraps of words. He used so many expletives, insults and terms all straight off the office for political correctness' index, that even Bill Burr's fourteen-minute rant against the city of Philadelphia sounded like a best man's speech at a wedding. Cowed by the violent verbal eruption, Murat and Paule dived back into their car and sped off to the nearest police station, engine roaring, to report the accident. As for Nico, he collapsed and was quickly surrounded by a cluster of people.

7. RESURRECTION

IT WAS EARLY MORNING WHEN THE DOOR OPENED TO NICO'S hospital room. A friendly nurse in her fifties entered, waking Nico and Schopenhauer next to him with a trilling voice: "So, good morning gentlemen, I hope you've both slept well, time to wake up and have your medication."

His head still in a fog, Nico didn't quite register what was going on. But the old man turned to face the wall. Approaching Nico's bed, the nurse glanced at her clipboard: "Today we're doing your colonoscopy. So no breakfast for you, but please swallow these laxatives."

Now, Nico was fully awake:

"Colono...what?"

"Your intestinal flushing," said the nurse brightly.

"Er, I thought I had some kind of head injury."

The woman took another look at her clipboard. "Intestinal trauma—says it right here!"

"Well, there's nothing wrong with my stomach. It's my head that hurts a bit."

Glancing one more time at her notes, the nurse held them in front of Nico's nose. Her tone was friendly, but exceedingly firm:

"That can't be right. Colonoscopy! It's written right here. And the files don't lie. If it says here that you're due a colonoscopy, then that's what I have to do."

Old Schotenhauer turned to face her. "Well, if he doesn't want it—I'll have one!"

"We'll come to you in a moment, Mr Schotenhauer," muttered the nurse.

Nico smiled at her pleasantly, but with flashing eyes: "Maybe you picked up the wrong file. My name is...Klaus."

"Er, am I in some kind of asylum?" She exclaimed, as the friendly mask slipped off her face.

Schotenhauer intervened with a raised forefinger: "In the world of appearances, strict determinism prevails!"

Irritated, the woman smacked a pill cup on the old man's night table. "Please swallow these, Mr Schotenhauer!"

He was very happy to oblige, greedily guzzling the medication. Then he pointed to the grilled windows, a rather strange sight for a hospital room, and continued with another pearl of wisdom: "In the intelligible world there is neither space nor time and therefore no causality."

At that point a vibrating tritone sounded from Claudia's smartphone, up to that point unnoticed under Nico's bed. Schotenhauer and the nurse simultaneously looked in the direction of the noise. As for Nico, he leaned over the armrest to peek beneath the bed, his head upside down. He could see his girlfriend's smartphone on the floor. The display was still illuminated; a just-sent message appeared on the lockscreen. With some effort, he fished up the phone and sat upright with it in bed, looking at the message:

Congratulations! Your Article 436763232320: Klaus Kinski Collection has been sold.

The nurse hissed: "Mobiles are only permitted on silent on the ward. This isn't an Apple store, after all!"

But Nico wasn't listening. He had unlocked the screen, opened the online auction house app and feared his heart might stop. As though stunned, he let the phone fall on the hospital floor, where it shattered into several pieces. He stammered: "Yeah, well...that's unbelievable...that fucking whore."

The nurse was horrified: "Excuse me?"

Nico sprang out of bed, tore the cannula out of his arm and yelled at the nurse: "People only regard bad behavior as a kind of privilege because no one is punching them in the mouth!"

Still dressed in hospital gown, he embarked upon leaving the hospital, slamming the door of the room shut with a loud bang. The nurse was left standing there in total bewilderment. "But a colonoscopy is a really sensible preventative measure for anyone over the age of thirty-five," she called out after him in genuine concern,—her eyebrows twitching skywards as she discovered Claudia's red G-string on Schotenhauer's bed.

———

Swearing and repeatedly flicking his hands up towards the sky, Nico dashed out of the Charité hospital and in the direction of Invalidenstraße.

"I'll send them back where they belong, those cretins!"

He crossed the street without checking for traffic and an approaching taxi had to slam on the brakes to avoid hitting him. The driver called out of his window:

"Are you tired of life, or something?"

With the famous Kinski-esque twist, Nico turned around slowly on his heel and with a diabolical stare, worked himself up in a lather over the audacity of the man who dared to address him. "That's unbelievable! He's crazy! He's completely mad, this idiot!"

"Hey, have you lost the plot?" asked the taxi driver in total seriousness.

But Nico was still bellowing: "First remove the log from your eye. And then see how you pull the splinter out of my eye!"

"Where did you escape from, dude?" The taxi driver shook his head. Nico took a deep breath to collect himself. Reverting to the old, submissive Nico Pacinsky, he spoke to the taxi driver as though nothing had happened: "Could you maybe take me to Charlottenburg?"

"Doesn't look as though you've got any cash on you, son," said the taxi driver.

"My wallet is at home. I'll pay you when we get there. I promise," Nico assured him.

The taxi driver thought for a few seconds. But as a Berliner, he'd given lifts to even stranger passengers during his twenty years behind the wheel. "Okay, jump in.—Hold on though: I hope you're wearing jocks underneath that."

Nico opened the door of the Mercedes and looked down at himself for the first time. Now he noticed that he was still wearing the white hospital gown—and no jocks. The taxi driver looked at him pityingly and got out of the car swearing under his breath in Turkish. "Hiyarin Oglu!"

He opened the boot to fetch a roll of disposable plastic seat covers. Deftly rolling one cover out, he pulled it over the headrest of the back seat on the right and in a single sweeping movement, spread the rest of the plastic out over the seat. Nico got in and Mustafa closed the door behind him. The taxi sped off and Nico noticed how after just a few seconds, the skin of his naked backside began to sweat.

———

Meanwhile back in the hospital room, the door opened a crack. Magnus Max, carrying out the orders of his master Verne Zog and armed with a bunch of flowers, entered the room and peered cautiously into the empty bed in front of him, as old Schotenhauer spoke: "He made off in something of a hurry just now. Cursing like a fishwife!"

Magnus hadn't clocked that there was someone else in the room. "Ah, good day sir."

"Mornin'," replied Schotenhauer.

"Well then...I'm looking for, for my brother. Nico Pacinsky," lied Magnus.

"Your brother? Identical twins, eh?" The old man laughed at his own joke, which Magnus didn't find at all amusing.

"I don't appreciate jokes about my physicality, noble squire!"

"Banality takes on all forms, to hide behind them: it cloaks itself in magniloquence, in bombast, in tones of superiority and elegance and in hundreds of other forms," countered Schotenhauer.

Magnus Max pulled a Smith & Wesson 500H double-action pistol out of his side holster, —one of the largest revolvers ever made,—and pointed it at the old man. "You'd be well-advised not to provoke me."

"OK, OK. Simmer down."

Magnus waved his weapon around: "So, perhaps you'd like to tell my girlfriend Susi here, where Mr Pacinsky disappeared off to."

"How the hell should I know that?" the retired philosopher exclaimed.

Magnus cocked the gun, climbed onto a chair and pointed it directly at Schotenhauer's head. The old man almost had a heart attack.

"I really have no idea," Schotenhauer was adamant. "He scarpered as soon as he heard the word colonoscopy."

"Are you shitting me?" said Magnus threateningly.

"He left that phone," Schotenhauer tried to offer the diminutive hitman something, and pointed at the shattered smartphone. A nurse had come by to pick up all the bits and place them on the night table with Nico's other belongings.

"He saw a message on it and totally lost it," said Schotenhauer.

Interested in this piece of news, Magnus hauled himself up on the side of the table with just one arm like Stallone in *Cliffhanger*, gathered up the pieces with the other free hand and inspected the pile.

8. NUGUNGA PYO 6ESEO GUTOMULEUL DAKKANAEYAHABNIDA!

IN THE COOL NEIGHBORHOOD OF KREUZBERG, IN FRONT OF THE COOL Korean restaurant Kimchi Princess, was a melee of cool people with cool drinks in their hands and cool gluten-free rucksacks on their backs. A punk who moved to the capital from Hameln or Bielefeld, wearing a real leather coat with a huge patch sewn onto it with the phrase *Fuck America—Fuck Capitalism*, was just withdrawing some cash from the ATM to buy the latest editions of the satirical magazine *Titanic* and an electronics mail order catalog at the station kiosk that wouldn't accept his EC, Visa card or Apple-Pay. Just along the way, on the forecourt of the huge Al-Khattab Mosque, erected on the ruins of a Bolle supermarket, two Greek mime artists were performing. Their aim: to show the audience by way of expressive movements and gestures how EU interest rate policies were benefiting radical parties in their homeland. Of course, neither they nor their passing onlookers fully understood the content of the presentation. But the show was nevertheless nice to watch and had a certain aesthetic value. Moreover, the two mime artists displayed a slice of the Kreuzberg attitude to life: Anything and everything can be politicized, even if you're clueless about the actual mechanisms.

Inside the restaurant, built out of old shipping containers, there were just as many hip people from all continents as outside it. It was loud, the atmosphere dominated by part-time vegetarians sizzling their organic beef on hotplates brought to their table. As they prepared their food, many of the diners blustered with their friends over the connection between the repression of the working class and omnipresent consumerism. The feasting over, such people ordered an Uber with their latest-generation iPhone and retreated to Mitte, to their refurbished historic tenement block apartments financed by their parents from southern Germany.

At one of the tables sat Christoph Gräve. The oddball artist fit right in here, and even though he'd never admit it: He only liked this place because he could usually expect to be recognized by people who'd seen his plays. Gräve enjoyed something of an underground cult status among a handful of culturally-aware Berliners who would've naturally rejected him and started calling for a boycott had his productions enjoyed any success beyond the city's borders. Gräve was in the process of enthusiastically outlining his latest project idea to two women from the Culture & Censorship Authority at Berlin's governing Senate. It was the same story he'd shared with Nico at the interview. The approval of Waltraud Beermeyer-Stöpsel and her colleague Irmgard Al-Hassani was necessary to secure large subsidies from the Senate to Gräve and the Ballhaus-Ost. The director was tense as a result and spoke even faster than usual.

"...ultra-fast races! Mega-hot babes and boys! Thrilling action! —And I'm calling it: *The Quick and the Enraged!*"

Irmgard and Waltraud exchanged a speechless glance. With a nod of his head, Gräve waited for their positive response to his pitch, "It's great, don't you think? Not cheap to produce, I'll admit, but..."

Irmgard interrupted him with the following, "Well, this is the situation, Mr Gräve. The new senator for culture has decided to withdraw all funding from your establishment if you don't produce a few hit shows soon."

Waltraud joined in: "So that's why we'd like to encourage you to have a good think about which play is going to be your next,— and discuss its content with us in advance."

Gräve's voice almost failed him. "Are you cutting me off? Please remember—who produced *Schindler's List,—The Musical*? Or the *Transformers-Monologues*? That was me!"

"No one wants to cut you off," Irmgard did her best to smooth down his ruffled feathers. "And rest assured: The Senator hasn't forgotten your past successes!"

"But you've not been getting the audiences recently," Waltraud added before delivering the final blow: "For that reason, from now on all creative decisions at the Ballhaus-Ost must be signed off by Irmgard and myself."

Gräve started hyperventilating, "You're subjecting me to a creative castration?!"

"We want a new beginning, Mr Gräve. Together with you."

The director gasped. "And what about my new play *The Quick and the Enraged*?"

"Well, I'm sorry to say it, I think we need to consider alternative material," said Irmgard. At that moment an exceedingly attractive Korean waitress approached the table to serve the raw meat for the grill and a few side dishes. As she scattered the little bowls across the table, Gräve jerked sideways and had to vomit so violently that even the most hard-core Kreuzberg partygoers looked up from their tables and stared pityingly at the director. Waltraud coolly handed him a serviette, and the Korean waitress issued a crisp order over her left shoulder:

"Nugunga pyo 6eseo gutomuleul dakkanaeyahabnida!" (Someone needs to clean up vomit at Table Six!)

9. THE DESTRUCTION OF THE TEMPLE

To the observer, the scene in Nico's living room was bizarre and über-decadent. Claudia and her mother were conducting an extremely strange fetish session in the midst of Nico's Kinski collection. Both women were dressed as vermin exterminators chasing an older swinger couple through the apartment. Strapped to the pest controllers' backs were pressure spray canisters affixed with huge black rubber dildos secreting some kind of steaming fluid. Their two clients had a rare fetish known as formicophilia and were bound together like the Human Centipede.

Playing her part to the max, Erna screamed in disgust at the insect, threatening to exterminate it. Using the spray canister, she showered the clients with a *toxic* solution made earlier out of sugar water and porridge. Pretending to be in the agonizing throes of death, the front female part of the centipede emptied her bladder and bowels, while the back male part came in orgiastic twitches. Still bound together, they sank to the floor and played dead.

But then suddenly Nico was standing in the room and the entire scene froze, as though someone had hit the pause button on an off-the-scale weird porno video. Erna, Claudia and the

centipede fetishists looked in silence at the living room door. Nico
had just walked through it. He was still wearing the hospital gown
and obviously nothing else under it but his birthday suit. The two
fetish clients protested that they'd booked the clinic games for
next Tuesday and that they wouldn't be paying for the premature
appearance of the handsome young stud in hospital attire.

"Nico, what are you doing here?" Claudia asked in a matter-of-
fact tone.

"Me? What the hell are YOU doing?" was Nico's response.

Claudia was silent for a moment. "We...we're earning a bit of
cash on the side."

Now, Nico properly registered what was going on. Up to that
point, he hadn't noticed the orgy. "I don't give a crap about your
porno business!—It's the Ebay stuff I care about! Did you sell my
Kinski collection?"

Claudia's mother Erna intervened: "All this frippery? You can
be happy we got such a good price for this trash!"

Nico fell silent and for a few seconds, he regarded the scene
like a still life painting in a gallery. He felt a wave of unbridled
rage surge within him. It would only take the slightest spark to
unleash itself. Instead, he suddenly turned around and made for
the door, hanging his head in despair. What else could he do?

Erna turned to her daughter and said in Romanian: "Off he
goes, the loser."

Nico understood the word *loser* and instinctively grabbed an
umbrella from the stand by the door. His anger erupted with a
battle cry. With a powerful turn, he hit the display case containing
Kinski's hat so hard that the thick glass shattered into a thousand
pieces sending the shards across the entire living room. Then he
tried to smack Erna over the head with the umbrella, missed her
by a hair's breadth and slashed open the suede sofa with the tip.
With a grimace, Erna sprang sidewards and crashed into the other
glass case, smashing it into pieces. When the human centipede

began to panic, total chaos broke out. The two clients were bound together so tightly with a thick metal and leather harness that it was impossible to free themselves without help. And since the two fetishists obviously wanted to escape in different directions, they ended up crawling through Nico's apartment completely out of control. As they did so, they pulled over pretty much everything and anything in their way. Nico meanwhile used the umbrella like a baseball bat to hit all the Kinski paraphernalia out of the cases and off the walls and in a superhuman frenzy, whacked them at Erna and Claudia who took cover behind the sofa. "He didn't say shut your mouth—he took a whip and cracked her in the mug! You stupid sow!" yelled Nico.

Grabbing one of the huge black dildos, he turned his attention to the centipede. After several hefty blows at the kidneys, he sent the plastic phallus flying in Claudia's direction with a guttural roar. But she caught the missile, plucking it from the air like a footballer going for a touchdown. The movement sent her stumbling backwards into the shelving unit, which also imploded burying her in debris. With an animalistic roar, Nico threw himself once again like a wrestler onto the centipede. Driven by fear and horror, Claudia and Erna managed to stagger out of the apartment. Eventually the Human Centipede was also able to wrestle itself free of Nico and scurried as best it could behind the fleeing women. Nico pursued them with threads of spittle dangling from his chin like a rabid wolf. Nico left the apartment and slammed the door shut. This in turn toppled a yucca palm marking the end point of the tornado of infernal rage that had ravaged the apartment. A blanket of silence descended over the chaos.

A short time later, the ottoman sofa opened and the diminutive person Magnus Max climbed out, wheezing, his head flushed bright red. He'd only wanted to install a few surveillance cameras in the apartment when he'd been surprised by Claudia, her mother and the two clients. He managed to hide inside the couch at the last minute. He'd heard everything.

"Holy shit!"

Without wasting any more time, he gathered up a few papers and sealed envelopes from a side table, stuffed them into his pockets and bolted, as quickly as he could, from the scene of devastation.

———

The taxi driver who'd brought Nico home was still waiting outside the house. He was pacing the pavement impatiently, having a conversation with himself: "I knew it. A freeloader. But no, I just had to be Mr Nice Guy yet again..."

The door of the tenement block opened and the taxi driver hoped that this time, Nico would be heading over to him with cash to pay his fare. But instead, he saw something that surprised even him. And he was a Berlin taxi driver. First came Claudia and Erna dressed as sexy pest controllers. Clearly in a panic, they sprinted down the nearest side street. They were followed by the human centipede, scarpering around the same corner.

A few seconds later, Nico finally emerged from the block and approached Mustafa the taxi driver with a smile, still dressed in his hospital gown. "Here you go, my friend. Thanks for waiting. What's the damage?"

You could've knocked Mustafa over with a feather. "€47.50."

Nico handed him a €50 note. "Keep the change. And thanks again!"

"Do you need a receipt, son?"

Nico negated with a chummy tap on Mustafa's shoulder. Unnoticed by both men, Magnus Max slipped out of the building and dived into his double-parked Bentley. He started the engine and floored it.

"Speedfreaks," Mustafa thought to himself.

Nico went back into the house, whistling contentedly, while Mustafa, shaking his head, returned to his taxi, where he found an agitated businessman waiting to be taken to *Artemis* in Halensee. Competition between the city's many brothels was fierce, and Mustafa was paid €20.00 for every customer he brought there. At the end of every month, he paid the cash into a Deutsche Bank savings account to pay for his daughter's education.

10. ASCENSION DAY

THE SNOW-COVERED, POINTED PEAKS OF THE ALPS SURROUNDED A gigantic estate secured with barbed wire fences and surveillance cameras—a breathtaking panorama of staggering natural beauty and human ingenuity. Alongside the manor house there was a kidney-shaped swimming pool. Dressed in a brown bathrobe, Verne Zog lay on a sun lounger catching some rays. His pasty, bare legs were crossed. The Ashera cat was sitting on a little table beside him, being lovingly stroked by Zog.

From the door of the summerhouse, Magnus Max appeared on a red self-balancing Hoverboard and entered the pool area. "Noble Master Zog, I have no more doubts. It's him!"

"Magnus, faithful friend and companion, wonderful that you have returned from the capital unscathed. Is there concrete, empirical evidence for your bold theory?"

"I laid my hands on Nico Pacinsky's girlfriend's mobile phone and thoroughly analyzed the data during my return journey."

Magnus took the patched-up smartphone out of his pocket and called up the auction house app. On the screen appeared the selling form for the article *Klaus Kinski Collection*. Magnus held the phone out for Zog, who although he was fascinated by this information, wasn't completely convinced:

"Interesting. But not really watertight. You know how terrible it would be to get this wrong! We need to be absolutely sure before we attempt a casting!"

"But noble master, what I experienced in his apartment—the orgy—the torrent of rage, the collection, I have no more doubt. But of course, I will conduct further investigations should you so wish."

Magnus performed a 180-degree turn with the hoverboard and was about to speed off through the hydropneumatic door, when Zog ordered him back: "Wait. What does this Nico Pacinsky do for a job?"

"Not much really, it would seem: twelve years in the army. Currently registered unemployed. Unhappy in love. His girlfriend is a sly one—she's got fingers in all his pies—and in a lot of other places as well, if you get my drift."

Verne Zog started to get impatient. "Magnus! What do Mr Pacinsky's future plans look like?"

"He wants to get into the theater. I found a good dozen unopened rejection letters from various establishments. He's applied to numerous theaters, operas, agencies etc. and been given radical short shrift from all of them."

Verne Zog considered this, chewing agitatedly on his thumbnail. "So he really does want to be an actor? We should take advantage of that!"

Magnus nodded. "He even appears to have responded to a job advertisement at the Ballhaus-Ost and attended an interview there. So far, he's not been rejected or accepted."

"Get Christoph Gräve on the phone immediately!" ordered Zog without further hesitation. He picked up a remote control and pressed a button. The staggering Alpine panorama projection disappeared and was replaced by dozens of digital screens showing scientific analytical data, share prices and surveillance videos from all over the world. One window showed a call being put through to Christoph Gräve.

After a couple of rings, the Berlin theater director picked up: "Yes, who is it?"

———

A few hours later the sun had gone down and Nico sat completely drained in his living room in the dark. All the bulbs had been broken and the wallpaper scratched from the walls. The floor was wet, because the radiators had been torn off the pipes and thrown through the plasterboard walls. Nico had evidently dedicated the last few hours to thoroughly dismantling his apartment so that almost nothing remained intact. All the furniture, but also his Kinski collection, had been atomized into such tiny pieces you could have sieved them through a tennis racquet. Now he stood up and meandered aimlessly through the ruins of his old life. All the while quoting from Bertolt Brecht's *To My Countrymen* and running a long butcher's knife over a grindstone in his hand. His voice was half an octave higher than usual and he spoke in a jarring style:

"You, who survive in cities that have died. Now show some mercy to yourselves at last! Don't march, poor things, to war as in the past. As if the past wars left you unsatisfied: I beg you—mercy for yourselves at last! You men, reach for the spade and not the knife! You'd sit in safety under roofs today. Had you not used the knife to make your way. And under roofs one leads a better life. I beg you, take the spade and not the knife! You children, to be spared another war. You must speak out and tell your parents plain. You will not live in ruins once again. Nor undergo what they've had to endure: You children, to be spared another war. You mothers, since the word is yours to give. To stand for war, or not to stand for war. I beg you, choose to let your children live! Let birth, not death be what they thank you for. You mothers, choose to let your children live!"

Yet again, Nico was overcome by a violent fit of rage. Spotting a photo of Claudia and himself on the floor, he stabbed it so hard the tip of the knife broke off in a flurry of sparks and flew into the ceiling.

Somewhere under all the debris the landline telephone had survived and emitted a plaintive ringing sound. With wild, jerking movements Nico freed it from the detritus and was just about to destroy it like everything else but then changed his mind and answered it, screaming: "Who dares to call?" into the receiver.

It was Christoph Gräve calling him from his office, sucking with obvious great pleasure on his e-pipe. After the disastrous dinner with the two ladies from the Senate, he'd been put in a much better mood by the mysterious call from his old acquaintance Verne Zog. "Hello. Christoph Gräve here, from the Ballhaus-Ost theater. Mr Pacinsky, is that you?"

"I'm not sure what to say to that," said Nico.

"Er...I was very impressed by our recent conversation here at the theater!" Gräve lied.

"Great. Pleased to hear it. But I don't need any free applause."

"My colleagues and I would very much like to welcome you onto the team at Ballhaus-Ost."

Nico was so shocked he dropped the receiver.

"Hello? Hello, Mr Pacinsky? Are you still there?" asked Gräve.

But Nico needed a few seconds to collect himself. After all, it appeared that his life dream was about to be realized at that precise moment. With some effort, he pulled himself together, picked up the receiver and reverted back to his own voice: "Sorry. The line went dead for a moment."

"Sure, no problem," said Gräve. "I'm having breakfast at the

Café am Neuen See tomorrow. Why don't you join me and we'll deal with all the paperwork then? Let's say, 10:00 am?"

"Yes. Er...I...absolutely, thanks a lot," stammered Nico, totally perplexed.

"No, thank YOU. See you tomorrow, Mr Pacinsky."

"See you tomorrow."

Nico hung up and thought for a moment. But then a diabolical grin spread across his face.

"Nico,—I think you need to get some help." It was the voice of Claudia, who had suddenly appeared in the doorframe behind him.

With the Kinski-esque twist, Nico turned to her with eyes stretched wide. Globules of drool dripped from the corners of his mouth and his voice changed back again to the jarring falsetto, "No, I don't need any help, you she-goat. I'll help *you*. I'll help the world! And with my willpower, make an eternally lasting impression on it! But you and your mother, just see where you end up! I hereby banish you from my temple."

Slightly unnerved, Claudia stepped towards her barely recognizable boyfriend. "Nico,—who do you think you are?" she asked.

He looked back at her, his eyes flickering: "I'm the person I have to be.—I'm Klaus Kinski!"

RASKOLNIKOV'S TRAUMA

Spotify Playlist 2

11. SO CLEVER

Some Euries may recall the strangely brilliant television arts program presented by Alexander *Kluge*—incidentally, German for 'clever'—broadcast late at night on private channels in the late nineties and early noughties. In it, universal genius Kluge—a germanic mixture of Ben Franklin and Dick Cavett, legal scholar and graduate of the Fritz Lang school of filmmaking, sat hidden somewhere behind the camera addressing other universal geniuses with a soft angelic voice posing *clever* questions that his interview partners never actually answered.

Especially memorable performances were delivered by Peter Berling, who never appeared as himself but always played someone else. The actor and medieval historian, who had also featured in several Herzog-Kinski productions, was almost always picking a fight with Kluge. And not forgetting of course—the great dramatist Heiner Müller (perhaps the German Norman Mailer). His response to Kluge's question,—"what he associates with the moon"—was worthy of a Nobel prize. First, Müller took an indulgent pull on his cigar and had to cough. He then made a redolent pause to consider what he actually did associate with the moon. Müller took a second drag on his cigar and coughed once more. His eyes were mildly glassy, but bright as buttons, and he gave a half-smile. Then he began to answer, "The memory is weak, almost milky. But I see my mother at the garden fence, and there's some sort of commotion. Grief. Cars are going by. This was a time when there weren't as many cars as there are today. I also remember a truck collecting something large...what it was, I can't say exactly. I walk towards my mother, and she tells me that President Hindenburg has died."

There's a pause. One second. Two seconds. Alexander Kluge pursued the original question, "And, er, what does all that have to do with the moon?"

Heiner Müller looked up at the ceiling, puffed on his cigar again, coughed, thought. One second. Two seconds. "Well *I* think that's got something to do with the moon."

Another of Kluge's more bizarre guests was none other than our hero Nico Pacinsky, invited onto the program after his initial success in Christoph Gräve's production at the Ballhaus Ost theater. In the role of the actor Klaus Kinski at the time when *Fitzcarraldo* was being filmed, Nico was expected to answer a number of questions in a dialog with Kluge. But just like so many other priceless treasures of TV culture, the Betacam tapes were completely destroyed in the great electromagnetic incident at the Berlin Adlershof archive.

There is however a stenographic transcript recently found by estate researchers in the attic at the Kluge Foundation. But, owing to the traumatic eruption of violence at the close of the interview and also due to the apparent insanity of both protagonists, this transcript was immediately confiscated by the Central Committee for Culture in Berlin-Wilmersdorf and held under lock and key ever since. However, we are able for the first time to reproduce an, at least to some extent, coherent thought protocol compiled by our proofreader and equal opportunities officer Stanislav Würfelstein. He used to work as an interview cutter for Kluge's production company DCTP and prepared the interview tape for broadcast. But the program never went on-air...

A ticker starts running against a black background,

'Nikolausz Günther Nakszynski, born 1926 in Zoppot, Danzig, is seen as a natural acting talent. He's already appeared in more than fifty films and plays. These include cooperations with David Lean, Bertolt Brecht and Werner Herzog. He's currently working with Herzog on the operetta-style film *Fitzcarraldo*, with a screenplay long thought to be unworkable. Klaus Kinski reports on the jungle ordeals and the *slave driver* Werner Herzog...'

"Herr Kinski, yes? You're currently shooting the film *Fitzcarraldo*, most of which is set in the jungle. What's it like working there with a man like Werner Herzog?"

"Well, you clearly haven't read my book then have you? I don't want to talk about that god-damned slave driver anymore!"

"But you're still working with him nevertheless?!"

"What's the point of these idiotic questions? Have you any idea how much I'm being paid to do it? I'm doing it for the fucking cash! And nothing else."

"As Bertolt Brecht says: the capital always wins, doesn't it? Although that doesn't necessarily have to mean the accumulation of funds, but also a capital consisting of knowledge, talent or suchlike. As in the case of you and Herzog, is that right?"

"Are you trying to provoke me? Just hearing the name Herzog gives me a brain hemorrhage. This asswipe of a *filmmaker* is so utterly talentless yet arrogant beyond measure..."

"Whereas you're regarded as a natural talent, correct?"

"A talent of nature? Natural talent? I'm epochal, I'm monumental...nothing more!"

FLORIAN FRERICHS

"And you've made great films and plays with great names of the film and theater world..."

"I've made moronic movies for moronic producers, yes!"

"For example, you played Jesus Christ,—back then in the Deutschlandhalle arena, wasn't it? Why?"

"I *am* Jesus! *You* are Jesus. Even I don't know whether Jesus existed or not. That means, he's existed thousands, millions of times. But not the official Jesus of the church. After all, and I'm not spilling any secrets here when I say that the church has made Jesus the second biggest whore after me."

"And what exactly did you hope to achieve with this play?"

"Ha, well you might as well ask a bird why it flies! Why a bear's a bear! It's a natural necessity, you understand? Why are you doing this interview here?"

"Is playing particular roles a natural necessity for you?"

"I don't know where you're going with this. Particular roles? It's meaningless. I mean, I don't even read the scripts most of the time."

"Nietzsche says for example that Goethe was no Faust, right? He created the character because it was necessary for him to do so at that particular point in his life."

"I tailor the roles to suit *me* and not the other way around. So it would appear what you say is true, I'm a natural talent. But I am me. And I am everything! Goethe also said this: I could have been anything in my life. From a murderer to whatever."

"When you said that to Brecht, he hired you on the spot, is that right?"

"Precisely! You see, *that's* what I call true genius!"

"*Nothing is true. Everything is permitted.* And because you are you, you can be anything as long as you're given the opportunity?"

"Well, I must say I think it's very healthy when I'm understood."

Staying in the role of Klaus Kinski, Nico casually pulled a

pistol out of his jacket. An old Walther PPK from 1931. He began to dismantle it, carefully examining the barrel of the gun before fixing Kluge with his piercing gaze: a scene straight out of a spaghetti western!

To be continued...

12. SO PLUMP

A FEW WEEKS BEFORE THE ALEXANDER KLUGE INCIDENT, NICO again found himself at the practice of his psychologist Dr Vary Plump, sitting on what was by now a rather worn, but exceedingly comfortable wine-red leather couch. You know the kind: a couch that invites the sitter to sleep rather than talk. Set at the heart of the ultramodern shotcrete house with windows barred from the outside, the couch felt like a cliché from a cheap novel (not like this one). But that was probably wholly intentional. The Sigmund Freud books in the built-in bookcases, the understated glass table with the Montblanc biro pen placed on it—nothing was there by chance. The scene was set perfectly! Nico noticed the grilled windows once again. Had they always been like that, or had the metal bars only just been put there? Nico desperately tried to recall, but then allowed himself to be distracted by Dr. Plump's nipples, which he thought he could make out vaguely but unmistakably through her cashmere sweater. Or was this also just wishful thinking on the part of a profoundly disturbed lunatic?

For some reason the handsome red-haired psychologist, who was an interesting blend of Jessica Rabbit and the B movie icon

Ilsa, had always had a bit of a thing for Nico. But her feelings were not of a romantic or even sexual nature. Her fondness was much more an amalgam of sympathy, maternal feelings and a certain fascination for psychological degeneration, rather like not being able to look the other way when passing a pile-up on the highway. Although it should be said that Dr. Plump was genuinely trying to help Nico ease his neuroses.

In any case, Nico also hadn't so far thought of Dr. Plump as a potential sex partner. For sure, he'd clocked her curves, which she cleverly accentuated by apparently concealing them beneath ostensibly subtle clothing. In fact those curves had lodged themselves so firmly in his consciousness that they sometimes flashed up in his head on the few occasions that he and his girlfriend Claudia indulged in a spot of intercourse. But then he always promptly dispelled thoughts of Dr. Plump from his mind's eye.

Of course, his idol Klaus Kinski would've wasted no time in making a play for the psychologist. And for her part, Dr. Plump would've probably responded positively to a man like Kinski. But had Nico already progressed that far? Yelling, rampaging, offending other people and berating them unnecessarily, he'd been working on all these things in recent weeks, applying them with some success and certainly making a few enemies in the process. At last! But would he take the final step and become the full Kinski package? Could he one day feast on all the plums just like his idol? Clean every carpet? Peel every peach? Pop every cherry?

That's just crazy, the thought blitzed through his head. He *was* Klaus Kinski! And no one else! Unnerved by Nico's invasive and neurotic thoughts and feelings, he decided to go a step further and launch an experiment. He regarded Dr. Plump's body so that she would not only notice his gaze, but also feel it. The

63

experiment was a success, although she tried to gloss over it with her next psycho-philosophical statement. Nico thought he could detect a slight reddening of her cheeks and he smiled inwardly. If his eyes could elicit such a response in her face, what might be going on in her panties?

Well, his megalomaniacal assumption happened to be on the nail: her lace briefs from H&M, available as a twin pack for €12.99, were eighty percent acrylic and therefore bad at absorbing any kind of moisture;—which, alongside the excitement unwittingly evoked by Nico's wandering eyes, also resulted in a certain degree of discomfort for Dr. Plump. It was all she could do to deploy her vastly superior intellect and defuse the situation with a monolog:

"You see, Nico, our brains are basically the same as they were 50,000 years ago. The DNA of homo sapiens has changed only slightly, if at all. If we used a time machine to bring a baby from the Stone Age to contemporary Berlin and allowed it to be raised by a regular family, the child would like exactly the same things and have the same problems and experiences as all other children in our society today. But that also means that our entire sensorium and the processing of absorbed information still functions according to highly archaic models. Up until five minutes ago, so to speak, people's lives depended on such decisions as: Do I have to fight against this herd approaching my waterhole? Or can I find a way to manage with it? Do I have to bring my family to safety? Is this a fight or flight situation? Human life always depended on such decisions, that were based on *information*. And like few other creatures on this planet the human being, blessed with an above-average-sized brain, learned to make decisions grounded in available information. This enabled him to improve and prolong his life and establish a totally new form of global society. We're now living in extraordinary times. Just a few seconds ago on the timeline of humanity any information from the past and the present can be called up by anyone, at any time and in any place.

Moreover each and every one of us has the ability to connect with anyone electronically and exchange information in a matter of milliseconds. The dependence on information has become a billion-dollar business that certainly comes with many advantages and conveniences, but barely any research has been conducted on how it's impacting upon our species. As I said: our bodies rely on the flow of information. Now, for more than two decades we've been placed in a permanent state of fear and alarm: terrorists, migrants, men, viruses...all potential threats to life. Bad news sells, because we're *addicted* to it like a heroin junkie. And we haven't learned to differentiate what information is crucial to our lives and what perhaps doesn't affect us at all. For example, nuclear power plants were decommissioned in Germany because in Japan, 9,000 kilometers away, one of fifty-four reactors exploded following the most severe earthquake in the nation's history. Violent earthquakes are more or less an impossibility in Germany, but since then Germany sometimes even has to import energy from the neighboring countries in which we have absolutely no control over the security of the nuclear plants. A mistake that's solely based on the fact that we haven't learned to cope with the *flood* of information and that we're immediately relating every piece of bad news and unfortunately also every piece of misinformation to ourselves and our own environment, even where there's no verifiable or merely a secondary correlation. Our brains function like a search engine algorithm: The more frequently a piece of information is called up, the higher it climbs in our internal rankings. If, for example, we're repeatedly hearing about a particular source of danger that's potentially lethal for just a few people in the world, we'll automatically consider this to be relevant to ourselves as well and conduct ourselves accordingly, because we perceive the threat of death for the few as a danger to us too. And this *sensed* knowledge, which spreads like wildfire via the media, then shapes politics, business and social interaction.

Our entire human culture is influenced by it and possibly even shaped by it. So the information industry has gained a new creative quality. If newspapers, TV broadcasters, the Internet etc. were originally naively intended as vehicles for the sharing and dissemination of information, they now create completely self-contained collective truths, that also have a serious bearing on real life. For this reason, in future you'd better switch off the television before you go to sleep, Mr Pacinsky!"

Enthralled by her own intellect, a shudder ran through Dr. Plump's electrified body and she sank back in her chair, her energy spent. For a moment she was tempted to light a cigarette, but then thought better of it and refocused on her patient Nico Pacinsky.

But he was fuming inside. What he'd have most liked to do to people like her, people who thought they could administer some kind of truth suppository by blustering on at great length like that, was punch them in the face. But he didn't dare raise a hand to such an intimidating woman, and instead imagined he could smell the viscous secretion that had formed in her panties during her monolog through her black suit trousers.

Indulging in this thought for a moment, he noticed an already pretty impressive swelling in his own trousers, presenting itself to the public gaze in the form of a denim tent. Nico attempted to conceal it by adjusting the material somehow. But the Kinski in him wanted to exhibit the boner with pride. So he smiled in mock embarrassment while endeavoring to direct the psychologist's gaze towards his pants. But Dr. Plump's practice was continually attended by dirty old men with erect penises, who sent her irritating dick pics via WhatsApp. A hardened professional like Dr. Plump was never going to show any interest in Nico's genitals.

Instead, she turned the conversation back to the original subject of the meeting: "Mr Pacinsky, what exactly happened last week?"

Nico hated being addressed by this surname, but he decided to play along with it for the time being. The shrink could take him for whoever she wanted. He himself knew better, and maybe he'd get out of the session quicker if he just told her what she wanted to hear.

"I had a huge meltdown," he admitted.

"Properly facing up to things is part of the therapy," said Dr. Plump. "So that's why I'd like you to give me a detailed account of the incident."

"I reduced my life to rubble and ash."

"And why did you do that?"

"I don't know...because I wanted to? Because I could? Since the car accident I feel...changed."

"How's the acting career progressing?"

"I'm starting work as an extra at the Ballhaus Ost. Maybe it's a ticket to a new life."

"How did your girlfriend Claudia react to the violent outburst?"

An electric shock ran through Nico's body at the mention of that name. In a millisecond, the rage took over all hormone production. Adrenaline and norepinephrine poured into all the blood vessels in his body and switched the neurotransmitter to attack mode. As though stung by a tarantula, he screamed, his face distorted in anger and spittle foaming in the corners of his mouth: "I sent her to hell, where she belongs, the stupid cow!"

But to Nico's astonishment, Dr. Plump didn't react. She neither looked up from her clipboard of notes, nor did she at least acknowledge his justifiable outrage with the slightest twitch of a muscle. Had he only imagined his own screams? Had he,—just as Nico would have done in the past,—simply swallowed his anger and kept it bottled up inside?

"You're very hurt by the sale of your Kinski collection, aren't you?" asked Dr. Plump.

"Yes, sure..."

"Of course, I'm not allowed to take sides in the matter. But it is highly conceivable that your self-discovery and self-definition will be much easier if you first stop channeling your own life through that of your idol. This could serve as a fresh start and bring your true personality to light."

Nico couldn't think of anything he'd rather do in that moment than to pick up a baseball bat and lay waste to Dr. Plump's office. But then the psychologist took his hand and looked him straight in the eye: "Nico, these days, anyone can be whatever and whoever they want to be—there's really no shame in that anymore. But just face up to the facts. There are many people in the world like you. And the vast majority of us think that's completely normal."

Nico was genuinely confused.—What did the psychologist think she knew about him? "I don't quite understand the question..." he said.

At that moment, the mechanical alarm clock on the sideboard went off and Dr. Plump jumped up from her chair: "Our time's up for today. We'll see each other at the next session."

She hurried out of the room to swiftly change her panties before the next patient appointment. As she crossed the waiting area on her way to the bathroom, Nico could hear through the thick concrete wall as she greeted that next patient, "Hello, Mr Gräve! How are you today? Go into consultation room four. I'll be right with you."

Gräve? Did Nico hear that right? Like the three-quarters crazy theater director Christoph Gräve from the Ballhaus Ost? Was this some kind of strange coincidence? Only when he got up from the couch did Nico notice how slack his body was after every session. As though he'd been injected with a muscle relaxant. He glanced one more time at the bars on the windows, opened the door to the waiting room and peered out. The only patient sitting there was a man of short stature and Nico greeted the stranger with a cursory nod. Magnus Max looked up from his Trader Joe's pick-of-the-week deals pamphlet, straight out of a plastic-wrapped direct mail package and said, "Vegan mince is on special offer!"

13. THE DOTTED LINE

THEATER DIRECTOR CHRISTOPH GRÄVE WAS SITTING HAVING breakfast on the terrace at the *Café am Neuen See*. The trees shimmered green, there was a tinkling of birdsong, the sun was doing its thing and it was almost unbearably hot even at such an early hour. It was one of those Berlin summer days without so much as a tepid breeze to provide some relief. You could cut the air with a knife. A few ducks bustled about down on the lake, and Gräve, lost in thought, watched the rather clumsy waiters as they went about their work. *Service wasteland Germany,* he thought to himself and wistfully recalled his time in Los Angeles, a place with a true service *culture* in his view. Gräve's yearning for America was almost pathological and in reality, solely due to his perpetual failures at home. Although up to that point he'd never been asked to produce anything from or even in California, the thought of that desert region in the far West remained a pleasant utopia to which he could escape in a kind of mental masturbation whenever things went tits-up at home—yet again. Nevertheless, he was almost nominated for a student Oscar back when he was just starting out as a director. If only the scatterbrained producer of his lyrical arthouse gangster drama

Soya Milk with Added Calcium hadn't missed the official submission deadline.

As he opened his laptop to make a note of something, he caught his reflection on the screen. He was a total wreck: dark rings under the eyes, a crumpled shirt and a repetitive twitch in his left eyelid. Days of sleep deprivation due to high levels of coffee consumption paired with the urgent desire to finally commit a new masterpiece to paper had taken their toll. As he brooded over the laptop extracting single words now and again, he took powerful draws on his cigarette as though he couldn't wait to light the next. But then he remembered what he was drawing on—an E-pipe with an especially large liquid container. Elderberry flavor with extra nicotine and caffeine aroma. Delicious, but ugh...he wondered just how low he had sunk. Next, he stared at the plastic bottle of alcohol-free beer on the table in front of him. It seemed to be a reflection of his very self: dull, flat, —and almost empty.

As though hoping to pimp the insipid hop nectar, he took a packet of ibuprofen out of his jacket pocket. But this box too was just like his creativity: all used up. He swore loudly in French, because he thought it sounded especially artistic, and crumpled up the plastic blister pack in frustration, throwing it into the lake behind him where it landed with a loud smack. Now he felt like an artist again. A little bit, at least.

A rainbow child accompanied by both his fathers had been observing things from the next table and intervened with appropriate indignation: "Dad, dad, that man's a polluter!"

One of the two fathers, fast arriving at a state of agitation, reacted in a predictable way to the child's horror—by arguing for the preservation of the flora and fauna of the metropolis for future generations. "Listen here! That packaging isn't biodegradable and for that reason, it doesn't belong in a lake!"

"You're a terrible person," the other Dad joined in. "Because of

71

people like you, the plastic density in the oceans of the world has risen by many percent in recent years. Our Joschka-Malte should grow up in a healthy world. Not in a polluted one."

Gräve ignored the three of them and tried to refocus on the business of capturing his ideas in writing.

"Hey, we're talking to you!" insisted one of the Dads. "Go immediately to the lake and pick that up before a grebe comes along, swallows it and dies a horrible death!"

At that point Gräve exploded; he couldn't concentrate any longer on the words on the screen in front of him. He jumped up from his seat and yelled like Al Pacino in *The Scent of a Woman* (or any of his other movies, for that matter):

"WOOOHHAAAA!!"

The climate-friendly family started in unison and the child began to cry. Without another word, the three of them stood up, the Dads shaking their heads, and sat at another table, far away from Gräve. He smiled a sardonic inward smile, drew on his vape and used a stick to fish the empty ibuprofen packet out of the lake, depositing it in an overflowing garbage can. Grinning, he nodded once again at the fathers and their son, all of whom turned away. That meant they didn't notice when a gust of wind blew the empty blister pack out of the garbage and into the beak of a passing grebe. The bird carried the plastic waste back to the lake. But that's nature for you.

Seconds later, Nico came around the corner and took a seat at Gräve's table.

"Nico. Glad you could make it," the director greeted him.

"What was all that about just now?" asked Nico.

"Take a look around you, Nico. What do you see?" was Gräve's response.

"Erm,...I..." stammered Nico.

"Coffee shop revolutionaries, eco-Nazis and menstrual cup advocates!" Gräve launched his rant. "These people protest against chlorinated chicken, but not against Putin. They force everyone around them to eat vegan and organic, but have no problem snorting drugs from South American workhouses."

"I'm in a bit of a hurry," Nico interjected.

But Gräve was in full flow and there was no stopping him: "Eco-citizens with trendy beards and band T-shirts from Primark with a penchant for everyday sustainability,—or perhaps the pansexual female vegan who's against genetic engineering and for gender mainstreaming. Or the educated and tattooed hipster Dad who *understands* the nationalist Alternative for Germany party: He's in favor of radically regional produce and against the global financial markets.—What we're seeing here is the emergence of a completely new mindset defined by the great prohibition habitus, noble-minded indignation, moral posturing and the perpetual outrage of all political camps over simply everything. For twenty years, the leftwing-green mainstream and conservative law-and-order citizens have nothing greater in common than in the demand for more and more prohibitions, more regulation, more state, more surveillance, more control. *Identity policy* and *identitarian movement*: it doesn't just sound similar, it *is* similar!"

Nico sprang up from his seat like a bolt of lightning and pelted Gräve's face with everything on the table: knives, forks, cold coffee and a bowl of half-eaten soy yoghurt with fruit and oats. "Grääävvveee! You fucking moron! You don't just need your face kicked in, you asshole, you need to be locked up, you've totally lost the plot!"

A blanket of silence descended on the entire café. As though in a beautifully choreographed ballet, all the ducks, crows and grebes took to the air at the same time, chattering as they did so. A majestic sight. Nico growled:

"Just give me the fucking contract already, so that I can ejaculate my name onto it, you wanker!"

Stunned by this outburst, all Gräve could do was to silently take the two-page contract out of his greasy leather bag and place it on the table in front of Nico.

Nico gave it the once over, striking through a paragraph in two places, and Gräve expected another meltdown. Braced and ready to defend himself, he observed his new protégé. The latter calmly signed his name at the foot of each page and as a reminder of his eminent lunacy, rammed the fountain pen so hard into the document it was pinned to the wooden table.

"So, I'll see you in the morning at the Ballhaus Ost," said the freshly-baked actor in a pleasant tone and performed the Kinski-esque twist in order to exit the scene like Nosferatu, hovering above the ground.

Gräve leaned forward to read the signature of his new colleague. There it was, in spidery letters: *Klaus Kinski*. All the synapses in the brain of the director immediately began to emit electrical impulses and then, fueled by Nico's apparent madness, he experienced a bolt of inspiration. Highlighting all the notes on his laptop, he deleted them with a tap on the backspace key. His fingers flying, he typed the title of his new idea: *They will claim that I was dead....* Suddenly fired up, he hastily began jabbing words into the keyboard.

Unnoticed by Gräve and Nico, Magnus Max, Verne Zog's willing lackey and hitman, had observed the meeting between the two men with great interest from a nearby table. He had followed Nico as he left the café after the contract signing.

Gräve stayed at the *Café am neuen See* for the entire afternoon, working like a man possessed on his new idea for a play, in which he aimed to channel Nico's firm conviction that he was Klaus Kinski. So he didn't notice the storm brewing in the skies over Berlin and when the first bursts of lightning lit the sky in the distance. One bolt even hit the West-Berlin TV tower. An initial harbinger of the unfettered power that would soon enter the city.

14. PHANTOM OF THE LATE AFTERNOON

NICO'S APARTMENT LOOKED AS THOUGH IT HAD BEEN HIT BY SEVERAL bombs. There were bite and scratch markets in the wallpaper, most of which was hanging off the walls. The air was full of fibers from the carpet, which had been shredded beyond recognition. Even after the initial meltdown, all the furniture, fixtures and fittings had evidently been subjected to such a frenzy of raw, destructive violence that you could almost inhale the cupboards, chairs, wash basin and toilet. Fragments of Nico's Kinski collection jutted out from the rubble in places. The scene was reminiscent of news footage broadcast in the wake of air strikes on a terror regime, when framed pictures of the vanquished dictator emerge from the debris of what had minutes earlier been somebody's home.

Claudia and her mother, each armed with a plastic bucket, were combing through the mess for anything salvageable to sell on Ebay. Like the rubble women of Berlin, they were also trying to restore some order to the ravaged apartment. But where to start? Erna hated her prospective son-in-law all the more now. After all, that *loser* had ruined all her plans.

She only wanted one thing: to somehow claw some cash

together and then get out of Berlin, back to Transylvania. And although Claudia had initially supported her mother's plans and even considered making a fresh start in Romania herself, she now noticed, following Nico's transformation, a recurrent tingling sensation whenever she thought of him.

Claudia no longer liked the way her mother talked about Nico; always putting him down and making him feel worthless. Claudia had even dared to defend Nico against Erna. After all, the people from Ballhaus Ost had called him about a possible job at the theater. Maybe the days of lethargy and moping about were finally over, even though he might have gone a little bit crazy in the process. Maybe some people need to do that to really show what they're about.

But Erna remained unimpressed and emphatically repeated her plan: it was necessary to flee this tenth circle of hell before she and her daughter were completely appropriated by the demon Nico. The devout Catholic kissed the image of Jesus hanging around her neck and crossed herself three times. But it wasn't just that Erna saw Nico as the spawn of the antichrist, she also perceived Berlin to be the vestibule to hell itself. She only had to think of her clients, who demanded that she, as a domina, perform all manner of conceivable and inconceivable sexual acts. She was probably the only dominatrix in the entire city whose emotional pain was the same as her clients' physical pain. CBT and T&D were just some of the more harmless things she was paid to do. And now she'd also dragged her own daughter down into the abyss along with her. How had she sunk so low?

As for Claudia, she had a soft spot for dissolute Berlin with all its bizarre, eccentric inhabitants. Nico was now one of those. And if other men wanted to pay her to play rough with their penis and balls and withhold ejaculation,—what of it? She enjoyed it, and most of her clients deserved what they got. In short, Berlin was anything but perfect, but she'd grown used to the city and learned to love it,—just like Nico.

Claudia noticed a broken picture frame lying on the floor. In it, an old holiday snap of the two of them. She picked it up and looked sadly at the image from long-forgotten, happy days.

It was one of those Berlin summer days when searing midday heat gave way to Biblical rainfall and storms in late afternoon. Claudia looked out of the window. The sky was closing in on itself, and she observed the dark blue clouds scudding by, bringing winds that whipped the poplar tree tops into an orgiastic dance. Then there was a click as the front door was unlocked. Erna emitted a cry of horror: He was back! She feared Nico's new unpredictability. Both women looked in the direction of the living room door, waiting for Nico to appear at any moment. But no one entered. Anxious seconds passed, until a whistling gust of wind through one of the open windows blew through the apartment and thrust open the living room door. With an infernal roar, a bolt of lightning struck close by. At the same time, all the lights in the entire apartment went out. The women clung to each other and Erna whimpered in fear.

As Claudia and her mother continued to look towards the door, the scene became drenched in sepia tones. Scratches and specks flitted through the air, and on the edge of the apartment you could make out the perforations of a film reel! It may sound unbelievable, but that's exactly how it was.

Or better, more or less how it was. It all depends on the perception of reality or more specifically with the recollection of the perception of a reality. To cite an example: If you drive at a speed of thirty kilometers an hour in a red cabriolet with its roof open in a thirty kilometer zone, many passersby when questioned will recall that the car was traveling at breakneck speed. So, in the heads of witnesses something has manifested itself that actually never happened, but that nevertheless represents a truth for each individual. In the same way, the characters in this story perceive events that don't necessarily represent the scientific and empirical truth, but the personal experience. *I'd rather be vaguely right, than totally wrong* as the Bavarian entertainer and Bush Senior's brother-by-another-mother Franz Josef Strauß once said.

Erna glimpsed herself in a shard of mirror on the floor. She and her daughter suddenly appeared to be wearing monstrously thick makeup that enhanced the contours of their faces many times over. Their movements were no longer fluid but always slightly jerky and somehow too fast. Their voices could no longer be heard, instead there was the sound of an organ somewhere, playing an impressionist piece of music. The living room was still full of wrecked furniture and decor, but now everything seemed painted on and without parallel lines. Claudia and Erna were in a movie scene from the German expressionist period, and their eyes widened in shock and terror as the huge shadow of a hunchbacked figure appeared on the wall still hanging with the shredded remains of Nico's Nosferatu poster. The shadow wandered slowly and menacingly through the living room until it disappeared into a corner, without revealing its human source.

Further seconds passed and seemed to stretch into eternity. Outside, the lightning struck as though from a magnesium flashlight bulb. True mortal fear crept across the faces of Claudia and Erna, frozen into distorted masks. Then a figure entered the room, not supported by moving limbs but hovering five centimeters over the ground. It was Nico, but ashen-faced, bald, with large pointed ears, long fingernails, two exceedingly sharp incisors and wrapped in a black cloak. But instead of biting the women or attacking them in any other way, Nico simply enquired what they were doing there.

Hadn't he banished them unequivocally from his consecration site? He looked at the few surviving Kinski memorabilia in the plastic buckets. And while Erna made a last ditch attempt to explain herself, Nico screamed at the top of his voice that she should just take all the stuff with her, sell it or give it to the poor, he didn't give a damn anymore. Then he went into the bedroom, exiting through the door on his left, leaving the women standing there.

Claudia asked Erna politely but firmly to leave her and Nico alone for an hour. She gave her mother a €20.00 bill to fund a pleasant afternoon in the *Hecht* bar. Erna had to warn her daughter once more about the loser demon Nico, but then she grabbed the note. She wasn't about to pass up on the chance of a few little afternoon drinks at her daughter's expense. Erna touched Claudia's cheek as she left.

15. JACK D. RIPPER

When Claudia entered the bedroom, the look and feel of the scene and the setting changed. The world no longer looked like an old silent movie to her. Her surroundings now appeared rather more like the backdrop for a sexploitation movie by the Spanish director Jess Franco. A bedside lamp in the corner drenched the room in a blood-red light, stylizing and exaggerating all the colors in the space. Everything felt a bit out-of-focus, as though the world was being viewed through nylon pantyhose.

Nico stood half-naked in front of the shattered wardrobe, its door hanging off its hinges. The full-length mirror was cracked in several places. He reached into the wardrobe and pulled out a crisply pressed, old-fashioned coat on a hanger. A short cape had been sewn onto the garment, which was reminiscent of late nineteenth century English fashion. Nico began to put it on.

"How did the interview with the theater people go?" Claudia asked him.

"It was satisfactory," Nico's response was cool.

Claudia smiled and was about to offer her apologies for the humiliations of recent months, when Nico pulled a pair of leather gloves out of the pocket of the coat and put them on. Fixing Claudia with a morbid gaze, he grabbed a bowler hat out of the wardrobe and jammed it on his head. With the uncertain tone of a wannabe axe murderer, he reprimanded her. "Get undressed now!" Claudia didn't quite understand at first, but then Nico made his demand clearer by drawing a long, very sharp-looking knife from his inside pocket.

He repeated his order that she undress, and it pleased her to finally get the chance to play a submissive role. Smiling mischievously, she obeyed his command. First, with the help of a seductive little dance, she removed her sweater. She was braless underneath, revealing pear-shaped C-cupped breasts. Her nipples were already erect, and when she glanced again at the knife in Nico's hand, which lent him a perversely outmoded masculinity, she noticed how the blood began to pool and pulse through her inner and outer vaginal lips. With a single movement, Nico rushed at Claudia and pressed his crotch tightly against hers; she could not contain an ecstatic cry of lust. He held the knife against her carotid artery and moved the tip along her veins, down between her breasts to the button of her denim skirt, which he removed with a precise cut. With a rapid flick of the hand, he pulled down her skirt so hard that her panties came along for the ride, revealing her part-shaved vulva with the butterfly tattoo.

Nico slid the knife slowly downwards barely touching her skin. As he reached her genitals there was a faint metallic sound as the blade skimmed her clitoris, pierced with a bar. Nico stimulated her carefully with the cold steel, which set her on waves of ecstasy. The slightest movement of her body would have resulted in injury, so she had to bear his touch without being able to move a single muscle. But then he released her and buried his face between her lips, eliciting another euphoric cry. He circled her clit with his tongue for just a few seconds before she was finally able to release the pressure valve and come so hard a torrent of sweet-sour vaginal fluid gushed from her Skene's glands and over Nico's face.

Claudia's legs trembled like those of an animal exhausted by a long desert migration within sight of a distant waterhole. Slowly, Nico inserted two fingers inside her and located her G-spot. Claudia jerked in ecstasy, but Nico just smiled, pressed the knife into her hand and brought it up to his own neck. As he leaned forward to kiss her, the blade nicked a thin, shallow cut in his skin. In the same moment, his other hand made a grab for her backside, spread her cheeks and slid his forefinger into her anus, which was drenched in vaginal fluid.

Claudia came again, hard, but this time without ejaculating. She kissed Nico feverishly, savoring the taste of her own juices. But then, pushing him away, it was her turn to point the knife at him, a barbaric expression on her face. "Undress!" *she* was the one issuing the orders this time. Nico smiled and began removing his Jack the Ripper costume. Then the two fell upon each other, stumbling into bed, devouring each other like two crazed carnivores, while their bodies seemed to merge into a single mass. After a few minutes, Claudia straddled Nico. All the while holding the knife against his throat to prevent him from sitting up.

Of course, she had no idea that the whole time he was thinking about Gwyneth, Christoph Gräve's suicide girl assistant. That was the only way he could maintain his erection. Because actually, he'd long began to despise Claudia and her affected posturing. Although he couldn't bear her mother, because she perpetually exploited him and his kind-hearted nature. If he was completely honest he'd prefer the honesty of a freeloader to the passive-aggressive hypocrisy of Claudia that he'd had to put up with over the past few months. Gwyneth on the other hand, with her thoroughly decent aura, awakened a desire in him the likes of which he had never felt before and that went beyond basic sexual attraction.

To turn up his torment even more, Claudia was bending so far forward that her perfectly-formed breasts dangled right in front of his face, but it was impossible for him to reach them with his mouth for fear of slitting his throat. Nico wasn't going to put up with that for long. With a hefty jerk of the hips, he manipulated her into a submissive position, winning the upper hand and penetrating her all the while. Fucking her at a ninety degree angle, his cock stimulated her Gräfenberg zone along the Halban's fascia. This put Claudia in a sustained orgasm-like state, similar to the rare PSAS syndrome. She felt as though she was leaving her existential sphere and entering a world of new sexual consciousness. Everything around her became numb and dazzling as though in a near-death experience. The hormones released by her body had reached their critical point; she was on the brink of an overdose of her body's own drugs. As she entered a parallel world of lust and pain, she thought she could at last understand the universe and above all reach out and *touch it*.

She knew exactly what she needed to do next. She looked at her hand, which was still holding the sharp knife. Then she drew in her lower abdomen so closely that her vagina clenched so tightly around Nico's penis, the slightest move would trigger his orgasm. At that moment she stabbed him from below into his neck and pushed the blade so deeply into the wound that the steel bored through his open mouth, his palate and from there into his brain.

A gigantic fountain of blood sprayed into her face and eyes. The world turned red! Claudia was no longer able to recognize what was happening around her, but she thought she could see Nico's body undergoing a transformation as he groaned and screamed in pain: his veins were pumping, his muscles inflated, horns sprang from his skull. A long, powerful tail emerged from his rump, and a leathery pair of wings unfolded themselves from his spine. And so he hovered through the room and Claudia lost consciousness—not least due to total dehydration from the non-stop orgasm.

16. IT PULLS LIKE PIKE SOUP

CLAUDIA'S MOTHER ERNA LIKED SPENDING TIME ON STUTTGARTER Platz. Here, West Berlin was still West Berlin—or in other words the *genuine* Berlin as she remembered it from the early nineties. Not this tourist Disneyland between Mitte and P'Berg that now looked like any other European metropolis.

Between amusement arcades and soft porn movie theaters lurked a handful of sex workers, waiting and hoping for a trick or two; alongside drug dealers and soccer-playing kids, an Arab clan was selling a newly-repaired Mercedes AMG S Class 6.5 with blue underside lighting to a Turkish clan. Top condition, fourteen years old, well looked-after, new MOT, €35,000. In cash, of course. Ciaooooo, *old man!!!* The deal was sealed without any major bother, and one of the proud new owners floored the accelerator to set the brachial sounding V12 engine roaring, causing the wheels to spin on the rain-slicked road and forcing several passengers to cower at the prospect of an imminent crash. As long as clan members didn't fire their submachine guns out of the car windows in celebration—of whatever they might be celebrating that day,—this boys-and-their-new-toys posturing was tolerated by both the police and the general population.

The rain was still pelting down; the clouds were getting steadily thicker. Other fancy motors by the likes of BMW and Mercedes were haphazardly parked in front of the bar *Zum Hecht (To the Pike)*.

An advertising board, sponsored by a leading Berlin brewery, was chalked with the words: *37 beers meet your daily vitamin C requirement.*

This bar, directly on the square locals called the Stutti, was a true original. Despite the smoking ban, it was always full of people puffing away, the price of beer hadn't gone up since 1967, 1.50 in any currency, with a shot of schnapps thrown in for double that. In short, the pub was one of the hallowed hangouts of the West Berlin pleb-elite. A large sign hung on the wall bearing yet another pearl of wisdom for the proletariat: *You drink, you die— you don't drink, you still die. So drink!* Genius!

It was the kind of place where if you scratched a nail on one of the dark brown walls, you'd be scoring through a thick film of filth. The dirt that had collected here over the decades was composed for the most part of cigarette tar and evaporated fat from the fryer. The curry meatballs and liver kebabs were an open secret in the locality, even getting a mention in the 1991 trucking association guidebook to Berlin. It was highly likely that the fat in the fryer hadn't been changed since then.

Anyone keen to observe genuine old Berlin lowlife going about their daily routines would always find them here. Many students whiled away their afternoons in the bar drinking just a glass of soda, watching all the comings-and-goings and jotting things down in a notebook. An hour in the *Hecht* gave psychology and sociology alumni more material for their studies than an entire term at the Free University, aka the rust and silver bower. At the *Hecht*, original phrases and profound aphorisms for the next assignment were always part of the experience: *Keep your chin up, even though your neck is dirty.*

A game of darts was going on in one corner. But the five inebriated men with swollen, scarred faces rarely missed the treble twenty. These guys were true professional alcoholics, not the kind to play any kind of drinking games with. Unless you got off on being humiliated with a few authentic taunts such as: "I thought you were standing upright, but you're holding onto the glass, aren't you?"

In another corner, a sloshed woman who could barely stand was trying in vain to get the jukebox working. She growled at it with a classic smoker's rasp: "Alexa! Play something by The Ramones!"

The response from the jukebox was cold. "Sorry. I'm not Alexa. I'm a jukebox."

At a table in the corner right at the back of the bar sat the German splatter movie director and level ten drinker, Olaf Ittenbach (the German Hershel Gordon Lewis, without any humor), whose oeuvre included such masterworks as *Legion of the Dead* and *Beyond the Limits*. He was, as per usual, no longer in command of himself. He actually needed to be drunk to function as a director, because otherwise he'd be unable to bear the brutality of his own screenplays. Alongside him sat another man sleeping off his hangover, his head in a lake of schnapps and puke. But Olaf didn't mind, he carried on chatting to the sleeping man like a blabbering waterfall, "...and then I actually did leave the special effects prosthetics in the car. But it was 40 degrees Fahrenheit in the shade, and the fucking things just melted. When I stuck them onto the actors' faces the next day, they looked pretty crazy...my best work to date..."

Erna Rosetzki was sitting at another table nursing a glass of red. She was surrounded by four men of advanced age, all vying for her attention. They clearly knew each other, as all four begged Claudia's mother to sing to them. "Go on, give us a tune darling!"

As soon as the *Blitzkrieg Bop* finished in the jukebox, Erna took a deep breath and unleashed her incredible voice, like a drunk opera diva, on the second aria of the *Queen of the Night* from Mozart's *Magic Flute*. "Hell's vengeance boils in my heart, death and despair blaze about me! If Nico does not through you feel the pains of death, then you will be, no, my daughter nevermore. Disowned be you forever, abandoned be you forever, destroyed be forever all the bonds of nature, if not through you Nico will turn pale! Hear, gods of revenge, hear the mother's oath!"

The four sots were frenetically applauding Erna when suddenly, a voice could be heard from somewhere beneath them. Erna and her adoring public couldn't make out where it was coming from at first. "So, the show's over. Leave me alone with this dear lady now, please."

As though following some kind of choreography, Erna and the winos all peered simultaneously under the table and saw Magnus Max fixing them with a serious gaze.

"Dude, you've got a face like a pair of hush puppies: it'd feel good to stick your feet in," one of the men had a go at rattling him.

But Magnus Max didn't rise to the provocation from the old guy with the sour smell of alcohol on his breath. Instead, he casually pulled out his Smith and Wesson 500H Double Action pistol from a side holster under his jacket. He cocked the weapon and raised an eyebrow. The men got the message and scarpered without another word.

Magnus climbed onto a chair at Erna's table. She peered at the diminutive man's face and had a sudden thought. She was convinced that the person of short stature sitting opposite her had to be the love child of her affair with Nicolae Ceausescu. As far as she knew, the baby had been put up for adoption immediately after its birth in hospital.

Magnus didn't know what to make of this woman. Could she be a double agent sent to put him on the wrong scent? But a penetrating gaze into her agitated eyes were enough for him to know that she was just another Berlin fuck-up. But one that he'd definitely be able to use to further the interests of his venerable master Verne Zog.

Removing his smartphone from his pocket and without saying a word, Magnus showed Erna some video footage from a surveillance camera in Nico's apartment. Flabbergasted, Erna saw herself and her daughter talking about Nico. Erna kept referring to him as a good-for-nothing demon. As the footage drew to a close, Magnus stuck the phone back in his pocket and looked at Erna in silence.

"You're monitoring his apartment?" she asked. "So you're with the police?"

"You could say that," began Magnus. "But that doesn't have to concern you. Because you already seem to know why we're interested in Mr Nico Pacinsky..." He glanced conspiratorially to the left and right before continuing in whispered tones, "We'd very much like to involve you in our investigations."

Erna, who sensed an opportunity to be rid of Nico once and for all, didn't hesitate: "What do you need me to do?"

Magnus rejoiced inwardly; he knew she'd be easy to ensnare. "Well, for starters, make sure your daughter and Mr Pacinsky stay together."

"What? Why?" asked Erna in shock.

"Now I'm not a one for big explanations," replied Magnus Max.

"But why?" insisted Erna.

"Didn't you hear what I just said? I'm not a fan of unnecessary explanations!"

But as Erna still looked baffled, he rolled his eyes and relented. "To give us continued access to him through her."

"For how much longer?"

Magnus wasn't used to answering so many questions. He

could sense a spike in his adrenaline level, which is already slightly high in people with microsomia.

"The operation will last as long as it takes, until my boss, the venerable and unimpeachable Master Zog, can accomplish his plans with Mr Pacinsky."

"Holy Jesus!" Erna spluttered. "That's all a bit vague, don't you think?"

Magnus ran his hands through his hair and took a few deep breaths to calm himself. He took his phone out again. "Give me your PayPal address."

"What? Why?"

That did it. The dwarf slammed his fist down so hard on the table it sent the glasses flying and hollered, "Just give me your fucking PayPal address!"

A group of Harley riders at the bar, who'd been waiting all day for a bit of drama, looked over at the pair with great interest. They were hoping for the chance of a punch-up. And to knock about a little guy like that would be a first for them. As two of the bikers ambled over towards Magnus and Erna, the latter was in the process of divulging her PayPal details. "OK, OK. Calm down mister. My PayPal address is affmilf69—all in one word—at gspotmail dot ro."

Magnus Max typed the letters and numbers onto his phone, as two of the beer-fueled rockers swayed towards the table. "Everything alright, Erna? Is the big guy giving you grief?"

Before Erna could say a word, Magnus Max interjected, "Well, I've just transferred €10,000 to the reputable lady via PayPal."

Erna snatched her phone out of the fake Louis Vuitton bag and read the message that had just flashed up on the home screen: "You have received a payment of €10,000." She couldn't quite believe her eyes.

Magnus Max grinned a grin of superiority. "On that note, I'll leave you and this...*high-end* establishment in mutual understanding, OK?"

Erna could only stutter. "Er...yes. Of course!"

Magnus jumped down from his chair and left the bar. The two bikers watched him go, their mouths open in surprise, before returning to what Harley riders liked doing best: drinking, scrapping and sharing fuel-related anecdotes with other petrol heads.

———

Outside, the rain started pelting down as Magnus stepped out of the door. He pulled up the collar of his coat to keep his clean-shaven nape dry. The Bentley on the parking lot in front of the bar opened its doors automatically as he approached. A small ladder unfolded itself by the side of the door and he got in. From the glove compartment, which contained all manner of guns and cartridges, he fished out a bottle of disinfectant and sanitized his hands. Then he pushed the start button and while the 12-cylinder engine with more than 600 BHP began to purr, the seat automatically moved into a position perfect for the diminutive driver. Back in the day, Verne Zog's movie production company had commissioned Ferdinand Piëch (main shareholder of VW and grandson of Ferdinand Porsche) to personally design and build the car so that it could be also driven by little people. Magnus accelerated the vehicle with a pedal on the steering wheel and sped off into the dark, rain-sodden night.

17. SENATE AUTHORITY FOR CULTURE AND GOOD TASTE

BERLINERS ARE ONLY ABLE TO BEAR THEIR BEHEMOTH OF A CITY BY assigning ribald nicknames to the many hideous buildings in it. The phenomenon known in linguistics as Berolinism or Berlinism, denotes a Berlin slang term for buildings and local customs. There are numerous examples of this. The best known are probably the *Golden Lizzy* for the Victory Column in the Tiergarten park, the *Washing Machine* for the Federal Chancellery, and *Erich's Lamp Shop* for the no longer extant Palace of the Republic.

A rather less well-known building was a gigantic concrete brutalist monstrosity in the district of Steglitz, which Berliners called the *Mice Bunker* because it used to host an animal testing facility. The Supreme Regional State Authority for Culture and Good Taste took up residence here in the 1980s. The structure was grey and bulky with numerous superfluous blue wastewater pipes sticking out of the facade like the canons and embrasures of a mediaeval castle. Ominous and intimidating, the building thrust itself upwards into the murky sky, its many floors linked by labyrinthine pedestrian bridges. Thick black smoke rose continually from several pipes and a row of gigantic, black-white-

and-red banners hung on the facade, from top to bottom. They bore the oak leaf emblem of the Senate Authority.

Christoph Gräve took in the sight with a certain sense of unease. He was totally worn out yet again, his vape dangling from the corner of his mouth. He was holding a can of Monster Red Bull (new flavour) in one hand, sipping it non-stop despite the vape. Under the other arm, he was hanging onto a stack of printed paper. Stopping for a moment at the entrance to the Senate Authority, he took a last deep drag on the vape before putting it in his pocket. He was just about to step through the door, when he shot a reverent look upwards at the preposterous concrete colossus with a sense of awe. Swallowing hard, he finally stepped over the threshold and entered the glass revolving door.

———

Gräve walked into the lobby, in the centre of which a zig-zag pattern had been inlaid into the marble floor, buffed up to a smooth shine. To the rear of the hall, a seemingly endless corridor led to another dauntingly large space lined on either side by Corinthian-style concrete columns. This room was a pantheon, dedicated to the fallen heroes of public broadcasting with an eternal flame burning at its heart. More black-white-and-red banners hung on the walls, bearing the insignia of the TV and radio licensing service, financed by the Senate Authority. A quote by Fritz Pleitgen (imagine the exact opposite of Conan O'Brien) was emblazoned in large letters on the concrete wall facing the entrance: *Your contribution makes a difference.*

Gräve made his way to the desk of the concierge, who was just spreading out his breakfast in front of him and on the point of tucking in to his filet mignon with steamed carrots and mashed potatoes, just delivered from Borchardt's in a Maybach.

The director stood at the counter and noticed that the

concierge cut a rather menacing figure in his military-style uniform. "Good morning. I'm here to see Irmgard Al-Hassani and Waltraud Beermeyer-Stöpsel."

The concierge looked up at him in annoyance, a thin trickle of steak blood appearing at the corner of his mouth. "Do you have an appointment?"

Gräve responded with a stony-faced lie. After all, working with actors was his business and he'd learned a few useful tricks over the years. "Of course. Why wouldn't I?"

"And what's it about?" enquired the concierge. The meat juices were running bloodier over his angular chin.

Gräve smiled and held up the wedge of paper. "Script consultation."

The concierge picked up the phone and dialed an internal extension number. "Hello. I've got somebody here called Mr..." He looked at Gräve quizzically.

"Christoph Gräve," said Gräve.

"There's a Mr Kristopher Greife here for you. He says it's about a script."

The women on the other end of the line seemed to be talking. Gräve could only hear the faint sound of agitated voices. Then the concierge hung up the phone and said coolly: "Ninth basement floor, Room 237. Elevator is at the back on the left.—I'm giving you clearance to enter."

Gräve didn't think it would be that easy to gain access to the ladies. Thanking the concierge politely, he headed for the elevator, the doors of which opened as though on command. He'd never seen such an elaborately designed elevator. A red light shone in his face, pushing up Gräve's pulse. The ninth basement had already been selected. The rear and sides of the elevator consisted of high-resolution retina displays showing a panorama of Hieronymus Bosch's *The Garden of Earthly Delights*. The doors closed and an elevator jazz version of Twisted Sister's *Burn in Hell* could be heard. Slowly, the elevator started to move. And with the movement of the vehicle, the digital triptych by Hieronymus Bosch moved too, taking Gräve downward through the painting. Upon arrival at the ninth basement, the doors didn't open straightaway. Gräve was already starting to feel nervous but after a few seconds, they parted to the sound of a high pipping sound, releasing him to step out into the corridor.

He took another slug from his can of Red Bull, before throwing it over his shoulder and beginning the search for Office 237. The endless, windowless corridors were decorated with all manner of framed posters advertising theater, movie and TV series productions subsidized in the past by the Senate Authority. As he walked past, Gräve's gaze fell on posters for projects such as *The Old Woman and the Flute* by the transgender director Rosa Wurst, *The Sea in My Thoughts is a Komodo Dragon* by the Georgian dissident Iosseb Bessarionis dse Dschughaschwili, and *The Pink Panther*. He had to smile at the sight of the latter poster, because he knew the director of the work personally. The movie by the Uzbek poet, human rights activist and filmmaker Sbstyslw Prgyxsdebslow was about the Turkish boxer Muhammed, whom everyone just called Ali. Ali was gay and didn't just have to fight against the prejudices of his family and the boxing world, but also against his own feelings of resentment towards the Jewish husband of his female promoter. The husband helped him secure a residence permit for his Angolan lover who, as it turned out, was HIV-positive and had also infected Ali with the deadly virus. But even before the illness could take hold, Ali's brothers ended his career with an honor killing. They couldn't tolerate having a homosexual as a brother. When it came out, the movie scooped the Golden Bear for best film at the Berlinale, the Teddy Award for the best LGBTLC+ film and the Silver Bear for the best lead actor. Nevertheless, for the Berlin art world it was a big scandal that Moritz Bleibtreu (the German Shia LaBeouf without cool girlfriends), in his role as a blind boxing coach who trained his protégé through hearing alone, hadn't even been nominated! And with these thoughts whirling around his head, Gräve arrived at Room 237. He noticed with surprise that the key, on a ring marked with the number of the room, was still in the lock and the door was slightly open. A murmuring noise could be heard coming from inside. Gräve sidled up to the door and tried to peer through the crack, but he couldn't make anything out. He could hardly bear the tension. Bracing himself, he pushed open the door cautiously. Inside, he was prepared to encounter all manner of perversions and every humanly-possible horror. Instead, he saw the full extent of the aesthetic abyss: Waltraud Beermeyer-Stöpsel sat in the spartan, windowless office and squinted over her glasses at her old thick-screened monitor, while Irmgard Al-Hassani poured coffee from a glass jug into a thermos.

"Someone forgot to take the key out of the lock," said Gräve by way of announcing himself.

"Ah, Mr Gräve. Come in. We were *not* expecting you."

Gräve nodded, approached the large chipboard desk and threw his script onto it with a deliberately sweeping gesture. The tatty cover page flecked with coffee and nicotine stains bore the title *They will claim that I was dead...*

"Your new play, I presume?" enquired Waltraud.

"My new masterpiece, exactly!" answered Gräve.

"Didn't we talk about the fact that we'd like to be involved right from the outset? You should've submitted a treatment first for us to authorize," insisted Irmgard.

"With all due respect, you've probably got no idea how a creative process works," countered Grave.

Waltraud rolled her eyes in faint annoyance. "Well go ahead then, enlighten us."

"I was just inspired and going with the flow. I'm not going to waste my energy on a *treatment*. When Dionysian forces fertilize

Apollonian forces within the soul of an artist, then there's no stopping him;—all he can do is lay the foundations that bring the heights of human rapture to life!"

Irmgard and Waltraud exchanged a look that said, we've always known it, this guy is off his rocker!

"Well, that's not how it works here, I'm afraid. But seeing as though you're here, let's hear a basic plot outline."

Gräve allowed himself a moment to catch his breath. "The entire story is a modern adaptation of the hero's journey of Odysseus by Homer, coupled with the fragmenting characteristics of Gonzo journalism and a hint of the fourth sonnet collection by Lothar Frohwein." (Don't even ask who that is.)

Irmgard poured herself another coffee and said, "OK, that sounds interesting. So what happens?"

Gräve began speaking effusively, accompanying his words with untamed gestures, "A young man is the total loser. He doesn't have a proper job or any hope of getting one, his girlfriend cheats on him. But then—BAM!—he's involved in a serious car crash that triggers an even more severe neurotic episode and henceforth the man believes himself to be—Klaus Kinski!"

A silence descended of the kind that if a needle had been floating in space, you'd've heard it. Both Irmgard and Waltraud had to swallow hard. But Gräve was just getting into gear. "Wait, it gets even better. He's so convincing in his role that one day, Werner Herzog calls and says he wants to make a film about Kinski's life, with him in the lead role."

Waltraud was so shocked she nearly dropped her cup; there followed yet another deafening silence. She was just about to express her misgivings about the idea, when Irmgard got in first, "That's ingenious!"

Waltraud looked at her colleague with wide, questioning eyes and shook her head so subtly it was barely noticeable. Signing on a docket, Irmgard authorized the entire estimated budget and called on him to start work on the production right away. The perplexed but happy director left the office without a word. The two women sat back down at their shared desk.

"What was all that about, Irmgard? That was just complete nonsense, and Gräve belongs in an asylum!"

"Of course, Waltraud, you're absolutely right!"

"So why did you give him a blank cheque just like that?"

"Well, think about it. We're both civil servants for life."

"Yes, so?"

"Nothing can touch us. Gräve is just an *employee* at the theater. Another disaster like the last play, and we'll be rid of this imbecile forever. And no one will give a fig about any of his past work. And in any case, this garbage won't even make it as far as the rehearsal phase. They're never going to find a suitable actor. No one can be Klaus Kinski—apart from himself!"

Waltraud considered Irmgard's words and sipped at her coffee. "OK, sounds like a plan."

The two women looked at each other with devilish grins and looked forward to the day when they'd watch Gräve fall on his face once and for all.

18. FIRST DAY AT WORK

It was already 9:28 am when Claudia Rosetzki woke up under the torn sheets in Nico's bed, still naked and drained after the night of unbridled lovemaking. She was confused; her eyes wide, she sought out Nico who was already awake and sitting next to her, flicking through a porn magazine with the simplistic title *Big Tits*. She reached for his head and felt for horns. Not finding any, she came to her senses and noticed the late hour.

"Shouldn't you be on your way to your new job at the Ballhaus Ost?"

Nico answered her in a snarling Kinski voice: "The Ballhaus is a *theater*. They run on a different time there; most of the staff are still in bed asleep. After all, we're talking about genuine artists. In any case, what are clocks to me? Nothing—they should be set to my time!"

Claudia leaned over Nico to kiss him. But he shrugged off her advances, stood up and headed for the bathroom.

As he stood under the shower, it occurred to him that his morning routine hadn't changed in years. Like any other morning, he was about to switch on the radio and imagine himself standing on the all-important stage. But now, he was actually an actor. He was Klaus Kinski, the greatest thespian ever to have trodden the boards. So he didn't need the radio anymore. He tore the plastic sucker off the glass panel and smashed it on the shower tiles. In a frenzy of curses, he clawed at the shattered pieces until his hands bled.

Fresh out of the shower, and without exchanging another word with Claudia, Nico left the apartment. He walked at an easy but purposeful pace, taking his usual route past the Savignyplatz arches and up onto the S-Bahn platform. His train arrived at the exact same moment; he could hardly believe his luck. Two pretty girls who can't have been older than eighteen shot him cheeky grins. He boarded the train, its doors now actually opening to a sound straight out of Star Wars, and the two girls followed. The three of them flirted for a while before the girls got out at Zoo station.

Nico hesitated. Should he go after them? Hadn't Kinski seduced a whole host of women on the Berlin public transport system in his time? Well at least that's what he claimed in his autobiography. But as he was still pondering his course of action, the doors closed and the train pulled out of the station. Nico told himself that once his genius had come to light, he'd be inundated with tryst opportunities.

Exiting the S-Bahn station at Schönhauser Allee via the steps to Greifenhagener Straße, he walked by the same stores as he had done on his first visit to the Ballhaus-Ost. But this time, he passed through the crowd without any problems. Perhaps it would be better to say that he paid no heed to others. If they didn't want to be barged, then they'd better just get out of his way. And look, the tactic was working! Whereas before, he was always bumping into people trying to be meek and polite and allowing them to pass, now they stepped aside for him, like a shoal of fish avoiding a predator.

Walking by a block with a forest of children's buggies at its entrance, he passed a slim Swabian woman and a hefty Franconian woman locked in a dispute over antiquated southern German customs in their faintly ridiculous dialects. As he strolled by, they both shot Nico a look warning him against any kind of mockery. Not that he was in the least bit interested in these migrants from the south.

When he finally arrived at the theater, he was in good spirits. But he still had to stop for a moment at the door and collect himself before entering. He inhaled deeply once more and stepped into the foyer. Gräve's delectable assistant Gwyneth was sitting at a bistro table flicking through a German real estate auction catalog. Noticing Nico, she jumped up from her chair, hugged him and greeted him warmly in English. Nico realized on the spot that he'd do anything for this woman;—he'd fallen for her at first sight. As she planted a kiss on his cheek, the two of them held onto each other for just a moment too long. The feeling was clearly mutual.

"I was so happy when Christoph told me we were gonna work with you!" said Gwyneth. Both sensed a moment of indecision, which passed as though in slow motion. Then Gwyneth steered Nico towards the corridor that led to the offices, and led the way.

"Christoph's new play got Senate approval just this morning. So he has other plans for you now."

Nico got a sinking feeling: *Other plans?* Just another shitty internship? No stage role? No extra job? Luck didn't appear to be on his side, even as Klaus Kinski. Nico began gearing himself up to either sock Gräve in the mug or get down on his knees and beg for a role. What would Kinski do? They arrived at the door to Gräve's office. Gwyneth knocked and entered without waiting for an answer. Nico followed her in silence and with a queasiness in his gut.

Gräve's office had meanwhile become a garbage dump of screwed up paper, cans of Red Bull, vapes and empty plastic salad containers from the supermarket swarming with fruit flies. The director himself was hunched over his old Macbook and was happy to see Nico. "Ah, Nico! Wonderful. Do come in."

Gwyneth excused herself as Gräve went on, "Nico, I'll keep it brief. I've got big plans for you."

"Well sure, I'd expect nothing less," replied Nico, again surprised at his own cockiness. Gräve took a script from one of the many piles and handed it to him. "Forget the extra job you applied for!"

Nico read the title of the script *They will claim that I was dead...* and said: "They lie!"

Gräve was lost for a moment. "Excuse me?"

"*They lie.* That's how the quote ends," Nico attempted an explanation.

"What quote?" asked Gräve.

"Well, the title on the script *They will claim that I was dead— they lie.* That's the complete quote by Klaus Kinski. Er...so...*my* quote, I mean."

Gräve's eyes widened, making him look even more rabid than before. He stood up from his desk and prowled around the room as though hunted by his thoughts. "Turn to page twenty-nine."

Nico did what the director instructed, and then looked up at him:

"That's the poem *Detractors* by Francois Villion."

Gräve nodded like a junkie on speed. "Read it out."

Nico thought for a second before beginning to read. "In lime, still unslaked, in iron pulp, in salt, salpetre, phosphor blazes..."

Gräve interrupted him by swiping the script out of his hand. At that moment, both men felt their adrenaline levels surge into the red zone. "No! Don't just read it! *Perform* it. Like your idol."

Nico was ready to ram a knife between Gräve's ribs. But he didn't have one in hand, and so he decided to channel the unleashed torrent of rage elsewhere. He put on a grandiose performance, metamorphosing both physically and mentally into Kinski. Freed from all societal inhibitions, he plumbed the throaty depths of his voice and let Gräve have it—at top volume.

Nico was already familiar with the following scene. Because it was the exact same situation that played out in his head before he rammed the Smart into the back of the Mercedes. It was as though, before this cataclysmic moment that would change his life forever, he had created a connection with Gräve's art that extended far beyond his conventional understanding of space and time and the relationship between the two.

"In lime, still unslaked, in iron pulp, in salt, salpetre, phosphor blazes, in urine of female donkeys in heat, in snake poison and in hag's spittle, in dogshit and water from the bathtubs, in wolf's milk, oxen's bile and latrine flood: In this juice detractors shall be stewed. In the brain of a tomcat which does not fish anymore, in the drivel, spouting from the teeth of the rabid dogs, mixed with monkey's piss, in quills, pulled out from a hedgehog, in the rain barrel, already floating with worms, croaked rats and the green slime from mushrooms, glowing like fire in the night, in horses' snot and also in hot glue: In this juice detractors shall be stewed."

For Gräve, Nico's performance was pure cosmic energy of the kind not seen on Planet Earth for decades. The ensuing silence was deafening. Nico stood there, trembling and white as chalk, his entire body taut, his rigid arms stretched upwards. Spittle foamed from the corners of his mouth and the burst vessels in his bulbous eyes tainted his gaze a fiery red. A tear ran down Gräve's cheek; the performance had left him profoundly moved. He began to clap, slowly at first, and gradually picking up the pace to frenetic applause. Finally, the two men embraced.

19. THE GREATEST PLAY OF ALL TIME

THE WEEKS THAT FOLLOWED WERE DEVOTED TO REHEARSALS AT THE Ballhaus-Ost. Nico threw himself into the work, fired up like never before. In doing so, he immersed himself more and more deeply in his role, both on and off the stage. Explosive altercations were therefore preprogrammed and also an intentional part of the preparatory phase to put everyone involved in the right mindset. Nico seized every opportunity to castigate Gräve, who reveled in the role of the slightly more passive, but no less spiteful Werner Herzog. With an obsession to detail without precedent at the Ballhaus-Ost, the two men and their entire team readied themselves for the play's grand opening.

Gwyneth, constantly at Gräve's side performing a key function in the organization, found herself falling head over heels in love with the fledgling actor Nico,—treading the boards for the first time, in an epochal main role to boot. He felt the same way about Gwyneth. His girlfriend Claudia, who didn't suspect a thing, was meanwhile busy with her mother redecorating Nico's apartment, where Claudia at least planned to stay for a while yet.

But something Nico either didn't realize or was completely ignoring, was the exceedingly strange fact that the start of Gräve's play mirrored the events of his life in recent weeks right down to the last detail. His crucifixion dream with himself on the cross, the car accident, the hospital sex with Claudia. It was all there, in *They will claim that I was dead….* The play was about a young man who, following a car accident, believed himself to be Klaus Kinski. How could Gräve have known about all that? Nico certainly hadn't mentioned any of it to him. And who was this mysterious Verne Zog who played a key role in the play? Nico was about to find this out soon, at least. With every day that passed, more actual events found their way into Gräve's play. Or was it the other way around? Did the scenes of the play find their way into reality? Nico didn't really give a damn about all that. He wanted success! He wanted sex! He wanted fame and fortune, bread and circuses! He was Kinski!

The second meeting between Nico and Gräve at the *Café am Neuen See* also became a scene in the play. In rehearsal, Gräve read out his own lines from the script, "… more regulation, more state, more surveillance, more control. *Identity policy* and *identitarian movement;* it doesn't just sound similar, it *is* similar!"

And Nico responded exactly as he had done at the time: "Grääävvveee! You fucking moron! You don't just need your face kicked in, you asshole, you need to be locked up, you've totally lost the plot!"

Then both men came out of their roles and discussed the scene. Gräve said: "Yes, not bad. But perhaps you could stretch the *asshole* just a bit more and make it bigger? That'll enhance the dramatic effect, I reckon."

"Yeah, OK," came Nico's honest, completely unflustered response. Switching back into his part, he hollered: "Grääävvveee! You fucking moron! You don't just need your *face* kicked in, you assssssshole, you need to be locked up, you've totally lost the plot! —Is that better? I put the accent on *face*, instead of on *kicked in*."

"Perfect," was Gräve's only comment.

The unlikely couple spent hours together at the laptop wringing the best out of the scene. They conducted dress rehearsals, spoke to set designers, and appointed other members of the cast. Both men were gripped by the same vision, to finally bring something genuinely important to the stage.

On one occasion during work on a particular scene, Nico and Gräve were almost at the point of strangling each other. Nico was wearing his *Fitzcarraldo* costume, a tattered, ill-fitting white suit, and Gräve was pointing a wooden musket at him. Nico raged, "Ah Werner, you're so insane you need your face smashing in, you wanker!"

In an almost perfect imitation of the calm and nasal tone of Werner Herzog, Gräve replied in accordance with the script: "Klaus, I've got nine shots in the Winchester. You carry on like this, you'll get eight bullets and the ninth's for me!"

Nico came out of role and went into total meltdown, "No, no, no, Christoph, you imbecile! I can't work like this. Herzog's not an Upper Franconian, he's from Munich. Go on, do it again. And make a bit of effort, or I'll smash your ugly face in, you repulsive freak of an artist."

This outburst actually did the trick. It spurred Gräve on to master Herzog's voice register and dialect so perfectly that he could've fooled anyone. He could've dialed a pizza delivery line pretending to be Werner Herzog ordering a double pepperoni with extra cheese.

On the eve of the premiere, Irmgard Al-Hassani and Waltraud Beermeyer-Stöpsel from the Senate Authority for Culture and Good Taste attended the dress rehearsal incognito. Slipping in through the back door, they accessed the theater pit through a rear entrance and eavesdropped from there. They were horrified to discover that the play was actually rather good, the performances outstanding and the set design ingenious. Speechless and shaking their heads in disbelief, the two women left the rehearsal after a little more than an hour, to retreat to their bunker in the ninth basement and consider their options. What could they do to hinder the success of the play at this eleventh hour? As they made their way out of the theater, they collided with a small figure in the darkness, someone who'd also concealed himself to observe the actors: Magnus Max. The ladies excused themselves politely, but Magnus had no time for any kind of pointless chitchat and remained glued to his binoculars, which were trained on Nico and his every movement.

The day of the grand premiere arrived. The Ballhaus Ost was completely sold out for the first time in months; every last seat was filled. As well as Mustafa the taxi driver, the audience also included all the characters from the story so far, for example Dr. Plump the psychologist, Schotenhauer the senile patient, but also of course Claudia and Erna, as well as all the characters that will appear as the novel progresses, and those deleted from the manuscript by the author. The lights were dimmed and the audience fell silent. The curtain went up to dramatic, jarring music by Györgi Ligeti—to reveal two crucified women, one white, one black. Then Nico appeared on stage, carrying a glowing neon-red plastic cross and accompanied by six SS men, six Japanese men and six Italians:

"Wanted—Jesus Christ. Accused of seduction, anarchic tendencies, conspiring against the state. Distinguishing feature: scars on the hands and feet."

———

At the close of the performance, as the curtain went down, a rapturous roar went up from the audience. The standing ovations lasted minutes. The theater world hadn't seen such a wave of ecstasy at a premiere for a long while. Many spectators wept in realization of the greatness and dimension of the historic moment, others laughed in joy and savored the experience. Then the curtain went back up and all the actors walked to the front of the stage, bowing and smiling. At the center of the group stood the overjoyed figures of Nico and Gräve, their arms wrapped around each other.

Nevertheless, when he spotted a man in the audience not clapping frenetically enough, Nico was ready to explode. But Gräve held him back and encouraged him to enjoy this extraordinary moment. The Senate ladies Irmgard and Waltraud sat in the front row, an indignant expression on their faces. They weren't applauding. They now knew that they'd be dealing with this Gräve character until their retirement;—and with him, many more terrible theater productions.

Later that night, the audience long gone and in their beds, the door of a quiet backroom at the Ballhaus Ost,—evidently used as a storeroom for cardboard boxes,—flew open and Nico and Gwyneth fell inside, their bodies entwined, their lips locked in a passionate kiss. They landed on top of one of the boxes and started tearing off bits of clothing. Like all suicide girls, Gwyneth was covered in tattoos. There was a pistol on both of her inner thighs, a jazzy planet constellation around her belly button and all manner of Japanese characters across her back.

Nico had never been with a dark-skinned woman before. Her skin felt different, which made it all the more exciting. When he spread her thighs to go down on her, he was surprised by the juicy pinkness of her vulva. Her clitoris was much larger than Claudia's, and he sucked it until Gwyneth could no longer bear it and straddled him hard until their simultaneous climax. The sex wasn't especially spectacular, but it was honest and driven by genuine affection. They shared another kiss, got dressed and went home.

The next morning, Nico and Gräve met for breakfast on the roof terrace of the *Motel One Flagship* hotel on Breitscheidplatz.

Gräve was first to arrive, and found the table covered with a range of newspapers and a few editions of specialist theater and culture magazines. All were effusive in their praise for the play, with particular plaudits for Nico—a total unknown who slipped with apparent ease into the shoes of Klaus Kinski. Gräve breakfasted in the pleasant sunshine, grinning with pleasure and pride at the rave reviews.

Before long Nico appeared through the glass door and headed straight for Gräves table. He was wearing ostentatiously large sunglasses. In a state of frenzied agitation, he started yelling the moment he saw the director, "This rag says I was brilliant!"

"But that's wonderful," said Gräve.

Nico reached the table, made a grab for all the papers and magazines and sent them flying over the veranda down towards the Memorial Church. "I wasn't brilliant... —I was *monumental!*"

Gräve had to laugh out loud and took a large gulp of coffee. His protégé Nico Pacinsky was evidently totally serious about believing he was Klaus Kinski. Method acting at its best! Gräve began fantasizing about the delicious successes that awaited, after all, he'd be milking this cow for some time to come. Kinski still had selling power, even today. Yesterday evening was the ultimate proof of that. He picked up a serviette and wiped a drop of coffee from his mouth. Then he said to Nico: "Hey, my friend Alexander Kluge called today."

Nico was beyond shocked. "Are you serious?"

"Yes, yes. He'd like to interview you on his program."

Nico was still reeling. "I hope you just said yes."

"Well no, I wanted to discuss it with you first."

"What is there to talk about?!" Nico raged.

"Well, he doesn't want to interview you as Nico Pacinsky...but as Klaus Kinski." Gräve was wary of Nico's reaction.

He burst out, "But I *am* Kinski, you moron!"

Gräve nodded, picked up his phone and tapped in a few

FLORIAN FRERICHS

commands. "I've just sent you Kluge's number. Call him. He'll meet you at short notice."

Nico looked at his phone as Alexander Kluge's contact details appeared on the screen with a quiet peeping sound. He unlocked the phone immediately to call him. It rang a few times, then he heard a voice as soft as an angel's.

"Yes, this is Kluge, yes?—Yes?"

110

20. CLEVERER

To one day meet the universal genius Alexander Kluge was one of Nico's long-held dreams. That he was now going to be a guest on his program to be personally interviewed by the great intellectual heavyweight himself,—that just blew his mind. He needed to channel his inner Kinski even more for the purposes of self-protection.

We're back in the place where this chapter began, in a recording studio where Alexander Kluge is interviewing our hero Nico in the role of Klaus Kinski. We'll pick it up where we left the conversation, at the point where Nico was dismantling his Walther PPK from 1931.

"You once said you were like an animal born in a zoo. What do you mean by that?" asked Kluge.

"That I'm in prison in the midst of this so-called civilization. That I'm chafing my skin on the bars of my cage. That I want to escape. To get away. The South American jungle is very good for me right now. The flies are the only thing bothering me of course. And that filthy director—what was his name?"

"Herzog?"

"That's it. He's a pain in the ass! That's why I'm screaming at him sometimes non-stop for twelve, twenty-four or even forty-eight hours to make sure that narcissistic murderer doesn't ruin everything. But what I wanted to say was that this so-called civilized humankind, which is complete bullshit, and its ridiculous rules,—it all seems so...meaningless!"

As he was talking, Nico reassembled the gun and loaded the magazine with several, old and rusty-looking bullets fished out of his jacket pocket.

"But in spite of that, each and every person claims to know the truth, don't they?" philosophized Kluge.

"It's meaningless. I mean, it's not without meaning, people give it a meaning,—but it all just doesn't make any sense!"

Kluge reflected on the latter sentence for a few seconds but then went for a change of subject. "What was your favorite role to date?"

Nico exploded: "How am I supposed to answer that! Why ask me a question like that!"

"Who would you most like to play?" Kluge tried a different tack.

"Paganini. Beethoven. Stalin. People of my caliber."

"Why do you hate the director Herzog so much, after all, you've done some of your best work with him?"

Nico sighed. He was bored of talking about Herzog. But then he quoted a paragraph from Kinski's autobiography *All I Need Is Love:*

"His talk is cumbersome, sluggish, fussy, pedantic, choppy. The words fall from his mouth like rubble. It goes on and on, flushing out his brain snot. Then he writhes, bullshit machine that he is; an old model whose off button doesn't function anymore. I have to punch him in the face. No, I have to knock him unconscious. But even unconscious, he would keep talking. Even if someone cut his vocal cords, he would keep talking like a ventriloquist. Even if somebody cut his throat and separated his head from his torso, words would issue from his mouth like foul gas."

Nico cocked the hammer of the Walther PPK and aimed the gun at his interviewer. Unmoved, Kluge asked in a calm, analytical tone, "What's your plan?"

"I don't have to always provide an explanation for everything, do I?" came Nico's laconic counter-question.

"Aha! *The Liberation of Expression from the Necessity of Meaning,* —yes? Sounds like something Schlingensief (the German Basquiat) would say…" Kluge was still offering his analysis as several bullets from Nico's pistol slammed into his chest and ripped his body apart. Parts of his liver became embedded in the plasterboard wall behind him forming a bizarre backdrop reminiscent of a work from the early design phase of Gustav Klimt. Kluge slumped off his chair and onto the floor. From there, he rasped his last words—for the moment, "Is this your way of recalling the Dada movement?"

Nico's Kinski-esque response was, "I don't understand the question…"

———

At the same time, a clandestine live feed of this rare interview recording flickered on one of the many monitors in Verne Zog's bunker. The venerable master sat in his chair and stroked his Ashera cat with a malevolent smirk. Another screen showed footage from the dress rehearsal for the play, while yet another showed the audience in raptures after the premiere. The huge desk in front of Zog was covered in piles of newspapers extolling the Gräve-Pacinsky stage success at the Ballhaus-Ost.

Thus spoke Zog, "Magnus, it's time. Get Mr Nico Pacinsky on the line."

Zog's adlatus appeared on his red self-balancing hoverboard.

He stepped off it and took up his place in an allocated spot to the left of Zog. On the touchscreen PC in front of him, he launched a conversation encryption program as well as an IP blocker. Then, on an ancient-looking green rotary dial phone from the Reagan era, he dialed Nico's mobile number. It rang.

Nico's mobile started vibrating just as he was leaving the Alexander Kluge studios and walking from Kluckstraße in Tiergarten via Lützowstraße to Kurfürstenstraße. Past glorious old Wilhelmine blocks, street whores and parks full of children and drug dealers. Although the call came from a withheld number, he nevertheless picked up. "I'm not giving any more interviews!" he yelled.

"Hello, am I speaking to Nico Pacinsky?" enquired Verne Zog on the other end of the line.

"No!" growled Nico.

"So who am I speaking to then?" Zog wanted to know.

"Ah, that's unbelievable! *You* called *me*, remember?" Nico spluttered. There followed a pause lasting several seconds, leaving Nico wondering whether the call had ended before it had even begun.

He was just about to hang up, when Verne Zog asked, "Should I call you Klaus?"

"Yes, that's my name."

"OK then, Klaus. I've heard about your formidable play and your intense dramatic power."

"Er, I don't understand the question!"

"That'll be because I've not asked one yet," said Verne Zog.

"I'm not sure I know how to respond to that…" answered Nico, increasingly irritated.

"I have a screenplay that's been waiting to be filmed for decades,—but thus far I've not found an actor that would even come close to meeting my colossal expectations."

"What's the fee?" Nico ventured.

"As much as you want it to be," said Zog smugly.

"Alright. What's my role?"

"This is the greatest heroic saga since the beginnings of humanity. What I plan to do with you is nothing less than create the greatest movie of all time and immortalize the life of my best fiend on celluloid: The life story of Klaus Günter Karl Nakszynski, also known under his jester pseudonym Klaus Kinski."

Slowly but surely, it began to dawn on Nico how he knew the calmly intellectual, nasal voice of the caller, and he started to get nervous. "Who are you?"

Verne Zog gave a dramatic pause, and for the first time it occurs to us that the man sitting in his chair shares a certain resemblance with Christoph Gräve. But with gray hair and a gray mustache. "I...am Werner Herzog!"

MY BEST FIEND

Spotify Playlist 3

21. ANDY AND UDO

IT WAS A COLD WINTER MORNING IN 1978. BERLIN WINTERS USED TO be so bone-chilling that even Russians from the Siberian tundra had trouble enduring them. The cold was wet and damp and penetrated through numerous layers of Goretex to the core.

Harald Schmidt was still Chancellor of the Federal Republic at that time, and the German youth was doing John Travolta with epileptic movements. The streets of West Berlin were filled with Opel C Kadett, VW, Citroën Ugly Ducklings and Mercedes W123 cabs. Men wore thick fur coats with extravagantly turned-up collars, and women did the same. People went shopping at Bolle and Meyer around the corner, and condominiums were doled out as a sort of welcome gift if you became a naturalized West German deserter. It was the time just *before* punk.

At Winterfeldtplatz, not far from Ku'damm, there was a music club called *Dschungel*. Storytellers still boast to this day about how they were there back then. Then you get to hear anecdotes about how great it all was when they hung out with Bowie, Nick Cave and Iggy at the *Dschungel* on Nürnberger Straße. But this quickly betrays the blurriness in the retrospective,—to put it kindly. At the time, the club was not located on Nürnberger Strasse, but on

Winterfeldtplatz. The visionary Bowie was so far ahead of his time that Berlin already pissed him off in '78 and he recorded the third album of his Berlin trilogy *Lodger* in Los Angeles instead of in the city. Nevertheless, Berlin continues to adulate itself with the fact that the artist of the century once briefly resided here and recorded his allegedly most important albums at Hansa Studios. Despite this, the city did not manage to name a street after him after his death, because it violated the bylaws of the Tempelhof-Schöneberg district council to name other streets after men. After all, there were already far too many in Berlin bearing the names of Prussian military men. And who ever stood for machismo and exuberant militaristic masculinity more than the intersexual Ziggy Stardust?

On an advertising pillar in front of the club, the film *Suspiria* by Dario Argento was being promoted, in which the young Udo Kier also had a guest appearance. The witch-horror flick was shown at the Metropol Theater and soon fell victim to an indexing in Germany.

The outside facade of the club was covered with all kinds of political and non-political posters. A few amateurish graffiti from the early days of the street art movement rounded off the picture and were a horror for pretty much everyone at the time.

From the metal door to the *Dschungel*, a young woman with a hippie haircut rushed out and collapsed on the cold floor laughing wildly, where she then tried to take a nap. Two policemen in green uniforms approached, bent down to her and picked her up. Immediately the lady began to clamor that she would not resist, and yet the fascist system wanted to deprive her of sleep. One of the policemen replied that she should please not make any *fisimatenten* (shenanigans) and just come along if she did not want to freeze to death. But the woman only got more upset and slurred through a memorized politicizing text from her AStA (hardcore leftwing fraternity), which, however, could no longer be reproduced at the time of going to press. Overcome by the realization that there was nothing more they could do, the police officers put the woman back on the ground and left.

In 1978, the *Dschungel* was not yet the cult club it became after it moved to Nürnbergerstraße. Although it was the middle of the day, there were still some extremely drunk and overtired young people dancing in one corner. At a table in an alcove, two men sat eating their breakfast, which consisted essentially of Bloody Marys. A real aura surrounded them, and they clearly stood out from the other guests. This was partly because they were sitting directly under a spotlight, which gave them something of a halo, and partly because they were extremely well dressed. They were already clearly buzzed, or rather they *still were*, because they hadn't left the club in over twenty-four hours. One, whose name was Andy, was American, about fifty years old, and wore thick dark sunglasses. His white-blond shaggy hair hung crisscross in his face as he smoked a thin cigarette, which he sporadically brought to his mouth with his ring and middle fingers.

The other was a thirty-four-year-old German named Udo, who was such an exceedingly handsome and attractive man that even Barbie's Ken would have turned green with envy. His full head of hair was brown, and his big, bullet-round shining eyes were a bright blue. He snuggled ever-so-slightly against Andy, and the two occasionally laughed together. Andy asked him, "Udo, my dear. Can you please once again repeat my favorite line from the movie?"

Udo shook his head with feigned embarrassment. His English was marked by a heavy German accent, "Sure, Andy.—*To know death, you have to fuck life—in the gallbladder!*"

They both laughed heartily, and Andy stroked Udo's cheek. "Beauty is a sign of intelligence."

Udo countered perkily, "Nevertheless, I was a total failure at school."

They laughed again when another man appeared from the darkness of the adjacent hallway. Udo stood up devoutly and extended his hand to him.

"Ah, hello Werner," Andy, who had remained seated, greeted the tall man.

"Good afternoon. I am really very pleased to make your acquaintance!" Udo stuttered reverently.

The man who stepped out of the darkness was none other than Verne Zog. And he looked exactly the same in 1978 as he would over forty years later. Clearly, the noble master did not age. He greeted Andy and Udo with a slight bow. He spoke slowly and deliberately in his nasal voice and slight Bavarian accent. "I greet you, Udo.—Andy, I am a big admirer of your art. I think its shattering use of nonchalant metaphysics elevates our reality to an entirely new level. I think your work will remain in the collective consciousness for centuries to come,—just like the cave paintings on the Indonesian island of Sulawesi."

Andy smiled kindly and waved it off. "Well, the idea is not to live forever,—but to create something that will."

Verne Zog finally sat down in the still vacant Thonet chair, and Udo said, "Werner, we have a present for you."

Udo dug out from behind his chair a one-meter by one-meter painting stamped on canvas that showed in pop art the faces of Verne Zog and Klaus Kinski on the set of *Aguirre, the Wrath of God*. Andy commented on the painting: "I'm an equal admirer of your art. And when I heard we were gonna meet here in Berlin, I was inspired to do a series on you and some of your film's characters."

Zog accepted the picture and was genuinely impressed: "Like the leader of the Indian tribe of Pokavalucha said, when he was offered beer and Lederhosen by Bavarian pioneers conquering the west, I'm flattered and honored to a sheer infinite extent."

Andy wanted to get to the business part of the conversation. "So,—you wanna make a movie with my friend Udo, yes?"

Udo smiled kindly at Zog, who emphasized the adjectives in the following eulogy in a way that only a true language connoisseur could do. He left a significant pause between each word, so that his monologue took on an inner drama and tension that could only be described as nerve-wracking. "Yes, Andy. I saw Udo's performance in your films *Flesh for Frankenstein* and *Blood for Dracula* and I think it was shocking, harrowing, distressing, percussive, upsetting, convulsing, shaking, frightening, brutally intimidating—and also very good. So, basically everything I seek in an actor.

Udo intervened: "Thank you, Werner."

Verne Zog and Andy paid only half-hearted attention to him. The actual conversation took place only between the two alpha males.

"And what do you have in mind for him?" Andy wanted to know.

"I will very soon reinterpret one of the most fascinating and angst-inducing fairy tales that ever came to life on the silver screen: Nosferatu—phantom of the night!"

Udo was immediately enthusiastic: "Oh, I love this movie!— Max von Schreck was a great inspiration when I prepared myself to play Dracula in your movie, Andy."

Udo smiled kindly at both men, but only Verne Zog gave him a casual nod, as if he were nothing more than an annoying but necessary burden. Andy, meanwhile, took another cigarette from his shiny gold case and offered one to Verne Zog as well. The latter declined, but pulled an old Red Army gasoline lighter from his pocket and used it to light Andy's cigarette. Andy asked Udo to get some whiskeys for everyone from the bar, and Udo immediately complied with the request.

As soon as he was out of earshot, Andy continued the conversation in a whisper: "Well, Werner, maybe you know that I have an exclusive contract with Udo. And only very rarely I lend him out to close friends and people I can really trust.—Why should I allow you to make use of his...capabilities? What do I get in return?"

Verne Zog smirked as if he had seen through Andy long ago, "I don't think that there is anything or any good that I could provide to a man of your wealth and social standing."

Andy bent over and grabbed Zog's knee with his left hand. "There are many things in this world I can't possibly possess."

At that moment, Udo returned with three whiskey glasses, placed them on the table in front of Andy and Verne Zog, and wanted to know, "So, did you come to an agreement?"

Andy and Zog looked up at Udo with piercing looks.

Fifteen minutes later:

In a gothic-style private fetish studio, whose interior could have been the set of a Dracula movie, the dark walls were decorated with stone reliefs of mediaeval rulers and the leaded windows with depictions of biblical rituals. Various chains and ancient-looking hand and foot shackles hung on two walls. The huge bed in the middle of the hall had a wooden frame with carved demons and underworldly animal creatures. Udo was already almost naked tied to the bed with leather straps, but a loincloth still covered his intimate zone. In his mouth he had a freshly slaughtered thigh bone, which was fastened behind his head with another leather strap, preventing him from speaking. The bone was still bloody, and some muscle fibers were hanging from it.

Andy and Verne Zog came staggering into the room tightly embraced, kissing passionately. They fell on the bed to the left and right of Udo and at the same time began kissing him on the bone in front of his mouth. As they did so, they pulled off the scraps of flesh with their teeth and gobbled them down like hungry lions. They kissed with their mouths wide open, and the fresh blood from the flesh flowed along the corners of their mouths with their saliva. Udo moaned completely out of his mind, so that his sounds came through the open window into the streets of Schöneberg, where schoolchildren were making their way home. But they were no longer surprised by anything anyway.

A full-blown swelling was now emerging from under Udo's loincloth. His animalistic sounds under the bone became even more violent, however, when Zog and Andy simultaneously pushed their heads toward the center of his body and began to give him a double blow job. As best he could, Udo tried to hold back his ejaculate, but after only a few seconds it was too late. The secretion mixed with the blood from Zog's and Andy's mouths to form a pink slime, which Andy greedily swallowed.

Just at that moment, the door flew open with a loud crash and Magnus Max stood in the room. He, too, already looked exactly as he did forty years later. Udo and Andy stared in amazement at the dwarf, who had kicked the door off its hinges with great force and now stood before them with a serious face. For Andy, at least, it would have been a novelty to involve a midget in lovemaking. For that very reason, he was delighted to see the man in the mini pinstripe suit with the doctor's bag under his arm. But the joy lasted only a moment, because immediately afterwards Andy and Udo were hit by curare arrows from Magnus Max's blowgun, and both lost consciousness instantly.

Verne Zog thanked his old friend for appearing on time and wiped his mouth clean with a handkerchief. The ceremony could begin. Magnus placed his doctor's case next to the bed and together with Zog hoisted the unconscious Andy next to the bound Udo. With leather and metal straps Andy was now also fixed to the bed. Magnus Max opened the suitcase and brought to light a blue sky disk and two jars. The disk would go down in the tabloids decades later as the *Nebra Sky Disk,* when robbers managed to ambush Magnus Max in Saxony and steal it from him. They later claimed to have found the ancient piece during illegal excavations in order to escape the much more punishable offense of dwarf robbery.

Magnus took out two more ancient South American masks from his bag, which he and Verne Zog put on. Now they looked like strange shamans from another dimension. Then Magnus opened the preserving jars and plucked out an eyelash from both Andy and Udo with tweezers, which he dropped into the buckets. He placed the sky disk between Andy and Udo on the bed and looked at them both through the mask for another second. "Those two will certainly take care of us for quite a while."

Verne Zog, however, instructed his friend and lackey with a quick glance to please be quiet now. Magnus winced slightly and moved to a corner at the other end of the room so that he was now standing behind Zog. The latter strutted like a conductor into the center of the room, spread his arms, and began to recite a pagan exorcism: "Gang ut, nesso, mid nigun nessiklinon."

The sky disc began to glow and give off a dazzlingly bright light.

"Ut fana themo marge an that ben, fan themo bene an that flesg."

The masks of Zog and Magnus also began to glow. Neon yellow streaks ran down their carved faces like thick raindrops and tears. Verne Zog's voice grew louder, "Ut fan themo flesge a thia hud, ut fan thera hud an thesa strala! Drohtin, vethe so!"

The masks showed wild patterns that moved as if in a 3D video mapping, but never repeated.

"Eiris sâzun idisi, sâzun hêra duoder. Suma haft heftidun, suma heri lêzidun."

The sky disk was now floating in the middle of the room and right between Udo and Andy, when suddenly ultra-bright bundled light beams emanated from their mouths, ears, eyes and noses, flowing directly into the open preserving jars.

"Suma clûbodun umbi cuniowidi: insprinc haftbandun, infar wîgandun."

The bright light outshone everything for a millisecond. Then there was a deafening bang, and in one fell swoop the glow from the masks went out, and no more rays of light came out of either Andy or Udo. Silence fell, and Magnus Max and Verne Zog took a moment's breath. They took off their ancient larvae; both were drenched in sweat.

There was a knock at the door, and the landlady's thin voice could be heard, inquiring about the occupants' well-being. Magnus answered that they were playing boules and preferred not to be disturbed. That was enough for the landlady, and she left.

Magnus held the jars against the light and looked at the viscous and faintly neon pink glowing ectoplasm of Andy and Udo. He screwed them shut with the appropriate lids, took two blank stickers from his pocket and stuck one on each jar. Then he labelled them with a black felt-tip pen: *Udo Kier* and *Andy Warhol*. He stowed them in his leather doctor's bag and then, looking at the lifeless bodies on the bed, asked his still rather exhausted noble Master Zog, "That's it for those two, isn't it?"

"Yes. They will remember a tremendous orgy of sex, drugs, and propaganda speeches, but in their remaining earthly lifetimes they will succeed in nothing of artistic or even intellectual value. They will find themselves from now on in a tremendous downward spiral of decadence and decline,—until death puts an end to their worldly bodies."

"So nothing changes for them," Magnus cheekily interjected. He and his master had to laugh heartily at that.

Then Zog looked again at the two exorcised on the bed and said with some disgust in his voice, "Come on, let's go. I am not a friend of soulless art. In their bodies, form and content now no longer correspond,—and I can't stand the sight of *L'art pour L'art* for three seconds."

Magnus nodded and packed his things. He walked down the two floors and out onto Nollendorfplatz, where the T-series Bentley Continental had been waiting for them with its engine running, already attracting a cluster of onlookers. Most of them had come from a Sunday trip to the flea market that had moved into the dead elevated Nollendorfplatz station, which also housed the Zille Museum. Magnus and Zog got into the car and drove off with the wheels spinning. First in the direction of Ku'damm and from there onto the Avus, past the ramshackle grandstands of former car races and at over 300 kilometers an hour in the direction of the inner-German border to Dreilinden at Checkpoint Bravo.

22. GUSION AGENCY

NICO WAS BACK ON THE COUCH OF HIS PSYCHOLOGIST, DR VARY Plump, and was now fully in Kinski mode. The success of Gräves' play had not only reinforced his neurosis, but cemented it in ferroconcrete. He now fully thought of himself as Klaus Kinski and had learned that whenever Nico Pacinsky tried to sneak up on him from the outside or the inside, he simply shouted him away.

"Those media freaks, at least, seem to be heavily into my performance in Gräve's play. I don't know what to make of it," he said excitedly.

"But these are fantastic developments. I congratulate you," Dr. Plump tried to encourage him.

"Honestly, I don't give a shit about my success or the success of the play," Nico lied to himself and the psychologist.

"I think you're starting to come into your own. And that's good news, Mr Pacinsky," Dr. Plump recited her psychologist text.

"Pacinsky? Who is that supposed to be?" Nico exploded.

But Dr. Plump didn't answer, instead making notes on her clipboard. Nico tried to peek at the note with a raised eyebrow, but couldn't make out what she was writing down.

"What will the coming weeks look like?" Dr. Plump steered to the next topic.

Nico, however, became philosophical: "Well, Gräve's play with me in the leading role is so successful that we'll probably have to keep doing this shit for a while to milk the cow. But you know...it's not me as an individual that matters in the process. It's the audience we're prostituting ourselves to so violently! And that's where the problem lies, the audience is an ungrateful bunch of fucking cultural philistines! Some even dare to enter the stands coughing or even clearing their throat. And such a thing is unheard of. What are cough drops for? If it were up to me, they'd have them beaten up right away,—but that's probably not so *en vogue* anymore, as I hear...The Rolling Stones have hired the Hells Angels for their concerts. And there, everyone gets stabbed a bit if they can't behave. It's an educational issue: you don't bother other people, you know? If this hypothetical person then *still* misbehaves, then he gets fully stabbed, and I think it's just fair!"

Dr. Plump smiled, apparently not really taking her patient and his confused neurosis seriously. "You seem to be completely absorbed in your role."

Nico instantly cried out: "What's this nonsense? No! This is no role;—it is *me*, do you understand?—That's exactly why the mass murderer, slash screenwriter, slash film director Herzog contacted me."

Dr. Plump dropped the clipboard from her hand in shock. She picked it up with shaky hands and had to collect herself for a moment. Had she understood the name correctly? "*Werner Herzog?*"

But Nico was already raving on, "It was clear that he couldn't do without the Kinskian genius forever. You only have to look at the moronic films he made without my involvement, In-Tol-er-able!"

Dr. Plump bit her lip nervously and thought excitedly. Every cell in her body was in a state of alarm and excitement. Was this neurotic, whose health insurance always paid for the sessions without hesitation, telling the truth and in contact with Werner Herzog? Nico Pacinsky was not a notorious liar like other patients whose diagnosis was *Pseudologia Phantastica*. Everything he told her was his honestly perceived truth, that much she knew. And a war-criminal like Herzog could definitely be trusted to want to make a feature film about Klaus Kinski. Especially with an unknown actor who had suffered serious psychological damage.

Without elaborating on the thought, Dr. Plump stood up and said goodbye to Nico, telling him that the session was over. Nico, however, was more than a little surprised, since their session actually continued for another forty-five minutes. But Dr. Plump didn't want to get into a discussion and pressed a black button on her desk. Immediately, a cutout in the wall that Nico had never perceived as a door before opened, and a black Hulk named Samael strode through like the Terminator. The handsome, muscular man, who was always dressed in dark blue, acted as Dr. Plump's personal assistant. His member measured a proud thirty-seven centimeters and had already given her many a sore spot, but also various hours of fulfilled pleasure. However, it was not so much Samael's flawless body or his sexual virtuosity that fascinated her. Rather, she was interested in his psyche, which had developed a rather unique form of Oedipal self-hatred. Few, in fact, knew that the Afro-German had a gigantic swastika tattooed on his back and had long been considered St. Pauli's most brutal and insane neo-Nazi thug. In his confused Oedipus complex, Samael accused his mother of being a racial abuser and himself the result of it. Dr. Plump, however, concluded in her analysis that Samael was neither a true racist nor a National Socialist. Rather, because of his permanent dissatisfaction with himself and the circumstances surrounding him, his psyche had sought the greatest possible multiplier to constantly provide new fuel for self-destruction. And so Dr. Plump found it particularly appealing not only to observe his further development but also to influence it in micro doses of psychological intervention.

Samael reared up in front of Nico. Without another word, he got up from the couch and let himself be escorted outside with his tail between his legs. The door closed. As soon as Dr. Plump was alone in the room, she reached for the phone on her desk. She dialed an extremely long number that began with +1-310.

———

It was still the middle of the night when the phone rang in an office in Century City. The offices of the *Gusion Agency*, an agency for actors, directors and writers, were in the same building as the headquarters of Haim Saban and his Power Rangers, who were down in the basement waiting for their next assignment. All the desks on the eighth floor were empty. Only one lamp was still on in a separate office behind glass. There sat Guido Gusion, a forty-three-year-old, extremely handsome Semite with black, slicked-back hair and piercing blue, intelligent eyes. In front of him were two monitors, one of which was currently displaying the image of the website *Boxofficemojo* and the other the interface of *IMDB-Pro*. The Amazon Echo Show in front of it displayed current stock charts, and his iPad Pro in a wooden stand was running a feed from the site *Live-Leaks*. Guido was currently studying the revenues of several of his clients' films to be able to estimate their values for the next films. The ringtone of his phone was the melody of *Angel of Death*, a song by the American thrash metal band Slayer, of which Guido had been a big fan since his youth. The song provided a relentless description of the gruesome acts of concentration camp doctor Joseph Mengele. Guido drummed his fingers on his desk to the fast-paced music and then looked at the phone's display. He wondered, because an unknown number from Germany was displayed there. He answered it and greeted it with his standard greeting. When he then perceived Dr. Plump's voice on the other end of the line and the world, he rejoiced. But before he could inquire about the condition of his colleague and friend, she interrupted him, saying that she had an actor whom they urgently needed to observe.

"What business? Film...—or the other one?" Guido wanted to know.

"He's actually a stage actor," Dr. Plump admitted.

"Oh, I'm sorry, Vary. I don't deal with theater people."

"But this one's different. Believe it or not,—Werner Herzog wants to do a movie with him!" She excitedly recited the news and Guido's jaw dropped.

"What?! Is this verified intel?"

"Well, at least that's what he claims."

"What's the actor's name?" Guido now inquired, increasingly agitated.

"Nico Pacinsky."

Guido immediately typed a series of search terms on his keyboard, and various pages appeared in German, reporting the success of a certain Nico Pacinsky as Klaus Kinski. Guido rubbed his chin thoughtfully.

Dr. Plump looked around her office and then whispered into the phone:

"This might actually be the opportunity to get hold of him."

Guido was electrified by the thought and his breathing accelerated again. "If we manage to handle the situation correctly, then yes."

Both were silent for a moment, listening to each other breathe.

"Are you coming to Berlin?" Dr. Plump asked with some anticipation.

"Booking a flight right now!"

"Perfect."

Without another word, he hung up and nibbled excitedly on his thumb fingernail. He and Dr. Plump were looking forward to seeing each other again.

23. EAT A SCHNITZEL, BOY!

THE KU'DAMM WAS REDISCOVERED IN THE 2000S AND THEREFORE quickly degenerated into the shopping promenade of the new European chic scene and in-people. Here, they wore Dolce & Gabbana sweatpants and considered Ed Hardy T-shirts a sign of superior culture. The women were botoxed—as were their men. At every corner you met party mayor Klaus Wowereit or star hairdresser Udo Walz, who seemed to be prancing through the streets of Charlottenburg all day in a complicated choreography to really catch the eye of every visitor to Berlin. So people paraded day in and day out along Kurfürstendamm, their sports cars with flap exhaust pipes screeched at top speed, and anyone who had never been to Paris thought the West Berlin boulevard was a counterpart to the Champs-Élysées.

A BVG bus on the M29 line pulled up to the stop at Adenauer Platz and opened its doors. A number of diverse people from different cultural backgrounds got on and off. A Swedish family dressed in Fjällraven clothing and matching backpacks entered the vehicle, and the father, with a friendly smile, held out to the bus driver the ticket he had apparently just purchased from the ticket machine. He expected that it would now be stamped. This was a mistake. The bus driver looked at him dumbly while the Swede waited cheerfully for an official confirmation of admission to the public transportation system. After a few seconds of awkward silence, the bus driver snarled in his barking Berlinish tone: "Yeah, should I bite it, or what?"

The Swedes were confused at first, and the father looked at the bus driver uncertainly. He lowered the ticket and asked the BVG man in perfectly understandable tourist German what he meant. But the professional driver didn't feel like discussing it further and barked loudly like a dog without further warning: WOOFFF! The family flinched, and the father sat down helplessly with his loved ones on one of the cushioned side benches. As if he had to make up for the seconds lost in the conversation, the bus driver started up with such a jerk that the passengers held on convulsively. The Swedish family had sat down right next to Nico, who smiled at them in a friendly manner and then, like a true cosmopolitan, tried to comment on the situation in English, "Don't mind the bus-driver. Berliners bark, but they don't bite!"

The Swedish mother thought about it for a moment and then replied with a seriousness that is unique to Scandinavians when they joke, "Ah, you mean like the people from Eskilstuna;—they fish, but they don't eat it." Her family laughed briefly, but Nico had to scratch his head. Had what the Swedish woman just said made any sense?

The bus braked abruptly and all passengers had to hold on again. An elderly lady banged her head so hard against the stop signal switch that a laceration in the shape of that very switch appeared on her forehead. But only the Swedes seemed to care, because they were the only ones who came to her aid. All the other passengers continued to stare silently at their smartphones or newspapers, annoyed by the new interruption to the journey. The injured woman didn't even want any help, and shooed the Swedes away like annoying flies with a wave of her hand.

Through the front window of the bus, a pregnant woman with a stroller was about to cross the road in the bus lane. Apparently, she had overlooked the approaching bus. The bus driver opened the front door and shouted out with a deafening but impressive timbre, "This is a bus lane,—not Prenzl'Berg!" (Berlin's Silver Lake)

The approximately four-year-old child in the stroller leaned out of his seat and gave the bus driver the finger. The driver returned the gesture and drove as close as possible to the baby buggy with squealing tires to teach mother and child a lesson. Due to the jerky acceleration, the injured lady was now thrown with the back of her head against the unicycle of a hipster. But before she could hold on to it, the bearded man managed to bring his valuable vintage vehicle from anno 1900 to safety.

Nico asked the Swedes, "So, how do you like our city so far?"

They did not answer, but only smiled slightly moronically.

In the outdoor area of the Italian restaurant *Paulo Scutarro* at George-Grosz-Platz, Christoph Gräve sat at one of the fully occupied tables. Across from him was a real giant of a man: ex-bodybuilder, gladiator and Arnold Schwarzenegger's buddy Ralf Moeller. Very fit, with a cigar in his mouth and in the best of moods as always. Gräve was pitching him his play. "And then Kinski tries to kill Herzog, because he believes he still has a score to settle."

Ralf tapped him on the shoulder with such force that Gräve almost fell forward. The muscleman laughed jovially and was genuinely enthusiastic. "That's great cinema, of course, Mr Theater-Director!"

Despite a now aching shoulder, Gräve enthusiastically continued to present the content of his play: "But Herzog also wants to kill Kinski. For his part, he believes that the demon that once possessed Kinski now resides in the actor Nico!"

"Suuuuper! My friend, this all reminds me quite strongly of the early works of Ridley and also Roland! Wonderful!" Ralf hit the table with his huge paws in joy, and all the dishes jumped up an inch.

Nico came from the bus stop and walked across George Grosz Square to the restaurant with the numerous tables. He kept a lookout for his director and finally made him out in the crowd. At the same moment, Gräve spotted him as well and waved him over. Nico came to the table and they greeted each other in a friendly manner. Gräve introduced Nico and Ralf to each other: "Ralfi, Nico.—Nico, Ralfi."

"Call me Klaus!" Nico said, with some resentment.

Ralf Moeller laughed uproariously, half rose and pressed the clearly smaller Nico warmly and fiercely against his chest. "Hahaha! YES! Klaus! Wonderful. I've heard so much about you, my dear."

"Nico is the new star in the theater sky!" Gräve interjected. "And just as everything in life is not a gigantic coincidence or *necessary* in the sense of eternal recurrence, *we* found each other!"

"That's great. Der Arnold is also a huge Kinski fan!" Ralf added, taking another enjoyable drag on his cigar.

Gräve nodded with satisfaction, "Ralfi will be part of my plan to cast the role of Herzog in the play with ever-changing celebrities."

"What?" asked Nico with some horror.

Ralf, however, continued to smile amiably while Gräve elaborated on his plans, "Yes, next week Ralfi will take over my role."

"And the week after, either der Jean-Claude or even der Arnold. I'll make the introduction," Ralf interjected with verve.

Nico didn't know how to answer, "Well, I don't know how to answer!"

Ralf wanted to appease him, "Well, order something first, my dear. Eat a schnitzel, boy!"

"No, I..."

"Would you rather have strawberry cake?" Ralf asked in surprise.

"Well, I wanted to...," Nico stammered.

"Schnitzel it is then."

Ralf waved to the waitress, who was taking an order two rows away, and called out loudly to her: "One schnitzel for my friend here!—Christoph, you too?"

"No, thank you..."

But Ralf ignored him: "One strawberry tart with extra cream for the new star director—I'll pay for that. And for me, a double espresso with cane sugar to go with it!"

Ralf grinned again broadly and generously. He was a real teddy bear. But Gräve tried to pick up the thread from a moment ago: "Anyway, I'm planning some more pretty heavy gimmicks. We'll be selling out performances into the next millennium!"

Nico, however, was fuming: "Well, Christoph, that's what I wanted to talk to you about."

All of Gräve's facial features sagged forebodingly. "What's going on?" he wanted to know with serious concern.

"Well...I got a call from...Werner Herzog. He wants to make a film about Kinski's life—my life—with me in the leading role..."

Nico looked up at his director with puppy dog eyes. At the same moment, Ralf Moeller's loud laughter sounded again, "Hahaha! Just like in your play, Christoph. The boy really gets into the role. Ingenious method acting. Der Robert und der Al send their regards. Great! And such great writing, too."

He took the manuscript of Gräve's play from the table and leafed through it enthusiastically. Gräve, on the other hand, was slightly unsettled. Was Nico serious? Or was he really completely absorbed in his role?

Then the waitress brought the strawberry tart and placed it in front of him. Ralf took the espresso from her before she could put it down and drank the hot coffee in one go. "Thank you, my dear!"

Nico, meanwhile, pulled a 150-page pad of paper from his leather shoulder bag. "The contract arrived this morning by express messenger directly from Herzog's Alpine fortress."

Gräve looked at the contract in front of him and was perplexed. Ralf grabbed the heavy stack and leafed through it, skimming a few passages. Then Nico finally blurted out the full truth: "Anyway, it says in there that from now on I'm not allowed to accept any more engagements and I have to terminate all others with immediate effect if I want to be in Herzog's film."

"That's out of the question," mumbled Gräve, completely apathetic. In his mind's eye, he could already see his masterpiece collapsing like a house of cards.

"I don't want to let you down." Nico tried to placate him. He was strangely level-headed, although his adrenaline level was already rising. "But this chance is unique, you know?"

"Nico, you have no idea what you're getting yourself into!" Gräve hissed. There was a strange certainty in his sentence. As if he had known Herzog personally for years,—and feared him.

Ralf Moeller interjected, "Well, you two certainly have a contract, too, don't you?"

Gräve flew into a rage and jumped up from the table. "Exactly! And our contract will be honored, too!"

Nico immediately switched back to Kinski mode and yelled after the departing Gräve, "You're insane, man! I take a dump on your contract! With coke diarrhea!"

His director had already left the restaurant's terrace, but turned back over his shoulder and shouted, "You'll be at the Ballhaus in two hours! Right on time! We're sold out again today!"

Nico overturned the table and Ralf instinctively slid his chair backwards to avoid the projectiles from the place setting. Gräve's strawberry cake with extra cream landed on the tits of Desiree Nick (the German Amy Schumer), who was sitting at the next table giving an interview to a reporter from *BILD am Sonntag,* despite her recent reduction mammoplasty. Nico yelled after Gräve, beside himself, "You success-hungry scene stealer, you're out of your mind!"

Gräve, however, left without turning around again. Several guests began to whisper and pointed with feigned indignation at Nico, whom they secretly admired for his animalistic habitus. Nico, however, sat back down on the chair and looked at Ralf Moeller silently across the overturned table.

Ralf studiously ignored the outburst and asked with serious fascination, "Werner Herzog? For real?"

There came the schnitzel ordered for Nico, which looked so delicious with the lukewarm potato-cucumber salad and cranberry sauce that Ralf ordered another one for himself right away. After all, he needed protein. And lots of it. Then he picked up the overturned table with a movement that could not be surpassed in ease, took another pleasurable drag on his cigar, and gave Nico a friendly grin while several waiters spooned the strawberry tart from Desiree Nick's cleavage and ate it up.

24. THE BOY IS MINE

THE OLD NEW BUILDING IN CHARLOTTENBURG'S SAVIGNY neighborhood, where Nico lived with his girlfriend, was about to be completely gentrified. Most of the residents were young people from southern Germany who had never had jobs, but always had *projects* instead. Every morning they took the subway to Kreuzberg or Friedrichshain with their Macbooks under their arms and analog cameras around their necks to hang out in the relevant cafés, so no one would know that their parents couldn't afford the exorbitant rents in the really hip districts. The permanent and penetrating smell of home-rolled cigarettes and fair-trade coffee that wafted ever more strongly through the streets of Charlottenburg-Wilmersdorf at the time did not bode well for the district's long-established residents. At least a few real Berlin *Atzen* (Berlin slang for proletarians) still lived in the various courtyards and side wings. On the second floor of the front building, for example, lived a man with an old Slavic name that sounded good but could never be remembered. Wearing underpants and a bacon-covered undershirt, the chubby gentleman stood on a rickety ladder, trying to hang a framed picture of former Icelandic Foreign Minister Gundlaugur Thór Thórdarson on the wall, balancing his layers of fat like an artist on a tightrope. Why he hung the painting, we will probably never know. But it is extremely likely that he did not know exactly either and never asked himself the question. At the same time, on the third floor of the left side wing, Mr Meyer attached a rope to a metal eyelet on the ceiling. The extremely corpulent man put the noose around his neck and then climbed onto a chair.

Meanwhile, on the fourth floor of the central front building, Claudia and her mother Erna were preparing a traditional Transylvanian lunch. They were serving peppers stuffed with minced meat from various animals, accompanied by mashed potatoes with sauce. As in many rented apartments in Berlin, the walls were extremely thin, and one could eavesdrop on just about all the tenants through the electrical outlet sockets. So both women looked up, startled, when they heard the muffled sound of a rope tightening and a gurgling from the floor below them on the right. It was clear to them that somewhere in the building an apartment would probably become available again, into which either a shared apartment with students from the HTW-Uni or an experimental musician from Rhineland-Palatinate would then move.

Fortunately, however, in Berlin after the war the ceilings of the apartments were often stuffed only with straw, war debris and ashes, so that neither lamps nor anything else could be fixed in them. Therefore, the hook immediately tore out of the ceiling and Mr Meyer fell with a heavy thud on his hairy butt. Thus the friendly dog lover and bachelor remained with the neighbors for another twenty-seven years until his death in the great firestorm of Halensee.

Claudia was chopping onions, and Erna was stirring with a wooden spoon in the pot on the gas stove, in which a red sauce was simmering. They were just talking about Nico.

"It is up to us women to strengthen our men in their struggle!

After all, behind every successful man there is always a woman from Transylvania, as they say," Erna claimed and Claudia just nodded. "And Nico is such a wonderful man, you should appreciate that, my dear." Erna looked briefly at the ceiling.

"Yes, I do, too.—But what's wrong with you all of a sudden? The other day you wanted me to shoot him down!" Claudia said, increasingly suspicious.

"The play opened my eyes. He is such a sensitive and good-natured type of artist." Erna took out her smartphone, which had just received a message via a message service. This came from Magnus Max, who wanted to know if Nico would now sign the contract with Verne Zog. Worried, she turned her gaze once again to the ceiling.

"Say, sweetheart. That other offer he got...the movie with Werner Herzog...is he doing that?"

But Claudia shook her head in resignation:

"I have no idea. He doesn't tell me anything anymore. I only know that the contract with the Ballhaus-Ost stands in the way."

"Oh, nonsense...you have to tell him it's the right thing to do. Just think of the fee..." Erna insisted.

————

At the same time, in Verne Zog's bunker, the dwarf Magnus Max was watching the goings-on in Nico's apartment via live feed through a camera hidden in the kitchen ceiling, watching quite sympathetically as Erna tried to influence the complicated situation through her daughter. On the various monitors in the command centre, Magnus was able to observe every room via the surveillance cameras. He heard and saw everything that had been going on there for a few weeks. And he spent hours analyzing and evaluating the recordings for the noble Master Zog. So now he also saw Claudia trying to appease her mother. She wanted to visit

Nico today at the Ballhaus-Ost to talk to him and try to persuade him to accept Herzog's film offer. Using the computer's touch display, Magnus typed another message into a window and could see via the video feed that it appeared immediately on Erna's phone. Magnus knew, of course, that Erna was aware of him watching her. He reminded her of this as often as he could, in order to slowly but surely wear down the woman who was supposed to help him and the master in achieving their ultimate goal, and thus turn her into a passive enforcer of Zog's plans. Then a new window popped up on the tablet to Magnus' left, displaying an incoming video call from Christoph Gräve. He seemed hardly surprised and accepted the call with a swipe across the display.

Gräve was sitting in his car: an old but extremely well-maintained 1987 BMW 7 Series E23 with leather upholstery and air conditioning, which he had imported from California a few years ago after the EU abolished VAT on the import of classic cars and drastically reduced the duty on them. His cell phone was attached to the windshield by means of a suction cup, so that the front camera filmed him during the video call. Without further greeting, Gräve rumbled off:

"I want to talk to Zog right now!"

"Forgive me, noble Gräve, but the master is indisposed at the moment."

"Magnus. Get—him—on—the—phone. Now!"

"I'm afraid that's impossible. You'll have to make do with me."

The fake friendliness only infuriated Gräve even more. He yelled into the phone.

"Tell Zog that Nico is *my* actor! I have a contract for at least twenty-four more performances. If Zog wants to film Kinski's life, he'll have to find another performer, or at least wait until the play's season is over!"

Gräve raged with anger. Literally. He was crossing the bicycle-pedestrian-motor vehicle encounter zone at Winterfeldtplatz at thirty kilometers an hour - per wheel - when he spotted a Berlin police speed camera in the distance and immediately slammed on the brakes. Numerous papers and Red Bull cans flew through the car,—as if in a snowstorm. He managed to slow down to the prescribed 20 kilometers an hour at the last second and was so annoyed at the brazenness of the law enforcement officers to set up a radar here that he honked at the newspaper-reading policemen in the speed camera car and insulted them through the window as rip-off artists.

"Is there a problem?", Magnus Max asked.

"Yes...tell Zog that I expect his call back and insist on the fulfillment of the contract with Nico!"

"That is not an option incumbent upon you. You'd better remember who brought Nico Pacinsky to you at Ballhaus-Ost."

"Yes, but..." stuttered Gräve, a bit overwhelmed.

"Nothing but. You've had your success. Enjoy it while it lasts. But from now on, Mr Nico Pacinsky is ours."

"We'll see about that!" Gräve shouted at the end and then pressed the keypad to hang up. The screen that had just been showing the live feed went black.

Somewhat nervously, Magnus chewed on the dead skin on the side of his ring fingernail bed and thought about the situation.

"What a fucking bastard..." he said to himself.

25. TXL

TEGEL WAS ONCE BERLIN'S PROUD LANDMARK AIRPORT, STRETCHING skyward in the glorious West Berlin architecture style of the 1970s. Even though, like much of Berlin, it was already obsolete when it opened, Tegel still transported tens of millions of people to all countries every year,—and a few of them back again. It ultimately had to be closed, however, because after fifty years of operation, the district's residents could no longer cope with the aircraft noise. Many had previously moved to the flight path to finally have a reason to really complain, which is known to be the Germans' favorite hobby.

Mustafa's Mercedes E-class taxi drove out of one of the tunnels leading to the terminal. He had Dr Vary Plump on board and told her in one go and without pause about his most absurd passengers, "...and then the other day: there was a completely crazy patient who wanted a ride without pants, only in a hospital shirt! Bare ass!"

Sitting in the back of the car, Dr. Plump rubbed her forehead. "Yeah, well...I think you can let me out here."

"What? You said your friend flies British Airways. They all arrive at Gate A unless they make an emergency landing. Then

Gate B! And then there was that lunatic a few months ago who thought the devil lived in the Pergamon Museum. What nonsense! He sits in the Currywurst Museum on Friedrichstraße."

Dr. Plump felt an aura begin to form in her head, the precursors of a severe migraine. She had such attacks again and again, especially when she was exposed to political issues that did not coincide with her own convictions.

The cab stopped at Gate A. "So, here we are!" Mustafa rejoiced. "That's €39.80."

Dr. Plump took a two-euro piece out of her pocket and gave it to Mustafa, who looked at her in amazement. "That's missing a little bit!"

"The remaining amount has already been settled with PayPal, right?"

Dr. Plump got out, and Mustafa did the same. He called after her, "Wait a minute! No PayPal!"

She held up her smartphone, slightly annoyed, and felt the migraine aura spreading from the right side of her head to the left. "I booked you through the Uber app, didn't I?"

"But Uber as such doesn't operate in Berlin. Thank God!" Mustafa raised both hands briefly to the sky. Dr. Plump unlocked her phone and held the Uber app in front of the cab driver. "But it says here: *the amount was debited from your account*."

Mustafa now understood the problem. "Yes. You can book cabs via Uber. But I can only be booked through the cab app,— not through Uber."

At the same time, Dr. Plump's eyes fell on the Uber advertisement on the side of the cab. "But you even advertise it!"

"It's just that anyone who pays well can put their stickers on it..." Mustafa tried to placate.

His passenger, however, finally wanted to leave for the gate. "Listen. I have to pick up my colleague..."

Mustafa smiled kindly. "Then you better pay now. I've had this happen before. I don't know why Uber has my cab in their system. You'll just have to email them and request a refund. Anyway, I only take cash."

Dr. Plump took another heavy breath. Then she tapped Mustafa's chest with her index finger. The sky instantly turned blood red, and hot lava flowed along the car feeder roads while sparks and sulfur rained everywhere. Mustafa wondered for a moment,—but then his eyes widened in shock. Dr. Plump's index finger entered his chest hissing like a soldering iron, and he groaned in pain. He could not escape, but had to watch helplessly as Dr. Plump's hand burned deeper and deeper into him. He looked into her face. It had contorted into a brutal, demon-like grimace that bellowed, gurgling and deafening, "Better...—sign...—up...—with...—Uber."

The poor man could just nod, he was so filled with pain and fear. The next moment, however, everything was back to normal: no demon face, no hole in his chest, and no limbo around him. Dr. Plump talked to him completely calmly, "Uber is the future of transportation. Now, a receipt, please."

Mustafa scratched his head in confusion. Was he losing his mind? Had the many psychopaths he took from A to Z every day in his Benz finally short-circuited his brain? Dr. Plump gave Mustafa two twenty-euro bills from her wallet. Apathetically, the cab driver accepted the money, then quickly filled out a receipt on his pad and gave it to the psychologist. She walked away hurriedly, but turned around briefly with a slight smile. Mustafa noticed it and got into his car in a daze.

"Amcik suratli..." he cursed and drove to the nearest cab stand.

Dr. Plump entered the airport through the sliding glass door. She tried to make out where the passengers were arriving in the maze of signs on the ceiling. Some of the displays seemed to be defective and showed nothing but a jumble of letters. That's when she spotted a police officer shuffling casually through the aisles with both hands on his *Heckler and Koch submachine gun Five*. Friendly, she approached him. "Excuse me, please."

The officer nodded with a frown, raised his gun a bit and seemed to expect a terrorist attack from the woman. The psychologist pointed to the fancy display boards, "Do you possibly know where the passengers who just landed at Gate A3 are arriving?" The policeman replied grimly: "Of course I do!"

Then he turned on his heel and went down the stairs to the restroom, leaving Dr. Plump baffled. Immediately afterwards, someone tapped her on the shoulder from behind. She flinched slightly and turned around. In front of her stood Guido Gusion, who greeted her warmly and gave her a kiss on the cheek. She returned the kiss, slightly irritated.

"That's how you do it in Europe, isn't it?" Guido asked. There was no doubt that there was an erotic tension between the two.

"Ehh...yes. Of course.—How was the flight?" Dr. Plump inquired politely. Side by side, the two walked toward the airport restaurants.

"Well, the damn TV in front of me didn't work, so instead of staring into a black hole for ten hours I decided to get a good night's sleep."

As if seeing her for the first time, Guido noticed Dr. Plump's glowing red hair, and she noticed his deep blue eyes.

"You must be hungry. We can grab a bite here at the *Red Baron* and discuss our next steps," Dr. Plump suggested. Guido agreed, and shortly thereafter, over lunch together, the two discussed how they would proceed to finally find Werner Herzog and liquidate him.

26. THE GREATEST THESPIAN FÜHRER OF ALL TIME

NICO ENTERED THE FOYER OF THE BALLHAUS-OST AT A TAUT marching pace. He seemed extremely upset. Even when Gräve's assistant Gwyneth greeted him behind her counter with a cheerful smile, his mood did not change. She gave him a kiss on the mouth. But he left her with the statement that he had to speak to Christoph Gräve immediately and went on in the direction of the corridor to his office.

In the meantime, Gräves' office looked like a nightmarish garbage dump. Like the kind of place you see in dramatic documentaries about Africa. One almost expected to see a couple of Angolan children somewhere in a corner behind the desk looking for usable scrap metal with a stick. Gräve himself was sitting at the table covered with papers and beverage cans and kept taking greedy puffs on his e-pipe. At the same time, he was on the phone trying to negotiate with a tamer, because he now wanted to have animals perform in his play.

"What?—How can a lion cost so much money? That's more than Dennis Franz and Alyssa Milano put together!"

Angrily, he slammed the receiver down on the phone. Without knocking, Nico entered.

"Ah, good that you're here!" Gräve greeted him.

"So...I'm sorry about our argument about the contract earlier," Nico began. "But we need to find a solution so I can work with Herzog, too." He wiped a stack of papers off a chair and sat down.

Gräve looked at him sadly and sighed. "That damned devil of a Verne Zog!"

"Who?" Nico wanted to know.

Gräve folded his arms and looked at Nico seriously for a moment. "Let me tell you the story of a boy who wanted to be a director," he then began. "Full of ideas, creativity and fire. It was in Berlin Kreuzberg in 1978. Amidst early punks, migrants and some old school drunks, I got out of the subway station at Schlesisches Tor smoking and walked across the street towards a squat. I was eighteen years young at the time, just graduated from high school and had absolutely no money. But that didn't matter. I entered the old building, which still had various war damages. There were a hell of a lot of them in Berlin at the time. A friend had given me the address, and I can still see it in front of me: In the basement there was a shop window that read: *Private Theater and Film School Verne Zog*. I opened the door and entered a room whose walls were completely painted black. The room was lit only by a few thick red candles. A few pieces of sports equipment such as bars and punch bags were attached to the walls, and there was a smell of hashish and menthol. On the floor, on a large Persian carpet, sat eight men and women from Berlin's alternative scene. I didn't really like people like that, but they were listening to their mentor giving a lesson. There was something spiritual about it, because it was Verne Zog himself who was lecturing. I sat down on the floor with the others and listened fascinated to Zog's explanations."

Gräve pulled on his electric pipe before he disguised his voice and, as Verne Zog, reproduced what the latter had recited to his students at that time: "It is of decisive importance that in the selection of the actors both the ordering and logic-birthing forces of the god Apollo and the wild, orgiastic and destructive energies of Bacchus are taken into account. Almost all of us who feel the creative forces within us know these demons and the inner struggle they wage within us.—Verne Zog had such a nasal, Bavarian tone," Gräve now continued again in his own voice. "We hung on his lips and listened spellbound to his words. I became his student. My mentor was a genius in the art of directing. We rehearsed incessantly with numerous mimes the most diverse pieces of world literature and also worked out our own scenes and dialogues. He gave me tips that still influence me today and help me in guiding the actors in a scene. From him I learned how to really *work with* actors. And very soon I got the hang of it. On a small Kreuzberg backyard theater stage, we rehearsed again and again. Under his aegis, I celebrated my first small successes. That feeling when a performance is over and you can take a bow together with the performers in front of an applauding audience...nothing has ever made me happier. Verne Zog initially stood by me in all situations like a father figure. I became more and more self-confident and was soon directing larger performances quite confidently. But everything in life comes to an end, and so there was a big row between me and my teacher. Because whenever I discovered new talents, Verne Zog interfered and summoned the young actors to his office to *advise* them. To this day, I have no idea what exactly he did with them, but after he was done, they were good for nothing! Completely talentless! The actors were just staggering around the stage in an uncoordinated manner and brought me to the brink of despair. I confronted Verne Zog. We argued, for I reproached him because his advice was destroying my finds. When I arrived at Schlesisches Tor the next morning, several fellow students were already standing in front of the closed doors of the theater school, peering through the shop window. I jerked on the door and squinted through the mail slot.—The premises had been completely emptied! The school no longer existed. And our training under Verne Zog had abruptly ended."

Gräve and Nico looked at each other silently for a moment. Then Nico said, "Really a nice story, Christoph.—But we should now please think about how we can dissolve our contract."

"Nico, you don't understand. My mentor... his name was...*Verne Zog*! And he's one of the 100 most influential people on the planet according to *Time Magazine*!"

"I see," Nico said, a bit puzzled. "Then how come I've never heard that name before? Verne...how?...Zog?"

Gräve paused meaningfully and smiled. Through the still-open door, he saw that Gwyneth was lingering in the hallway, listening to the conversation. He rose from his chair, closed the door, and continued talking as he wandered across the room. "There was no Internet back then. No permanent mass multimedia. Hardly anyone in the alternative scene even had a television. I knew the name *Werner Herzog* by hearsay, but I had never seen a picture of him or any of his films."

Once again, Gräve's narrative took him back to West Berlin in 1978. At a wild party in the *Dschungel,* young people danced to *One Way or Another by* Blondie and moved with the blinding disco lights. In one corner, a very young Tilda Swinton sat with Lou Reed, sharing a joint. In the same corner, but a little further away, young Christoph Gräve stood talking to an extremely drunk man. Udo Kier. Both were holding a Schultheiss beer in their hands and Udo slurred, "I'll tell you one thing: never work with that Werner Herzog. He gives good blowjobs, but when he's done with you, your career is over."

Gräve did not know Werner Herzog. "Herzog... is that that gay porn producer?"

Udo laughed uproariously and had to hold on to the bar to keep from falling over. In the process, he grabbed the tit of Romy

Haag (David Bowie's transvestite girlfriend), who was drinking a whiskey and didn't feel further disturbed by Udo.

"Sorry, sweetie! Anyway,—since the encounter with Herzog I've only been shooting shit. I can't remember any more texts...Herzog has robbed me of all my creative powers. I think I'll go to the monastery now." With that, Udo raised his bottle, toasted Gräve and took a big swig.

Gräve, however, felt reminded of his mentor Verne Zog by the strange story. "Hmm...I knew a guy like that once."

Udo talked himself into a rage: "And then this criminal director didn't even cast me in the role of Nosferatu, but that stupid Klaus Kinski again!"

He pointed to a picture on the wall. It was the very work of art that Andy Warhol had given Verne Zog when they first met in the *Dschungel*. Gräve stared at the painting from a distance and could not believe his eyes. He slowly walked closer to the canvas, and Udo followed him.

"That idiot even forgot the picture Andy painted especially for him," Udo said. "Now it's hanging here."

Gräve pointed perplexedly at the man next to Kinski in the picture. "That's Verne Zog!"

Udo didn't quite understand. "Huh? Who?"

"Well, that guy there next to Kinski!" Gräve groaned.

Udo belched vigorously. "This is the man who consumes so much energy that he has to tap others! Werner Herzog."

He put the bottle to his mouth again, but it was empty, so he threw it in a high arc into the corner in frustration. Before it hit the floor, however, Iggy Pop had already caught it in midair and casually set it down on the table. As if nothing had happened, Iggy continued to spread peanut butter on his toast. But Gräve stared in disbelief at the picture of Herzog and Kinski on the wall.

Nico, who had followed Gräves' story spellbound, was completely perplexed: "Then this...Verne Zog...is Werner Herzog?"

Gräve nodded, and it took Nico a moment to internalize this information. "And what does that mean now?"

"I never saw Verne Zog or Werner Herzog again," Gräve said with a shake of his head.

But Nico started shouting: "That's why you don't want to let me go. Because you still have a score to settle with him!"

"No, it's not like that," Gräve affirmed, confidentially placing his hand on Nico's shoulder.

But he cried out, "Don't touch me!"

He jumped from his chair and wanted to leave, but Gräve played his hitherto secret trump card, "A few weeks ago, however, I got a call from Verne Zog. After decades. He told me about a young man who I absolutely had to hire at the Ballhaus-Ost,—and who believed himself to be Klaus Kinski!"

Nico turned on his heel by means of the Kinskian screw and blurted out, "What do you mean, *believed*?"

"The call came one day after you auditioned with me as an extra. That can't be a coincidence," Gräve insisted.

"I *am* Kinski, you stupid pig!" Nico exploded.

Gräve tried to calm him down: "Yes, Nico. You're doing a wonderful job. But because of the thing with Zog or *Her(r)*-Zog... well, I can only warn you!"

"There is no more Nico. I...am Klaus Kinski! And that you both need the Kinskian genius for your purposes is the best proof of that. But Herzog, or whatever his name is now, pays the better fee." With that, he left the office in a rage.

Gräve was still calling after him, "Nico, wait!"

But Nico stormed out the door and bumped into Gwyneth in the hallway, who had overheard the conversation. She tried to stop him, imploring him that he couldn't just leave her and the theater and leave everyone out in the cold. He grabbed her around the waist and began kissing her frantically. So they stumbled into a storage room of the props department, where they fell tightly embraced on a red chaiselongue sofa that stood to the left of the entrance door. Nico animalistically ripped open her blouse. Gwyneth was not wearing a bra, and he immediately began sucking on her long, dark nipples. Then she reared up, brutally threw him off her and catapulted herself on top of him.

"You finish this with *us*!"

She bent down to him and kissed him passionately while pushing the thong under her skirt aside. With a flick of her wrist she had already opened Nico's pants and let his hard cock slide into her wet vagina. She rode him only a few seconds, when suddenly Nico's girlfriend Claudia stood in the doorway.

"Uh-huh...I had a hunch," she said monotonously.

"Who's she?" Gwyneth wanted to know.

"My girlfr...whatever!—Gwyneth,—Claudia. Claudia—Gwyneth," Nico introduced the two women to each other.

"Hi, Gwyneth. I think we briefly met at the premiere," Claudia greeted her rival.

Gwyneth smiled. Her breasts were only half hidden by her ripped blouse, and the pierced nipples of her A-cups continued to stand erect. She greeted back in a friendly manner, "Oh, hi. Nice to see you again, Claudia."

Nico straightened up next to Gwyneth, who slumped backwards into the sofa. Claudia sat down between them, to both of their surprise. Without giving Nico another look, she let her two hands slowly slide over Gwyneth's belly until she finally touched her breasts. She gave a muffled moan. Nico bent down and kissed Claudia on her open, lustful mouth while still massaging Gwyneth's breasts. She tasted the aroma of her nipples in Nico's mouth and undid the button of Gwyneth's skirt. Then she grabbed Nico's hand to guide it along the Suicide Girl's belly into her panties. So Claudia and Nico slid together along Gwyneth's vulva and felt the thick hair growth, which was limited to a small field by shaving. Claudia let her fingers circle around

Gwyneth's clit, which was already swollen with blood, while she gripped her nipple much tighter with her other hand and pinched it between her thumb and forefinger. Nico's middle finger slid along between Gwyneth's outer labia, which he then spread using his ring finger and entered her between her inner lips. Her G-spot was considerably lower than Claudia's, but it was all the more sensitive, and Gwyneth moaned in ecstasy. Hands moved up and down her panties with increasing speed as Nico was grabbed by the shoulder from behind. He turned around and saw that Gräve was standing right behind him.

The director put his arm around Nico's neck and pulled him to him. The two men started kissing each other, and while Nico's right hand was still inside Gwyneth's thong, he undid Gräve's belt with his left. Claudia pulled the leather strap out of the tabs, and Nico undid the remaining buttons of Gräve's pants, sliding his free hand into them. This allowed him to satisfy Gräve and Gwyneth at the same time, and Claudia looped the belt from Gräve's pants around Nico's neck like a noose. She began to gently choke him while she deftly managed to remove her own pants. Then she sat down on Gwyneth lying under her, whose face she began to ride with her already dripping wet vagina, gently at first, but then becoming more and more violent.

———

In the next moment, however, the image of the foursome orgy changed into that of a surveillance camera on a laptop. This in turn was located on a desk in room 237 of the Senate Administration—the office of Waltraud Beermeyer-Stöpsel and Irmgard Al-Hassani.

Both women stared spellbound and also somewhat impressed at the increasingly wild debauchery in the Ballhaus-Ost. Then, however, the laptop closed before their eyes with a clicking sound.

Behind it was Magnus Max, who had shown the video to the senate ladies.

"Where did you get that?" Irmgard wanted to know.

Magnus Max grinned with satisfaction. "Well...the noble Master Verne Zog just has his eyes everywhere."

Waltraud thought out loud, "If this gets out...*Senate funds wild sexcapades at Ballhaus-Ost.*"

Magnus instantly jotted down this headline on his notepad.

Irmgard, on the other hand, was seriously concerned. "Could we possibly be *disgraced* for something like this?" she asked her colleague. Then she turned back to Verne Zog's servant, "And who were you again?"

"Max. Magnus Max."

"Is that a stage name?" Waltraud wanted to know.

"No, it has something to do with my physique.—My penis was already close to forty centimeters long when I was born."

The two senate ladies were mildly surprised and of course did not want to offend the dwarf. A few seconds of silence followed. Then Magnus snorted out, "Hahahaha...I had you going there for a moment, didn't I? Hahaha."

Irmgard and Waltraud wrestled a tortured smile from themselves.

"...in fact, it was forty-five centimeters!" said Magnus Max.

Both women had to take a deep breath. "What can we do for you now, Mr Max?" Irmgard then asked.

"I believe we have a common agenda," the dwarf replied. "Namely, to make sure that the play *They will claim that I was dead...* by Christoph Gräve is cancelled once and for all."

Waltraud, however, immediately voiced her concerns, "That's a double-edged sword. After all, we want this nonsense to come to an end. But the success unfortunately proves Gräve right."

Her colleague Irmgard added, "The Senate Chancellery doesn't look at quality, but only at ticket sales. Nobody understands why people go to see it at all,—but that's the way it is. If we cancel the play so easily now, the senator won't be happy at all."

"And Gräve would then probably arrive here with an explosive belt to blow us all up," Waltraud interjected truthfully. "But what do *you* actually care about the play being cancelled?"

Magnus paused for another significant moment before continuing.

"Even if it's really none of your business, the noble master Verne Zog is the rightful discoverer and thus owner of the main actor Nico Pacinsky and now needs his services in his own cause."

Irmgard got nervous. "Is this for a government-sponsored production? And has it gone through the committees? Is there a regional connection? Otherwise, we cannot and *must not* support you and the project at all. Not in any form."

Magnus Max smiled audaciously. "Ladies, let me put it this way. We better find a way together to either cancel or void Mr Pacinsky's contract with Ballhaus-Ost. Otherwise, the video you just saw will go viral." He held up his note on the pad. "You've just provided me with the appropriate headline yourself."

Magnus packed his laptop and notepad into his backpack, jumped off his chair and went on his way. He wished them a good day and left the women silent and thoughtful.

27. THE ASSASSINS

THE NEXT MORNING, NICO HAD ANOTHER APPOINTMENT WITH HIS psychologist, Dr Vary Plump. He was sitting in the waiting room, leafing through a tabloid magazine in which all sorts of celebrities were gushing about him and Gräves' play. He had hardly ever seen any of them in the audience, but if you could fill a few square inches in the tabloids, German *celebrities* were actually never too shy to do a little gonzo journalism. They spouted off the most adventurous generalities, which were then peppered by the journalists with information copied from some other tab. Such fabricated articles were then usually garnished with hypocritical moralism and virtue signaling.

This time it was not the receptionist who called Nico, but Samael, Dr. Plump's personal assistant, who accompanied him into the room and to the couch. Through another door that Nico had never noticed before, Dr. Plump entered the consulting room. Once again, he noticed the barred windows as Samael left the room again. Thoughtfully, he greeted his psychologist, "Good afternoon, Doctor Plump."

"I'm glad you could make it, Mr Kinski."

Nico was pleased with the recognition. "No problem, you're welcome."

"Where were we yesterday in the meeting?" Dr. Plump wanted to know.

Nico thought for a moment. "I think we were interrupted when I told you about the call from despotic film director Werner Herzog and his offer."

"Right. So tell me, why do you think he contacted you again after so many years? Your last movie together was in 1988, correct?"

"Well, you see, everything this lunatic did after that was complete junk. Worthless filth. Garbage. Crap. Trash. Rubbish. Nonsense. How do you say, *Toxic Waste*. Nobody really wanted to see that. And so now he has to make another movie with *me* so that he doesn't lose all credibility at some point."

"How do you explain that you—that is, Klaus Kinski, have not made a film since 1991?" Dr. Plump tried to test Nico.

The latter, however, gave her the Kubrick stare and grinned insanely. His left eye twitched twice, then he escalated into a schizophrenic-like rage, "Werner Herzog only staged my death in '91 to get publicity for his film *Cobra Verde*, which was delayed. He brainwashed me out of my memory of everything I had experienced as Kinski and forced the persona of Nico Pacinsky on me. But since the car accident, my true self is finally finding its way back to me. So in the end it was Herzog who was responsible for all the humiliations that happened to me during that time."

A long pause of silence followed. Then Dr. Plump nodded. "That sounds very plausible."

Nico felt vindicated. "Absolutely."

The psychologist leaned forward and whispered to him, "I'm not really allowed to say something like this,—but if I were you...I'd get back at Herzog."

Nico nodded and leaned forward in his turn. However, he did

not whisper, but only roared himself even more into a rage. "Exactly! I'll tell you what. I completely don't give a shit about the fucking movie he wants to tap my genius for again. I will, however, find a way to see this scumbag suffer. And I'll take the fee, of course."

Dr. Plump smiled with satisfaction and leaned back in her chair again. Then she pressed a button on her desk. The door opened, and Guido Gusion entered.

"Good afternoon, Mr Kinski."

"This is Mr Guido Gusion. He is an amazing agent from Hollywood and will be assisting you from now on. He'll represent your affairs and advise you."

Guido came closer and shook Nico's hand. "Great pleasure to meet you. I heard awesome things about you. We will make sure everything you wish for will be taken care of in regards to your next movie project with Mr Herzog."

Guido put his hands in the pockets of his suit trousers and pushed his jacket aside. This allowed Nico to see that the man from America was carrying a holster on his left and right, each containing an antique flintlock pistol with gold inlays made by *Penel Freres St. Etienne*. "I see, you come prepared," Nico remarked.

"You bet." Guido nodded confidently. "So, may I assume we have a deal?"

A few seconds passed, during which Nico looked closely at both Dr. Plump and Guido Gusion. Then he decided. "You know what?—Let's do this!"

Guido took a chain with a crucifix out of his pocket and gave it to Nico. "This will be our sign."

Nico looked at the chain, which must have been something like a high-tech tracking device, and he, Dr. Plump and Guido conspiratorially shook hands.

THE DEVIL'S VIOLINIST

Spotify Playlist 4

28. GOETHE, SHAKESPEARE, MOZART, KINSKI

IT WAS A WONDERFUL EARLY SUMMER'S DAY IN 1808. IN WEIMAR, the metropolis of German poets and thinkers, a man was sitting at a small wooden table in a handsome garden area that was strictly designed and yet almost wild in its individual plots. Between them were tall sunflowers, magnificent rose bushes and blossoming fruit trees. In front of the man on the table were various papers, next to them was an inkwell with a quill and a beer mug. The man was the polymath and poet prince Johann Wolfgang von Goethe —unmistakable by his clothes and hair.

He knew just about everything there was to know in 1808. But if you looked closely, you could see that the man bore a very close resemblance to the actor Nico Pacinsky. He was watching a young and beautiful girl working in the garden. Minna was cutting roses and watering them, her curves standing out through her white dress. Minna was impersonated in this scene by Christoph Gräve's assistant Gwyneth. Goethe called out to her with a smile, "A little more water for the roses, Minna."

Barely concealed, he rubbed his crotch as the girl bent even lower over the plants. Minna perceived this, but nodded to him pleasingly and smiled at him from a distance.

A little apart from Goethe sat a visitor. Mephistopheles, who was also immediately recognizable from his clothing and headgear. Here he was played by the theater director Christoph Gräve, whose eternal role model was Gustav Gründgens (watch István Szabó's movie *Mephisto*, which is about Gründgens). He observed Goethe, who was gazing at Minna and said, "Whoever makes such an old goat into a gardener should not be surprised about dirty laundry by the ton."

Goethe, however, was not bothered by this. "You only live once, Schwefelbart. And that must be enjoyed. I will let the inamorata's pretty butt glow in all tones of my color theory!"

Mephisto grinned. "Do you not overestimate your quill's power of action, old friend?"

The poet prince comprehensively grabbed the bulge of his pants. "And if the sack also becomes limp,—nothing that a strumpet's devotion could not compensate for!"

"The young ladies' poison can easily lead an old man like you to death," Mephisto pointed out.

"Old man? Young as ever in heart, mind and loins. Full of creative power and juice!"

Minna did not hear the conversation, but noticed the attention of the two men and again greeted them amiably. Both gentlemen waved back, and Mephisto grinned slowly. "Pretty. But you will probably destroy her with it!"

Goethe waved him off. "There are many girls every day. Me, on the other hand, only once in all times. She will not be mourned, but I will still be bewailed long after the last fanfares call."

"Are you that sure?" Mephisto tried to provoke him.

"Sure? No. Who would ever be sure of anything in your presence, dear Nobiswirt! But Schiller's end taught me to appreciate life in pleasure and burden—and to feed my demon as he fed me!"

There was a short, painful cry from Minna, who had

apparently hurt herself on a rose thorn. She put the finger in her mouth, sucked on it and made sure she was being watched. Goethe trembled inwardly at the sight of the beauty.

"So your xenia aren't that tame, old scoundrel!" Mephisto stated.

"And you are never so full, friend Hadessprout, that you could tame yourself in me! Hardly can there be another demon, insatiable as you!" replied the poet. The girl at the other end of the garden was lolling herself before resuming her work. Once again, her magnificent body was visible through her clothes.

"Even in the circles of hell there is little without equal. But you are right. Hardly anyone comes close to your Mephistopheles' art."

Goethe looked at him suspiciously. "Hardly anyone? Surely no one can be compared to you—to us!"

Mephisto was struggling. He was indignant. Finally he jumped up. "No, none! And this for proof!"

The demon stomped across the plants and pounced on the girl. He kissed her unrestrainedly, and she returned his desire, for she had sought to amplify the voluptuous looks of the two men all the while. While she and Mephisto made moaning love to each other on the lawn, Goethe rubbed his crotch with his left hand. With half-closed eyes, his right hand wrote the title of his latest book on the paper in front of him, *They will claim that I was dead...*

In an English bower in 1591, the moaning continued; two men could be seen there on the bed making wild and unrestrained love. They were Christopher Marlowe and Henry Howard. The latter was just being penetrated from behind by the former. Howard was impersonated by Christoph Gräve and Marlowe by Nico Pacinsky. Then the door flew open with a loud bang, and the couple on the bed started up in fright, but without breaking away from each other. The intruder who strode in the door held a drawn rapier in his hand. It was William Shakespeare, played by

Verne Zog. The naked Marlowe in bed found his composure surprisingly quickly. "By St. George's lance, hardly can you call this a fair fight, noble Shakespeare. Your rapier in hand—against mine in this man!"

Shakespeare's face was drawn with hatred. "I will no doubt shut your mouth more successfully with this steel than your stylus was able to do with this warm brother!"

Howard was breathless with fear and lust alike, but remarked, "His weapons are without fault, my lord.—I can swear to that."

Shakespeare struck with his rapier, but the pair, still wedged together, managed to roll aside by a hair's breadth. Marlowe raised his hand defensively. "Old friend! Must this feud go on forever?"

Shakespeare's face was drawn with genuine disgust. "The hollow crown offers a head only the space in the swing of its bow! This honor is mine, and mine alone!"

Marlowe straightened up, keeping his playmate planted on his middle and his arms around him. In this manner, he walked a little way toward Shakespeare and pleaded, "William! Brother! Take thou the glory while thou leavest me the pleasure. Put thy name on my plays, I shall not mind, but end the drive, that I may still drive this pretty play to the end."

Shakespeare plunged his rapier through the man's back and pinned them both to the wall behind. His face showed triumph, but only for a moment. Then his eyes widened when he saw a handwritten manuscript lying beside the bed, its first page showing the title of the book: *They will claim that I was dead...By Christopher Marlowe*. Shakespeare took the first page with the title and tore it up. As he did so, he looked into the man's dying eyes and spoke with contempt, "Christopher Marlowe....No name for eternity!"

Shakespeare threw the scraps of paper at the dying couple, who still had the rapier stuck in them. Then he pulled the bloody metal from the bodies, which then collapsed dead on the floor, and a fountain of blood slapped his face. He took the manuscript under his arm and disappeared outside through the door of the bower. The air escaped from the lungs of the stabbed men in a languid sigh that continued in 1791 Vienna, where a rattle could be heard in a classically furnished bedroom where the curtains were drawn. Only a single candle on the nightstand provided some light, and a concert grand piano stood in the background. On the velvet-covered bed lay a heavily breathing and apparently dying person: Wolfgang Amadeus Mozart, here embodied by Nico Pacinsky. The door opened and Antonio Salieri, played by Christoph Gräve, entered. He seemed genuinely concerned about the great musician. "Doctor Brandner gave me news of Herr Mozart's imminent demise—and so I immediately hurried to the Rauhensteingasse."

But Mozart rasped bitterly: "Salieri,—you are an Italian dog! A cabal against me—the only genius in this room."

The accused was horrified. "A cabal? Your mind must already be clouded."

"Yes, from your poison!" Mozart rasped and pointed his finger in the direction of the window. "I will now go to Himmelpfort." He coughed heavily and could hardly breathe.

Then Salieri saw a scrawled score on paper lying on the piano. Slowly he approached it. "Your last will and testament, my dear sir?"

The dying Mozart became a little nervous. "You'd better leave that alone!" But Salieri took the score and read it. The heading read: *They will claim that I was dead....* Salieri rolled up the pieces of paper and put them in his coat pocket. "A new opera, I suppose..."

Mozart became panic-stricken. "What are you doing?"

"I think I'd better leave the sick gentleman alone now," Salieri said and left the room.

The exceptional musician, who was losing his battle with

death, called hoarsely after him, "You have no idea what that is. But you have always been a thief. Piss on your sheet music!"

With the slamming of the door, the gust of wind blew out the candle, and with it the light in Mozart's eyes went out. His last breath became the heavy breathing of a man obviously completely beside himself with deeply felt rage marching through a South American jungle. It was Klaus Kinski, played by Nico Pacinsky, who, armed with a machete, slashed his way through the green thicket in fury, yelling over and over again. He wore the dirty and wrinkled costume of Fitzcarraldo from the film of the same name.

He was not alone, for he was followed by a Peruvian native who carried the actor's numerous heavy bags and suitcases on his back like a pack mule, playing his pan flute again and again as if commenting on Kinski's shouting.

"*Whatever the cost, it's film or death.* How can a person express himself in such a foolish way? At the same time, he tolerantly squints both eyes, out of joy at the outgrowths of his megalomania, which he considers to be genius. Sure, he honestly admits that sometimes he himself gets dizzy before his own insane ideas, which, however, would simply carry him away. You know what I mean?"

Of course, the Indian didn't understand a word of what the white devil was saying. Then a goat got in their way, and Kinski became completely hysterical. "Get out of my way, you stupid pig of a goat, or I'll kill you!"

The goat looked at the choleric man for a few seconds, chewing silently. Then it urinated, gave a relaxed bleat, maa and trolled off into the next bush. Kinski chopped down a few vines and branches that got in his way with his machete and continued bleating, "I've never met such a humorless, stubborn, uptight, unscrupulous, mindless, depressing, boring, big-headed person as Herzog in my entire life. Right?"

The native smiled as if in affirmation and played his jingle on the pan flute.

"He completely unconcernedly cannibalizes the most witless, stupid, uninteresting punch lines of his boasting, and then finally collapses,—like a sectarian before his idol,—to his knees before himself; where he fanatically perseveres until someone bends down to him and lifts him up from his humiliation before himself."

The Indian tripped over a root on the ground and collapsed under the weight of the bags.

"Watch out!"

Kinski wanted to help the Indian, but he was able to get himself up again with some effort. So they continued to make their way, and Kinski cursed under his breath, "Everyone can clearly see that he considers himself extremely cunning. And that he stalks me at every turn and desperately tries to probe my thoughts. That he is racking his brains to see how he can outsmart me on all points of the contract. In short, that he is determined to trick me."

The last sentence obviously enraged him to such an extent that he hacked the next vine dangling in front of his face into small shreds like a maniac and still hit it when it was already on the ground.

Then an impacting rifle bullet tore the bark of a tree. While the Indian took cover, Kinski looked around, his limbs twitching in all directions like those of a wild animal. Out of the blue, Werner Herzog, played by Christoph Gräve, stood in front of him and pointed his Winchester 73 at him. Kinski was impressed for a moment and had to swallow: "Werner! What are you doing?"

The Indian dropped his bags and suitcase and hurried away.

Herzog was dead serious. "Klaus, if you leave the film set now, you and I will never do another motion picture production."

"That's such bullshit. The film is insured, you asshole," Kinski rumbled.

"No, because you've already broken too many contracts. No insurance company in the world will take us anymore."

There was no denying what Herzog was saying, and Kinski had to take a breath. "That's outrageous. Werner, I'm leaving now. Finish that shitty movie with Jason Robards or Mick Jagger. I'm out of here!"

Kinski prepared to leave, but Herzog loaded the Winchester with a dangerous click and took another step toward Kinski so that he could not possibly miss him.

"Klaus, you can't. The film is more important than us. It's more important than our personality or our life."

"Chatter, chatter, chatter. Man, Werner, you're so insane that you should have your face smashed in, you wanker!"

"Klaus, I have nine shots in the Winchester. If you go on now, you'll have eight bullets in you, and the ninth is for me."

Kinski realized that the director was serious. He remained rooted to the spot. At the same time, he was boiling inside. The two of them fixed each other in a silent stare-off like in a Corbucci Western, waiting for their counterpart's next move. The tension literally tore them apart. After a few seconds, however, Kinski suddenly cried out, as if stung by a tarantula: "Help!!! Police!!! Help!!!"

Of course, there was not a single police station within a radius of more than a thousand kilometers, and Herzog looked at him with his eyes wide open. "You're going to claim you're dead!" With that, he pulled the trigger! Bang!

29. ART IS WORTH MORE THAN TRUTH

NICO PULLED HIMSELF UP OUT OF BED, DRENCHED IN SWEAT. NEXT to him lay Gwyneth and Claudia, who slept naked and cuddled together, covered only with a sheet. He rubbed his forehead and raised his hands to the sky, wishing that this madness would finally stop. He reached for a glass of water on the nightstand and drank it down in one go. Then he stood up and pulled the bathrobe, which was lying next to the bed, over his naked body. He did not close it, so that the two ends of the cord dangled back and forth like a lateral extension of his own hanging. Lost in thought, he was about to leave the bedroom for the bathroom when the voice of his mother-in-law-to-be, Erna Rosetzki, sounded from a corner.

"I always thought you were a loser."

Nico was startled and looked up. Only now did he notice that Erna was sitting in an armchair in the corner, and had obviously been doing so for quite a while. She had clearly been an observer at the merry threesome with Gwyneth and Claudia.

"Uh, Erna? What are you doing here?" Nico wanted to know.

She looked at him openly and stared through the open

bathrobe at his midriff. She was honestly impressed. "I had undeniably underestimated you."

Nico tied his robe and whispered: "Erna, what are you doing in my bedroom?"

She didn't answer right away, instead getting up from the armchair and taking Nico by the arm to lead him out into the newly renovated living room. Together they stepped through the bedroom door, and Nico closed it extra quietly so as not to wake Claudia and Gwyneth.

"Do you need money?" he wanted to know.

"No, Nico. I just wanted to talk to you." Erna sat down on the sofa and signaled him to do the same. After a moment of hesitation, Nico complied with the request.

"I know I haven't always been nice to you," she began, "and, trying to sell your Kinski collection..."

Nico interrupted her immediately, "Yes, Erna, that really annoyed me,—but now I don't need all that stuff anymore. I *am* Klaus Kinski!"

Erna smiled mildly. "Exactly. We have art so that we don't perish from the truth."

Nico was struck for a moment by the Nietzsche quote and had to think about it. "I'm totally with you on that. Absolute knowledge leads to pessimism. Art is the cure for that. My remedy!"

Erna took Nico's hand. "And that's exactly why you *have* to make the film with Werner Herzog."

Nico pulled his hand away and looked at her suspiciously. Then he stood up and paced around the room while his thoughts began to race. "What do *you* get out of it?" he wanted to know.

Erna answered honestly, "You know, that girl there in your bedroom is my everything. Of course I want a good life for her. So many opportunities have passed me by myself."

She took a whiskey bottle from the drawer of the new Ikea

coffee table, a hiding place that Nico apparently didn't even know about yet. She poured herself a big gulp and emptied the glass in one go. Then she offered Nico some of the Trader Joe's booze, too, but he declined with slight disgust.

"Ever since I've known you, you've been obsessed with Klaus Kinski and Werner Herzog," she continued. "Do you want to let a chance like that go by? And end up like me? Opportunityless and left behind?"

Nico looked at her pityingly. No, he definitely didn't want to end up like that; old, addicted to gambling and alcohol. Erna poured herself some more whiskey and drank the next glass down as well. She got up from the sofa and came close to him—too close. He backed away, but Erna patted his face maternally. "I did a lot of bad things to you and behaved badly toward you. I want to apologize for that."

"Fine, thank you," Nico said. "But why are you so concerned about me doing the movie with Herzog? Tell the truth."

Erna shook her head. "Truth? Art is worth more than truth. You of all people must know that."

Nico's breath caught at the new quote. She stroked his cheek again. And he couldn't believe it himself, but she had him. He decided at that moment to simply break the contract with the Ballhaus-Ost and Gräve. "Good, Erna. That's the way it should be."

Animated by his decision, he suddenly became tame and realized that he somehow liked Erna after all. He took a deep breath and then nodded to her. Erna smiled with relief. As she did so, she looked at the ceiling, where one of Magnus Max's cameras was located behind a small hole. Nico didn't notice and, after giving Claudia's mother a hug, left the living room.

Erna stared at her smartphone, where a message from Magnus Max had just appeared: *Will he do it?*

She typed the answer immediately: *I think so.*

Magnus' answer followed immediately: *I'm on my way!*

A new message from the PayPal payment service appeared on the display: *€10,000 received from magnus@verne-zog-ltd.org.*

Erna was visibly delighted with the renewed windfall, and Magnus knew how to fire her up further. *€100.000 extra when the contract gets signed!* he wrote.

Claudia's mother looked up at the camera on the ceiling and sent Magnus an air kiss.

Nico, meanwhile, stood in front of the bathroom mirror and looked at himself. He seriously wondered who he was and opened the lid of his right eye with his index finger and thumb. He stepped very close to the mirror and could observe Gwyneth in it through the open bathroom door, lolling briefly in her sleep. Actually, he didn't give a damn whether he was really Kinski or anyone else,—and in the awareness of this cognition, he finally realized the scope of his decision: He would make a film with Werner Herzog, no matter what the cost. With or without the blessing of Christoph Gräve. A Kinski just doesn't stick to any contracts. So he took another breath in the satisfying feeling of relief at having made a decision. Then he put on his pants and shirt, combed his hair and was about to brush his teeth when suddenly a deafening, repetitive hammering noise rang out. Hastily, he spat the toothpaste into the sink and hurried back into the bedroom. Gwyneth and Claudia sat up in bed, terrified. Roused from their sleep, they no longer understood the world. The noise became so loud that their eardrums threatened to burst, even though they were covering their ears. A glaringly bright light penetrated through the half-open bedroom window, and the hammering from outside became louder and louder.

A strong breeze whirled all the papers and curtains in the entire room. Nico hurried to the window and looked out. His face showed the realization that the time had come. He looked once more at the shocked faces of the two women, then grabbed the crucifix on the nightstand that Guido Gusion had given him earlier and hung it around his neck. Without looking back another time, he opened the window fully to climb out. The two women in bed screamed in terror. Just then the bedroom door opened, and Erna came rushing in. She went straight for the window from which Nico had just climbed out and disappeared. Erna stuck her head out and could just make out a rope ladder where Nico was disappearing into the clouds at that moment.

30. ALPINE FORTRESS

THE NIGHT WAS ILLUMINATED BY A BRIGHT FULL MOON AS NICO WAS pulled up hanging from the rope ladder. He grabbed the crucifix around his neck and twisted the small crown of thorns on the crucified so that the red-blue LEDs embedded in it lit up briefly three times. Then he hid the pendant under his shirt and climbed the ladder fully up to the helicopter, through whose side window Magnus Max could be seen at the controls. The helicopter was a Mil Mi-26, the largest helicopter in the world, decommissioned by the Soviet Army and converted into a luxury aircraft. The logo of *Werner Herzog Filmproduktion GmbH* was emblazoned on its side.

It took course towards the south and finally disappeared completely in the dense cloud cover over Berlin.

———

At the time, Dr. Plump and Guido Gusion were already sleeping side by side on an oversized, custom-made replica of Mies van der Rohe's Barcelona Couch in Dr. Plump's apartment. Her dwelling was a stylish new building beyond measure in the style of rationalism: the walls were made of bare reinforced concrete. On the wall above the bed hung framed portraits in pairs of various prominent personalities that Gerhard Richter had personally painted for Dr. Plump: Edison and Tesla, Mary Stuart and Elizabeth I, Shakespeare and Marlowe, Mozart and Salieri, Jagger and Lennon, Che and Fidel, Trotsky and Stalin, Jackson and Prince, Stallone and Schwarzenegger, Nietzsche and Wagner, Madonna and Courtney Love, Herzog and Kinski.

A cell phone vibrated on the nightstand. The cross-shaped, semi-transparent high-tech super-smartphone from the company *VatiCom* was blinking and showing a 3D rendering of the very cross that Nico had just hung around his neck on the holo-display. Still a bit drowsy, Dr. Plump grabbed the phone, but when she realized what app had just been launched, she was immediately electrified. Guido also woke up and looked at the device with flashing eyes.

"It begins!"

Both smiled as if intoxicated with wide-open, feverish eyes, and Dr. Plump grunted excitedly, "Fuck me, Guido! Now!"

Guido turned around with a jerk and landed on top of her. He complied with the instruction energetically, and while she bit his nipples with teasing ferocity, the Barcelona couch extended two side arms to the right and left, turning into a cross on which the two made love in every possible position.

The Alps were a majestically brutal, intimidating, cold and inhospitable sight. In the distance, Nico saw a heavy fortress built of impenetrable reinforced concrete towering among the snow-capped peaks. This was secured by high walls with barbed wire, surveillance cameras and self-fire systems, as well as anti-tank barriers and anti-aircraft missiles. As the helicopter approached, several automated searchlights stretched into the sky to accompany it. It had just broken through the cloud cover, descended slowly and landed on a special platform on the fortress, which then began to descend into the interior of the building. So Magnus Max and Nico finally arrived in the belly of the structure and exited via an automated gangway. They entered a high-tech airlock and were immediately surrounded by a dome made of Plexiglas that shot out of the floor and completely enclosed them both. Various probes and jets hissed loudly and menacingly. After analyzing their bacterial, viral and chemical load, the computer released the two men, and the Plexiglas lowered into the floor.

Nico was so impressed by all this that he followed the dwarf as if in a trance. Magnus, for his part, praised Nico.

"Thank you for coming along so easily and without further resistance." So they walked side by side through the confusing network of underground corridors, whose meter-thick walls were adorned with framed original vintage placards of Werner Herzog's films. But some frames also held announcements of opera and theater performances staged over the centuries by Verne Zog. Magnus watched as Nico studied the posters.

"The noble master is enormously looking forward to meeting you!"

Nico nodded.

"And I'm delighted to finally see Herzog again today. Because, of course, there's so much to sort out before I get involved in a new collaboration."

Magnus flinched and stopped.

"We thought we could sign the contract with you today!"

But Nico waved it off.

"Not without my lawyer or agent."

They walked on and came to an elevator whose doors opened instantly. Magnus climbed in grimly, but Nico hesitated to follow him. Of course, he was just playing it all out. After all, he really wanted to work with Herzog, and the revenge mission he had embarked on with Dr. Plump and Guido Gusion also had to be accomplished. How he could reconcile the two was not yet clear to him, but he convinced himself that he would find a solution. He played with Magnus Max and his intentions. After all, this media business was like the girls, they want you all the more if you don't show any interest.

"Let's be clear, I'm not signing anything today. I'll be happy to meet with the master for a preliminary discussion, but I'm not committing myself contractually at this point."

Magnus rolled his eyes, took one deep breath, and sighed to himself, "Actors..."

The two looked at each other silently for a moment through the still open elevator door. Then Nico got in, too, and Magnus pressed the button for the forty-eighth basement floor. The elevator music was reminiscent of the soundtrack to Herzog's film *Aguirre—the Wrath of God*. Nico was pleased about this. After all, he had had all the music CDs and vinyls for Herzog's films in his collection. Many of them were sought-after rarities.

Magnus explained, "The music is a live broadcast of the Krautrock band Popol-Vuh, which we have garrisoned on the fourth floor. They essentially only do our elevator music now when we don't have a current film production."

Nico contemplated. "Didn't the band leader Florian Fricke pass away a long time ago?"

"Hahahaha...You will have a lot to learn about the noble Master Zog, my clueless friend."

"Master Zog?" Nico asked, thinking about the story of Christoph Gräve and his acting teacher in 1978.

Magnus Max, however, corrected himself, "Uh...Herr Zog...Herzog!"

With a deep metallic sound, the elevator arrived at the bottom and the doors opened. They had arrived. Nico stepped thoughtfully out of the high-tech vehicle and walked into the main control center of the creative epicenter. The hall had a gigantic boulder to the wall to one side. The floor was made of the finest and most polished Carrara marble. To the other side, the room opened into a huge window overlooking a wide valley where a meadow shone green and lush in the sunshine. A massive wooden desk with various monitors was in front of it. Verne Zog's bunker world would have made all dictators of the twentieth century turn green with envy—and all Bond villains as well.

Nico was confused looking through the panoramic window, "I thought we were underground."

Magnus smiled, took a small, metal Apple TV remote control out of his pocket, and triumphantly pressed a button on it. Immediately, the alpine panorama changed to a deep-sea view. Various fish and several sharks swam by, giving the impression that they were now underwater. "That's the beauty of the entertainment industry," he commented. "Everything is a big illusion."

By now they had crossed the hall and arrived at a lounge-like seating area. Magnus signaled Nico to sit down, and he did so after a second of reflection. "What time is it, anyway?" he asked. "I think a coffee wouldn't be bad right now."

"Of course. We have Kopi Luwak from Indonesia—or Black Ivory from Thailand," Magnus offered.

"Okay...And what's the difference?"

Magnus raised an eyebrow at his ignorance. "Kopi-Luwak beans were predigested by stray cats—Black Ivory beans, on the other hand, by elephants."

Nico inevitably had to swallow. "I think I'll have a Coca Cola."

At that moment, a voice sounded whose origin Nico could not make out at first. It was the Bavarian nasal, calm voice of Verne Zog. "The way you have just pronounced the word *kola* indicates that you assume that the term is spelled with a *C*. But this misconception is not only widespread, but also wholly misleading and dangerous. In fact, the invention of the kola drink goes back to the northern Scandinavian natives of the Kola Peninsula, who once cultivated the kola nut among themselves and brought it with the first Viking excursions to America to the Naskapi tribe. From there, it reached the pharmacist John Stith Pemberton in the nineteenth century, who misunderstood the pronunciation of the Native Americans and made kola with a *K* into *cola* with a *C*. This then gave rise to the *Coca Cola Company,* since alliterations in the field of manufacturing mass-produced goods simply imprint themselves better on the collective consciousness of consumers."

Magnus Max delivered an ancient-looking medicine bottle on a tray, which he placed on the table in front of Nico. He produced a bottle opener, opened it with a fizz and poured some of the kola it contained into a glass precooled with liquid carbon dioxide. Nico was about to take a sip when suddenly Verne Zog stood right in front of him. He was so startled that he almost dropped his ice-cold kola glass.

"Good evening. I'm Werner Herzog," the man introduced himself.

Nico rose devoutly. "Yes…good evening. I am Klaus Kinski." They shook hands.

"Let's sit down." Zog settled into his majestic armchair, and Nico again took a seat on the smaller model opposite.

"Coffee, noble master?" Magnus enquired.

"I'd love some Kopi Luwak, please. Thank you."

"Sure. Coming right up," Magnus disappeared through one of the various hydropneumatic doors at the other end of the room.

"Well, my dear, I have big plans for you," Zog continued. "Have you then already read the contract I recently sent you?"

Nico tried hard to switch into Kinski mode, but it was difficult for him to succeed, as he was impressed by the presence of the noble master.

"Honestly, no. I don't read that kind of stuff. That's what my lawyers do. I'm interested in two things: the money and the script. And the latter, after all, I haven't gotten to see yet."

Verne Zog couldn't help but grin at the Kinskian demeanor. Magnus returned and brought his master the coffee he had ordered. He had overheard Nico's last sentence and stood by Zog in Nibelung loyalty. "Please understand, it has already been proven by hundreds of experts that the noble master is the most creative and excellent person since the beginning of time. Therefore, you will get the script only when he deems it appropriate."

Verne Zog took a sip of coffee and then continued, "That is correct. So, of course, the formal writing of a screenplay is pure waste. I usually write the text passages to be filmed only in the morning before the shooting at the catering truck."

"And how am I supposed to learn the lines?" Nico asked.

"You'd better leave that worry to me, the master director Werner Herzog, who is above reproach and who I am because I have to be."

Nico took another sip of the old-fashioned kola, which tasted great due to its high cocaine content, and then leaned back in his chair. "Well, just tell me what exactly you're up to."

"Good.—I want to film in a metaphysical way the ordeal and story of Klaus Günter Karl Nakszynski, also known by his juggler pseudonym Klaus Kinski," Zog explained.

Nico became impatient, "Yes, well, I already know all that. And in the process, of course, they can no longer do without my epochal and monumental genius. But what is it about in terms of content..."

Verne Zog got to the point, "A young man is a total loser. He has no real job, no prospects, his girlfriend is unfaithful to him. But then: BANG! He has a serious car accident, which results in an

even more severe neurosis, and from then on the man believes—
he is Klaus Kinski!"

Silence. Nico had to swallow. He had already heard the words
in exactly the same order from Christoph Gräve's mouth. And
what's more, this was also his own life story, although the neurosis
that had imprisoned his mind since his accident prevented him
from admitting it.

He was searching for words, but Verne Zog was really turning
up the heat now. "Wait and see, it gets even better. He is so
convincing in his role that one day Werner Herzog calls him to
make a film with him about Kinski's life."

"That...that sounds kind of familiar," Nico said thoughtfully.

Verne Zog, however, was enthusiastic about his own pitch. "Of
course. It's the oldest story in human history, and so it's deeply
rooted in all of us."

Nico, however, was honestly confused and his thoughts raced.
What was happening here? "It...it's exactly *the same* story that
Christoph Gräve and I staged as a theater play at Ballhaus-Ost,"
he stammered.

Magnus Max was beside himself with indignation, "You better
not dare to question the noble master!"

His noble master, however, calmed him down immediately.
"It's all right Magnus. I think a little more detailed explanation is
needed now. *We do not get rid of God because we still believe in
grammar,* is my favorite quotation of the German philosopher and
dynamite researcher Friedrich Nietzsche. For the moment when
man began to say *I am,* that is, to conceive of his own existence, is
the origin of language and thus of the great misunderstanding
about our universe. Who understands himself as being, projects
also into all other things that they are. However, by doing so, we
exclude all other states of being from our perceptual horizon."

Nico couldn't quite follow. "Aha...Can I have another cola?
With two fingers of whiskey, please."

Magnus nodded, somewhat annoyed, and dodged off again through the hydropneumatic door. Nico now wanted to get down to the essentials.

"So, in terms of the contract..."

Verne Zog interrupted him immediately. "We'll get to that. First, please understand the scope of our undertaking. I am concerned with nothing less than the cinematic staging of the world formula!"

"The world formula? Did you possibly breathe a little too much high-altitude air this morning?" Nico commented cheekily.

Verne Zog nodded. "That may very well be. But it doesn't change the advised risky game."

"It doesn't quite make sense to me what the *world formula* has to do with the movie."

In the background, a great white shark rammed its snout against the digital picture window, trying to break the glass with its mouth wide open. Magnus Max returned with a new kola and a bottle of 1926 *Macallan Fine and Rare Whiskey* and looked at the window, shaking his head. "I beg your pardon, master. Programming error."

He pressed the Apple TV remote again, and the underwater panorama changed to a view from a moon station. Through the window, there were now vast fields of gray sand and a black sky hung with stars, while the Earth rose majestically in the background.

Verne Zog leaned over to Nico and held onto the table. "E is equal to mc squared! Energy is equivalent to matter. If we think this model once to the end, then there is only a certain amount of particles. These consist on their part of compressed energy. Since the universe expands to all appearance, matter must dissolve sometime again in energy.—And what follows then?"

"Uh...A new big bang?" asked Nico.

Verne Zog was enthusiastic. "A big bang, yes! But in the last consequence this must also mean that this process has already taken place infinitely often. Therefore, every conceivable and unthinkable situation has already existed endlessly many times. Beyond that it *will* also still exist continuously. But at the same time all variations of it exist in parallel realities!"

"I see. So in a parallel universe we're sitting here with Madonna and Pope Kierus preparing for an S&M orgy?" Nico tried to provoke his counterpart.

"That is absolutely correct! Since you have just devised this situation, it has now *become* a parallel reality," Zog continued, extremely agitated.

"Okay. And so that's why we're shooting the film congruently with Christoph Gräve's play?" Nico scratched his head.

"Yes, by this we symbolize an all-embracing philosophical theory, we can convey a new understanding of truth to mankind by means of art and thus prepare it at least spiritually for the next evolutionary stage of Homo Sapiens Sapiens. As we are not allowed by law to do this also physically."

Nico commented on his director's obvious madness with slight irony, but was secretly completely thrilled himself, "If only Richard Wagner and Friedrich Nietzsche were here today. I'm sure they would be very happy about these ideas."

Magnus Max and Verne Zog looked at each other. They knew that the mentioned personalities were of course present at this moment. But just in a slightly different way that only they understood so far.

"Will you please allow me to plant another philosophical thought in your head?" Nico asked with all due politeness.

Verne Zog nodded. "Of course."

Nico literally burst out of his chair and threw the precious whiskey bottle against the digital panorama window, which instantly developed a deep crack. He nagged, "You're completely insane, man! To just shit like that in front of my feet! As if I should care! Me, you or any other stupid sow! That's just great! This is so shallow and deep at the same time, pointed to a single line, that it would not surprise me if we ourselves were all just part of a great play!"

Enthusiastically, Verne Zog looked at Nico. He was overwhelmed, happy and relieved to have his long lost friend back with him. Tears came to his eyes and he slowly started to clap. Just like Christoph Gräve did after Nico had recited the Detractors poem. Zog's ovation increased, and Magnus clapped along. His master gave Nico a fatherly hug. "Klaus, it's really you. I've missed you, my dear."

The emotional outburst also softened Nico's heart. His eyes as well became watery and he warmly embraced Verne Zog in turn. "Yes, Werner. Let's make this movie, damn it!"

"Wonderful, Klaus!"

Then Nico broke away from the embrace. "Werner, there's only one problem: Christoph Gräve doesn't want to terminate the contract with me. I would break it, of course, but..."

"There are no problems, only thorny opportunities!" Verne Zog intervened. "Even though a contract is, of course, a sacred covenant to be protected. Who would know that better than you and me? However, I still know Christoph Gräve from long before..."

"Yeah, he told me some funny story about your acting school in Kreuzberg in the seventies," Nico said.

Verne Zog did not elaborate. "One can talk to Christoph," he said confidently. "He's a reasonable person. We'll arrange a meeting between the three of us and negotiate your transfer fee.— Magnus, please contact Christoph Gräve and set up a mediative meeting with him at the Savoy Hotel in Berlin."

Magnus Max was immediately alarmed. "But master! The capital is full of envious people and enemies who want to kill you.

You should not expose yourself to direct publicity or put yourself in such great danger."

"I will disguise myself so that no one will recognize me," Verne Zog decided, clapping his leg joyfully as he stood up, and then said elatedly, "Magnus, please escort Klaus out, and take him back to Berlin-Charlottenburg."

Magnus was shocked. "Noble Master Zog! I wonder if I could speak to you privately for a brief moment?"

"Is that really necessary?"

"Yes!" Magnus pulled Zog's arm emphatically and indicated to Nico, "Excuse us for a moment, please."

The master and his adlatus disappeared through the soundproof door and entered through a side passage into an underground film studio where several other dwarves were already working on various sets. All sorts of spotlights, dolly rails, tripods and other film equipment were stored here. On one side of the hall was a large green screen cavern and on the other was a catering kitchen with various beverage refrigerators. A giant LED screen mounted on the ceiling could be lowered when needed. It was connected to the latest version of the Unreal Engine, in which Verne Zog had stored high-resolution 3D scans of all the cities and landscapes as well as the interior views of all the houses and apartments on earth. This meant that he could use his quantum computer to create all the backgrounds in real time as required, and no matter what scene he had in mind, he didn't have to leave the bunker world.

Magnus took a seat on a dolly from the *Panther* company. "Master Zog, I don't quite understand. We are letting Nico Pacinsky go?"

"Yes, it is necessary. For one thing, although the Kinskian demon is strong in him, it has not yet fully developed and therefore needs some time. For another, we cannot do anything with him without a proper contract. For the distribution chain, a complete record of all legal positions is essential. Otherwise, we would not be able to exploit the film, especially in the larger territories. Even if the theatrical manufacture is of course only a by-product of our colossal project, the monetization can refinance at least a part of our expenses."

Magnus puffed. "Yes, but the fact that you want to go out in public does not please me at all. There are too many entities out to get you. And especially now with Cardinal Kierspe as pope!"

"Magnus, don't worry about it. Udo has long since given up, and no one but he would have the strength and power to actually become dangerous to us." Zog patrimonially patted the shoulders of his old friend. Then he turned and walked through another hydropneumatic door into his bedroom, where a previously unbroadcast, specially produced episode of the series *Seinfeld*, in which the Swedish band ABBA made a guest appearance, was waiting to be consumed on his Trinitron tube TV. These sets simply had the most authentic black levels.

His lackey Magnus was seriously worried about him and said more to himself, "I don't know how to protect you out there."

But the master director was already gone, and Magnus was left alone in the studio. While thinking about how he would be able to build a shield around the noble master, he went back to the study, where Nico was still sipping his cocaine kola. Magnus motioned him to follow, and together they again traversed the jumble of corridors reminiscent of Maurits Cornelis Escher's depiction of *Impossible Figures*. Finally, they reached the helipad, where the Mil-Mi 26 was already being refueled and readied for takeoff by some dwarves. As Nico climbed in via the ladder, he looked around one last time and then took out his crucifix from under his shirt. Stealthily, he turned the crown of thorns again, and it lit up three times. But two souls continued to fight in Nico's chest, that of the neurotic Nico Pacinsky, who desperately wanted to make a film with Herzog. And that of the insane Klaus Kinski, who simply wanted to liquidate the greatest filmmaker of all time. Who would prevail?

———

Guido Gusion and Dr. Plump had listened attentively to the entire conversation between Nico and Verne Zog on their smartphones. Now the display showed that the transmission had ended. With a triumphant look, Dr. Plump looked at Guido. "We've got him out in the open! The time is nigh!"

Guido, electrified, packed his suitcase with various assassin weapons of all kinds and sizes. Then he closed it and, breathing heavily, looked up at Dr. Plump, who was glaring at him with glowing eyes.

31. POPE KIERUS THE FIRST

A FEW MONTHS EARLIER, A NEWSFLASH HAD FLICKERED ACROSS ALL
the world's television and computer monitors. The German state
owned ZDF station ramped up its fee-financed machinery for a
special broadcast. In the capital's studio, located in the former
socialist Free German Youth (FDJ) building, various hair-and-
makeup artists quickly put the finishing touches on news anchor
Petra Gerster (the German Megan Kelly), to whom the tax payers
were so grateful for her fearless commitment to finding the truth
that they paid her fourteen thousand euros per broadcast. Two
red breaking news bars ticked through the picture at the bottom
and top. At the top it said: *White smoke in the Vatican!* And at the
bottom the ticker showed: *Apparently new pontiff elected. Are we
pope again? Who will be the new one?* The special edition of the
Today program began with a bombastic fanfare jingle that Hans
Zimmer had written especially for the occasion, and for which he
received a ridiculous fee of only three hundred and fifty thousand
euros.

Stupidly, the editors in charge had not read the contract from
Zimmer's U.S. agency William Morris Endeavor thoroughly
enough. That's why they hadn't noticed when they signed it that

the clever American agents, who cared deeply about the talent of their clients—after all, they got ten percent of every deal—never made total buy-out contracts with TV stations as a matter of principle. Such one-time fees were only common among the Europeans, who often wanted to sign their creatives not only meagerly, but without repeat fees. For this reason, Hans Zimmer's fee was due pro rata each time the fanfare was played anew.

The ZDF presenter looked into the camera with an affectedly serious expression on her face.

"Good afternoon, ladies and gentlemen, we interrupt our program *Hitler's Head Hair* for a special report from the Vatican. The history program will, of course, be continued at a later time and, starting next week, will be repeated every twelve hours on all special-interest channels.—Apparently white smoke is rising from the chimney of the Sistine Chapel. This indicates that a new Vicar of Christ on earth has indeed been elected."

The live image of the chimney was displayed.

"Vatican insiders and experts are predicting a neck-and-neck race between Nigerian Cardinal Francis Arinze and German Cardinal Udo Kierspe, formerly known as Udo Kier. Either would be a sensation. For while Arinze would be the first black African pope, Kierspe would be the first openly homosexual one. And, the former actor, who was Andy Warhol's muse for a long time, would also be another German at the interface between God and humanity after Pope Benedict. So are we going to be pope again? Here is Jürgen Erbacher with a special report on Cardinal Udo Kierspe."

The newscaster nodded smugly into the camera. Then a montage of photos, newspaper reports, and film and television clips from the life of the cardinal and ex-actor Udo Kier played. Above this was the voice-over commentary by the expert Erbacher.

"Once he was a celebrated actor and bon vivant. But an

encounter with one of the most important filmmakers of all time brought him back to the Church and into the fold of God."

An archived interview recording from 2016 was superimposed, in which Kier made a personal statement at the Vatican. "Werner Herzog is the reason why I initially entered the monastery. An audition with him in 1978 led me to give up acting. I switched to the Vatican, however, because of all the fantastic orgies."

Udo looked mischievously into the camera with his bright blue eyes, and the expert's commentary intervened.

"Since Kierspe's entry into the Pope's Council, where he quickly rose to become an important politician and thus one of the most powerful whisperers of the Curia of Petri, the *fantastic orgies* and debauched Easter feasts have become legendary."

Another interview snippet followed, showing a half-naked hysterical Kardashian sister atop one of Cardinal Kierspe's Easter concelebrations. She was surrounded by several equally half-naked men from the Swiss Guard, showing off their well-toned Sistine Six packs.

"Woooohoooo! Easter rules!! Man, I'm telling you, these dudes know how to Parteeeyyy! Wooohoooo! Udo! You Rooooock! Jesus is awesooome..."

This was followed by footage that had apparently been made in secret with a hidden camera and was supposed to show something like an exorcism. Vaguely recognizable on the low-quality material was also Cardinal Udo Kier, who was witnessing a demonic expulsion.

"But not everything around Cardinal Kierspe was always so *awesome*," the commentator continued. "A scandal rocked the Vatican in 2010, when it became known that Kierspe was apparently intensively involved with exorcisms and demons. Thus, criticism of the German became increasingly loud. Not a few even doubted his state of mind. Today, however, Kierspe seems to have been largely rehabilitated. But will his performance be able to convince God's jury? Or will he succumb to the other finalist—his African archrival Cardinal Arinze?"

32. REQUEST REJECTED

IN ROOM 237 OF THE SENATE ADMINISTRATION, IRMGARD AND Waltraud went about their work. Using a thick red felt-tip pen and a stamp from the authorities, they censored texts that had been submitted by various artists for approval. Irmgard, however, began to have doubts as to whether they were really doing the right thing. After all, art was supposed to be free. Just like thoughts. In addition, they prevented many more projects than they made possible. And when an application was actually approved, it was always by the same people who had been making culture out of the public eye for years and who were getting rich at state expense for it.

While Waltraud couldn't believe what her colleague was suddenly saying, and, miffed, decorated a few more submission forms with the thick rejection stamp, she explained to Irmgard that they were both fulfilling an important duty. "We have been entrusted by the highest authority with the worthy task of preventing *bad art*. The state-legitimized filtering system is an important body to ward off entertainment. For *entertainment* is, of course, the greatest danger to the further moral development of the German national body. And the threat posed by the type of the eternal artist has still not been completely banished." She hammered the next stamp onto the paper with such brute force that the red ink immediately souped through to three other applications below. She read her colleague paragraph nineteen of the Senate Film and Theater Funding Act, "It is written that funding assistance may not be granted if the artist's credentials or new project may offend moral decency and /or offend religious feelings.—However, artists of all kinds, but especially writers, directors and actors are nothing more than a bunch of insane drunks who look for trouble all day long and thus completely disqualify themselves for the democratic formation of will!"

The phone rang, and Irmgard picked it up. She listened to the voice on the other end of the line for a few seconds and then decided to turn on the speaker so Waltraud could listen in.

It was Magnus Max, who—as usual—was sitting in Verne Zog's bunker in front of numerous monitors and also got a live feed of Irmgard and Waltraud by means of a surveillance camera in the ceiling. "That dress looks wonderful on you, Irmgard," he commented.

The two women looked around in embarrassment, but could not spot the camera that was watching them anywhere.

"What can we do for you today?" Waltraud wanted to know.

"Well, you surely remember our joint agenda to cancel the play *They will claim that I was dead...*, I suppose.—There will be a meeting tomorrow at 3:00 pm at the Savoy Hotel between Werner Herzog, Nico Pacinsky and Christoph Gräve."

The two ladies of the Senate were stunned for a moment. Then Irmgard stammered, "*The* Werner Herzog?"

"Yes, the congenial writer, film-, theater-, documentary- and opera-director, producer, explorer, adventurer and ornithologist— my noble and beyond all doubt master Werner Herzog."

Irmgard remembered the first meeting with Magnus Max, when he had already spoken again and again about his noble master. "Didn't you say last time that you were working for a certain...Verne...so and so?"

"You'd better leave the formulation of such stupid questions to people who know how to do it if you want Gräve's play to be stopped," Magnus Max hissed. "Just follow me unconditionally, and everything will turn out for the best."

"Very well. What can we contribute to the meeting of the *great artists*?" Waltraud wanted to know.

"I would like you to act as a positive reinforcing catalyst and encourage both Mr Pacinsky and Mr Gräve to sign the replacement agreement so that the actor will give up the play and move to our film project."

Waltraud's voice began to vibrate. "And you think that would end Gräves' play once and for all?"

"That's absolutely correct," Magnus Max trumpeted.

Irmgard made a handwritten note. "Good. Tomorrow, then...you said 3:00 pm at the Savoy?—We'll be happy to come and give the gentlemen a good talking to."

"Wonderful."

Clack. Magnus Max had hung up and Irmgard and Waltraud remained puzzled. "Werner Herzog?! This is getting crazier and crazier!"

"Well, that's wonderful. Once the play is canceled, we can calmly get rid of the director as well."

The two cultural guards laughed maliciously, and suddenly the lights went out in the entire ninth basement. When it came back on after a few agonizingly long seconds, the janitor was standing in the doorway, sucking on a beer bottle. It was Wolfgang Wendland, singer of the punk rock band *Die Kassierer*, who had been ordered by the employment office to change the fuses in the senate administration. In protest against the fact that he was expected to do physical work, Wendland took advantage of a legal loophole and always performed the work completely naked and usually with an erect penis, which, however, hardly stood out under his gigantic beer belly. So the former candidate for chancellor of the Anarchist Pogo Party of Germany, whose slogans were *Booze, Soak, Guzzle—all day long!* and *Work is shit!*, surveyed the indignant faces of the two ladies and delighted in their disgust. He slurred, "Sorry. We just had a fuse failure here. Everything's back up and running, though."

33. HOTEL SAVOY

THE NEXT DAY, NICO AND GRÄVE SAT TOGETHER IN THE LOBBY OF the Hotel Savoy in Berlin-Charlottenburg and drank a coffee. Gräve had doubts that Verne Zog would really show up and suspected that Nico had only met a double in the Alpine Fortress. Nico, however, insisted that he had talked with the real Werner Herzog. Gräve immediately corrected him. The man's name was *Verne Zog*. Under Nico's shirt, the crucifix pendant transmitted every word into the headsets of Dr Vary Plump and Guido Gusion, who were heavily armed and well hidden on a veranda above the hotel lobby. Guido was assembling one of his Assassin firearms and installing a scope on the AR500. Through it, he could see Nico, who looked up at their hiding place on the veranda and nodded once, unnoticed by Gräve.

Then, suddenly and to the surprise of all concerned, the two senate ladies Irmgard and Waltraud stepped up to the table. Guido handed Dr. Plump the rifle so that she could look through it herself and identify the two strangers. She stated that the women looked old, nasty and frustrated. From this she correctly concluded that this could only mean one thing—that they must be representatives of some Berlin authority. When she took a closer look at the wardrobe of the two ladies, which seemed to come from the old clothes collection, she realized that the troublemakers must come from the cultural sphere. Guido was about to abort the mission, but Dr. Plump insisted on staying and waiting. Such an opportunity would not arise again so soon.

Irmgard and Waltraud sat down unbidden with Nico and Gräve in the still free armchairs. "We have come to give you moral support in your negotiations with Herr Herzog."

"How do *you* know about that?" Gräve wanted to know.

"We are the supreme district senate administration for good taste and culture," Waltraud replied. "And therefore also know about everything that's happening culturally in our city. But without further ado, of course we also pursue our own agenda. Or to put it more clearly, we care very much about your fate *after* your creative period at Ballhaus-Ost."

Gräve was about to get up and leave the hotel, annoyed, when Nico grabbed him by the sleeve and pointed in the direction of the main entrance. As if in slow motion, they could see the door open. A gust of wind chased through the lobby. Immediately after, Magnus Max, dressed in sunglasses and a dark suit, entered the Hotel Savoy. He had a radio button in his ear, a mic on his lapel, and a black briefcase under his arm. He was followed by ten other dwarfs in the same getup. As if in a ballet, they spread out around the hotel and secured the lobby and all access routes to it.

———

On the porch, Guido Gusion was startled. "Damn it! Security Dwarves!"

"Don't worry. We are in a superior position. They cannot see us," Dr. Plump reassured him.

"The room is filling up. I hope we brought enough bullets!"

Dr. Plump answered this only with a wry smile and a raised

eyebrow. Of course she had taken enough cartridges. Then she started a high-end digital binocular, while Guido turned his attention back to the scope on his gun. They saw a tall gaunt man following the dwarves, who had pulled his slouch hat low on his face and kept his head lowered so that his countenance could not be seen. Guido nonetheless unsheathed his rifle. Beads of sweat ran down his forehead.

"Is that Herzog?" Dr. Plump asked excitedly.

"I can't fully ID him. Damn!" Guido hesitated, and his hand shook slightly. He looked up from his rifle, "Let's wait and see."

———

The man in the floppy hat headed for the table where Magnus Max had now also positioned himself. Gräve, Nico and the two senate ladies held their breath as the slim man sat down on the chair that was still free. Gräve was frozen to a pillar of salt, and all the others looked up in awe and tension at the man, whose face they could not yet fully recognize. Then he took off his hat. It was indeed Verne Zog, alias Werner Herzog. A curse escaped Gräve. "Holy shit! You haven't aged a single day!"

"Thank you, Christoph," Zog nasalized. "It's very nice to see you again after such a long time."

Guido's and Dr. Plump's breathing was even faster now, and their hearts were racing in sync. Because of the number of people sitting downstairs at the table, Guido just couldn't get a clear shot. "It is him. But there are too many others in the line of fire," he noted in frustration.

"Then kill 'em all!" Dr. Plump tried to encourage him.

"We can't do this. We're on a papal mission!" said the son of Hasidic Jews.

"God damn it!" she replied.

———

Down at the table, Verne Zog gave a friendly nod to the Senate ladies and said, "I think I need no introduction; my reputation should precede me. I am pleased to make your acquaintance. My adlatus and faithful servant Magnus Max has already told me of your formidable achievements in the field of Berlin public culture."

Gräve snorted contemptuously, and Waltraud and Irmgard were so impressed that they merely stammered to themselves, unable to get out a complete sentence. They offered each other the second person singular of the personal and possessive pronoun (the polite form of address), but Nico grew impatient and looked nervously at the porch above them. "So, let's go. No more of this banter. We don't have forever, after all."

"Very true, Klaus." Verne Zog nodded at him. That he addressed him as *Klaus was* noticed by everyone at the table.

"So, I get a bunch of money to make a movie with Werner about my life. Do you understand? But since I signed such a gag contract with Christoph Gräve and the Ballhaus-Ost, there will be a transfer fee due—and it's being negotiated now!" Nico banged his fist on the table, bending the nail on his ring finger so that tears came to his eyes in pain.

Gräve took over the conversation, "All right. I'll be completely honest. Verne, you and I still have a score to settle. And I want it settled with interest and compound interest. In return, I'll then discontinue the theater production of *They Will Claim that I was Dead…* and let you have the leading man, Nico Pacinsky."

Nico's gaze again wandered nervously to the porch, where Guido and Dr. Plump continued to wait for a clear shot. Magnus Max noticed Nico's nervousness and watched him all the more closely.

Irmgard, meanwhile, wanted to make herself important. "Well, if it helps, the Senate can certainly cover part of the cost of your film, Mr Herzog."

And Waltraud interjected. "Then you might be able to refinance the transfer fee in advance. However, a regional effect of 125 percent would have to be achieved. In which federal state are you registered, Mr Pacinsky?"

Verne Zog declined with a friendly nod. "Thank you, that is very thoughtful, but my financial resources exceed the gross domestic product of the Federal Republic of Germany by several thousand percent."

The nervous heads of Irmgard and Waltraud constantly bounced up and down in front of Guido Gusion's targeting optics. Like Muppets, they kept twitching through the picture, thwarting any possibility of a fatal shot at Verne Zog.

"Kill them, Guido!" Dr. Plump demanded, increasingly tense.

Guido, however, only looked up at her, annoyed.

Downstairs, the waiter, who bore a resemblance to the young Helmut Berger, brought more coffee for everyone. Nico took a sip and grumbled "Well, Christoph, just tell us how much money you want and that's it. I don't have forever either, you know?"

Christoph Gräve also took a mouthful of coffee and then turned to Verne Zog, "Well, first of all, I want an explanation of what you did with my actors back then, and why they all played like shit afterwards. Udo Kier had the same problem with you, by the way."

Verne Zog answered bluntly, "Dear Christoph, first I exorcised the performers, then I freed their creative demons, captured them, archived them, and incorporated them over the following decades to increase my own creative power and prolong my life."

There was incredulous silence at the table. Then everyone except Gräve let out an unbridled snort. "Yes, wonderful!" Irmgard said with a laugh, and her colleague Waltraud added, "Well, he has a sense of humor, too!"

"I don't think it's so funny," Gräve mumbled to himself.

Irmgard hissed back, "That's why you're not a global super star like him."

Offended, Gräve passed over this remark and made his next demand, "Well, fine. My second postulate: I want 250 billion dollars transfer fee for Nico!"

All those present stopped laughing. Nico raged. "Christoph, what are you doing, you stupid pig?"

Verne Zog, on the other hand, remained completely unmoved. "Two hundred and fifty billion? You shall have it, of course, my dear. Absolutely no problem at all."

"What, really? Should I have said 500 billion?" the shocked Gräve asked, and Waltraud became quite dizzy at the mere mention of such a sum.

"That...that...that's almost as much as the annual catering budget of the Public Classical Music broadcast station!"

Verne Zog sipped the coffee, but immediately spat the drop back into the cup. His sensitive taste buds had instantly analyzed that the beans used here to make the caffeinated hot beverage had not been predigested by any animal, so at best a mediocre aroma could emerge. To Gräve he said, "One djinni always fulfills three wishes. And I am your djinn today, dear friend."

Gräve narrowed his eyes and then trumpeted, "Good...demand three. I want a starring role in your film!"

Nico exploded again, "Tell me, Christoph, have you completely lost your mind?" Immediately afterwards, however, a thought occurred to him, "That's actually not such a bad idea!"

Verne Zog drummed his fingers on the table, clearly pleased. "So we're in agreement then. Magnus, will you please bring us the contract?"

Magnus Max left his strategic position and stepped up to the table. He opened the briefcase, took out a heavy stack of paper and handed it over to his master together with a *Tibaldi Fulgor*

Nocturnus, the most valuable pen of all times, which was designed in parts according to the angular size Phi and thus symbolized the principle of the golden ratio. The exclusive piece was not filled with conventional ink, but with the bluish blood from Leonardo Fibonacci's smoker's leg, whose numerical sequence named after him was originally only intended to describe the growth of a rabbit population, but in fact turned out to be an almost inexplicable universal growth pattern in nature. The further one progressed in the sequence of numbers, the more the quotient of the successive numbers approached the values of the golden ratio. It was not until the twentieth century that Verne Zog's creative work succeeded in helping his own critical theory of aestheticism to achieve a breakthrough and in contrasting the golden ratio with another aesthetic system of reference.

Verne Zog opened the contract, which was marked in several places with a yellow sticky note, and filled in the blanks with his pen. "Two hundred and fifty billion dollars...Or euros?"

"What is the exchange rate at the moment?" Gräve wanted to know.

But Verne Zog did not dwell on such trifles.

"So Euro. Then...leading role in the film...date...signature." He put his signature under the contract and handed it to Gräve. Both artists smiled at each other with relief and satisfaction and shook hands. Nico, however, looked nervously up at the veranda again. And this time Magnus Max followed his gaze. It was just the moment when Gräve, for his part, wanted to sign the contract.

Guido still had no clear field of fire, and Dr. Plump's patience wore thin. "Fire the gun now!"

"No!"

She aggressively grabbed his rifle, and a shot rang out. The uranium-hardened bullet from the silenced gun whizzed through the lobby and almost silently pierced the top of Irmgard's skull. Her head disintegrated in a red cloud of blood and brain fragments before Gräve could sign the contract. Chaos broke out throughout the hotel, killing a total of fifty-six residents and staff. Waltraud, splattered with the blood of her colleague, cried out in panic, but was unable to stand up in her state of shock. So she sat bolt upright at the table, the cup with the decaffeinated coffee and Irmgard's bone splinters in it still in her hand. Completely motionless, as if frozen in a pillar of salt, she screamed through in one go without taking a breath. All the security dwarves, including Magnus, pulled out their guns and started firing wildly around the area. Nico took cover under the table, while Magnus Max tried to get his noble master to safety through the back door.

Now there was no turning back, so Guido Gusion switched the rifle to automatic and continuous fire. He fired several volleys downward. Magnus Max instinctively made a pike to intercept a bullet meant for his master. Wounded, unconscious and bleeding, he remained on the ground.

Verne Zog shouted in wild desperation the name of his longtime companion, with whom he had spent almost the entire twentieth century. But Magnus, in his unconsciousness, did not hear him. Two other dwarves grabbed Zog and hastily smuggled him outside, one firing several times at the porch above them, clearing the way for the master director's rescue, at least temporarily. Dr. Plump was hit and tumbled down over the railing. She hit the ground hard, while Guido was able to liquidate two more dwarves who toppled over side by side to the left and right.

Only Gräve remained completely unmoved and cool in his chair, while the panicked Waltraud next to him was still screaming like a banshee without stopping. But Gräve was not bothered by this and sipped his coffee, which was so bitter that he had to put two packets of cane sugar in it. He commented laconically that he had always said that there was something not quite kosher about this Verne Zog, but no one listened to him.

The next moment, Waltraud's chest exploded as a ricochet from behind shredded her lungs. She crashed face-first into the coffee table, and her soul was instantly transported to hell, where numerous theater directors and screenwriters who had taken their own lives because of her were already waiting to pounce on her with wild roars. The remaining dwarves collected the corpses and carried them outside like busy ants to the vans they had come in.

However, when they went to rescue their friend and leader Magnus Max, they came under continuous fire from Guido Gusion. Two more dwarves lost their lives. At the same time, Nico came out from under the table and was about to run away when he was pierced by a bullet. One of the fatally shot dwarves had accidentally pulled the trigger of his gun one last time while falling. Nico cried out in pain and hit his head on the ground. The shot had pierced his shoulder. So he was only slightly injured and not life-threatening. Now Gräve also cried out in horror. But before he could rush to the aid of his protégé, the remaining dwarves seized the unconscious Nico and carried him at lightning speed toward the exit. They had to cease their attempts to rescue Magnus Max because he was lying directly in the line of fire.

Suddenly it became quiet. The dwarves had escaped outside and had even been able to save Nico and Verne Zog. Body parts and blood, however, decorated the entire hotel. The smokers from the *Times* cigar bar attached to the lobby were the only guests who had survived the massacre, as they were separated from the rest of the world by a bullet- and vaporproof door. So their nicotine addiction had ultimately saved their lives after all. Next to the unconscious Magnus Max, Dr. Plump, who was also badly injured, slowly regained consciousness. Guido Gusion rappelled down from the veranda and examined his girlfriend's wounds. A broken and exposed bone protruded from her coat sleeve, and her calf was shot through. They agreed that they had to leave immediately. Dr. Plump's eyes fell on the unconscious Magnus Max beside her. He was still breathing, so she motioned for him to be taken away. Guido nodded, picked Magnus up off the floor, and with some effort threw him over his left shoulder. With his right arm he helped Dr. Plump up and supported her on their way to freedom.

From the corner with the armchairs, Gräve called out to them, "Hey! Hey, you! Who the hell are you?"

"We're the good guys," was Guido's terse reply.

"I bet," Gräve said, but the two paid him no further attention and fled as fast as they could through the lobby toward the exit. Gräve remained behind, staring after them as they left the hotel through the main entrance in the direction of Fasanenstraße.

THE BIGGEST WHORE EVER

Spotify Playlist 5

34. THE POPE'S SON-IN-LAW

THE VATICAN IN ROME, THE ANCIENT AND RELIGIOUS BUILDINGS
towered mightily. There was the Sistine Chapel, here St. Peter's
Square with St. Peter's Basilica. In a back room in the Apostolic
Palace were the naked and shapely bodies of a man and a woman.
They were Adam and Eve in the Garden of Eden in an oil painting
by the Austrian painter Wenzel Peter. The breathing of several
people could be heard softly in the background. In the large room,
whose walls were decorated with all kinds of biblical frescoes and
pictures, the oil painting with the naked bodies extended into
reality, because the entire wide hall was filled with numerous
barely clothed men, women and intermediate beings, who did not
move in the slightest and apparently waited silently.

A few wore masks and lacquer and leather replicas of antique
armor and uniforms. It was a completely surreal picture, because
for minutes absolutely no one moved, and everyone seemed to
stare spellbound in the direction of the entrance gate. Suddenly, a
low moan and the crack of a whip could be heard from a separee.
The large wooden door, adorned with heavy gold inlays, opened,
and Pope Kierus the First strode through. A slight murmur went
through the hall.

Kierus stomped tightly towards a pedestal, climbed up and then turned around with a sweeping move to his audience. Those present now finally viewed the man in his full glory. He was clad in his papal rainbow robes, already stained with numerous spots, and he carried an old leather riding whip in his right hand. He cleared his throat and paused meaningfully while his audience held its breath. Finally, with his heavy German accent, he spoke in English to his disciples, "My dear friends. We have waited for so long, but finally I proved that we could do it. Finally I have the power I righteously deserve. And I will make sure that my papal term goes down in history as the biggest and longest lasting orgy since man learned to fuck one another!—So please...let's get ready to ruuuuummmmmmble!"

With a loud crack, Udo swung the whip as a signal that it could now start. And it did. An orgy never before surpassed in decadence began to the music of Madonna's song *Deeper and Deeper*. While four transvestites approached each other and formed a phalanx, five nuns of advanced age formed a group and charged at everything that was not nailed down. Having taken out their teeth, they managed to clamp the hard cocks so tightly between their jaws that most of the gentlemen ejaculated immediately, even before their penises could penetrate the throats of the virgin ladies. Several men held down a ladyboy who screamed with laughter like a fury, while a woman in a handstand tickled the soles of his feet with her tongue. Pope Kierus, meanwhile, made himself comfortable in a wheelchair on the platform, from where he could easily observe the festivities. He hummed along with the Madonna lyrics.

"Deeper and deeper, and deeper, and deeper—sweeter and sweeter, and sweeter, and sweeter... Daddy couldn't be all wrong—and my mama made me learn this song..."

There was wax play here, whippings there, rubber toys everywhere. The entire BDSM alphabet was represented—and a few umlauts to boot. Pope Kierus, sitting in his wheelchair, gave several bursts of fire from a giant black dildo like at a Rammstein concert while being fellated by various people at the same time. He moaned to this exactly as he had once done while dying in the movie *Flesh for Frankenstein*. "Aaah! Aah! Ah! Ah. Ah? Aah? Aaah?"

In the background, several mugwumps ran around looking for new consumers of their stuff. These critters, which came from the heroine-soaked brain of William S. Burroughs, were a bizarre-looking alien species that appeared gaunt and reptilian. They had strange antennae on their heads that secreted a whitish, viscous liquid when you sucked on it. This stuff was highly nutritious and at the same time extremely toxic, so you had to be careful not to overdose yourself. Just as Pope Kierus was enjoying a mugwump drink, the red phone, which had a video display and a camera, rang on a side table next to him. A number from Germany was displayed.

Slightly annoyed, Kierus picked up the phone and asked who dared to disturb the papal peace. On the other end of the line, a heavily exhausted, panting woman could be heard. It was Dr. Plump, who appeared on the display quite battered but still extremely attractive. She had two band-aids on her forehead, a bloody bandage on her leg, and what appeared to be a homemade splint on her broken arm. She looked as if she had just come from war, which in a strange way gave her an Amazonian erotic aura. Pope Kierus perceived her injuries and instantly let go of the mugwump's antenna. Shocked, he inquired about her health and whether her mission might have gone awry.

The psychologist stammered that everything had gotten out of control because suddenly Herzog's security dwarves had appeared everywhere at the Savoy Hotel. Pope Kierus instantly sat up in his wheelchair and asked, eyes wide open, if they have at least liquidated the enemy.

Dr. Plump struggled with the truth. But then she admitted that the target had been able to escape in the hellish chaos that had broken out.

While a few more Vatican servants were still working on his genitals, the pope threw a gigantic tantrum, a bit like Bruno Ganz as Adolf Hitler in the Führerbunker in the movie *Der Untergang*. He screamed, "This can't be true! That was an order! An order! How dare you fail and then call me instead of immediately doing yourself in or launching a new attack? Bunch of amateurs! Bits and pieces of shit you are!"

All the participants in the orgy turned their eyes to Pope Kierus. The pope's son-in-law, dressed in drag, and an elderly nun began to cry and ran outside the hall, where they committed suicide together.

The pope next wanted to know if at least Guido Gusion had fallen honorably in battle against Herzog. Dr. Plump answered in the negative, but she and Guido had been able to take possession of the person of Mr Nico Pacinsky. It was not yet known whether they could really get to Herzog through him, but they would certainly be able to find out in the next few hours. She and Guido had also had Herzog's private adlatus Magnus Max in their care for a short time, but unfortunately they had lost the dwarf.

Dr. Plump ran her hand through her stringy hair, for she knew that the Pope's reaction to this must result in wild shouting. Kierus could not believe his ears. He was raving. How was it possible for a ridiculous dwarf to slip away from two experienced assassins so easily? Dr. Plump dodged the question, explaining that it was all a bit confused. Finally, however, she began to tell what had happened after the failed attempt to assassinate Herzog at the Savoy Hotel in Berlin and how the loss of the dwarf Magnus Max and the capture of Nico Pacinsky could have happened.

"After we had collected ourselves to some extent, Guido and I left the hotel. Guido supported me and carried the unconscious Magnus Max on his shoulders. We had to leave the theater director Christoph Gräve behind, because we already had so many other problems to take care of and we could not accurately estimate his value for the operation. Our rented Porsche Cayenne S was parked in the parking garage of the Ludwig Erhard House. Latest model, of course. 440 hp. I opened the car's tailgate with the remote control so that Guido could plop the unconscious Magnus Max into the trunk with a jerk. We managed to escape before the police showed up, and during the drive we discussed whether we should take me and also the dwarf to a doctor. But since we both had gunshot wounds, that would have been unwise, since such wounds must always be reported to the authorities. So we decided to take care of the injuries ourselves in the parking lot at Olivaer Platz. Magnus Max had only been grazed and was obviously unconscious not because of the wound but because of his fall. As a psychologist, I naturally also have enough knowledge in the field of human medicine to be able not only to sew up a gunshot wound, but also to treat my own open fracture and my leg puncture. Guido bought an electric stapler, two meters of metal wire, a pair of pliers and some white spirit at *Conrad Elektronik* (Germany's Fry's Electronics) on Wittenbergplatz, which was more than adequate as medical equipment.

But when we got to Olivaer Platz, we found that all the parking spaces had been removed in the spirit of *Berlin's traffic turnaround.* Guido therefore backed up the Porsche Cayenne at full speed and made a U-turn with the handbrake to drive back toward Ku'damm via Fasanenstrasse. In doing so, he accidentally cut the lane of a lowered AMG S-Class with blue underbody lighting. The occupants felt provoked as a result and raced after us to restore their honor. When the next traffic light showed red, both vehicles had to stop and the driver of the Mercedes pulled up to our side. They lowered the side window and screamed murder, but because our Porsche was so well insulated, we could only hear fragments of their rare or even dead language. When the traffic light turned green again, Guido stepped fully on the gas and left the antique market criers in their pimped posh car from fourth ownership behind him. Magnus Max in the trunk was pressed against the rear wall of the vehicle by the acceleration, while the Cayenne bravely fought its way to the next traffic light. Of course, the light turned red just at that moment, forcing Guido to brake hard again so as not to endanger passersby. This caused Magnus Max in the trunk to be thrown against the back row of seats. Since in Berlin really every traffic light turns red as soon as you reach it, this process repeated itself a few more times.

Unfortunately, Guido overshot the stop line at the traffic lights at Ku'damm, corner of Nürnberger Straße by half a meter, and so our vehicle protruded a small distance into the crosswalk. While passers-by were crossing the causeway, a mime artist entered the intersection. He had a lit torch in his hand, used it to light several smaller torches, and then began a dance and juggling performance for the waiting cars. Apparently, he had unfortunately overlooked the fact that our Cayenne was a little over the stop line. So he tripped against the fender during his performance, and his burning flares crashed onto the hood. Immediately, the kerosene leaked out and ignited the front of the Porsche. Guido and I jumped out of the car in a panic, and as best we could with my injuries. Guido cursed wildly, but I had the presence of mind to pull the fire extinguisher out from under the seat with my still-functioning hand and smothered the fire. The hood was completely charred and the rest of the car was covered with white powder from the extinguisher. A little later a policeman came to question Guido, me and the mime artist about the course of events. He made notes on his clipboard, and the Luxembourg street performer accused us of having crossed the sacred stop line—the last bastion that still separated civilized society from total car anarchy.

The policeman took a stern tone and explained that the

situation was perfectly clear. After all, the Berlin Senate rents its city-owned street crossings to internationally recognized artists and artistresses, so you can't just drive into it. It was therefore a case of trespassing in combination with serious endangerment of pedestrians. We, however, insisted that the juggler had set our car on fire, and therefore wanted to have his personal and insurance data in order to report the resulting property damage to the car rental company."

Pope Kierus gradually became indignant and shouted into the phone, "I don't give a damn about this crappy Porsche Cayenne! The Vatican has the Sistine Company Package with Sixt and is therefore always fully insured. *Without* deductible in case of damage. What about the midget?"

"Yes…well…that was because…the artist had to leave because he still had a performance in front of a floor grinding machine rental shop window. The policeman dismissed him without pursuing the question of guilt any further. Just as he turned the corner, the tailgate of the Porsche opened, and the bloody Magnus Max jumped out screaming hysterically. He ran off and disappeared around the next corner without us being able to do anything about it. For a moment we didn't know what to make of this situation. The policeman, however, broke the silence and remarked warningly that we had obviously transported a dwarf. He therefore asked to see our dwarf transport license, which we would have had to apply for six months before the transport, and for which one would also have had to take a dwarf transport driving lesson at a local Berlin senate test center."

In the Apostolic Palace, Pope Kierus had something like an epileptic seizure from anger and slumped in his wheelchair. After a few seconds he regained his composure and even managed to speak. "I just want to finally get hold of Herzog, to restore the natural order of things," he gasped. "We need to get to him while he's out of hiding—and before he warps back to his alpine fortress."

Dr. Plump rubbed her temples. "Yes, my pope.—But I wasn't quite done yet. After we had distracted the policeman from us with the old your-shoelace-is-open trick and thus managed to escape, we were able to tend to my wounds in the heroin parking lot at Nollendorfplatz. It was actually only allowed to stop there for the electric refueling of battery-powered vehicles, but since there was no one from the Law and Order Office to be seen at the time, we dared to use it illegally with a vehicle with an internal combustion engine anyway. After I had hurriedly stitched up my injuries there and splinted the open fracture, we were driving back towards Zehlendorf when Guido got a call on his American cell phone. He took it out of his jacket pocket and held it to his ear, although this behavior is of course highly immoral and dangerous while driving. But the phone call was extremely short, and Guido could not believe what the chief rabbi of the New Synagogue on Oranienburger Strasse told him: they had Nico Pacinsky! We immediately turned around and took the Tiergarten Tunnel in the direction of Central Station. The whole way, we kept asking ourselves how in the world Nico had gotten there."

35. RABBI ROTTWEILER

THE WONDERFUL MAGNIFICENT BUILDING OF THE RESTORED NEW
Synagogue in Berlin with its impressive dome was, as always, well
secured by the Berlin police. Bored officers, clutching their
submachine guns, were loitering between the armored barriers,
waiting for an assassination attempt or the end of the day. Then
the coked-up Porsche Cayenne with Guido Gusion at the wheel
came hurtling along and, with a screeching full stop, stopped
right in front of the entrance to the Jewish house of worship. The
policemen, of course, immediately awoke from their lethargy,
raised their weapons tremblingly, and ran somewhat headlong
but nevertheless purposefully to the car. When Guido rushed out
and jumped onto the sidewalk, all the guns were immediately
pointed at him. The foremost policeman even aimed at Guido's
head. "Don't move!"

Guido instantly put up his hands and stopped.

"Get down on the ground!" another policeman shouted.

Guido, however, did not understand the excitement and only
affirmed with his hands still held up. "I'm Jewish!"

The policeman thought for a moment and then pointed his
MP at Guido's waistband. "Show us your cock!"

Slowly, Guido put down his right hand and unzipped his dark blue *Alex McQueen* jeans. As he did so, his eyes were fixed on the policeman in front of him. Careful not to make any wrong moves, he took out his little Guido, which wasn't so little at all, and showed him off to the law enforcement officers as requested. After what felt like an eternity, the policeman, relieved, put the gun down again and called over his shoulder to his colleagues, "It's okay! He's a Jew!"

A relieved murmur went through the ranks of the police officers, who lowered their weapons and secured them again. Dr. Plump also got out of the car. Guido pointed to the building in front of him and politely asked the policeman, "Is this the entrance to the New Synagogue?"

"Yes. But, sir, this is a security area. You cannot park your vehicle here. But we can valet for you, while you have your mincha, if you want." Guido thanked him and threw him the key. The policeman was also extremely polite. He handed him a valet ticket in return. While Dr. Plump and Guido entered the synagogue, the policeman drove the burnt Porsche around the corner into a parking lot.

———

Chief Rabbi Hektor Wiesengrund-Rottweiler was sitting at his desk. He was a thoroughly pleasant presence, spoke with a slight Hebrew accent, and invited Guido and Dr. Plump to come in. The rabbi and Guido knew each other from earlier, when both had lived in Sherman Oaks in the Valley of Los Angeles. After Guido introduced his colleague and friend Dr. Plump to him, they exchanged a few pleasantries before the psychologist steered toward the real topic at hand: Nico Pacinsky.

The rabbi looked at both of them for a moment with a mild, worried expression and wanted to know what kind of Schlamassel they had gotten themselves into. Guido, however, took the clergyman's hand placatingly and assured him that everything was fine and that he had nothing to worry about. Dr. Plump indicated that they were on a secret mission from the Vatican, which, of course, only made the rabbi more worried. He wanted to know if Guido's father knew that his son had converted to Catholicism.

Guido vigorously objected. He would never give up his birthright to be a Jew. But he wanted to help to bring the mission, which he was not allowed to name further, to a successful conclusion. He said he was proud that the Vatican and the pontiff had entrusted him, as the only Jew in history, with such an important but highly secret mission. The rabbi nodded his understanding and then began to explain that a few hours ago an alarm had been raised because a young and completely naked man had appeared in front of the synagogue. That in itself would have been nothing unusual, after all, this was Berlin-Mitte, but the things that the naked man had said in his delirium had been quite borderline.

————

A few hours earlier:

In front of the synagogue, the same policemen were guarding the Jewish house of worship that we had already met when Guido and Dr. Plump arrived. Around the corner came Nico staggering. He was completely naked, and his bullet wound had apparently been freshly stitched. Babbling confusedly, he staggered right into the security barrier of the synagogue: "The Kinskian demon. He wants him. Herr Zog is not a Herzog. He is a demon without a daimon."

A policeman stepped up to him. "Hey, what are you doing here? Get out of the security zone now!"

Nico, however, continued to walk apathetically toward the policemen. "E equals mc squared. We live in a theater reality."

"Get down on the ground!" shouted one of the cops.

The policeman was followed by five other security guards with their submachine guns drawn and cocked. But Nico paid no attention to them. One of the lawmen stared at Nico's naked midsection and then shouted to his colleagues, "That guy doesn't have a foreskin!"

A relieved murmur went through the ranks of the police officers, who now lowered their weapons. One passerby, however, pointed out, "As far as I know, Muslims don't have any either."

Immediately, all weapons went up again and aimed at Nico. The squadron leader called the chief rabbi by cell phone so that he could make a decision on how to proceed with the confused young man.

Back in the chief rabbi's conference room, Rottweiler went on to explain that poor Nico had been completely frozen and had been feverishly babbling about people like Werner Herzog, his Alpine Fortress and the theater director Christoph Gräve. But also the name Guido Gusion had been mentioned, and therefore Rottweiler had of course first informed his old acquaintance Guido, instead of the police.

Guido wanted to know who else was informed about the matter. Rottweiler looked at him paternally and just shook his head: no one, of course.

Dr. Plump asked where Nico was now. Rottweiler let his eyes wander from her to Guido and back. He pondered hard, trying to figure out what was going on here. But then he decided that his friendship with the Gusion family, whom he had known for over three decades, ran deeper than any doubt about Guido's story. Rottweiler rose from his chair and headed for the door. Dr. Plump and Guido followed him and took the elevator underground. Together they entered a tunnel. Again and again, signs posted on the walls pointed the way through the branching system of tubes in Hebrew.

"I didn't know there were underground tunnels here," Dr. Plump said, somewhat taken aback.

"Of course. 4,000 years of pogroms make you a little...meschuggene and paranoid," was Rottweiler's laconic reply. "In case some really bad Schlamassel happens upstairs, we also have a direct high-speed train line to Israel down here."

Dr. Plump was thrilled.

"Really?!"

"No! Of course not," Rottweiler laughed. "Ah, these Germans. They just don't get the Jewish shtick."

Rottweiler and Guido grinned. Dr. Plump, on the other hand, was somewhat crestfallen. "Well, laughing is not a German matter..." she commented, and the two men laughed again. Then they reached a metal door, behind which was apparently a padded cell. Dr. Plump and Guido looked through the barred window and spotted Nico, wrapped in two tallits, sleeping on a bed in the middle of the room. Rottweiler took a key out of his pocket and unlocked the cell.

Dr. Plump told all this to her boss, Pope Kierus the First, via the papal video phone network. The Pope was still in the middle of his orgy, but it had come to a complete halt because of the phone call. The story Dr. Plump was telling him was already going on far too long, and he was getting more and more nervous. Time was pressing. At some point the pope had to take care of his numerous guests again, who were waiting for further sex instructions and those potency pills did not work forever either. In any case, someone had to get hold of the criminal director Herzog.

Pope Kierus inquired, "So, what have you done with the boy Nico? Does he know anything about the whereabouts of Werner Herzog?"

"Nico is unresponsive so far, unfortunately," Dr. Plump said. "But Guido has taken him to safety at *Bonnie's Ranch*. And I've made contact with one of his friends in the meantime. I'm with him now, and we're about to go and visit Mr Pacinsky together."

Kierus calmed down again and continued in a more conciliatory, almost tearful tone, "All right, Vary. Please understand, I have waited so long. You must keep trying—and you *must* succeed. I want my soul back!"

"Of course, most holy father!"

They both hung up, and the picture on the videophone went out. Dr. Plump had conducted the entire telephone conversation from Christoph Gräve's office in the Ballhaus-Ost. Gräve himself was sitting at his desk, white as a sheet. He looked at Dr. Plump, stunned, and could not yet grasp the full scope of the situation. Everything he had enacted in his play seemed to be becoming reality. Or was he simply going gradually insane because he had spent too long looking into the abysses of Kinski and Herzog? *When you look into an abyss, the abyss also looks into you, and he who fights with monsters must be careful not to become a monster himself,* Gräve's favorite philosopher Friedrich Nietzsche had already known.

Dr. Plump, however, assured him that they would surely find answers to all these questions, as soon as they had apprehended the super villain Werner Herzog. But first they would have to find him. And Nico would be the key. The psychologist left the office and signaled Gräve to follow her. Apathetically, he got up, and the two drove in Gräve's BMW through the evening city toward Berlin-Wedding. There, in the Wittenau district, was the Karl Bonhoeffer Mental Hospital, popularly known in Berlin as Bonnie's Ranch. Officially, the facility had already been closed in 2006. Secretly, however, privately wealthy psychologists were able to continue using the facility for their own research and detention purposes in exchange for a high monthly rent payment to the state lottery company, which served the Berlin Senate as a cover for a variety of shady activities.

On the trip, Gräve wanted to hear all about Dr. Plump's encounter with Rabbi Rottweiler to distract himself a bit from what he thought he would face in the mental hospital. Judaism was Gräve's personal fetish. While he himself was not devout or even religious, this more than four-thousand-year-old community of people and faith held a great fascination for him. Of the handful of Jews he had met in his life, pretty much all were multi-talented geniuses. He remembered a real estate agent who wrote symphonies in his spare time that went straight to his soul and made him cry because of their melancholy mood. Or this extremely pretty brunette Ukrainian woman who had appeared as a substitute singer in several of Gräves' plays. Her main occupation was housewife and mother, but on her weekends off she had trained her voice in such a way that she would have upstaged even Maria Callas. Moreover, Gräve was secretly convinced that today's German cultural scene was so subterraneously bad because, due to the Nazi regime's persecution and extermination of Jews and the state and societal resentment that still existed in some cases, there were hardly any Hebrews left in Central Europe at present.

Then he often imagined what it would have been like if the world had been spared the German Terror. What if Billy Wilder, Fred Zinnemann, Peter Lorre, Otto Preminger, Robert Siodmak, Ken Adam and Gräve's numerous other idols had been able to stay in their German homeland? Would Hollywood be in Berlin today? A case can be made for it...

36. BONNIE'S RANCH

A LARGE OLD BUILDING COMPLEX FROM THE END OF THE NINETEENTH century with brick clinker facade and Prussian caps decorating the windows with round arches rose menacingly and coolly into the summery but overcast Berlin evening sky. Brownish ivy climbed up the facade, and classical spires adorned the roof. Trees stood in the background, while in the foreground a freshly mowed meadow shone with an almost surreal lushness. Lemon butterflies fluttered by in their evening mating flight, and a few bees still buzzed somewhere nearby. The whole area presented an extremely incongruous picture. Natural idyll met four-meter-high fences with NATO barbed wire. Surveillance cameras and warning signs rounded it all off. A plaque embedded in the facade bore the name of the facility: *Karl Bonhoeffer Mental Hospital*.

A siren sounded, and two yellow warning lights on the fence flashed. One of the gates opened, and a car drove through. It was Gräve's old BMW 7 Series. The luxury classic car came to a stop in front of the main building next to the burned Porsche Cayenne that also parked here, while the gate closed again in the background. The passenger door opened, and Dr. Plump got out.

FLORIAN FRERICHS

Gräve followed the dangerous beauty, who only seemed more attractive because of her bruises, toward the building entrance. He activated the retrofitted locking mechanism by pressing the radio remote control in the car key. The alarm honked and flashed once briefly. Then they both disappeared inside the building, where Guido Gusion immediately met them in the hallway.

He was accompanied by Dr. Plump's assistant Samael, who carried a leather doctor's bag. They greeted each other politely, but then Samael noticed the Porsche, which had been damaged by the fire. Puzzled, he asked what had happened, but Dr. Plump only replied coolly, *"Don't be gentle—it's a rental."*

She and Guido exchanged a pained, knowing look. They made their way through the seemingly endless labyrinths of corridors that rose like diseased convolutions of the brain over several levels. One could easily guess that the walls here had witnessed immeasurable human suffering. The group of four went to Block F, where on the sixth floor Nico was housed in a cell. Dr. Plump wanted to know from Guido whether he had already had the opportunity to speak with the patient, but the latter only replied that he had wanted to wait until she and Christoph Gräve were present. Samael added that Mr Pacinsky had been extremely aggressive when he was admitted by Mr Gusion, and that even such a heavy sedative as Lexotanil had had little effect. He therefore hoped that perhaps Christoph Gräve, as a close friend of the patient, could have a calming influence.

Finally they stopped in front of one of the numerous doors, which all looked completely the same and could only be distinguished from each other by their six-digit assignment code under the windows. Samael asked Christoph to take a seat in the waiting area behind the door opposite until they would ask him to come to Nico's room. Gräve just nodded and disappeared into the room, which still contained old magazines from 2006—full of reports about the soccer World Cup in Germany. Gräve shudderingly recalled that the World Cup had been the starting point of the new German national consciousness, which brought flag-waving back into the *Volksgemeinschaft* from the dingy rightwing corner and equated the performance of soccer players with the performance of the *Volkskörper*. For him, it was only a matter of time before people would be cheering for soldiers again instead of footballers. For suddenly, even ordinary citizens no longer felt any shame when waving the black-red-gold banner, as had until then actually been part of the good ol', cross-party tone of the Federal Republic's consensus society. Gräve felt dizzy at the thought, and he put the issue of *Stern* back on the table.

———

Samael, meanwhile, pulled a key attached to a chain with a snap hook out of his pants pocket and unlocked Nico's cell. He hesitated for a moment and looked questioningly at Dr. Plump and Guido before pushing open the heavy door, which was padded from the inside. As he did so, he put his free hand to a baton attached to his belt. The three entered. The dark room was sparsely lit only by a twinkle light on the ceiling. At the other end of the surprisingly large room, Nico was lying on the bed where he was restrained with a straitjacket. He looked wildly at the three people entering.

"Good afternoon, Mr Pacinsky. How are you?" Dr. Plump greeted him.

Nico screamed, "He wants my soul! And that's what you want!"

"Please calm down. You have suffered a severe trauma."

"Herzog! He is the trauma!"

"Do you remember what exactly happened?" Dr. Plump asked as she moved closer to the bed.

"Of course, what a stupid question! Only someone who is completely clueless—or malicious—could ask that," Nico raged.

"You think I'm clueless?" Dr. Plump asked.

"No! Evil! All together!"

Nico looked at the three of them, shrugging his head wildly, and Samael stood protectively in front of Guido and Dr. Plump in case the patient should break free. Then Guido Gusion joined in the conversation: "Your friend Christoph Gräve is waiting next door. He would like to pay you a visit."

Nico became instantly silent and calmed down. "What, Christoph is here?"

"Would you like to see him?" Dr. Plump asked.

"Yes, please. He had warned me about Herzog, but..."

Guido gave Samael a sign. He disappeared outside and locked the door, only to open it again a few moments later and return with Christoph Gräve. "

"Christoph!" Nico called out weakly, but visibly pleased.

"Nico, jeez...I told you better not get involved with Verne Zog!"

"Yes, Christoph. I guess you were right," Nico murmured meekly. "I should have kept doing the play with you instead of shooting the film with Herzog."

Dr. Plump wrote something down on a clipboard, and Gräve took a deep breath before speaking, "Nico...I have to tell you something that might upset you. You're talking about a film shoot. But you didn't make a film at all. There was no film shooting. We were still together this morning at the Savoy Hotel when an assassination attempt was made on Verne Zog. You were wounded."

"What nonsense," Nico shook his head. "I got hit by a falling crossbar on the film set in Herzog's Alpine Fortress while we were shooting an orgy. That's why I'm here...isn't it?"

Dr. Plump, Guido and Gräve looked at each other. There was a tense silence, and Gräve even had tears in his eyes. He turned to the side to hide his emotions.

But Nico insisted, "Right?—Christoph! Talk to me! What's going on here? What's going on with *me*?"

Hesitantly, Gräve turned back to him and finally got up the nerve to tell him the truth: "Verne Zog has most likely exorcised you—and robbed you of your creative juices and powers!"

Nico couldn't help but laugh in disbelief. "Please, what?!"

Now Guido Gusion joined the conversation: "Mr Pacinsky, all this might sound a little weird to you. But we have been tracing the tracks of Mr Werner Herzog for quite some time now. According to your friend Christoph Gräve, however, his real name is Verne Zog."

"Okay...but what the fuck is going on?" Nico shouted.

"It all adds up," Gräve said excitedly. "After all, at first I couldn't believe myself what Dr. Plump explained to me, but now it all makes sense. After so many years, I finally have answers."

"You are not sick," Guido said. "You are not insane. You aren't suffering from amnesia or any other brain injury. But to get to the point, Werner Herzog—or Verne Zog—is a demon hunter. And he tried to get hold of your demons, too."

"No shit!" Nico said, starting to feel a little queasy. He looked at Gräve from wide eyes and whispered, "Christoph, get me out of here."

"You will be free very soon," Dr. Plump said. "However, you have suffered severe mental trauma, and it may worsen after we tell you the whole truth. So it's better if you stay strapped in for the time being."

She nodded to her friend Guido Gusion, and he began a more detailed explanation, "Verne Zog steals the demons of creative people. There are two demons in every person, one is good—and one is evil. Yin vs. Yang. Apollo vs. Dionysus. God vs. the Devil.

235

The principle is as old as mankind itself. But in some people, one demon is stronger than the other...Verne Zog and his alter ego Werner Herzog, however, do not have *any* demon at all! He's a freak of nature. That's why he must feast on others' to satisfy his own never-ending thirst for creativity."

"Christoph, what are they saying? They are completely insane! Take off the shackles before they do something to me!" Nico begged his friend.

Gräve, however, shook his head slowly and barely noticeably. "Why do you think Herzog has directed more outstanding films, documentaries and plays than any other director in the history of mankind?"

"That's right. We can finally put all the pieces together," Guido interjected. "Verne Zog collects demons for Werner Herzog—his alternate persona—to devour. He's done it for centuries. And he might have exorcised yours before he threw you out at the synagogue."

It became silent. Nico's thoughts raced. But then he finally remembered that he was Klaus Kinski and didn't have to put up with such nonsense any longer. "This is just another trick of yours to get me back to the theater, you stupid pig!" he shouted at Gräve.

Resignedly, Gräve shook his head and dropped into a chair against the wall. He lowered his eyes, because he knew what had to follow, and it was better not to watch.

Dr. Plump switched to a businesslike, medical tone, "We will now test to see if Verne Zog has already fully exorcised you."

Samael opened his leather doctor's bag and took out an ancient-looking mask, which he handed to Guido. Guido put it on, and Dr. Plump approached Nico with a pair of tweezers. It was the same exorcising instrument that Verne Zog and Magnus Max had used.

"What are you up to? Help! You're insane! Nurse! Help!"

"Take it easy. It won't hurt." Dr. Plump plucked out one of his eyelashes, but at the same moment something unbelievable happened: Nico's face suddenly turned into a blood-red demon's face, which bore a devilish resemblance to the face of Klaus Kinski. Horns sprouted from his skull and long tusks shot out of his teeth.

Guido commented succinctly, "Well, obviously he did *not* exorcise you."

Nico's arms and legs, riddled with throbbing veins, tensed to the point of bursting, and with a violent jerk he burst the shackles that pinned him to the bed.

While Dr. Plump was still trying to take cover, Nico, with a powerful backslap, knocked Guido's exorcism mask off his face, which shattered into a thousand pieces. Large amounts of blood immediately poured from Guido's facial orifices, and with his skull shattered, he collapsed dead. Samael wanted to strike Nico in the kidneys with his baton to get hold of him. But the demon whirled around and kicked Samael in the stomach with his cloven hooves so forcefully that the man was thrown against the thick concrete wall. The wall collapsed completely, burying Dr. Plump's assistant under heavy rubble and debris.

The psychologist met a similarly unfortunate fate. Nico punched into her chest with his bare hands and with bestial force tore her heart out, which he immediately stuffed into his huge maw and gulped down. Blood rained down on the sickroom as if from a sprinkler system.

Gräve feared for his life and wanted to soothe Nico. "Nico…Calm down, my dear…We can dissolve the contract with pleasure…"

But the demon strode slowly and menacingly toward Gräve, who held out his hands to defend himself. With a superhuman leap, the monster threw itself at its director. Gräve, however, executed a 180-degree backspin under his opponent, grabbing Nico in mid-air and flinging him behind him with full force, sending him flying headlong into the wall with a deafening crash.

But the demon was not yet out of action. On the contrary, he rose anew with a seated forward spin and built himself up threateningly in front of Gräve. A barbaric fight to the death began. Gräve was first able to give Nico a few heavy blows to the kidneys, which visibly caused the Kinski demon pain. He cried out loudly and spat a torrent of blood. However, with a downward 360 karate double spin, he pulled Gräve's legs away immediately after, causing him to hit the ground and break several vertebrae. Nico wanted to end the fight by throwing himself on Gräve with a Seated-Senton, but he made a ground roll despite all the fractures and brought himself to safety at the last second.

The demon hit the hospital floor hard with his rump. The linoleum ground cracked under its weight and a hole opened up in the concrete. Gräve straightened up with the last of his strength, took the monster in the stranglehold that policemen used, and squeezed the air out of him.

With howls and almost superhuman energy, however, Nico got back to his feet and knocked Gräve off, sending him flying into a corner of the room. The latter darted over the hospital bed and landed with a heavy roar on a side table with medical equipment. The director quickly got back up, grabbed several scalpels that he had taken with him in the fall, and hurled them at Nico like a knife thrower.

He intercepted the projectiles with his arm, in which they got stuck. Both opponents charged at each other, and an insanely fast bareknuckle fistfight began that could hardly have been surpassed in brutality, and which even Connor McGregor or Mike Tyson would not have survived. In lightning-fast combinations, the blows rained down on the respective opponents. At first it remained completely unclear who would have the upper hand, because both landed and received the heaviest of hits. The skin on their hands burst open from the force of the hooks, and they already had open fractures on their faces as both opponents simultaneously lunged for an almost superhuman blow with wild expressions on their faces and eyes wide open. Thus they simultaneously placed and conceded such a violent head blow that they crashed to the ground together, unconscious. Icy silence followed.

For a few minutes, the scene remained absolutely quiet and completely peaceful. Then, however, a dazzling light shone from outside through the cracks in the door, slowly pouring into the room and spreading like a liquid until it finally enveloped the two unconscious fighters completely. Nico and Gräve came to at the same time, but still visibly battered. However, Nico was no longer a demon. Incredulous and with open mouths they stared in the direction of the light source. They could not believe their eyes, for out of the cloud of light surrounding them peeled the silhouette of an overweight man who casually had a cigarette in his mouth. He had oily hair, a sparse beard, and a face scarred by pimples and acne. His tattered jeans and dirty white jacket were stained and obviously hadn't been washed in a while. The man from the light had neither time nor leisure for such trifles. Through the lenses of his metal glasses, he looked down at Gräve and Nico, who were still sitting on the floor. From his jacket pocket, he took out a small medicine bottle and sucked a strong nose of coke from it.

"Oh, my God!" Nico shouted. "Is that... ?!"

The overpowering voice of the man answered, "Yes—it is I."

"Holy shit! Rainer Werner Fassbinder!" Gräve groaned in disbelief.

But Fassbinder said, "I have come to tell you that you are both completely insane."

"Look who's talking," Nico commented.

Fassbinder went on to explain. "Klaus Kinski is dead. And

Werner Herzog lives a relatively normal life in Los Angeles. Everything you have put together is complete humbug."

"But the shooting," Nico interjected.

"And the demon hunters," Gräve added as he pointed to the bodies of Dr. Plump and Guido. Nico and Gräve nodded in unison, one as if in confirmation of the other.

"It's all made-up nonsense," Fassbinder shook his head. "You're both inmates of an insane asylum, and you're both experiencing a severe collective psychosis."

The two lunatics looked at each other, stunned.

"What should we do, Rainer?" Gräve wanted to know, but Fassbinder only smiled.

"I do not offer solutions, only knowledge. And you both know yourselves long since what you have to do."

With a grin, he turned around and floated away like a ghost through the closed door of the room. With his disappearance, the dazzlingly bright light also went out.

Nico looked at the badly battered bodies of Guido Gusion and Dr. Plump.

"Good grief! What are we going to do now, Christoph?"

"Well, if Rainer Werner Fassbinder says that we are insane— then that must be the case..." Gräve stood up, reached out his hand to Nico, who was still sitting on the floor, and helped him to his feet.

"But what does he mean that we knew what to do long since?" Nico asked.

Gräve thought for a moment. "Finding the truth through art. —We have to stage something new."

"Another play, perhaps?" Nico asked.

Gräve nodded with a wild expression on his face, the kind only artists have when they are inspired by a new idea.

At that moment, however, Guido Gusion, Dr. Plump and Samael stood up. Together with Gräve, Nico and Fassbinder they lined up and bowed. Raging applause rang out, which increased to frenetic proportions. In standing ovations that lasted for minutes, the Berlin scene audience celebrated the performance of the completely insane theater piece in the Ballhaus-Ost entitled *They will claim that I was dead...* directed by Christoph Gräve and starring Nico Pacinsky.

37. BEHIND THE SCENES

AFTER THE CURTAIN CLOSED AGAIN, THE AUDIENCE WENT TO THE foyer to celebrate properly—as after every performance of the play so far. In the meantime, word of the wackiest play of all time had spread around the globe, and critics, celebrities and ordinary people from all over the world made the pilgrimage to Prenzlauer Berg to get their hands on one of the rare tickets while the play was still running. Rumors were already circulating in the press that Gräve and Nico were planning only a few more performances and would then devote themselves to other projects.

A team from *Spiegel TV* documented the crowd and captured a few voices of various celebrities. Steve Buscemi, for example, stated, "It's really unbelievable what the guys and gals have brought to the theater stage. So many twists and turns! I wish we would dare to do that again on TV.—It's still a secret, but I can reveal that much: I'm currently working with the Coen brothers on an adaptation of the play for an international streaming service." Then he pulled a pair of black sunglasses from the pocket of his jacket, put them on, and headed off to join the like-minded revelers.

Bela B. Felsenheimer from the German punk band *Die Ärzte*,

who had been on friendly terms with Christoph Gräve for years and regularly exchanged rare, forbidden horror DVDs and videotapes with him, said "Of course, as a film buff, I was particularly pleased with the guest appearances by Fassbinder and Udo Kier. Also, the splatter factor is somewhere between Lucio Fulci and the Paris *Grand Guignol*. What does the inclined critic say? Two cocks up!" Bela grinned broadly and pointed both middle fingers into the lens.

Then the most successful man of all time stepped in front of the camera. He was the most highly decorated bodybuilder, the best paid actor and the most successful Austrian politician export in the twenty-first century. His hydropneumatics were getting old and squeaked now and then, but his red-glowing artificial eye could still teach you to fear. He spoke with an Austro-American accent, "My friend Ralfi Moeller and all the others did an amazing job. And a theater piece with such a great production value and so much action is really something very special. But also the fact that this is an environment friendly production, which saves more carbon dioxide than it consumes, impressed me deeply. Now please excuse me. Somewhere at the party is Sarah Connor. She makes such terrible music that I have to turn it off before her unborn son goes to the resistance."

Pamela Anderson made a point of being photographed or filmed only with a ring light, but otherwise kept herself surprisingly accessible and tame. "Really great! My friend Christoph Gräve is such a genius! I heard that 3.42 percent of the net proceeds of the play will go to the Sea Shepherd organization, which is committed to saving whales, as I have been doing for a long time, as you know.—But now, if you'll excuse me. I have to get to the bar. *Free drinks!*"

Only when Pamela turned and sprinted away in slow motion could it be seen that she was carrying a red lifeguard buoy as a handbag, which she tossed into the bowl of strawberry punch, securing the rest of its contents. She yelled, "Dibs!"

"Rest assured: All rumors that our lead actor Nico Pacinsky would leave us before the end of the season to enter the film business are untrue," Gräve lied into the camera right, left and center. You could see it in his face, too, because he had a pretty bad feeling in his stomach at the thought of the production's future. He quickly turned his attention to another topic. "Please understand: our play is unique in the history of theater—perhaps even in art in general. Namely, the drama builds up like one of those Russian Matryoshka dolls."

Then the interview was interrupted, because wild, inarticulate shouting could be heard from a corner at the other end of the hall.

"Is that Mr Pacinsky?" asked the *Spiegel TV journalist*.

"Yes...Sounds like it. But we mustn't disturb him in the process. Through these tantrums, we can make sure he stays in character." Gräve indicated to the journalist to keep quiet and follow him. The camera crew crept up on the predator as if it were an animal documentary. The closer they got to the roar, the more of what Nico was saying became audible:

"... this complete dumbing down of the audience, which doesn't even understand that the Nico liberation is pure cynicism and a swan song to the decadent individuality and freedom-hostile *democratic* western society. A society that equates and even prefers a mouse like Nico to a lion like Kinski!"

Gräve knocked on a beam to his right and peered around the corner, where Nico was raving away. The *Spiegel TV team* followed in his footsteps.

"Christoph. We're having a conversation here," Nico rumbled. Ralf Moeller sat in front of him on a folding chair and nodded with amusement.

"Ah, Ralfi. There you are," Gräve called out delightedly.

Ralf Moeller replied, "Nico is just explaining to me that my purely commercial value could just as well have gone to him."

Gräve was shocked. "But...but Ralfi. I thought you said you were playing *pro bono*."

Nico exploded: "Exactly! *I* would have taken money for it."

The ex-gladiator Moeller noticed the TV team even before Nico. He quickly fixed his hair and put on an even wider grin. "Oh, look, *Spiegel TV!*—Hold the camera on me...Running?—Good. Then three, two, one: I've never had such enormous fun. After all, it's my very first theater production. But I guess I'll have to tell my agents to look around for more. Ah, there's Nico. Nico, look, it's the ladies and gentlemen from *Spiegel TV*. Say something, my boy."

Nico looked somewhat hesitantly at the camera and gave Ralfi a pained smile.

The *Universal Soldier*, on the other hand, was as effusive and benevolent as ever. "Well, my boy, now tell the TV audience at home: what did you think of my performance in the play?"

"Well, that's a strange question," Nico expressed himself indignantly. "I can't give an answer to that. Only the audience can."

Ralfi took Nico in his arms with a flourish. "Yes, they did cheer and applaud!"

"Well, I have to..." Nico tried to avoid the camera team. "I have something important to clarify with Christoph Gräve."

He was about to turn around when the journalist behind the camera called out. "What's the truth about the reports that you were actually contacted by Werner Herzog to film the life of Klaus Kinski with him?"

Nico turned on his heel with the Kinskian screw and shouted angrily, "That scumbag Herzog is a great director. One of the greatest of all time, perhaps. So you can answer that question for yourself, can't you?"

Ralf Moeller laughed jovially.

"Well, my boy. Now you do the film with Werner first, and then you'll both be set for the rest of your lives. I hope I get a guest appearance."

As if caught, Nico and Gräve looked into the camera.

"So, it is true after all?" the journalist immediately asked.

Gräve hesitated for a moment, then took the reporter by the arm and pulled him a bit away from the camera. They walked a few steps through the hallway backstage, and Nico followed them, while Ralf Moeller stayed behind and devoted himself to the finer things in life. He lit a cigar and, as if from nowhere, a group of female bodybuilders appeared and started posing in front of him, wanting to be judged by The Gladiator.

"All right, yes, it's true," Gräve whispered to the journalist. "We will end the season early. I have agreed with Herzog on a very high transfer fee for Mr Pacinsky. But I would ask you not to publish that for the time being until we can put out an official statement."

The journalist thought for a moment and then demanded: "I get the story exclusively, though, right?"

Gräve looked at him in disgust. "Yes, whatever."

With that, the press hack was satisfied, and he and the camera team left. Confused, Nico approached Gräve. "Christoph, what are you talking about? The contract with Verne Zog hasn't been signed at all."

"Uh...what? Yes, of course it is," Gräve replied. "We were at the Savoy Hotel together with Werner Herzog this morning, weren't we?"

"Verne Zog," Nico insisted.

"Tell me, Nico...what are you actually talking about?" Gräve wanted to know.

Nico was now also unsettled, but tried to encourage himself: "Well, the shooting, the assassination, the assassins! I was hit, and many dwarves were killed!" He tore his shirt down a bit to show the wound on his shoulder for proof. But there was nothing there.

Gräve stepped a little closer to him, looked deep into his eyes and grabbed him by the uninjured shoulders. "Nico, that was in our play. I think you either have a severe psychosis—or you're a damn good method actor."

Nico was in a daze. He felt a panic attack rising inside him.

"No. That is highly improbable and absolutely not plausible!" a voice answered Gräve's last sentence, while another summer evening thunderstorm was brewing outside and the first flashes of lightning could be seen in the distance through the skylight windows.

Nico and Gräve turned their heads to where the soft Bavarian voice of the man came from, who now stepped slowly out of the shadows. In front of them stood Verne Zog, who nodded at them. Immediately after, Magnus Max, still looking a bit worn out, appeared. His shoulder was bandaged. A few scratches on his forehead bore witness to the previous shoot-out at the Savoy Hotel.

"We should find a place to talk so the noble master can give us clarification," the dwarf suggested.

"Yes...sure." Gräve nodded. He was still completely shocked by the unexpected appearance of his former teacher and secret idol.

Nico, however, ran his fingers through his hair as if in a frenzy and shook his head. It was all becoming too much for him. Screaming out of fear of learning something about himself that he didn't want to know, he ran away, while Gräve, Magnus and Zog looked after him wordlessly.

Nico stepped hastily into the dark back room where parts of the stage decorations were kept and where he and Gwyneth had made love for the first time. As he did so, he babbled unintelligibly to himself and kept rubbing his temples as if he had a severe migraine. He did not turn on the light, but he noticed for the first time that the window set far up in the wall, through which some moonlight gleamed, was barred with thick bars and there were no window openers. Confused and sad, he stretched on his toes to look outside, but he did not succeed.

In a state of dissolution, he sat down on a battered wooden box that stood in the middle of the room and put his hands in front of his face. He sat there like that, stammering incomprehensible phrases and words over and over again. Suddenly a tear ran down his red face and he began to sob. He quickly went into a violent crying fit, which was caused by real and deep mental injuries.

The door opened a crack and Gwyneth peeked in. When she saw the completely slumped Nico sitting on the crate, she stepped toward him and took his face in her hands. "Nico. What's wrong with you?" she asked, but Nico was sobbing so desperately that he could hardly speak at first.

Gwyneth took him tenderly in her arms and stroked his hair. Instead of calming him down, she encouraged him to finally let it all out and let his true emotions run free. She got this wisdom from her tattoo artist, where she got a new tattoo whenever she felt the need to have a good cry.

Only when Nico gradually calmed down after a few minutes did she ask him, "Do you wanna talk about it?"

He, however, merely stammered a few half-sentences.

"I...I—I just can't do it anymore...I don't know what...how...where...why...everything is spinning..."

Gwyneth wiped the tears from his face.

"It's alright, Nico. I'm here.—You're here. We're in this together. Whatever may come, your friends are with you!" But Nico went into a whining tirade, "I don't know...I don't know who my friends really are...who is who...are you you?—Am I me? Am I myself? Is anyone at all who they claim to be?"

Gwyneth tried to relieve his tension by giving him a kiss on his forehead. Then she lifted his face with both hands to look him in the eyes. She said nothing and left it to Nico to find words.

"I feel like a prisoner inside myself!" he said, trembling.

Gwyneth, however, assured him,

"Very soon, you will be free. I promise you. And then we can be together." Once again she gently stroked his cheek, and they looked deeply into each other's eyes.

"I love you, Gwyneth."

"I love you, too."

She hugged him and then stood up,

"I got to go."

But Nico begged her,

"Please, don't leave me alone..."

But Gwyneth waved to him one last time and strode out into the deserted hallway, where no light appeared to be on. When the door closed behind her, Nico jumped up. "Hey, wait!"

He in turn sprinted to the door and opened it. But now the hallway behind the stage was brightly lit. Gwyneth was no longer in sight; instead, workmen, stagehands, and a few actors crossed Nico's line of vision. In one corner, he spotted Verne Zog, Magnus Max, and Christoph Gräve, who were obviously engrossed in a conversation.

"Christoph, where did Gwyneth go?" Nico wanted to know.

"Gwyneth? Doesn't she have her day off today?" Gräve asked back.

"No. She was just..." Perplexed, Nico looked around. Had he just imagined that? Was he finally losing his mind? Or was he a piece in a six-dimensional chess game that some otherworldly entity was playing with him? Yes, it had to be like that. There was no other explanation for all the madness that had been testing both his soul and his intellect since the car accident and seemed to be constantly expanding and rejecting all the boundaries of the conceivable.

Magnus Max observed Nico insistently. "Have you calmed down again, Mr Pacinsky?"

Nico nodded absently.

"Good, then let's talk in an undisturbed place. The noble master would like to present his theory to you as well."

"You have to listen to this, Nico," Gräve encouraged him, performing a gesture with both hands that was probably meant to signify *mind-blowing*.

38. GET TO DA CHOPPA!

THE GROUP OF FOUR ENTERED GRÄVE'S OFFICE, WHICH BY NOW looked like a Terry Gilliam nightmare: Piled among the furniture were mountains of paper, coffee mugs, empty organic vegetable soup jars, various hideous theatrical props that had found no place elsewhere, and two rust-free fenders for his BMW E32, which he had bought cheaply on Ebay to get his vehicle past its next MOT, which was due in October. The windows seemed to have been smeared with something like peanut butter or an alternative product to it, the trash cans were overflowing, and several large colonies of maggots were building an empire in their contents. The office gave the impression that Gräve was trying to channel the success of his play into the decay of his office as a way to compensate for the recognition he was receiving, as it was by now quite creepy to him. One of the theater props was an infinitely ugly and oversized, six-foot-tall beaver with yellow teeth and big, evil glass eyes, standing on its hind paws and looking like a psychotic creature from a forest planet—ready at any moment to wipe out humanity with a shot from its laser tail.

Magnus Max and Verne Zog were heavily impressed by the chaos. Magnus looked up at the ugly beaver, and Zog nodded sympathetically. "A truly formidable furnishing in the style of H.S. Thompson's Gonzo Feng Shui." Then he turned to Nico: "You once lived in an apartment whose interior was made entirely of foliage."

Nico nodded. "Yes...Back in Munich."

Gräve kicked over a huge pile of files with his foot and manically threw various papers aside. Beneath the chaos, a comfortable beanbag corner appeared, which had obviously not been used for some time and smelled of old coffee and cigarette smoke.

"One can really only praise you, dear Christoph. Your office reflects in a very playful way not only your art, but also your own state of mind, and thus reminds one of the runic writings of the ancient Germanic tribes, who also recognized the structure itself in chaos," lectured Verne Zog in his typical manner.

But Gräve commented ironically, "Thanks. I set it up that way myself. But let's sit down."

Everyone complied with his suggestion and took a seat in the beanbags. The coffee table in front of it consisted of two old touring car tires with a glass plate on top. Gräve had snatched the tires from Stefan Bellof's crew at the 1000 kilometer race in Spa-Francorchamps in 1985 in exchange for free tickets to the premiere of his Tannhäuser production. Bellof himself, who was the great German Formula 1 hope at the time, was unable to attend the premiere (because he died in a crash, caused by tire failure).

Magnus Max took the floor. "Now listen. The noble Master Zog has a theory which he intends to present to you."

"Yes, please enlighten us as to what is going on here!" Nico pleaded a little too tearfully, while Gräve found an opened bottle of sparkling water next to his beanbag and opened it. He drank a large gulp directly from the bottle, and Zog indicated with a clearing of his throat that he would also like to have some. Gräve found a few used disposable plastic cups stacked inside each other in the chaos, which he spread out on the table. He poured a little water into all of them. Verne Zog took a devout sip and enjoyed not only the refreshing fizzy drink, but also the passing of time, which he read on a large wooden clock on the wall, which came from the Goslar Clock Museum in the former Villa Schrader.

Nico, however, burst his collar. "Well, Werner, you stupid sow! Now finally let your thought fart out, before the inner rot eats you up completely."

Verne Zog looked at him mildly and started to speak. As he did so, no one noticed Nico reach under his shirt and covertly activate the crown of thorns on his crucifix pendant, causing it to light up briefly three times and begin transmitting the conversation to Dr. Plump and Guido Gusion.

"We make a mistake when we think of space and time as a continuous line," Zog began. "For this, too, is nothing more than falsely projecting out our own axis of life, which merely extends from birth to death. However, by doing so, we obstruct our view of the true nature of the universe."

"I'm going to punch you in the face, Werner, you asshole," Nico yelled. "Get to the point!"

———

At the same time, Guido Gusion and Dr. Plump were cleaning some of their assassin weapons in their apartment when suddenly the cross-shaped VatiCom smartphone on the kitchen table lit up and began to vibrate. Excitedly, they interrupted their activity, knowing that it must be a sign from Nico, who was probably in contact with Werner Herzog again. Via their smartphones, they were able to listen in on the dialogue between the four men on the premises of the Ballhaus-Ost. The two papal assassins were completely surprised to hear the voice of the director they were looking for. With a double-tap on the GPS bar in the VatiCom OS, they had the location coordinates transmitted to them.

Gudio Gusion couldn't believe what Google Maps was showing him. "Ballhaus-Ost! I can't believe he's still in Berlin! That badass son of a bitch! Let's get our stuff together. We got to go right now!"

In a rush, the two packed their weapons into several suitcases and loaded the Porsche Cayenne that was parked in the driveway of Dr. Plump's apartment.

———

Meanwhile, in Gräves' office, Verne Zog set about explaining his theory in more detail. "The dramaturgical principle of *They will claim that I was dead...* comes much closer to the true understanding of being than any philosophical or religious theory that mankind has yet brought to light. Only the best of the best have so far cracked this code and made it work for them: Mozart, Shakespeare, Goethe, Schwarzenegger, Herzog...to name only the most important."

Only now did Gräve notice that Magnus Max was in a physically poor condition, as he had apparently begun to bleed again under his bandage. "What actually happened to you?" he asked the dwarf and Magnus looked at his noble master Zog with a questioning look.

The latter nodded at him in confirmation. Only then did Magnus say, "I was shot at the Savoy when we wanted to sign the contract."

"Ha! I told you so," Nico snapped.

But Gräve shook his head, somewhat stunned. "Guys, the shooting was just a staging on our theater stage. That was part of the play!"

"Yes and no," Verne Zog replied, then floated the suggestion "Multiverses!"

"Multiverses?" asked Gräve.

Verne Zog stood up and walked toward a whiteboard on the wall that was written all over with completely jumbled elaborations of various twists and turns to Gräve's play. Zog wiped it all away with a sponge.

"Hey, I still need those notes," Gräve called out to him in horror.

Zog, however, shook his head. "Not anymore. The story continues to exist without being written down in all its forms and for all media known to us today and existing in the future."

He began to draw with a marker on the blackboard how he imagined the principle of multiverses. "It hasn't happened to me in my 507-year life either. But it seems as if two or perhaps even several parallel worlds have broken open and flowed into each other. The play and the reality we know have now become one. And they will probably also unite with our film shooting."

"And how does that happen?" Gräve wanted to know.

"I have only one explanation for this: the energy released when Herzog and Kinski's souls met again was enough to tear a hole in the space-time fabric we know and…"

"So I really am Kinski!" Nico interrupted him with a cry of joy. "I knew it."

"You are Kinski in the same way that I am Herzog," Zog explained. "Namely, in parallel universes. Thus, for example, I am also Martin Scorsese, Stanley Kubrick and Francis Ford Coppola."

"Michael Bay?" interjected Gräve, but Verne Zog shook his head indignantly.

"I think that's completely out of the question and highly irrational. Even my imagination doesn't go that far. Even if Michael Bay's films certainly know how to deliver entertainment and visual eye-candy to the inclined viewer."

Gräve strained to think aloud, "But...what's going to happen to us now? If the play becomes reality, according to the manuscript, the next thing we'll do together is shoot the film to *They will claim that I was dead...* in the Alpine fortress, right? With me and Nico in the leading roles. And Nico will then..."

He couldn't bring himself to say the last sentence fully. Therefore, Nico finished his utterance: "... I will die first and my soul will be absorbed by Zog!"

Magnus Max and Verne Zog looked at each other. Both knew that Nico was absolutely right with this conclusion, but Zog smiled at him just slightly mischievously. "Yes, my dear. But please consider this: A bee collects honey, and a dolphin swims in the sea. Not because they want to, but because it is a necessity of nature. I have this gift of liberating artists, and I apply it—because I have to."

Gräve defiantly interjected with a snort, "You're sucking talent from artists and using it for your own purposes!"

"But only for the good, of course," Zog replied. "Just look how far Udo Kier has come as a result of my exorcism. He was never really gifted as an actor. But now he's the pope! And that's only because I brought out his true self and harnessed it. Udo's flesh has always been weak and no match for his own demons. But today he celebrates formidable orgies in the Vatican!"

Nico shook his head before crying out, "No, no, no. Stop it now!" Slowly he moved backwards towards the door and pulled a long knife out of his pocket, holding it out to Gräve and Zog. "No one will *free* me or take advantage of my epochal genius for even a single second longer!"

"Nico, what are you up to?" Gräve shouted in horror.

Nico, however, increasingly talked himself into a rage. "I'm going to shoot my own film now. Without you. *The life of Paganini.*"

Verne Zog waved it off. "You tried that once before and failed. I consider your script for Kinski-Paganini, as I said at the time, to be absolutely unfilmable…Klaus."

Nico's hand was shaking. He looked from Zog to Magnus and from Magnus to Gräve when suddenly shots rang through the hallways of the theater. All four of them startled and, to their horror, heard terrible screams. Nico dropped the knife.

"The Pope's assassins are back! But how did they find us?"

"They are either unexpectedly well prepared—or they have read our script!" concluded Verne Zog.

Nico dared to open the door and peek out. Several volleys whizzed past him, but they were immediately answered by a deafening clatter. Apparently there was resistance, which seemed to keep the Assassins at bay for the time being. In a brief lull in the firing, the four men cautiously poked their heads out of the door, one above the other: Magnus Max below, then Nico, Gräve above, and Verne Zog at the top. Instantly, the exchange of gunfire flared up again, and they saw some stagehands fleeing.

"We need to get out of here as soon as possible!" Magnus shouted.

"But where to?" Gräve wanted to know.

"To the helicopter! It's on the rooftop."

Gräve thought for a second. "Okay, follow me. The fastest way to the roof is through the boiler room."

They waited for another lull in the firing. But when this occurred and the men started running, Nico, to their horror, went in the other direction—directly to where the shooting was coming from.

"What are you doing? Come with us if you want to live!" Gräve shouted.

"No. I'll stay here at the theater and fight," Nico said defiantly and started running. However, a loud machine-gun salvo forced him to turn back. Around the corner came limping a huge figure. Astonished, the four men saw who had apparently been firing counter-attacks all along and was now emerging from the smoke of the burning stage set: it was Ralf Moeller!

Ralfi had a Gatling gun tied around his body and had been wounded in the leg by a bullet, which he ignored. "Go!" he shouted. "You've got to get out of here while I can still keep them at bay."

Ralfi fired a new salvo towards the stage, from where Dr. Plump and Guido Gusion were slowly approaching. Gräve stretched his neck to see better and recognized the two assassins. "Them again!"

At well over 160 decibels of volume, Ralfi built a new shield of bullets and screamed at his friends:

"Get out! Get to da Choppaaaaa!"

Gräve, Zog and Magnus fled in the direction of the boiler room, but Nico remained stunned. Distracted by this, Ralfi was about to turn to him when he was hit in the chest by three bullets from the assassins and collapsed, fatally riddled. Nico was shocked. In the giant's fall, however, more bullets came loose from the Gatling gun, ricocheting off the metal struts of the theater roof and scattering in all directions.

Nico ducked and was not hit. Suddenly, however, Gwyneth stood in front of him, looking at him perplexed and with wide-open eyes. Bloodstains spread on her white shirt, and she collapsed before she managed to say anything. Her spirits were already leaving her, and Nico didn't know what to do. He looked to his right, in the direction where Gräve, Zog and Magnus had disappeared, and then to his left, where he could make out the approaching shadows of Guido Gusion and Dr. Plump. True, he had made a deal with them to eliminate Herzog together, but in their brutality they had just killed not only the greatest German world star, but also the love of his life.

Alone, he made a decision that would be of great, if not decisive, importance not only for him, but also for the further course of the history of our universe. With a determined look on his face, he picked Gwyneth up from the ground, threw her over his shoulder, and chose the path to the right—the direction his friends had taken to get to the helicopter on the roof.

———

More and more lightning flashed across the Berlin sky, and it began to rain. On the roof of the Ballhaus-Ost, Gräve and Zog had taken their seats in the passenger compartment of the luxury helicopter, and Magnus was sitting in the pilot's chair. While he played the safety video, directed by Jörg Buttgereit (the German John Carpenter) and featuring only corpses, he let the turbines warm up and the rotor blades began to turn. Then, with a jerk, the door to the stairwell opened, and Nico stepped out, the lifeless Gwyneth over his shoulder.

The helicopter was about fifty meters away from him, and Gräve was putting on his six-point harness, as explained in the video, when he spotted his friend in the distance. "There's Nico!"

Verne Zog ordered his adlatus Magnus Max via radio to open the doors as quickly as possible without interrupting the turbines' warm-up process. Magnus complied, and the rear cargo hatch opened electrically but agonizingly slowly. Just as it was fully open, Nico, breathing heavily, reached the vehicle and first deposited Gwyneth inside the helicopter. Verne Zog helped him as best he could. But Gräve was so shocked to see his longtime assistant bleeding and unconscious that all color drained from his face and he threw up. Nico now also climbed aboard the Mil-Mi-26 and collapsed on the ground, relieved to have made it.

Immediately afterwards, through the rear side window, they saw the door to the stairwell open again and Dr. Plump and Guido Gusion step out. The two assassins immediately aimed their weapons at the helicopter and fired several shots at the heavy aircraft, which in its luxury version weighed over thirty tons and could also carry almost as much payload. BANG! BANG! Two bullets penetrated the hull but missed our friends. Magnus radioed to his master that they needed to take off immediately, before a bullet could penetrate a rotor. The master acknowledged, and Magnus revved up the turbines.

Even before Nico could buckle himself or Gwyneth on, the steel colossus rose into the air with the cargo door wide open and accelerated to its maximum speed of around three hundred kilometers per hour in no time. Together, Nico and Zog held onto Gwyneth so that she would not be ejected through the open cargo hatch. Due to the violent downforce generated by the rotors, Dr. Plump and Guido were thrown to the ground on the roof and could not aim, let alone continue firing their weapons. Only when the Leviathan had already disappeared quite a distance into the sky were they able to get back up and aim. Dr. Plump fired again, but her bullets merely tore an air hole in the sky and could no longer pose a threat to the machine.

"They are too far away already," Guido declared resignedly.

"Jesus Christ, we were so close!"

Frustrated, the two looked after the ever-shrinking aircraft. The rain became heavier and drenched them completely.

———

Nico stood in the increasingly accelerating helicopter at the open hatch and looked down. There he could see the two assassins, who were getting smaller and smaller in the distance.

Magnus Max closed the electric door by pressing a button. Shortly before it locked completely, Nico had another thought. He stood with his back to the others so that they could not see him reach under his shirt and pull out his crucifix pendant. With quiet doubt, he looked at the piece of jewelry with the crucified man, his crown of thorns still flashing, for a second. Then his eyes wandered to his friends and his beloved Gwyneth, and he took heart: he yanked the necklace from his neck with a jerk and tossed the pendant out the closing door. Then he turned around, bent down to the lifeless Gwyneth and gently stroked her cheek, which was already getting cooler.

Looking up with tears in his eyes, he noticed Zog watching him. "Don't worry about her. Magnus will get her fixed. We have our ways and means."

Nico nodded. Relief and simultaneous worry were in his gaze, which wandered from Zog to Gräve. He felt that these two men were his true friends and that he would go with them down any path of destiny, even if it was marked by madness, folly and foolishness. Nico was now determined to do anything, sensing the truthfulness and rightness in the announced undertaking, and shouted as loudly as he could against the rotors and turbines: "Very well, friends. Let's make a movie!"

Gräve and Zog grinned at him, and the three men placed their hands over each other as an oath of allegiance.

THE
GREAT SILENCE
AKA. CORPSES PAVE HIS WAY

Spotify Playlist 6

39. CUT!

WE ARE ON THE THEATER STAGE IN A MENTAL INSTITUTION. ALL THE windows are barred, and the stage is lit only by a single coldly shining spotlight. Several heavy metal doors, secured with wire glass and surveillance cameras, lead in and out of the hall, but at present they are locked. In the background are a few empty beds that must have been part of a stage set. In front of it, there are about fifty empty chairs spread out in a criss-cross pattern. Obviously, the room was left in a hurry. The stage itself is stained with blood. The slowly approaching clacking of footsteps can be heard. The silhouette of a dwarf peels out of the darkness. It is Magnus Max, but he now wears a mustache. When he arrives at one of the pools of blood, he bends down and touches the red juice with his index finger. Thoughtfully, he holds his hand up to the light and examines the viscous substance, which has apparently already clotted a bit.

Suddenly, a voice is heard behind him. Christoph Gräve steps out of one of the numerous corridors leading around the theater room. He has one arm in a sling and a freshly stitched laceration on his forehead. He says: "What a huge mess!"

Magnus Max looks up. There is bewilderment in his gaze.

"Gräve! What are you doing here? Why aren't you in your room? The auditorium is closed for the time being."

Gräve, however, is not deterred and comes closer. "Have the police been informed?"

Magnus Max takes a deep breath. "No. But I don't see how that's any of your business."

Gräve wanders a little provocatively along the pools of blood, fixing his gaze on Magnus Max again and again. "Oh, it's very much my business. After all, I am the author."

Slightly annoyed, Magnus sends him a look. "What do you want?"

Gräve grins diabolically. "Freedom."

Magnus replies with a contemptuous snort. "Freedom?!"

"Yes, exactly. For me and my friends."

The two men pace around like two animals, leering at each other, ready to pounce the next moment. Magnus becomes indignant. "Are you even aware what you have done here?"

"Of course I do," exclaims Gräve. "Art!"

"A bloodbath is what you and your friends are responsible for!"

"Oh, it's all a matter of point of view," counters Gräve. "I see it more as...*four-dimensional* theater."

Magnus Max's face darkens. "I swear to you: If you ever want to see the light of the sun again, you'd better bury any memory of your play *They will claim that I was dead...*"

Gräve grins provocatively. "Just as you think, Herr director."

———

Suddenly someone shouted from the other side of the room. It was Verne Zog. "Cut!—Thank you! We'll go right on to the next shot."

Immediately, all sorts of technicians, stagehands and costume designers came running into the picture. All of them had genetic microsomia, also known as dwarfism. They set up the scenery as well as the costumes, hair and makeup of Magnus Max and Christoph Gräve for the next take.

The whole thing took place on a huge set in a film studio. It was part of the gigantic film complex in Verne Zog's Alpine Fortress, which we have already met. In total, the area of the various underground halls, offices, storage facilities and supply units amounted to over 750,000 square meters. This made the subterranean territory about three times the size of *Warner Bros.* studios in Burbank, California, and Zog commanded a work force of some 25,000 dwarves therein, who came from all over the world to the area carved into the mountains. In return, they enjoyed an almost overwhelming luxury that was otherwise usually denied to little people. In addition to many amenities and leisure activities tailored to the size of the workers, there was, for example, fresh orange juice every day, and once a month the bed linen was changed in the barracks. On top of that, Zog had already introduced his own cryptocurrency for his employees in 2007, with which he paid them princely wages. The Herzog dollar was only valid in the alpine fortress, but it was independent of the currency markets and thus free of any externally controlled volatility and inflationary loss of value.

At least, that's what he thought. Primarily, however, it was a clever ploy to tie the workers to the company in the long term. Through their work, most of them were able to build up a considerable fortune, but were forced to purchase all goods and services directly through Zog's mail-order company *HerzogPrime VOC* (Verne's Own Company). This in turn resulted in more and more dwarves following their relatives to the Alpine fortress to live and work. Zog granted great financial and personal freedoms, but had a strict immigration policy: only people under one meter could become naturalized citizens. For all others, there were short-term residence permits of up to four weeks per year, and in exceptional cases even less if their adult height was over 1.20m.

In 2020, however, a major catastrophe occurred down there when all filming had to be stopped during the dwarf pandemic, causing economic output in the alpine fortress to fall towards zero. Zog did try to counteract the economic decline with monetary gifts to the workforce and zero interest rate policies, but the result was an exorbitant and unprecedented decline in the Herzog dollar. Inflation not only devalued the assets of the dwarfs, but also exponentially reduced their purchasing power. The economic consequences for them were even more disastrous than the *Budweiser virus* itself, which cost the lives of around one percent of the workforce.

In order to somehow cover the enormous expenses during the pandemic and to be able to continue producing films, Zog felt compelled to demand a forced loan from the dwarves. He borrowed ten percent of the annual income from each citizen of the Alpine fortress and then programmed new money in Zog's state-owned Central Digital Bank to repay the loans after one year. Of course, the purchasing power of the money had more than halved in that time, and so Zog was able to repay the loans without much trouble, all the more so because he had in the meantime put part of his licensed library on YouTube and thus generated advertising revenues in the triple-digit billions.

The savings of the dwarves had retained their nominal value, but from now on the owners could only afford about half of it in the virtual Herzog Mall. Zog also applied a similar principle externally to further secure himself and his people financially. At the same time, there was an epidemic among the giants working for Costa Gavras at his Atlantis underwater studio in Greece. Zog lent the colleague horrendous sums to overcome the crisis and in this way bought into the assets of the studios there, which from then on had to commission all the services of their film productions from Werner Herzog GmbH und Co. KG.

In the described studio in the Alpine fortress, Christoph Gräve called out to his director Verne Zog. "Well, I'd like to have one more take, please. For the art!"

Zog stepped up to him. He was wearing headphones, through which he was receiving a live playback of the sound recordings of the sound engineer dwarf via radio transmission. In his hand he held a rolled-up paper binder containing excerpts from the script. "No, my dear," he told Gräve. "That was absolutely perfect. You internalized the essence of the character without any ifs or buts and turned it inside out for the scene. Formidable!" Then he turned to the script continuity girl, "The last take gets a marker—with asterisk and smilie."

"Will make a note," said the dwarf.

Nico, meanwhile, was sitting at the Video Village, where the images from the various cameras flickered across numerous monitors. He jumped up in horror. "Well, that's total bullshit, man! The script just doesn't make any sense."

Verne Zog took off his headphones and approached him. "Klaus, I'm afraid you haven't really understood my work yet."

He pulled Nico with him toward the catering cart, which was the world's only underground mini-McDonald's branch with organic meat and Fairtrade vegetables. Gräve followed the two and filled three paper cups with coffee at one of the thermos jugs with pump mechanism set up on a table. Of course, the pots contained only the finest coffee made from the best beans. But before these could be processed into the world's most aromatic instant coffee powder and packaged in *Nespresso capsules*, Zog insisted that they be pre-digested either by rare wild animals or noble primitive peoples threatened with extinction, so that the coffee would have the special aroma befitting the master's elevated level of taste.

"This is all completely convoluted brain crap made up by a mental patient!" Nico raged. Gräve distributed the coffee, and Nico only got more upset. "How is the viewer supposed to see through this? It all seems so...pointless!"

Gräve, however, stood by Zog: "Well, Nico. *They will claim that I was dead...* is just not an ordinary project. It's more of an experience."

Zog nodded. "Absolutely right. But it's far more than that. Remember, we're not doing *CSI Miami* here with editing frequency, the same plot points over and over, and Villain-of-the-Week stories."

"Yes, I understood that. But if we film Kinski's ordeal—my ordeal—there has to be a backstage sequence in the theater after our meeting with Fassbinder in the insane asylum. Not another scene in the insane asylum."

While Gräve was still thinking about it and freeing his arm from the prop sling, Zog replied, "Klaus, of course we don't shoot chronologically. Moreover, our film is not based on reality, but reality is based on our film."

"Which we're just shooting," Nico yelled. "That's exactly what gets me so upset; actually, the shoot isn't even necessary anymore, and we're just wasting our time here."

Magnus Max stepped in. He was taking off his glued-on beard. "Gentlemen, noble Master Zog: Set N14.B is lit, and the next scene would be ready."

"Wonderful. Thank you very much, Magnus."

Gräve grabbed two more half-McMatt sausage rolls from the McDonald's catering cart, stole the onion rings from another one and put them between the two halves of bread. As the four men made their way to the set together, he asked, chewing, "What are we shooting next?"

"So, according to the shooting schedule, what follows now is the scene of how, after our spectacular helicopter escape from the

Ballhaus-Ost to the Alpine Fortress, we revived Nico's love interest, your esteemed assistant Gwyneth Q. Brick, and brought her back to mental health," Magnus replied.

Nico was startled, because only now did he realize that he hadn't thought about the beautiful but dead girl since their arrival at the Alpine fortress. He was so carried away by the film shooting that such things seemed to escape him. "Uh...as far as I remember, we haven't even revived Gwyneth yet," he stammered.

"Exactly," said Verne Zog enthusiastically.

————

One floor below the film studio complex was a spacious high-tech laboratory equipped with numerous futuristic-looking medical devices. Gene splicers, centrifuges, electrophoresis devices, quantum computers and various particle accelerators were lined up like in a dystopian Frankenstein movie. This image was broken, however, by an extensive collection of ancient, mystical-looking artifacts scattered among them. For example, there was an original statue of the Roman goddess Diana, called Artemis by the Greeks, and various other priceless originals of classical antiquity.

The vaulted ceiling was painted with an iconographic potpourri of various film characters from the silent era. The artwork came from the initially completely talentless hands of an Italian beggar whom Zog had picked up on an opera tour through Lombardy in the early 1950s. By means of two exorcised demons, however, he gave the man the ability to add an artistic touch to his newly emerging laboratories in the Alpine fortress. After the newly minted artist had completed his service to Zog, however, there was no room for him in the Alpine Fortress. His height was well above the allowable Zog-meter, and so Pinin Farina was initially loaned to the *Cinecitta studios* in Rome before the designer rose to become one of the most important automotive designers in history. Numerous classics were associated with his name.

Zog's underground laboratories, where religion and mysticism merged with science and technology, would have been a real feast for any architecture buff. Numerous magazines offered Zog millions to print just a single photo of it. But Zog was never really concerned with exposure or even wealth throughout his life. Everything he did, everything he created, he did solely out of the impulse to produce great art. If the lowly plebs had so much as glanced at it, it would not only have disavowed the work, it would have dragged it down from the heights of Olympus to the level of the common man. For this reason, most film critics and moviegoers knew only Werner Herzog's popular culture work. His official filmography consisted exclusively of lowbrow rejects, which the noble master threw to the masses as opium for the people and thus financed his other ventures.

His real magnum opus, on the other hand, was known only to the dwarfs and Zog himself. These films were so good, no, outstandingly divine and free of any blemish, that they were not shown in public even once after their completion, because otherwise the audience would never have wanted or been able to see another film. In spite of all this, Zog felt so indebted to his colleagues in the industry that he didn't want to do that to them. In addition, there were also those works that human words are inadequate to describe. *The Frankenstones* or *Nosferaturbo III* can actually only be summarized and evaluated by means of a symphony. But since no human being has seen them yet or will ever see them, we are left only with the knowledge that for a fleeting moment in the history of the universe we existed simultaneously with those masterpieces.

These films were of such epochal visual power and strength of content that Zog decided after post-production to burn all film reels and storage media and to snuff up the ashes together with the best Peruvian jungle coke. Artist and work thus became one big high. He did have to undergo a nasal septum operation afterwards because the toxic particles had decomposed his mucosal tissue, but what did he have his underground dwarf Charité hospital in the fourth basement of the Alpine fortress for, after all?

In a back corner of the room was a transparent cryo-pod with all sorts of tubes and cables connected to it. Inside the device was the dead but perfectly preserved Gwyneth. The hydropneumatic door to the lab opened, and Verne Zog entered. He was followed by Magnus Max, Gräve and Nico, who immediately spotted his girlfriend and rushed excitedly to the pod. Gently stroking the plexiglass covering Gwyneth's face, he was visibly agitated. But Verne Zog reassured him everything would be fine, and Magnus could now begin the procedure. The dwarf nodded and stepped in front of a gigantic cabinet, which he opened electronically by fingerprint sensor. The shelves inside were overflowing with preserving jars, like the ones we've already seen in Andy Warhol and Udo Kier's Exorcism. Using a sliding ladder, Magnus climbed up the cabinet like a librarian and inspected the labels on the jars.

"Well, I would have Madonna here, for example. We met her on the *Who's That Girl World Tour* in Tokyo in '87…" With a hint of pride, he showed them the glass. "But then I'd also have Josephine Baker."

"New Year's Eve 1925 in Berlin," Verne Zog said somewhat wistfully, while Magnus also casually showed off this glass.

Gräve was thrilled. "Wow, I'm a huge fan of Humpty Dumpty."

Magnus, however, continued to rummage among the glasses. "Or maybe Leni Riefenstahl?" At that moment he lost his footing and dropped the glass, which shattered into a thousand shards on the floor. A brown, viscous soup spread on the floor. "Oh, no! Please forgive me, noble Master Zog."

He, however, reassured his loyal assistant:

"Not too tragic. The glass was obviously leaking. Leni has already turned brown. So we can dispose of her without the slightest hesitation." Immediately, a small wiping robot arrived and took care of removing the brown slime that had once been the creativity of the Riefenstahl.

Nico, who was still standing by Gwyneth, was getting impatient. "Can't we just restore her to the way she was before?"

"No, you can't," Zog said. "Her demons are extinguished with her death. But we can certainly improve her."

Gräve nodded thoughtfully. "So, like a post-mortem boob job, yeah?"

Zog looked at him a little piqued. "Not at all. We're not ghouls, we're *life artists*."

At that moment, Magnus Max had found something in the very back of the shelf. "Look, this could be something!" He pulled out a particularly old-looking jar, blew off the dust, and proudly presented it: "Margaret Hughes. The very first professional actress. This must have been well before my time with the noble master." He examined the label for a date and soon found it, "Ha! 1791!"

Zog nodded. "What a vintage..." he murmured with a nostalgic undertone.

"Whatever, you imbecile bums. But now hurry up," Nico was forced to say in order to maintain the nimbus of the insane super actor, even if it was quite exhausting.

Magnus came climbing down the ladder, balancing the preserving jar in his right hand. Then he stepped toward the pod containing Gwyneth and placed the jar in a kind of vacuum chamber on the side of the device. He pressed a button, and it closed with a soft hiss. From the cabinet below, he retrieved his leather medical kit and unearthed a replica of the blue Nebra Sky Disk, which he placed on the pod. He then handed out ancient South American masks to Gräve, Nico and Zog. The men put these on, and Zog nodded affirmatively to release the procedure. Magnus pressed another button on the control console, and some sort of can opener lifted the lid of the preserving jar with a hiss. Immediately, streaks of the now gaseous demon spilled into Gwyneth's pod, obscuring the view.

"What's happening to her?" Nico wanted to know, but Gräve elbowed him to silence him.

At that moment, Verne Zog stood in front of the pod like a conductor and began. He lowered his head and spread his arms: "In nomine Werner Herzog Dei et Domini nostri, intercedente immaculata Vergine Dei Genetrice Gwyneth Q. Brick, beato Klaus Kinski, beatis Apostolis Christoph Gräve et Nico Pacinsky..."

The sky disc began to glow and gave off a dazzlingly bright light.

"...et omnibus Sanctis, et sacra ministerii nostri auctoritate confisi, ad infestationes diabolicae fraudis repellendas securi aggredimur."

The men's masks glowed as well. Neon yellow streaks ran like thick raindrops and tears across the carved faces, showing wild patterns in motion—almost like 3D video mapping. The sky disc hovered in the middle of the room as ultra-bright focused beams of light emanated, penetrating directly into Gwyneth's mouth, ears, eyes and nose, driving the gaseous demon into her body. With a deafening bang, the sky disk sank to the floor, and then silence fell.

"And...did it work?" Nico asked nervously.

The men took off their masks and stared spellbound at Gwyneth in her pod, who did not move at first. A queasy feeling rose in Nico's guts. Was Gwyneth lost forever? At that very moment, however, she winced with a hissing inhale and widened her eyes.

Verne Zog shouted: "Cut! Thank you!"

Only now did Nico realize again that he was, after all, on a shoot in a film studio. Gräve, Zog and Magnus took a breath, but Nico remained in the scene. Once again, the set was populated by worker dwarves, who took care of makeup, costume and set design.

"I am impressed. Very good visual effect!" noted Gräve.

"Worked out wonderfully, didn't it?" Zog nodded with satisfaction. "I'll be at the catering truck preparing the next scene."

"I'll go with you on that one!" Gräve and Zog made off, while two dwarves rolled away the prop of the pod in which Gwyneth still laid. The young woman who had just been awakened, however, seemed completely confused. The light hurt her eyes, and her voice was so low and scratchy that hardly a sound escaped through the curved Plexiglas.

"Hey, Magnus!" Nico shouted. "Open that thing up and let her out."

Magnus stepped toward Nico and shook his head, but initially stopped his fellow dwarves from pushing the pod out. "You can't. Depending on how well she takes the demon, she'll have to stay in there for a few more days. We'll give her ciclosporin to prevent rejection of the demon implant."

Magnus released the pod, and the dwarves pushed it away. Nico's and Gwyneth's eyes fixed on each other as long as they could. Nico shook his head in bewilderment. "Was that all real just now?"

"Of course!" Magnus said. "Everything here is genuine. That's just how the noble master works. This is the Zog-*method-directing* he has developed and occasionally licenses to other fellow directors when they prove worthy."

"Unbelievable."

"We pulled a whole ship over a mountain with pure muscle power in *Fitzcarraldo*. That was all real, too. No tricks, no visual effects."

"I know. I was there," Nico insisted.

"Oh, yeah...right..." Magnus rolled his eyes.

Nico watched the dwarves leave the room with Gwyneth in the pod. "Where are they taking her?"

"The warehouse. To the others."

Nico was shocked. "To the others?"

Magnus grinned. "Follow me inconspicuously, please."

He went off, and Nico trotted after him as if in a trance.

The warehouse was a huge hall with numerous supporting round arches. The entire section was filled with hundreds of cryopods. Just then, the one with Gwyneth was parked among the others and tagged with a QR identification number.

"What the hell ...?" Nico saw the senate lady Irmgard Al-Hassani lying in a pod, whose head had been reconstructed with great difficulty from collected individual parts, implants and various foreign bodies. She now clearly looked better than before. In the pod next to her lay her colleague Waltraud Beermeyer-Stöpsel, and next to her rested Ralf Moeller. All were breathing, but seemed to be asleep.

Magnus was pleased by Nico's amazement. "You can never have enough extras, can you?"

"You guys are insane," Nico snapped.

"Completely wrong. The world out there is insane. And in case the madness makes its way down here, we want to be prepared." Magnus' gaze roamed over the vast field of cryo-pods containing an army of half-dead, sleeping people.

40. THE POPE IS ON THE PHONE AND WANTS TO TALK TO YOU!

ERNA AND CLAUDIA ROSETZKI PACKED UP SEVERAL SUITCASES IN Nico's apartment. Both were in a bad mood and also a little sad. There was an icy silence between them. Claudia in particular didn't know how to deal with the fact that her life partner Nico had simply disappeared after the last performance at Ballhaus-Ost and hadn't even said goodbye to her by phone or text. But since Gwyneth didn't answer the phone either, Claudia concluded that they had probably run away together and wouldn't be back anytime soon.

Claudia was sincerely in love with both Nico and Gwyneth. That her hopes for a future in a ménage à trois were so abruptly and brutally disappointed pained her. She now tried to channel this pain into something like hatred for her mother, with whom she was to return to Transylvania for good. Erna, on the other hand, tried to cheer her daughter up a little.

"We will surely find another prince for you, once we are back home in Romania..."

Full of incomprehension about her mother, Claudia shook her head while she angrily stowed away some handcuffs and riding whips in a suitcase. Erna continued to try to influence her daughter:

"The good thing about Nico's disappearance is that we can now start over somewhere else." Of course, she didn't tell her that Magnus Max had transferred a total of €120,000 to her PayPal account. Claudia just rolled her eyes and continued packing her bags.

The doorbell rang. Instantly, the two women jumped up. While Claudia rushed to the door, hoping it could be Nico, her mother prayed to the Lord in heaven that it might not be him.

Claudia looked through the peephole in the door and asked through the intercom who was there. A woman's voice sounded muffled directly from the hallway.

"Good evening, I am Dr. Plump. The psychologist of your life partner Nico Pacinsky."

Claudia was unsure how to respond.

"Yes, well... Nico is not here. What do you want?" The psychologist did not let herself be put off, however:

"That is not so easy to explain. But, if you want, we'll try."

"We?" Claudia asked wide awake, when at that moment her mother Erna joined and quietly begged her not to open the door for God's sake. Immediately after, Guido Gusion's voice rang out, and he stepped in front of the peephole so Claudia could see him.

"Hello, my dear. I'm Guido Gusion.—Your boyfriend's super successful and very handsome agent from Hollywood."

Claudia and her mother exchanged an incredulous glance with each other, but finally the two women could resist no longer, opened the apartment door and stood face to face with the two papal assassins, who smiled at them in an over-friendly manner. When Claudia noticed Dr. Plump's wide-open cleavage and that Guido Gusion was eagerly squinting at it, she realized that she herself hadn't had sex in almost a week. The psychologist, on the other hand, had immediately noticed Claudia's Lolita-like appearance. Apparently she was trying to compensate for a paternal attachment disorder. Guido opened the conversation:

"Hi. We want to help you retrieve your boyfriend!"

"Well, he's not my boyfriend anymore... I think," Claudia said with some melancholy in her voice.

"I'm sorry to hear that," Guido replied and started to enter, but Erna blocked his way with a determined look on her face:

"I didn't know that Nico has a manager in Hollywood." Guido reacted with a huff:

"I'm not his manager. I'm his agent—and therefore I receive ten percent of his net profits." Then he tried again to force his way into the apartment, but Erna did not move an inch from the doorway. She asked with all clarity and the best possible English:

"What do you want?"

Then the door to the neighboring apartment opened and the man with the complicated Slavic name stepped out to go to the nearest whorehouse. Suspiciously, he crept past the door to Nico's apartment and felt caught, although of course no one knew his destination, the flat-rate fuck palace Müllerstraße. For a moment, everyone stared at each other in embarrassment, until Claudia finally stepped aside, allowing Guido and Dr. Plump to enter the apartment. After some hesitation, Erna did the same. She sent a silent prayer to heaven and trusted in the power of God, who had always brought her through life somehow.

When the four of them entered the living room, Dr. Plump immediately noticed the numerous packed suitcases:

"Mother and daughter are probably going on a well-deserved vacation, yes?"

"No, we're going back to Romania."

Erna invited them to sit in the corner of the couch with a wave of her hand.

"Back to Romania? You are Christian-orthodox then, yes?" Guido asked immediately wide awake.

Erna grabbed the cross around her neck. "No, of course not. We are proud Transylvanians, of Southern German descent. We are Roman Catholics."

Guido grinned and thought hard.

"So, tell us why Nico's manager and his psychologist are visiting us?" Claudia wanted to know.

Dr. Plump and Guido looked at each other meaningfully. "Nico has disappeared. And we are very worried," Dr. Plump feigned.

Claudia nodded. "He must have run off with Gwyneth. No phone call, no letter…nothing. Not from either of them. The last time we saw them was at the Ballhaus Ost. Mother and I went home right after the performance, but Nico and Gräve were still backstage with Ralf Moeller and a team from *Spiegel TV*. And they were all never seen again."

At the name of the fallen gladiator Ralf Moeller, Guido and Dr. Plump exchanged a knowing glance. After all, he had died in the hail of their bullets.

"Well, we heard there was a…brawl after the show backstage…And we think that Nico was kidnapped. By Werner Herzog. The Antichrist himself!"

Claudia and her mother looked at the strange couple with some suspicion. Then Erna straightened up and grabbed her daughter emphatically by the shoulders. "Claudia, please. Let's go back to Transylvania. Right now! This whole thing is getting too scary for me!"

Claudia didn't know what to do. Follow her mother or try to find Nico? Of course, the circumstances under which her ex had disappeared and under which he had gotten the job at Ballhaus-Ost in the first place were extremely bizarre and strange. But that was precisely why she felt the urge to respond to Dr. Plump and Guido Gusion, because she was hoping for answers to the many questions that had arisen.

Guido sensed this and therefore quickly played his trump card. "Actually, we know the exact location where Nico is! And we can help you to get him back. But we need your help first."

Claudia listened up. Erna, on the other hand, was in despair. She just wanted to get away, to the airport and onto the next *Tarom-Airline* plane. "Who are you people?"

Instead of answering her, Dr. Plump looked at her silently for a moment. Then she took her VatiCom smartphone out of her pocket and dialed a number. It rang. The line apparently had a personalized dial tone, because the song *Don't stop believin'* by the U.S. band Journey was playing. The rock classic had already been used successfully by the CIA during numerous waterboarding interrogations of prisoners at Guantanamo in a continuous loop to boost the morale of the staff.

On the other end of the line, someone picked up. At first, only an indistinct shout was heard, and Dr. Plump hurried out into the hallway to be reasonably undisturbed. "Yes...Udo...Udo!—My pope, it's me. Let me put you on video."

She pressed a virtual button on the device, and immediately Pope Kierus the First appeared, obviously hard at work. He was drenched in sweat, had a crooked crown on his head and an orb with a cross in his hand to go with it.

"Vary! Have you got him at last?"

"No. Not yet, but..."

"I told you to please not bother me if you don't..."

"Udo!" Dr. Plump interrupted him. "We have two ladies here who may be able to help us. And they are Roman Catholics!"

Udo became silent, wiped the sweat from his brow and adjusted his tiara. "Oh. Well, in that case..."

Meanwhile, Claudia, Erna and Guido were silent in the living room. They could not hear the conversation between Pope Kierus and Dr. Plump. Erna was getting more and more scared and anxious. "Claudia, please trust me. Extremely strange things are going on here. We must..."

Just at that moment, Dr. Plump came back. She held her smartphone with the display toward her and said, "The Pope is on the phone and would like to speak to you." Triumphantly, she turned the smartphone around and held the display out to Claudia and Erna.

"Good evening, ladies!" sounded the voice of the Pope.

Claudia and Erna were equally speechless. Erna threw herself on her knees and crossed herself. Claudia followed her example.

"Most Holy Father!"

Udo grinned pontifically and nodded paternally. "Ladies, I don't have much time until the next sado-maso orgy, so I'll be brief: my guardsmen, the Berlin Protestant Dr. Plump and the American Jew Mr Guido Gusion, are on a holy mission. And they urgently need your help in doing so. Can I count on you, ladies?"

"Whatever you say, most holy father." Both women crossed themselves again and nodded submissively. Guido Gusion and Dr. Plump were satisfied, because the first step of their new plan to liquidate Herzog had worked.

41. CUT! TWO

MEANWHILE, THE MONUMENTAL SHOOT IN ZOG'S ALPINE FORTRESS progressed with constant madness. Just then, the noble master was preparing a scene with his actors Nico and Gräve. In the background, several dwarves were setting up a green screen and adjusting some LED Kinoflo lights on tripods, because the actual backgrounds were not to be created and inserted into the scene until post-production of the film.

"Okay, next we'll shoot the scene in the Ballhaus-Ost. You two get to know each other a little better now," Magnus said to Nico and Gräve.

"Yes, good. Shall we go through the text?" Gräve suggested. "Preferably from the moment we enter the theater stage to the point where Nico activates the giant papier-mâché phallus I get in my balls."

"Okay, let's do it!"

While the two virtuoso actors were rehearsing their lines, the scenery in their minds transformed into the very situation that can be read in the first chapter of this book (or in the first act of Gräve's play). The interior of the Ballhaus-Ost came to life before their eyes, and they felt completely transported back to the time when they did not yet know each other and their play *They will claim that I was dead...* had not yet found its way to them. The stage and the hall were completely empty, except for a few tripods and lamps. In the middle, however, hung several metal ropes, to which apparently some art object was attached, but which could not be completely made out in the darkness of the room.

"All right, I start. What do you see, my friend?" began Gräve.

„An auditorium and a stage—a very beautiful auditorium..." Nico reproduced exactly in the same tone as then.

"A stage! - But what do I see?" Gräve paused significantly.

"Maybe you see a play?"

Gräve laughed half madly, for he delighted in his counterpart's quick grasp. "A play! Yes! Exactly!—I see *my* next play!"

"And what's it about?"

Gräve was pleased about Nico's curiosity, started talking and walked back and forth on the stage in the following monologue. He pantomimed what his ideas were as he did so.

"Undercover police officer Brian gains access to the illegal street racing scene in hopes of tracking down the perpetrators of several truck robberies."

At that moment, however, the illusion in their minds shattered into a thousand little splinters and shards, because Nico fell out of character and yelled at Zog, who was sitting at the video village: "No, no, no...It doesn't work like that. I didn't set out to imitate reality."

"Klaus, what's wrong?" Verne Zog tried to calm him down. The two went aside to discuss things with each other. In the meantime, Gräve was sucking on his e-pipe and flirting with an extremely attractive dwarf from the makeup department.

"Werner, do you want to shoot one of those crappy pre-show documentaries?" Nico rumbled.

"Of course not..."

"Well, there you go. Then we have to modify the true events a bit."

Zog had to take a breath. He already knew this script interference from other shoots starring Klaus Kinski. "All right, Klaus. What do you have in mind?"

"Yeah, well, I don't know. We just need things that the audience wants to see. There should be big tits and giant explosions everywhere. And I should actually be screaming completely psychotic all the time and smashing everything."

Gräve overheard the conversation in the back and immediately interjected: "I think that's great!"

Verne Zog's enthusiasm, however, was limited. "Well, I would refrain from that for now, please. My instructions to you right now would be..."

"Now don't give me any stage directions, I can't stand that. I know what to do on my own."

"Of course. But we have to know..."

"Yes, technically. But don't tell me how to do it, I'll do it all by myself." Nico trudged through the studio, keeping his distance from Zog.

"No, not quite," Zog said.

"Yes! Completely alone. Or you go on stage for me and do it."

"Well, that can..."

"You always want half-measures. You're just afraid of consequences. And if someone gets upset..."

"Yes, but..."

Nico was now talking himself more and more into a rage: "You always seem to me like Gründgens, where Gräve said he was probably afraid of it, so he didn't do it. And that is...If you want to have an excited person, then you let him be excited! And otherwise you say he's not excited!"

"Well yes, it could be..."

"So!"

"But I don't want to be too…"

"So let's shoot it now!" Nico went into a kinski-esque tantrum.

"Yeah, I just need to…"

"Go ahead, turn on the camera and shoot that shit down!"

"The camera is not shooting now."

"I now play it the way I want, over and out!"

"Well, yes, but of course we need to know…"

Gräve was seemingly unconcerned by all this. He continued to flirt with the make-up lady and enjoyed his e-pipe and Kopi Luwak coffee. Meanwhile, the ferocity of the exchange between Zog and Nico increased exponentially.

"If you would just stop giving me your housewife instructions! Make sure…"

"Klaus, who is the director?"

Nico exploded and screamed, "You're not a director! You have to learn from me!"

"No, of course I'm not learning from you."

Now Nico finally snapped and threw everything around that got in front of his hands and feet. "You are a beginner!"

"Of course, I'm not a beginner."

"A dwarf director! But certainly not a director for me!"

All the dwarves in the room looked at each other indignantly.

"Now you better not insult me," Verne Zog demanded.

"Insult? Insult?! Well, you can't insult me any more than by directing me! That alone is an insult!"

"Now we shoot the scene here. And I'll give the stage directions."

"You can't just come to me and say *Mr Kinski… do you think?*…David Lean also did that and also Christoph Gräve. And you will do it too, my dear!"

"No, I'm not going to do that."

Nico went to another corner of the studio and yelled as loud as he could, "Well, we'll see about that!"

"I'm not going to do that, Klaus."

"We'll see about that!"

"What you did with Gräve and David Lean, I couldn't care less."

Gräve ate another delicious Polish coarse McSausage with cheese filling at the catering cart, and Nico came down a bit again: "You're not going to do it? Well, we'll see if you do!"

"Yes, yes..."

The two chased each other through the studio like two boxers. In the process, they had to dodge worker dwarves from the team again and again.

Nico raged on. "You're doing the wrongest thing you can possibly do. You behave so clumsily and so stupidly and you should actually already know that you can treat me very easily by just being careful with me. But apparently you've already heard that. You behave as clumsily as no one has ever behaved in my life at work. You stumble from one moment to the next, babbling and babbling and babbling...and your brain just doesn't work as fast as mine!"

Now Magnus Max stepped in to protect his noble master, "Stop it now!"

Nico immediately stopped his shouting and said to Magnus in a completely calm tone, "Shut up. You have no function here right now."

"No? This is my master and friend, the noble Master Zog!"

"Yes, that's different," Nico told Magnus in an absolutely friendly chatty tone. "This is private, but we're talking about the movie." With that, he turned back to Zog: "We're talking about the movie, aren't we?"

"You're having a conversation about whether or not my master is a director," Magnus said, richly displeased.

"Yes, I can express that as I wish!" Nico got excited again. "If you knew how work goes on in the theater or in the movies, I think one person has said that to another a thousand times."

"Well, that's a lot of private insults already," Verne Zog indicated.

"How then *private insults*? Private insults? Well, then I would have to be insulted all the time!" Nico said, insulted.

"Yes, you are."

"I'm not privately insulted. I am offended. At work."

"Fine, but what Gräve or David Lean or anyone else did, I couldn't care less..."

Now Nico shouted again beside himself: "You don't care, because you are megalomaniac! And you just have to get out of the habit, my dear!"

For a moment there was absolute silence, which was immediately broken by Verne Zog, "Cut! Thank you!"

The workers began to hustle and bustle again in preparation for the next scene. Only Nico was confused: "What? Was the camera rolling again?"

"Of course. This will be a key scene in the sixth act. You really did a great job, my dear," Verne Zog praised and left the stunned Nico standing there to talk to his script girl about the next shots of the Second Unit, which Zog of course directed himself. Nico threw up his arms in anger and left the set with a wild war cry.

42. MONTAGE

IF THIS WERE A FILM, WHAT WOULD FOLLOW AT THIS POINT IS A really palatable montage in the style of the eighties with the appropriate background music to illustrate the progression of the temporal component and to show a development of the characters, the narration of which would otherwise have taken up too much space in the work. A classic example of this method are training montages in which the protagonist is initially still a wimp without muscles, but then matures into a real professional athlete within minutes through hard building exercises. What, as a dramaturgically mature narrative, would probably have required its own mini-series, can be formulated extremely quickly by means of the montage and also gives the viewer the feeling of having gone through the development himself.

This technique was invented by Latin-German expatriate and image designer Secare E. Montag when he once accidentally bumped into Russian director Sergei Eisenstein in a hallway of the MGM, who was transporting the film reels of his latest masterpiece *Kamenistyy* (Stony). The film reels scattered all over the floor, and the entire second act of the film got so messed up as a result that Montag saw only one way out to help his friend

Sergei meet the deadline: radical cuts, punctuated with power music. The resulting sequence burned itself so deeply into the collective memory of viewers that more and more directors followed suit and also incorporated montages into their works, until the films finally mutated into one big montage without character development or dramaturgy at the end of the 1990s.

———

And if something like that works in film—why not in a novel?

So now we hear the song *Push it to the Limit* by Paul Engemann from the movie *Scarface*—the best montage song of all time—and in our mind's eye a sequence begins that shows the madness and insanity-filled filming of *They will Claim that I was Dead....* As we do so, we keep flashing back and forth in our minds between the filming in the Alpine Fortress studio and the original scenes we have already read about in other chapters of this book. Because let's not forget: Nico, Gräve, Zog and Magnus Max are currently filming the very book that you are reading at this moment. At the same time, they are filming Gräve's play, which in turn is based on Nico's life, but his life is based on this novel, which of course reflects Nico's biography in a purely documentary way.

So Nico and Gräve suddenly found themselves back at the *Café am Neuen See* signing their contract:

"Grääävvveee! You fucking moron! You don't just need your face kicked in, you asshole, you need to be locked up, you've totally lost the plot!"

A blanket of silence descended on the entire café. As though in a beautifully choreographed ballet, all the ducks, crows and grebes took to the air at the same time, chattering as they did so. A majestic sight. Nico growled:

"Just give me the fucking contract already, so that I can ejaculate my name onto it, you wanker!"

But of course Nico and Gräve weren't really sitting in the *Café am Neuen See,* but in front of an LED video wall in Zog's film studio. Filming was underway, and in the background a few extras were sitting at prop tables. But then Nico fell out of character again (or not) and, to the annoyance of his director, angrily stopped the take, yelling: "Oh, fucking hell! That extra back there is not in character at all and was thinking of something completely different. I can feel that. Get him out of here!"

Immediately, two dwarfs from the AD department came and led the man away in a police grip.

In another scene of the montage, Magnus Max entered the recovery room with the numerous cryo-pods inside. He approached the containers of Irmgard and Waltraud and opened them with the push of a button. With a hiss, the Plexiglas window came down, and the two senate ladies awoke. Their bullet wounds were halfway sewn up, but they now looked like Frankenstein's monsters.

"Welcome back!" Magnus greeted the two.

The ladies were still quite confused and therefore fell hoarsely croaking into old habits: "This has not been approved by the Senate authority. The motion is rejected!"

Magnus smiled with satisfaction, because the master already needed Irmgard and Waltraud in the next scene. Zog wanted to do without actors as much as possible and shoot the film with the real characters from Nico's life or Gräve's play. Therefore, he was glad that Magnus had been able to bring the senate ladies back to life.

So, another scene was shot in the studio: Christoph Gräve pitched his idea for the play *They will claim that I was dead...* to Irmgard Al-Hassani and Waltraud Beermeyer-Stöpsel in the Senate Chancellery. The dwarves from the set had done a great job, because the built set of room 237 of the Senate Department for Culture and Good Taste looked exactly like the original. The only downer was that Irmgard and Waltraud had apparently not yet fully acclimated to their new life situation and were drooling like brain-dead zombies. They were desperately straining their remaining brains to figure out why they were here in the first place and what was happening to them, but the camera was already rolling and they were right in the middle of the scene:

Gräve nodded, approached the large chipboard desk and threw his script onto it with a deliberately sweeping gesture. The tatty cover page flecked with coffee and nicotine stains bore the title *They will claim that I was dead...*

"Your new play, I presume?" Waltraud wanted to know, while a seam on her head slowly loosened.

"My new *masterpiece*, exactly!" replied Gräve.

"Didn't we talk about the fact that we'd like to be involved right from the outset? You should've submitted a treatment first for us to authorize," Irmgard insisted, a thread of saliva flowing from the right corner of her mouth.

"With all due respect, you've probably got no idea how a creative process works," Gräve countered, and Waltraud's left ear fell off—straight into her coffee cup. At this point, Nico interrupted the scene again and stormed onto the set, angrily shouting and gesticulating: "Well, Werner, you asshole, you can't be serious! Those two women are in worse shape than Oliver Reed was when we shot Pierce Haggard's *The Black Mamba!*"

The women looked at him, dazed and swaying slightly in their chairs, while several dwarves from the makeup department were already starting to fix them up as best they could. Gräve was quite uncomfortable with Nico's omissions towards his former adversaries. "Man, Nico, get a grip on yourself. They'll fix everything later in post-production."

Sitting at the video village, Verne Zog nodded with satisfaction, because the scene was absurd and slightly surreal, but it was in the can. So he could move on to the next set-up.

———

Meanwhile, in Dr. Plump's living room, a kind of mass was taking place: Erna and Claudia were initiated by Guido Gusion and Dr. Plump into the sacred and rare art of exorcising and imorcising demons. All four of them wore masks and practiced the procedure on a plastic dummy, like the ones used in first aid courses.

A little later: While Guido was polishing his assassin weapons again in a corner, watching the news ticker on the CNN channel, which reported on the disappearance of the brilliant theater director Christoph Gräve, Claudia and her mother Erna knelt before Dr. Plump, who was preaching, holding a cross and a Bible in her hands. Then the two crossed themselves and stood up. Dr. Plump handed Claudia, with great pathos, an old leather bag like the one Magnus Max had. In it were the appropriate exorcism instruments.

———

Nico meanwhile lingered again in front of Gwyneth's cryo-pod and eagerly placed his hand on the plexiglass above her face. Magnus Max stood a little apart and reassured him, "She'll be ready soon!"

Nico just looked at him silently and with glazed eyes, wishing that everything would soon come to a satisfactory end.—And with that, the song *Push it to the Limit* by Paul Engemann slowly fades out in our minds, thus ending this light but nevertheless content-rich montage sequence.

43. A BOMB UNDER THE DIRECTOR'S CHAIR

NICO WAS SITTING ON A LARGE ROUND LEATHER SOFA IN HIS LOUNGE in the Alpine Fortress, reading the *Benway* chapter in the novel *Naked Lunch* by William S. Burroughs. The luxurious room was completely furnished in the style of an eighties high-class living room, so even American Psycho Patrick Bateman would have enjoyed murdering people here and snorting large amounts of coke off of their corpses. There was a high-end *Akai* tape recorder that held a *best of Genesis* from their time with Phil Collins and a loose collection of various songs by *Huey Lewis & the News*. On the walls hung nude photographs of Nancy Pelosi by Helmut Newton, Zog had secretly commissioned to take. There was also a window, an augmented reality window to be exact, through which Nico could see right into Jurassic Park. Every now and then, a Brachiosaurus, a Dilophosaurus, and occasionally a couple of raptors would roam by and peer through the digital window, snarling.

The ingenious thing about these screens was that a lidar tracking camera was installed behind the display, which could capture and track the viewer's eye movements. Through this data, the image processor was able to constantly recalculate the parallax of the displayed views. This created the perfect illusion that it was actually a real window. Using an *Apple TV* remote control, the residents of the underground apartments in the Alpine Fortress network could choose between different views, all of which were of course based on famous film, theater or opera works. For example, if you wanted to feel like Dr Heywood Floyd in the Hilton on Space Station 5, you could turn on the *2001: A Space Odyssey* channel, and the windows would show a corresponding space view. After 10:00 pm, they also aired x-rated images, often based on Italian splatter and French erotic originals —or both at the same time. For example, there was the fuck-horror flick *Porno Holocaust*, which transported the room guest to a beautiful South Sea island where zombies coited, killed and ate their victims—in various permutations.

Many train and aircraft manufacturers would have gladly licensed this AR technology from Verne Zog for horrendous sums, but the master did not allow himself to be corrupted and retained the exclusive right to it for himself and the hotel chains and broadcasters connected to the Alpine Fortress.

There was a knock at the door. Nico didn't even look up from his book at first, but called out to the troublemaker: "Well, I don't understand the question!"

The door opened a crack, and Christoph Gräve peeked into the room. "Hey, Nico. Can I come in for a minute?"

"Ah, Christoph. Well, sure. Why don't you sit down?"

Gräve entered and took a seat on a brown leather chair opposite Nico. "I just wanted to check up on you...see how you're doing."

"Yes, thank you. So far everything is fine," Nico said truthfully.

"It's amazing how well the shoot is going so far, isn't it?"

Nico put his book aside and became indignant. "So, who do you think it's down to? Certainly not on this scheming, perfidious, deceitful, backstabbing *director*!"

"Yeah, all right. You're running the show here," Gräve said. "But then it amazes me how easy it all comes off."

"Well, don't forget, the dwarves are absolute full professionals," Nico pointed out. "They've certainly produced dozens of films here in the last fifty years."

Gräve took his smartphone out of his pocket, which had no reception in the fortress but was connected to Zog's own intra network. He called up an app, grinned with a shake of his head and held the display out to Nico. On it was the user interface of Berliner Sparkasse's online banking. Gräves' balance was €250,000,000,046.37. He still couldn't believe that Zog had actually transferred the full transfer fee for Nico to him:

"Two hundred and fifty billion euros!"

"Well, that's great," Nico was happy for his friend. "The years as a depriving artist under unemployed assistance level are finally paying off. By the way, my first royalty statement is also through. At least they pay on time."

Gräve continued to be dizzy from the sum in his account. He thought hard. "I should use the dough to found my own state. Without laws. Without a fixed structure. There is only one basic rule that governs everything in it: the art constitution!"

"Yes, yes, Christoph. Now stop daydreaming and let's finish the film first. Then we'll see what happens next."

Gräve put his phone back in his pocket and wiped the castles in the air from his mind's eye with a wave of his hand. He fumbled. "Yes. That's actually what I wanted to talk to you about."

"Well, go ahead and shoot!" Nico said impatiently.

Gräve narrowed his eyes and leaned over to whisper something in Nico's ear: "Doesn't it all seem a little strange to you?"

"No," Nico answered, like a shot.

"I think we're really making a great movie here. Of course, it's based on my play. But I can't shake the feeling that Verne Zog is up to something else..."

Nico looked at Gräve silently for a moment and then said coolly, "Yes, my exorcism, for example."

At that moment, Gräve realized that everything that was yet to happen had long since been written down in his own theater script. A lightning-like feeling ran through him, reaching from his head to his deepest guts. But before he could explore his realization further, Nico also leaned forward and whispered, "Christoph, do you seriously believe that a genius like me isn't prepared for everything?"

Gräve looked at him steadfastly. "You don't want to...?"

Nico grinned maliciously and finished Graves' sentence:

"Finally put into practice what I have dreamed of all my life."

"Win an Oscar?"

"No, of course not," Nico echoed in disgust. "What am I supposed to do with that, you simopath!"

Gräve looked at him questioningly. "What is a simopath?"

Nico took the book he had been reading off the sofa and pointed to it as if the answers to virtually all of mankind's questions could be found here. "A simopath is a fellow human being who is convinced that he is an ape or some other ape-like primate. But either way, I'm finally going to get back at Herzog for what he's done to me over the decades—and blow him up as the grand finale of the film. Just as the prophecy—your manuscript —predicted."

Gräve leaned back in his chair and looked at Nico in disbelief. "Man, are you crazy? This is reality and not our play."

Nico laughed psychotically.

"I've already installed a bomb under his director's chair, and I'm going to set it off by remote control the moment that low-life, stuck-up sociopath tries to steal my demon. According to the shooting schedule, that's in exactly…twenty-one hours and fifty-nine minutes."

Nico held up his *Tag Heuer Connected* smartwatch, which served as a remote igniter. A countdown was running on the display.

Gräve was now somehow taken with the fact that his actor had apparently internalized his play in such a way. "Uh…well…that's a bit ingenious."

"Of course. It's going to be the greatest movie ever," Nico said.

———

The conversation of the two became the image of a surveillance camera. Magnus Max sat in the old familiar bunker in the Alpine fortress in front of the various feeds sent to the numerous monitors. He watched and listened to the conversation between Gräve and Nico, while Verne Zog sat next to him on his throne and also followed everything live.

"Great! I knew I could count on the Kinskian demon," Verne Zog enthused.

"Noble master! We must act now on the spot and surprise him with the expulsion!" Magnus announced with growing nervousness.

"Everything in its own time, my dear Magnus. Klaus has always had a good sense of rhythm. I too want the apocalyptic confrontation as a grand and epochal finale for my film. But for that we have to make him believe that he can defeat me."

"Noble Master Zog! Even if you and your work are immortal— Werner Herzog is not."

"You speak in riddles, dear friend and companion—and yet you know the answers."

Magnus shook his head in despair. He was close to tears. "No, master. Should Herzog fall in battle...then...then you too must bid farewell to this persona forever."

Verne Zog smiled mildly. "That's exactly the plan."

Magnus had to swallow hard, and the first tears ran down both his cheeks. "But, master..."

"Everything comes to a well-deserved end one day. My work as Herzog up to now has been deeply satisfying. But it is time to put Werner to rest. If anything should happen to me in this struggle, you shall be my successor and assume responsibility for the Alpine fortress and its dwarf-people."

Magnus could not believe his ears and looked at his old companion with glazed eyes. "What do you mean by that, most noble and excellent Master Zog?"

"I wish to leave this earth with the creation of the greatest work of art in the history of mankind, which still goes far beyond the metaphysical content of *They will claim that I was dead...* and culminates in the total and final self-sacrifice of its creators and at the same time finds its origin in it. Should it come so far, I do not exclude myself from this fate."

Magnus had to digest that first. Then he said in a tear choked voice, "That means that...in the worst case I may not bring the noble master back to life?"

Zog rose and patted his adlatus fatherly on the shoulder. Then he left the bunker through the hydropneumatic door, while Magnus Max wept unrestrainedly. He knew that a change of times was imminent, and such a thing was always connected with pain and separation.

44. THE HIPSTER SACRIFICE

IT WAS ALREADY LATE EVENING WHEN DR. PLUMP AND GUIDO Gusion, standing at a digital whiteboard, explained to Erna and Claudia the plan to penetrate Zog's alpine fortress and free Nico.

"Alright. There are no transmission lines that go into the alpine fortress. We can not communicate with them," Guido elaborated. "The fortress is completely self-sufficient and even better shielded from the outside world than North Korea—with its own intranet and perfectly functioning infrastructure. So we have to find a way to lure Herzog back to the outside world. And you, Claudia, in your role as Nico's former love interest, are exactly the right bait for this." Claudia protested:

"Why don't you go yourselves!"

But the answer was simple:

"Herzog knows who we are and who we work for," Dr. Plump added. "But you're *just* Nico Pacinsky's beloved girlfriend paying her lover a visit on the set. You come with a legitimate coitus request that I doubt anyone can or will deny!"

"But how am I supposed to get in there? Just ring the front doorbell?" Claudia asked.

Guido nodded. "That is exactly what you will do."

"Isn't that very dangerous?" Erna wanted to know.

"Don't worry, we've organized security, which will serve as additional bait on top of everything else," Dr. Plump said, pressing a button on the whiteboard. The door opened, and two young Berlin-based hipsters stepped into the room. Their names were Dörte and Sönke, they each carried a gunny sack, and they had an analog SLR camera hanging around their necks. With blank stares, they simultaneously drank Yerba mate straight from the bottle and stood forlornly in the room while struggling hard to radiate total nihilism. They smelled of home-rolled cigarettes and Fairtrade coffee and wore T-shirts of punk rock bands they had never heard of. Dörte came from Chemnitz and had made a name for herself in the anti-fascist scene there when she had emigrated to Berlin-Wedding in protest against the state election results. Sönke, on the other hand, was the son of a Baden-Württemberg industrialist who was also a nonpartisan district administrator in the Backnang constituency. His son Sönke was a sympathizer of the Identitarian movement, because it got on his nerves to buy fruit from far-away regions of the world at Trader Joe's and other supermarket chains, while the German apple tree produced just as good, if not better fruit. Being an anti-globalization activist and a neo-fascist was no longer a contradiction in terms in the Berlin hipster scene.

The two freethinkers greeted Erna and Claudia with an ostentatiously averse nod of the head and managed to look as if they were about to pitch their next photo project. However, Dr. Plump forestalled this: "These two lowly artists are willing to sacrifice their demons for a good cause. They will entice Verne Zog to open the gate to exorcise them."

Erna crossed herself again. "Oh sweet Jesus."

Dörte, however, casually waved it off. "It's okay...I'm through with society anyway. We do have a new, totally *fancy* project, but..."

Guido Gusion interrupted her before she could spout any

more sermon. "If Zog takes the bait and lets you in, you will immediately get to Nico and steal his demon, as we taught you!"

"Oh, holy Lord in heaven!" Erna cried out and crossed herself a whole nineteen times. Dörte and Sönke took their iPhones out of their pockets and took selfies with particularly neutral facial expressions for their Insta group.

"The Kinski demon is the only thing Herzog ever wanted to possess," Dr. Plump explained. "Once you have exorcised Nico and taken possession of the demon for us, we will pick you up in the holy helicopter and fly you and Nico out to the Vatican. You'll be safe there."

Guido gave Claudia a crucifix pendant like the one he had once given Nico. "Through this device we can hear and track you. You simply need to activate it."

He demonstrated to her how to do it. Claudia took the cross and held it up to the ceiling light to look at it. Then she hung it around her neck and said, "God with us. For love!"

She crossed herself and her mother did the same with tears in her eyes. Erna knew that this important papal undertaking would further delay her departure for Transylvania and possibly put her daughter in great danger. Dr. Plump and Guido Gusion, however, were glad. Their mission could continue. Pope Kierus would be pleased.

———

Nico, meanwhile, had fallen asleep on the sofa in his lounge, with the Burroughs book resting on his belly. There was a short knock at the door, and Magnus Max looked in. "The next scene is coming up. Set rehearsal in eight minutes."

Nico woke up and was confused. "Yes, my director. I'm coming."

Magnus raised his eyebrow fleetingly, but then turned and

pulled the door shut behind him again. Nico rubbed his eyes, drank a sip of sparkling water and then went to the door. As he was about to close it behind him, he flicked the light switch at the same time.

The light goes out. Nico stops abruptly and opens the door again. In the dark, his room looks almost like a cell in an insane asylum.

He turns the light back on. Everything seemed normal again. He saw his lounge.

He turned off the light again. *Suddenly everything appears again as in a cell in an insane asylum.*

Nico repeated (*repeats*) the process a few times with always the same result.

He blamed the phenomenon on a sophisticated mechanism in the Alpine fortress that could probably transform the rooms for different uses by projection. Shaking his head, he smiled to himself and closed the door behind him. Leaving the light on, he went to the set, where he was already expected.

————

Magnus Max and Nico stood together in front of Gwyneth's cryo-pod. The dwarf began the wake-up procedure; he pressed several buttons and entered a numerical frequency into the control console's touchpad. It hissed, and the unit's Plexiglas lid slowly opened. Magnus and Nico waited, spellbound, but finally the redeeming moment came, Gwyneth opened her eyes and smiled at Nico. Magnus grinned proudly, but then left the two alone with their reunion. Gwyneth was still a little hoarse, and speaking was difficult for her. Her already British accent now had an old-fashioned edge to it—after all, she was revived with the demon of Margaret Hughes.

"What happened?" she asked.

Nico was about to tell what he had experienced so far in the alpine fortress, but then decided not to, after all, she knew Gräve's play. "Too much to tell you now, actually. I'm simply happy you're back!"

Gwyneth straightened up in the pod, and she and Nico hugged each other. Then she looked around, as best she could, at the strange surroundings of the lab. "Where am I?" she asked.

"We are in the Alps," Nico said.

"The Alps?"

"Yes. We are shooting the movie about my life down here."

Gwyneth was shocked. "You accepted Werner Herzog's offer?! Did you quit the theater play?" Her disappointment was impossible to miss.

Nico helped Gwyneth out of the pod, and Magnus brought her a bathrobe with the emblem of *Werner Herzog Filmproduktion GmbH.*

Nico ummed and ahhed. "Well, yes and no...It's complicated. But Christoph is here with me as well."

"Really?" Gwyneth asked with some surprise.

She seemed quite cold and Nico hugged her again. Then Magnus intervened, "We'd better take you to your room now."

Gwyneth nodded. Then Verne Zog joined in with vigor: "Aaaaand—Cut! Thank you! That one's in the can!"

Gwyneth was now completely confused. "Nico, what is going on?"

Immediately, some dwarves came and took care of Gwyneth's clothes and makeup. Nico did not react at first. Instead, Verne Zog approached Gwyneth and gently stroked her hair. "You did a great job, dear Gwyneth. The confusion on your face reminded me of the painting *Woman in a Hat* by Henri Matisse, whose Fauvism I have always admired throughout my life."

Gwyneth started to get scared. She wanted to escape. But how? And where to? Was this real? Was she dead? Was she dreaming? Was she trapped in Gräves' play? It felt like she had fallen into a deep hole and only come out the other side years later. The life she had lived so far felt to her like thinking about the time before her own birth; you know there was that time, but you weren't there and you had no proof that the past existed. That's when she made out a familiar face in the crowd: her old boss and buddy Christoph Gräve, who came running up to her pod, laughing broadly and hugging her warmly. Gwyneth was relieved. "Oh, Christoph, I am so glad to see you!"

"Likewise! I was really worried about you."

They embraced each other intimately one more time. But Nico intervened and wanted to move on to the next scene. After all, the shooting day only had twenty-four hours. "Yes yes...now save your sentimentalities for the really emotional scenes. Let's move on now, please."

Suddenly, the main alarm, which pierced through marrow and bone, blared, and all the dwarves ran frantically. The signal, which had previously only been used during drills on the annual Alpine Fortress Population Warning Day, indicated that either intruders from outside were at the gates, or that an air strike from an enemy film studio was imminent. Verne Zog was hastily escorted by several dwarves to the emergency exit, from where a rocket-propelled capsule took him to his ABC-proof bunker, located fourteen floors below the studio complex. Nico, Gräve and Gwyneth were left perplexed. At first, they assumed it must be another of Verne Zog's directing methods. But when Magnus Max also jumped onto his hoverboard in a panic and shouted to them to flee to their bunks immediately, they realized the seriousness of the situation.

"Get yourselves to safety. The noble master and I will bring the situation under control!" shouted the dwarf.

With that, he disappeared through the door of the emergency exit, and Gräve, Nico, and Gwyneth, still naked under her bathrobe, were alone.

"So...Maybe someone can get me some clothes?"

———

Zog and Magnus sat spellbound in front of the monitors in the bunker and could hardly believe their eyes. The surveillance cameras showed Claudia walking towards the main entrance of the Alpine fortress, accompanied by hipsters Dörte and Sönke. In her hand she held the strange leather bag with Guido Gusion's exorcism kit.

Magnus Max's amazement was the first to subside. "Noble Master Zog! This is the concubine of Lord Nico Pacinsky."

"Highly interesting. Another component for the apocalyptic finale," the master director rejoiced.

"But, I don't know the other two creatures. They look like they are pseudo-artists," Magnus Max speculated.

———

In front of the imposing main entrance with its numerous bars, surveillance cameras, Nato barbed wire, anti-tank barriers, self-propelled grenades and flag lights, the three intruders walked along the snow-covered access road, under which a thousand-meter-deep unsecured ravine lay to the right and left. Dörte took a sip from her Mate bottle, and Sönke shot photos with a Soviet Leica replica.

Of course, he was not impressed by the Alpine fortress. "Barbed wire and tank traps are so nineties. Totally the retro charm."

Then, suddenly, his camera burst. A defensive laser beam that Magnus had fired from the control centre had hit the bull's-eye, or rather the lens. Sören pretended to be very nonchalant, although at that moment he wanted nothing more than to return to his mother's bosom in Backnang. "Let's face it: lasers haven't been cool since the eighties."

Magnus fired a warning shot from one of the four eighty centimeter Dora cannons over the heads of the intruders, making a tremendous noise. Zog had bought these gigantic guns from the Krupp factories in the 1940s to prevent them from being put on the open market and thus possibly falling into the wrong hands. Sönke was so startled that he tripped over an ice floe and fell backwards. He almost slid over the edge of the bridge on the slippery ground, but at the last second managed to grab hold of a rusty steel girder sticking out of the concrete. With some effort, he was able to pull himself up on it. Claudia spotted a camera on a pole and spoke directly into it with her hands raised so that Zog and Magnus could hear and see her in the bunker. "Hello, please don't shoot! I'm the girlfriend of your actor, Nico Pacinsky."

Zog looked at Magnus and with a nod of his head gave him confirmation that he could answer. The dwarf then grabbed the stand microphone in front of him and pressed a button. "Who you are, of course, we know. But, who are your two companions?"

With a queasy feeling in her stomach, Claudia replied: "These are young artists from Berlin. Friends of mine...and also totally big Herzog fans. They have a project that they would like to present to you..."

A cold shiver ran through Verne Zog, and he shook with pure disgust. His face looked as if he had bitten into a lemon. Immediately he gave Magnus the order to liquidate these completely worthless *artists*. Never would he sink so low as to absorb the demons of such filth. Magnus knew what he had to do and pressed another button on the control console. On the monitors, they could watch as Dörte and Sönke were blown to smithereens by the Grjasew-Shipunov 30mm caliber Gatling guns. The unique reloading mechanism of this type of cannon, operated by rotating barrels around a central axis, had been learned by Zog during the American Civil War, then copied by Richard Gatling and introduced in Europe. A drone equipped with two M9-series flamethrowers banished the remains of the two hipsters to ash, which was sucked up by a small autonomous and self-controlled vacuum cleaner robot from the company *Robomopp*. The coal dust could later be used to sprinkle the courtyard driveway and as fertilizer for the in-house plantations.

Claudia cried out in despair. "No! Stop! Help!"

The crucifix around her neck transmitted all the events to the VatiCom phone in Dr. Plump's apartment without any latency. This allowed the two assassins to listen in on the massacre on their smartphones while sitting at the kitchen table.

"Well, they knew the risk," was Dr. Plump's laconic comment. But Guido felt sick and had to throw up next to the sofa on the expensive Persian carpet, while he and Dr. Plump, in the apparent safety of the secluded Grunewald property villa, continued to listen in on what Magnus Max was telling Claudia through the intercom:

"The noble master does not appreciate the pretentious arts!"

In Verne Zog's bunker, the noble master gave the order to his lackey to allow Claudia to enter and open the gates. Magnus Max let go of the intercom button. "But master! Probably the enemy sent her. Possibly she is even a Trojan horse."

"Very likely she is," Zog said. "And that's exactly why I never write anything like a script. Real life has sent us the ultimate showdown here."

Magnus looked at his master worriedly. After all, he knew Gräve's theater manuscript, and in it the arrival of the young woman did not bode well. Nevertheless, he followed his master's instructions and pressed the button to open the gate.

Directly in front of Claudia, sirens began to wail everywhere and yellow-red flashlights began to blink. Several searchlights and all the firing systems of the Alpine fortress were pointed at her.

One false move or mention of an incompetent film critic would have meant her certain death. The large, rusty metal gate, which apparently had not been opened in years, slid aside to reveal the Alpine Fortress, its disposal towers stretching several hundred feet high into the starry evening sky. Various airlocks with smaller security gates stood between it and the elevator that led into the interior of the underground complex at the end of the path. From one of the megaphone speakers, Magnus Max's voice rang out, "Enter."

Slowly, Claudia walked along the brightly lit and snowy path between the heavy iron gates. The procedure for passing through the locks took about four hours. She had to give blood, urine and stool samples, was completely x-rayed and disinfected. She was given a new wardrobe from the Herzog Collection, which was created in cooperation with *Canada-Goose*. However, the electronic helpers and sensors in the airlocks did not object to her crucifix pendant so as not to hurt her religious feelings—which is why Dr. Plump and Guido Gusion were able to continue attending the live broadcast.

45. MARTINI SHOT

NICO, GRÄVE AND GWYNETH WERE SITTING IN NICO'S LOUNGE waiting for the curfew to end, which had now lasted for over four hours. Gwyneth, meanwhile, was wearing a blouse and skirt that Nico had stolen for her from the costume car and was warming herself with a hot cup of tea. She did look like a living dead woman—but in a somber, thoroughly sexy-gothic way.

"I just can't believe how cold I am," she said.

Nico took her gently in his arms and pressed her against him to warm her. As he did so, his hand touched her completely hypothermic neck. "That's...probably a side-effect...Hopefully."

She broke away from his embrace and became serious: "Okay, guys. Let me get something straight: we need to get out of here. Right now. This place is dangerous and scary."

Gräve sucked on his e-pipe and poured himself his sixth espresso, which he drew from the gold-plated special edition *Elektra Belle Epoque* coffee machine.

"Gwyneth, we have a movie to finish. I know, it's all totally confusing and mysterious—but I'm convinced we're part of something really really big here!"

Gwyneth, however, shook her head. "I don't know what you guys are up to...But I want to go home. As soon as possible!"

Nico looked at his *Tag-Heuer Connected Smart Watch*: the countdown was running and had almost reached its end. He hoped the lockdown would be lifted soon so he could stay on schedule with the planned blast. There was finally a knock at the door, and Magnus Max entered. "We have someone here who would like to speak with you."

Behind Magnus, Claudia peeled herself out of the darkness of the hallway and entered the room. Magnus disappeared without another word.

"Claudia! What are you doing here?" Nico started up.

Claudia, however, rushed up to Nico and Gwyneth and embraced them both. She put down her leather bag with the exorcism instruments next to the bed. Nico didn't quite know whether to return her caresses. Gwyneth, for her part, greeted Claudia with a smile. "Hi Claudia. Nice to see you again."

Then they sat down together on the sofa.

The scene turned into one we've read before at the end of chapter three. Namely, the one in which Gwyneth, Claudia, Nico and Gräve are all over each other in a barred back room in the Ballhaus-Ost theater. And only now do we realize that the back room is the very one that Nico saw earlier when he turned off the lights. The back room in the Ballhaus-Ost was not only a projection in the Alpine fortress, but is also something that looks like a cell in a mental hospital.

Gwyneth smiled. Her breasts were only half covered by her blouse, and the large, pierced dark nipples of her A-cups stood erect. Without giving Nico another look, Claudia let her hands slowly slide down Gwyneth's stomach until she finally touched her breasts. Nico leaned forward and kissed Claudia on her open, greedy mouth while still massaging Gwyneth's breasts. She tasted the aroma of her nipples in Nico's mouth and undid the button of

Gwyneth's skirt. Then she grabbed Nico's hand to guide it along the Suicide Girl's belly into her panties. So Claudia and Nico slid together along Gwyneth's vulva and felt the thick hair growth, but it was limited to a small field by shaving. Claudia let her fingers circle around Gwyneth's clit, which was already swollen with blood, while she gripped her nipple much tighter with her other hand and pinched it between her thumb and forefinger. Nico's middle finger slid along between Gwyneth's outer labia, which he then spread using his ring finger and entered her between her inner lips. Her G-spot was considerably lower than Claudia's, but it was all the more sensitive, and Gwyneth moaned in ecstasy. Hands moved up and down her panties with increasing speed as Nico was grabbed by the shoulder from behind. He turned around and saw that Gräve was standing right behind him.

The director put his arm around Nico's neck and pulled him to him. The two men started kissing each other, and while Nico's right hand was still inside Gwyneth's thong, he undid Gräve's belt with his left. Claudia pulled the leather strap out of the tabs, and Nico undid the remaining buttons of Gräve's pants, sliding his free hand into them. This allowed him to satisfy Gräve and Gwyneth at the same time, and Claudia guided the belt from Gräve's pants around Nico's neck like a noose. She began to gently choke him while she deftly managed to remove her own pants. Then she sat down on Gwyneth lying under her, whose face she began to ride with her already dripping wet vagina, gently at first, but then becoming more and more violent.

While Gräve and Nico lay between Claudia's legs, they couldn't see Claudia open her leather bag and take out a yellow sky disc and an ancient-looking mask, which she put on. Next she unearthed a high-tech glass jar with all sorts of displays and cables—the Vatican equivalent of Magnus Max's preserving jars. Between her moans, she began to mutter, "Gang ut, nesso, m' nigun nessiklinon. Ut fana themo marge an that ben, fan themo bene an that flesg."

The sky disc began to glow and float freely in space.

In the next moment, the image of the Foursome orgy in Nico's room turned into that of a surveillance camera on one of the monitors in Verne Zog's bunker. The master and Magnus Max sat open-mouthed in front of it. While the dwarf stared in horror at the screens, Zog was enthusiastic, "Well, my dear Magnus, this is going to be a great scene. No scriptwriter in the world could ever come up with something like that. I have to say, it's really well improvised. So I suggest we just let the security cameras run, because they record at 200 frames per second at a resolution of 256K in RAW format, therefore they can be perfectly integrated with the rest of the footage if we hire a good colorist."

Magnus jumped up to rush to Nico's lounge. Zog held him back, whereupon the little man cried out in horror, "But, noble master, we must intervene now, before she steals the demon!"

"Wait! Steven Spielberg once said that after every day of shooting, he sweats and wonders if the scene he just shot will work the way he imagined. For the first time in my career, I feel the same way."

In the background, the monitors showed that rays of light were already beginning to emerge from the sky disk and outshine the image.

"Master! She wants the Kinski demon!" Magnus Max shouted.

Verne Zog pondered. "Is my director's chair still in the studio?"

"Yes. But..."

"Wonderful! You make sure that the concubine doesn't make off with our possessions. I'll join you in a moment! And take the two senate ladies with you! It'll be the perfect martini shot."

The *Martini Shot* is a filmmaking term for the last shot setup of the day to be filmed. The martini shot was so named because it refers to a post-wrap drink, or in other words, because there is unrestrained drinking after each day of shooting.

Electrified, Verne Zog exited the bunker through the door on his right to retrieve his director's chair, under which Nico had placed a small but highly potent amount of hexanitroisowurtzitane, the world's most powerful known chemical explosive. Magnus scaled his hoverboard and, electric motors howling, exited the bunker through the door to his left.

Nico and Gwyneth, meanwhile, were in full swing, oblivious to what was happening around them in their orgiastic screaming. The countdown on Nico's watch had now fallen below the two-minute mark.

"Ut fan themo flesge a thia hud, ut fan thera hud an thesa strala! Drohtin, vethe so!"

Gräve and Nico double penetrated Gwyneth—Nico from the front, Gräve from behind—while Claudia slid her wet vagina over the girl beneath her and continued with the exorcism steadily, as the papal assassins Dr. Plump and Guido Gusion had taught her. The crucifix dangled back and forth on her bosom. Suddenly, however, her breasts were seized by four more hands, and she was startled so violently that she almost fell off Gwyneth. Behind her, stark naked, stood the two revived senate ladies Irmgard Al-Hassani and Waltraud Beermeyer-Stöpsel, already releasing their lust juice from all orifices. Shocked, Claudia looked to the open door where Magnus Max was standing and undoing his belt. He walked towards the group and now pulled down his pants in his turn. He had not lied, the yard on the ninety centimeter tall man actually measured forty-five centimeters. Magnus took a chair, climbed on it and shoved his erect penis into Claudia's hungry mouth so that she could not possibly continue with the demon exorcism. The countdown on Nico's clock showed fifty-nine seconds left and steadily counted down as another person strode through the open door and recited the spell, "Eiris sâzun idisi, sâzun hêra duoder. Suma haft heftidun, suma heri lêzidun."

It was the voice of Verne Zog, who had taken a seat in his director's chair in the middle of the room and was continuing the exorcism. No one looked up at him for even a second, because the orgy continued uninhibited. Waltraud and Irmgard fingered each other's re-opening bullet wounds, Gwyneth had an anal-vaginal super-orgasm, and Gräve and Nico would have loved to penetrate each other, but didn't dare yet. Claudia had her hands full trying to restrain Magnus' meat cannon, and her vaginal fluid was dripping seemingly incessantly onto Gwyneth's face. The countdown on Nico's watch showed twenty seconds left.

Nico changed position under Claudia and was about to start sucking on her breasts when he noticed the pendant on her neck. Shocked, he realized that it was the same crucifix that Guido Gusion had given him. He looked up at Claudia and peered into the ancient mask she wore over her face. Astonished, he missed Gwyneth's hole, and she gave a scream of terror. Gräve and Nico were flung out and off her, respectively, and toppled off the sofa together.

The orgy came to an abrupt halt, but Verne Zog would not be stopped. "Suma clûbodun umbi cuniowidi: insprinc haftbandun, infar wîgandun."

The countdown had reached five seconds. The sky disk circled freely in space, spinning on its own axis. Ultra-bright focused beams of light emanated from Nico's mouth, ears, eyes and nose, flowing directly into the open high-tech preserving jar.

———

KABOOOM! At this moment, a small pyrotechnic effect ignites under Verne Zog's director's chair. All stage spotlights light up and outshine the scenery. Verne Zog is pulled up to the ceiling in no time at all via two wire ropes on pulleys, as if the explosion would hurl him into the air. In the process, however, he hits his head so hard against a three-point stage crossbar that it slips out of the improperly closed lashing strap, falls to the floor and buries the just copulating acting troupe of Nico, Gräve, Magnus Max, Gwyneth, Claudia, Irmgard and Waltraud. With another bang, the bulb of a spotlight explodes, and the fuses on the entire floor of the asylum blow out. It goes dark.

"Oh, my Zog!"

46. THE TRUE REALITY

WHITE, GLARING LIGHT BURNS INTO OUR EYES AS THE CONTOURS OF a table and the outlines of human-like beings slowly become visible. Muffled, but gradually more and more distinct, their voices can be heard. After some time, the world around us becomes visible, but remains blurred for a few seconds, until finally a kind of improvised interrogation room emerges. The windows are barred. We find ourselves in a mental institution. Magnus Max paces nervously from one corner to the other, sweating. He wears a mustache again. In another corner of the room stands the rather washed-up Dr. Plump. Magnus walks right up to us and yells. He has a bump on his forehead and a band-aid on his cheek.

"Holy crap, guys...what were you thinking?"

Now Dr. Plump grabs Magnus' shoulder and pulls him away. "That won't do any good. They're both in shock."

Magnus Max suddenly snaps, jumps around cursing wildly and throws a chair against the wall, which breaks into several pieces. "What a fucking mess! How could this happen?"

Dr. Plump wipes one of the greasy strands from her face and takes a breath. "Now, calm down and let's find a solution."

But Magnus Max cannot be restrained and yells at the psychologist, "I had put you in charge, Dr. Plump! This is all your fault!"

"Well, the play was *your* idea!" she shoots back. Of course, the psychologist is absolutely right. But because Magnus Max doesn't want to admit the blame for the situation getting out of hand, he leaves the room in a rage and slams the door behind him with a loud bang.

The worried Dr. Plump is now also looking directly at us. "Guys, you've put a huge pile of crap in our front yard!"

Then she, too, leaves the room. Only when she slams the door can we see who she and Magnus Max have just been talking to: Verne Zog and Christoph Gräve.

Zog wears a bloody bandage around his head and rocks apathetically back and forth. Gräve, staring numbly at the ceiling, has a freshly sewn laceration on his forehead. Both men are wearing straitjackets. In his head, Gräve hears the voice of his friend Nico Pacinsky in the role of Klaus Kinski reciting from Nietzsche's *Thus, spoke Zarathustra.*

"He sinks, he falls now—you sneer now and then; the truth is: He descends to you! His over-glory became his misfortune, his over-light goes after your darkness."

———————

The theater stage in the auditorium of the mental hospital is well known to us, because there is still the stage set of the room where the great orgy last took place. All the windows are barred, and the stage is lit only by a single coldly shining spotlight. In the background there are a few empty hospital beds and in front of the stage about fifty chairs spread criss-cross. A man, still standing in the dark at first, seems to be cleaning and tidying up. He has a large water bucket on a trolley in front of him, into which he repeatedly dips a mop and wipes the floor of the stage with it. The water in the bucket is blood red. Magnus Max comes in, approaches the man and speaks in a soft voice, "You did a good job. Now everything is clean again. Thank you very much."

The man turns around and we can see his face: It is Guido Gusion. He seems slightly mad and keeps twitching as he speaks. "Yes, sir. Thank you very much, sir. What a great play. What a great evening. Thank you so much for your confidence."

Magnus Max taps him on the thigh conciliatory but full of concern. "I think you're done here. Why don't you go to your room and get some sleep?"

"Yes, Sir. I will. Thank you, Sir!"

————

In the infirmary at the mental hospital, Erna Rosetzki is nervously and tremulously busy cleaning bloody utensils that appear to have been recently used. She is wearing a uniform that identifies her as a head nurse. Sitting in a chair a little further back in the room with her legs drawn up is her tearful and repeatedly sobbing daughter Claudia, who works here as a nurse. Magnus Max enters with a worried expression on his face. "Have you got everything sorted out so far?"

The woman, who is still in shock, does not get more than a brief nod of the head in response.

"Good, I think you can go home then." Magnus' words are not a friendly request, but an emphatic instruction. Erna nods, and she and her daughter leave the ward to change in the locker room and then head back to their apartment in Marzahn. Slowly, Magnus walks toward the back of the infirmary, where there are several morgue closets embedded in the wall. He climbs a small ladder, opens the first cabinet and pulls out the sled on which Irmgard Al-Hassani's body lies. The sled automatically extends a chassis, and Magnus rolls the dead body on the stretcher to the door of the station. Then he opens the second cabinet and pulls out this sled as well. On it lies the body of Waltraud Beermeyer-Stöpsel. He rolls this stretcher to the door as well, through which Dr. Plump steps at this moment and looks in horror at the mortal remains.

"Are you really going to go through with this?" she asks.

Magnus, however, is already making his way to the third cabinet. "Of course. What do we have our own crematorium for?"

Dr. Plump shakes her head. "We don't have to do that. It was an accident."

"And this accident would not only end your career once and for all, but also mine, if all this were to become public. So you'd better help me save your ass and get these two down to the ninth basement already!"

Dr. Plump takes a breath and then moves the first stretcher with Irmgard out of the room, heading for the elevator to the crematorium. Magnus Max has to take a deep breath before he pulls the last drawer out of the cabinet. On it lies the dead body of Nico.

THEY ARE LYING!

Spotify Playlist 7

47. WALHALLA

THE WALHALLA MEMORIAL IN DONAUSTAUF IN THE BAVARIAN district of Regensburg, which has commemorated personalities of *German Tongue* since 1842, was an imposing building modeled on Greek and Roman temples that stretched into the sunlit sky directly on the Danube. Its chunky appearance, in contrast to the ancient models, was based on the triglyph-corner conflict that had not been solved in this building. A detail that sometimes annoyed more sensitive viewers.

Around it stretched meadows and forests. Inside the temple, busts of various significant politicians, artists, generals and scientists were lined up. The building itself was in the hands of the Free State until the Bavarian crisis of 1965, which was triggered by a dispute over the Bavarian Hymn. But because liquidity was urgently needed after the calamity, Bavarian autocrat Franz Josef Strauß had some of the treasures of the Bavarian thesaurarium sold off and liquidated. Thus, the film director Werner Herzog, who was only known to a small audience at the time, was able to acquire the building and set up a refuge there for the souls and demons of deceased German film directors, with whom he soon fell out so violently that he abandoned the property with all the souls and other junk in it.

This explained the poor structural condition, the leaking roof, the leaden water pipes, and the Internet, which was still running at 56 Kbps. At least there was an enormous table in the center of the large hall, covered with sumptuous food and placed directly under the skylight, thus illuminated by magical-looking natural glow. Seated on the chairs upholstered with leather cushions were the gods of German cinema: Fritz Lang, Friedrich Wilhelm Murnau, Robert Wiene, Samuel Wilder (aka. Billy), Max Ophüls, and a strangely sick looking Leni Riefenstahl. They all seemed to be waiting for someone, staring spellbound at the huge wooden gate that opened at that moment. Glistening light flooded the entrance hall, and a figure stepped out of the darkness. It was Nico Pacinsky! There was absolutely nothing kinski-esque about him anymore and he seemed to be the soft, misunderstood Nico from back then again.

Slowly, he approached the table and looked around, fascinated. "Good heavens! Is this Valhalla?"

Fritz Lang, who was blind in one eye like the Germanic father of the gods, wore an eye patch. He smiled and nodded. "Welcome!"

Nico looked up at him. "And who are you? Are you...Odin?"

Fritz Lang laughed. "So to speak. I am the Deum Patrum of German film directing."

Nico was honestly confused, "Excuse me? Are *you* the real Werner Herzog?"

At that moment, Murnau jumped up in a rage and hurled a ball lightning against the wall right next to Nico. "How dare you?"

"It's all right, Plumpe," Fritz Lang placated him. "Calm down. It's not his fault. But first of all, may I introduce you? Here we have Leni Riefenstahl, Friedrich Wilhelm Murnau, Robert Wiene, Samuel Wilder—also known as Billy—and Max Ophüls."

Nico now thought he understood the reason for his presence in Valhalla. "Wow. I suppose I'm dead then, huh?"

Max Ophüls interpreted the situation hyperintellectually, "Well, one could henceforth also dub this a *play in the hereafter,* as an antithesis, so to speak, to the *play in existence.*" The Riefenstahl was annoyed by his *cultural Bolshevik* advances and let her passive-aggressive anti-Semitism show through, which Fritz Lang registered with disgust. The Riefenstahl said:

"Shut up, Oppenheimer! This is about the purity of body and mind!"

Billy Wilder, who was in Valhalla not entirely voluntarily because he didn't actually consider himself a German, defused the argument with a joke typical of him: "The good ones always die first. The others should be ashamed to be alive at all."

Robert Wiene held an archaic and ancient-looking urn upward into the sun's rays streaming in through the skylight. Some reliefs on the vessel bore the sardonic likeness of Klaus Kinski.

"Well, the body of Mr Nico Pacinsky has indeed died. But the demon that resided in you is now with us."

Nico gradually understood and tried to touch the urn with his fingers. "Is this the Kinski demon that Herzog is after?"

At Nico's mention of Herzog, such a violent pressure built up in the vessel that it threatened to burst. Robert Wiene quickly took it out of the light and placed it under the table so that Nico could not possibly reach it.

"What do you want for it?" Nico asked.

The gods looked at him silently for a moment. Then Lang took the floor: "We can give you back your life. With or without Kinski, just as you like. But we want something in return."

Nico took a breath. "I'm listening."

"There's a reason why German films have been churning out nothing but filth and garbage for years." Lang paused meaningfully, and Nico looked at him expectantly. "Zog. Verne Zog." he continued.

"Werner Herzog? But he's one of the most brilliant people ever," Nico shouted like a true fanboy.

Under the table, the vessel began to vibrate and hiss again. The first small holes appeared in the outer skin, and the lid and the bottom bulged outward. The mention of Herzog had apparently triggered something like a nuclear chain reaction in it.

"We don't have much time," said Lang, who looked at the vessel and then began to explain. "For Zog to capture the demons of artists and harness them for himself disturbs the natural order of things. Only this holy council here has the right given by me to do so. We collect the demons after the artists' worldly demise and then distribute them to other thespians and artisans in need. Just as we sent you the Kinski demon after your car accident to save your life. Verne Zog is a god, just like us. But he is renegade to us. Without him, our power is not complete, and we can do absolutely nothing for German motion picture art!"

Nico was flabbergasted and at first didn't know how to deal with these revelations. "What can *I* do then?"

"Only the power of the prototypical genius Klaus Kinski can get hold of Verne Zog," Lang replied. "Find Werner Herzog, the real one, and bring him back to us in Valhalla. We need him in our ranks by the end of December at the latest."

"December? What's in December?" Nico wanted to know.

"There's the announcement of the program for the next Berlin Film Festival! The lineup will again consist exclusively of arthouse films that absolutely no one cares about, but that still make you want to remove your guts with a red-hot knife!"

"Oh, my God, no!" it escaped Nico.

"Oh, yes! That would usher in a thousand-year empire of bad taste," Murnau got excited. "That must be prevented."

Leni Riefenstahl, on the other hand, muttered off the record: "Well, there are worse things."

Fritz Lang then regurgitated the ambrosia, and he threw up in a small metal bucket. A reproachful look in the direction of the dark goddess of propaganda films, whose visual skills were the model for so many Hollywood blockbuster directors, quickly concluded this brief but remarkably nauseating interlude.

Nico nodded resolutely and was now ready to return to Earth for the good cause. "I will find Herzog!"

The Kinski vessel vibrated more and more strongly and was finally about to burst.

"Take good care, though!" Lang continued. "Werner Herzog is not Verne Zog. Verne Zog is Werner Herzog, though. Reality is a theater stage! And the theater stage is no longer reality!"

"Shit, what's that supposed to mean?" asked Nico, whose despair was growing.

BANG! The jar under the table burst, and the Kinski demon hissed wildly and with much noise through Valhalla. In the process, it left a trail of devastation and finally entered Nico through his orifices. He cried out loudly, "Ahhhh...Werner! You stupid sow!"

Shaken by brutal pain, he reared up convulsively and fell backwards onto the floor, blood and saliva flowing from the corners of his mouth. Fritz Lang helped him to his feet.

"Take my depraved adopted son as a faithful fighter and companion on your dangerous journey." Then he gave a hand signal, and from a corner stepped a small, fat man. It was Reiner Werner Fassbinder, who was just injecting some morphine into his eyeball with a syringe, because that supposedly promoted visual understanding. Then he approached Nico: "Nice to see you again, Mr Pacinsky! I look forward to working with you."

Nico, however, still gasping, had to brace himself against the table and, plagued by severe pain, fell again with his butt on the floor. Shortly afterwards, however, he shouted out to Fassbinder in a buzzing Kinski voice: "*Mr Pacinsky*? I don't understand what you're trying to say!"

The wooden gate opened as if by magic, and the gods of German cinema showed the two men the way back to earthly existence.

"Good luck, noble knights of true German art."

Fassbinder extended his hand to Nico and pulled him outside with him. So they walked, staggering at first, but soon the dazzling light enveloped and swallowed them.

48. HEIL, ANSTALT!

MAGNUS MAX, THOUGHTFUL AND INTROVERTED, PUSHES THE corpses of Waltraud, Irmgard and Nico into the oven of the crematorium of the mental hospital. He watches silently as one by one they burn to ashes. With a small hand brush, he sweeps the remains into a grayish heap, which he in turn pushes from the edge of the oven into a golden cup-like urn. He reaches into the vessel with two fingers and pulls out a pinch of powder that was three people just a few hours ago. As he does so, Magnus muses to himself about the origin of all matter, which is ultimately just a remnant of the Big Bang. Since the renovation of the asylum, the combustion energy of the furnace has been converted into electrical power via a small turbine. He looks at the fine dust in the bright blue light of the ceiling lamp and wonders whether Nico's soul might now be traveling in the Berlin power grid. Then he takes a small medicine bottle out of his jacket pocket, opens the lid and sprinkles some of the white powder, which mixes with the corpse soot to form a light gray matter, on his fingers. He brings them to his nose and snorts the dust mixed with cocaine, opening his eyes wide and making a maniacal face reminiscent of the paintings of Gottfried Helnwein.

In a state of agitation, he looks around once to the right and once to the left. Hastily, he unzips his pants and masturbates over the cup with the ashes. When he then finishes relatively quickly, his face is completely distorted with perverse lust—also in the style of a Helnwein.

———

Christoph Gräve's cell in the Bonhoeffer mental hospital is strangely tidy and clean. Reddish rays of sunset filter in through the barred windows. On the walls hang pictures and posters of his idols: Nietzsche, Schlingensief, Herzog, Kinski. Gräve himself is sitting at a narrow wooden table, reading a yellowed, worn manuscript that was probably typed on a typewriter. It is as thick as the telephone directory of a major city. He hears a key in the lock and looks up. Dr Vary Plump enters and smiles at him somewhat pained. "How are you feeling now, Mr Gräve?"

"Quite wonderful! And yourself?" Gräve's statement is completely sincere, causing recognizable concern in Dr. Plump.

"I'm really very sorry about your friend Nico Pacinsky. How are you coping with the loss?" the psychologist wants to know.

"Oh, you know—he lives on forever in his performance in the play. Just like your two colleagues from the Senate."

He places his hand on the manuscript as if resting it on the shoulder of a trusted friend, and Dr. Plump steps up to inspect the thick tome more closely. "What are you reading?"

He folds the script closed so that Dr. Plump can read the title: *They will claim that I was dead...* "Oh, just an old manuscript from my student days."

Dr. Plump, however, is astonished. "I had no clue at all that your idea for the piece was so old."

Slightly manic, Gräve replies, "It's the oldest and at the same time the most up-to-date work of art in the history of mankind!"

Dr. Plump has to swallow. She points to the manuscript with her hand. "May I?"

"Yes, of course."

The psychologist flips through it and reads a few lines. "You did write the ending after all!"

Gräve grins to himself while Dr. Plump studies the last third of the thick book in amazement. Then horror enters her expression. "What...what is this?"

Gräve deliberately doesn't answer immediately to build up suspense. After all, he is a storyteller. Then he snorts out as if he were the joker, "It is the essence of reality and our perception of it."

Dr. Plump gets angry. "For God's sake, stop talking in riddles! Where did you get these pages?"

Gräve appears offended. "The question is not where I got them from, but why so few people understand them."

The psychologist snorts in annoyance, then turns on her heels and leaves the cell with the manuscript under her arm. Gräve jumps up and bangs his fists on the door while Dr. Plump locks it from the outside.

"Can you bear the truth then, Dr. Plump? If not, you'd better not read any further!"

With a fit of laughter, he collapses on the floor...

———

... and the manuscript lands on the meticulously tidy desk in Magnus Max's office, where he is going through some files. Dr. Plump is standing in front of him, and her boss reads the title of the script, slightly annoyed. Then he looks up at his employee, who has stormed into his office without knocking.

"Please, not this book again," he says, extremely irritated. On his desk is the cup containing the ashes, cocaine and ejaculate.

Dr. Plump points to the manuscript. "Look closely! This edition contains considerably more than the script of the play. Gräve and Zog apparently never presented us with the complete version."

Magnus rolls his eyes. "So what!?"With emphasis, Dr. Plump points to the open page, but Magnus has neither time nor leisure to concern himself further with the play of his inmates and strikes a serious tone: "Dr. Plump! I have just secretly and illegally cremated two female employees of the Berlin Senate and a patient. The stage play of these two lunatics is so up my ass!"

"But, Doctor Max! Read!" She again points vehemently to the page. Reluctantly, Magnus puts on his glasses and begins to read. After a few seconds, he pushes the manuscript away from him, annoyed. "Yes, I told you: total trash for pseudo-intellectuals. Just like the rest of the play. Valhalla with Fritz Lang and Leni Riefenstahl. Such out-and-out nonsense."

Dr. Plump turns a few pages. "Read on."

Magnus reads. Then he falters, and his jaw drops. "Holy shit!"

The psychologist nods as if in confirmation. The text Magnus has just read reads, *Then he unzips his pants and masturbates over the cup of ashes.*

Startled, Magnus looks around his office. "Did the crazies put cameras in here?"

Dr. Plump wrinkles her nose. "So you really ejaculated into the ashes of the dead?!"

Magnus tries to talk his way out of it.

"Uh, no, of course not. What do you think? But then, this isn't about me, it's about those degenerate elements who made it up!"

Dr. Plump flips a few more pages, looks for and finds a line, and points to the very dialogue they just had with each other:

So, you really ejaculated into the ashes of the dead?!

Magnus tries to talk his way out of it.

Uh, no, of course not! What do you think? But this isn't about me, it's about those degenerate elements who made it up!

Magnus Max is distraught. He looks around the room again fearfully and peers cautiously under the table, between papers and file folders, as if searching for hidden listening bugs.

Dr. Plump shakes her head. "I don't quite understand it yet either. But some wild conspiracy is going on here."

Magnus pulls out a bag from a desk drawer, fills it with some glue, and takes a few deep breaths in and out. Then he reaches into the cup, grabs a handful of the cocaine-ash-ejaculate mixture and snorts a large portion through his nose. He offers some to Dr. Plump as well, but she refuses with a disgusted look on her face. Magnus grumbles irritably: "I knew it right away: we should never have allowed the inmates to stage this play."

"Well, you played along with full zeal!" Dr. Plump replies.

"And you, too, I suppose!"

"I thought it would be a good way to allow the patients to act out their exuberant creativity in a harmless way," the psychologist confesses. "So what do we do now?"

Magnus thinks for a moment. "Talk to everyone involved again," he then says. Find out what the inmates know about *They will claim that I was dead…, and* I'll read through the manuscript to the end in the meantime."

Dr. Plump nods and leaves the office thoughtfully. Her worries are not unwarranted, for after her footsteps have faded, Magnus takes the thick manuscript and flips through it again in disgust. Then he squeezes it into the urn, douses it with lighter fluid, and pulls his Zippo out of his jacket pocket, adorned with a logo for *Werner Herzog Filmproduktion GmbH.* He opens and lights it, then sets fire to the manuscript in the urn. The firelight is reflected in his face.

———

The mental hospital has its own gym. A few evening rays of sunlight penetrate through the barred windows and shine directly onto a golden plaque on the wall. The writing on it reads: *Sponsored by Ralf Moeller*. Below it is a poster of the Universal Soldier. From one corner, the strained inhalation and exhalation of a man can be heard, training on a piece of equipment in the otherwise completely deserted gym. It is Guido Gusion, who seems to have regained his composure.

Dr. Plump enters and approaches Guido. When he notices her, the sweaty man stops pumping and straightens up, out of breath. He takes a sip of water from a plastic bottle and gives a friendly nod to his psychologist. For a moment, the two look at each other silently, but then he takes the floor: "That was wonderful, Dr. Plump! You were really great!"

"You're talking about the play, I assume?" Dr. Plump asks.

Guido is almost a little offended. For him, the stage romance of the two papal assassins was much more than just a performance in a play. For him, it was all real. "If it was just a performance for you, doctor..."

Dr. Plump is unsettled. Of course, she too felt a certain attraction between herself and Guido, as often happens between performers. "So for you it was more than that?"

Guido can't help smiling broadly. "Oh, now don't play dumb! You know perfectly well."

They both eyeball each other as Dr. Plump steps closer to Guido. "Tell me more about yourself, Mr Gusion."

"You know my file."

The sweaty man looks up at her. As if his most secret fantasies of the last few weeks were now becoming reality, the psychologist sits seductively on his lap. Guido doesn't quite know how to react when Dr. Plump grabs his head and licks a bead of sweat from his cheek. In a thin voice, he says, "Okay—I'll tell you everything."

49. GUIDO GUSION

"I MAY BE THE ONLY FOREIGN INMATE AT BONHOEFFER MENTAL Hospital, but before I was incarcerated I was actually a fairly successful media buyer in Los Angeles. Lalaland, you know: the Hollywood Sign, big tits, Beverly Hills, big tits, Hollywood Boulevard, big tits. I worked at one of the best media law firms in Hollywood, Bloom Hergott Diemer Rosenthal and Partners. Every day, grinning broadly and with my hair smartly slicked back, I signed the thickest contracts, worth millions. I couldn't stop shaking hands with other executives who all looked just like me. And just like me, none of them knew who actually had what job. But it didn't matter, as long as we diligently signed everything that came in front of our *Montblanc pens*. One of my clients was Haim Saban. One day we were standing together in his fancy office on the twenty-fifth floor of a high-rise in *Century City*, chatting animatedly and amiably. Then he revealed to me that he was sending me to Germany for a lucrative assignment. The very next morning, I took off from the LAX runway in a *Lufthansa* A340 and headed for Europe. Less than ten hours and various recent blockbusters later, the plane touched down at Munich's Franz Josef Strauss Airport. The moment the doors opened, the sweet

Southern California air of my homeland escaped the plane and the gases of German breath, charged with hatred and antipathy, diffused into the lungs of the passengers.

A cab took me to Unterföhring to the *ProSieben-Sat1 headquarters*. The ugly building, which dates from the 1970s, looked like an old factory for life belts and cardboard boxes. The gray walls, the gray cars, the gray weather and the gray, bad-tempered people matched it. The media group's executive suite consisted mainly of rooms that had apparently last been renovated more than twenty years ago. Dulled eighties chic met gray and brittle plastic. All the employees looked the part: They wore clothes and hairstyles from the seventies that were supposed to represent the nineties. I cleaned up all that. I went through hundreds of documents with a red pen, firing an army of office sitters left and right, and folded up the remaining employees on a daily basis. My client, Haim Saban, had previously bought up the majority shares in the group and entrusted me with the task of bringing some order to the store. I discontinued expensively produced programs and replaced them with content from our own library. It was the highlight of my career! I argued with a long, lean man with gray hair who had stolen his show from David Letterman and achieved something like cult status without an audience. I fired him, too, and expelled him from the building while I continued to go through the TV guide with a red pen in my ugly office. But he who flies high also falls low. When I was supposed to travel back to LA for a meeting, I entered the airport in Erdinger Moos unsuspectingly and went to the airline counter. A group of plainclothes police officers awaited me. Using a law from the Nazi era, I was arrested for subversive activities. The law enforcement officers triumphantly showed me an official-looking document and pulled out their handcuffs. The Germans really know no joke when it comes to their broadcasting stations.

I was put in a gray, sinister-looking concrete block with high walls, barbed wire, video surveillance, towers and bright spotlights that shone day and night. Everything was reminiscent of the border fortifications of the Berlin Wall. I was incarcerated in the Stuttgart Stammheim terrorist prison, and they had already thrown away the key when a public outcry ensued: At a demonstration jointly initiated by baldies in Springer boots and alternatives wearing Palestinian scarves, the concerned citizens of the brown-green-right-left-eco-law-and-order majority society gathered in front of the Reichstag to demonstrate against *injustice.* They fanatically shouted their slogans and bleated out diffuse world conspiracy theories. There were banners with inscriptions like: *Ami go home! Holgi, the fight goes on, freedom for Ulrike*xyr* and so on...

These five-quarter crazies were demonstrating not because I had been imprisoned using a law actually invalidated by Dr Josef Goebbels, but because German society feared for the memory of the RAF terrorists who had died in Stammheim prison and because the two Jews Haim Saban and Guido Gusion were winding up a German broadcasting family for profit. Meanwhile, the Bundestag reluctantly put me on its agenda, and a heated, fanatical debate unfolded, with various politicians seething with rage. As former terrorist friends and old-68-generation muddle-heads, of course, some MEPs of the Green Party were allowed to speak, crying with moraline that the legacy of the heroic RAF should not be soiled by moral trollops like Saban and me. After that, the speaker flew off to Thailand on vacation at EU expense to have his green-spelt pumpernickel polished once again. The next speaker was a lesbian fascist cunt from the *Alternative for Dumbfucks and Deutschland (AfD).* She stated that the German people and their TV stations were an inseparable community in the struggle for the greatness and security of the Reich—er, the Federal Republic, of course—and that the purity of the Ariogermanic program should not be tainted. She then drove

home, where she was already eagerly awaited by her wife from
Sri-Lanka and their four adopted black African sons, in order to
agitate together against foreigners over supper. The chancellor
held one of her famous, stirring speeches, that one must now roll
up one's sleeves and wait energetically. Parliament passed a few
emergency laws, and the German state bought *ProSieben-Sat1-
Media AG* back from Haim Saban for many times its original value,
in order to integrate the family of stations into its own fee-
financed state educational network. In *Century City,* my friend
Haim Saban, his executives and the Power Rangers could hardly
believe their luck, for we had made a horrendous profit virtually
overnight. Despite my absence, Haim and my colleagues
exuberantly danced a hora to Yiddish klezmer music by the band
The Kabalas. I, however, was taken to Berlin and shipped off to the
Bonhoeffer mental hospital. To you, Dr. Plump. And it was here
that I actually went mad."

―――

In the Ralf Moeller Memorial Gym at the Bonhoeffer asylum, Dr.
Plump is now sitting across from Guido, listening to his words
with a certain enthusiasm. "How exactly do you mean that you
have gone mad *here*?"

Guido rolls his eyes. "Of course, I just told you complete
nonsense. That was my story *before* real reality was replaced by
Gräve's theatrical reality."

Dr. Plump feels caught-out and annoyed with herself for
having fallen for the insane Guido, if only briefly. She makes a few
notes on her pad and puts on an artificial smile. "And what's your
real story, Guido?"

The inmate grins wildly. He's obviously pleased to now be able
to tell his story from a different perspective: "You know my true
background—at least if you've read Gräve's manuscript. I'm an

agent in Hollywood and have my own company, the *Gusion Agency*, where I work for various successful actors and get them the most coveted jobs in the dream factory. In the early two-thousands, I and my team rose to become a global player and the *Gusion Agency*, *GU for* short, made higher revenues than *CAA* and *WME* combined. But let's start from the beginning:

I was born the youngest offspring into a Jewish family of Sephardic origin that has resided in Palm Springs since the 1950s. My first childhood memories are of the wonderful mid-Century flat house where we lived. This was the American baby boomer idyll: green front yards, white picket fences, V8 battleships parked on the driveways. We had everything that made up the American dream and were the typical average Jewish family: mother, father, two boys, two girls—and a baby. That was me. I like to think back to the time when we all sat at the richly set dinner table and Father said the blessing, *Baruch atta adonai elohenu, melech ha-olam, ha-mozi lechem min ha aretz.* Then he broke the bread, and the loaf was passed around. Like all Jews, I was born a genius. Since the age of five, I have played the piano at international concert level. Friends and family always enthusiastically sat with us in the living room, where I composed the most virtuosic symphonies at our grand piano. By the time I was ten years old, I was already so educated through extracurricular activities that I regularly took over lessons when our class teacher was ill. I am still fluent in English, German, Yiddish, Hebrew, Bavarian, Aramaic, ancient Greek, and a rare Swahili mountain dialect. When I was twenty, I could usually be found in the reading corner of a library. I always carried with me a gigantic pile of books, which I read hard and intensely. During my studies, I wrote a major comment piece on the Middle East conflict that ended it for all time and won me not only the Nobel Peace Prize but also the Nobel Prize for Literature. I studied religion and psychology. Just like you, Dr. Plump. So it happened that I was the only Jew to ascend to the Pope's secret council and we met at the inauguration of Pope Kierus the First. In St. Peter's Square in Rome, thousands waited for the new pontiff's first public appearance. In a corner behind the balcony, the two of us stood together. We chatted animatedly and adored each other. While Udo Kier, who became Pope Kierus the First, stepped into the loggia of St. Peter's Basilica, happily waving the papal scepter in one hand and a rainbow flag in the other, we made love in a wonderful Roman-style room. Just as we climaxed together, the enthusiastic crowd outside cheered to welcome Kierus. At the Vatican we had a brief but intense affair, on the basis of which the Most Holy Father chose us to embark on a secret mission in his name.

We met him in a back room in St. Peter's Basilica, where we were his only guests. The pope accompanied his remarks with wild gestures, because the subject obviously stirred him up a lot. Then he initiated us into the secrets surrounding the eternal artist Werner Herzog, who has been wandering restlessly on earth for centuries. Besides you, Dr. Plump, I am the only secular person on the face of the earth who belongs to the initiated. We have been personally entrusted to put an end to the villain.

We parted ways for a few months after our first mission at the film festival in Telluride, Colorado, failed. However, as I was once again brooding over ancient books, files and artifacts that seemed to come from another universe, the ringtone of my phone rang out, the song *Angel of Death* by the thrash metal band *Slayer*. You were on the line and told me about the young actor Nico Pacinsky. I immediately flew to Berlin, where we persuaded Nico to betray the great master Herzog. Some pretty intense action-packed scenes followed, and we had sex every four hours. You, of course, are still in love with me to this day, while I'm on the fence about proposing to you, since you remind me all too much of my beloved mother with your red hair."

Dr. Plump looks at Guido in disbelief. "You see, this is the problem of method acting. It seems that you and other inmates have developed dissociative identity disorder, stemming from an inability to separate the emotions of the character on stage from your own in daily life."

At that moment, Udo Kier comes staggering into the gym. He is completely drunk, or at least he pretends to be. Immediately Guido stands up in awe and bows to him. He tells Dr. Plump to do the same. She complies with the request somewhat hesitantly.

"Most Holy Father!" Guido says full of respect.

"Boy, I told you, you can call me Udo..."

Dr. Plump chews her lip a little nervously. "But...you know you're not Udo Kier, right?"

"Of course I'm not Udo Kier *anymore*," Udo slurs. "But Pope Kierus the First."

Only now does Dr. Plump fully realize the damage the play has apparently done to the inmates of the asylum. Instead of the hoped-for progress in the patients' recovery, there seems to be nothing but glaring regressions.

She shakes her head. "I'm sorry. I thought you would have moved on from this by now. You may have been an actor once, but you're not Udo Kier. You are Helmut Berger." A moment of silence follows. Then Udo and Guido look at each other and burst into hysterical laughter.

"Helmut Berger! What nonsense. Is he still alive at all?"

"Herr Berger" Dr. Plump interjects. "You have been my patient in this asylum for a long time, and you keep taking on new personalities. Your first neurosis developed from the fact that you thought you were King Ludwig the Second. I was convinced we were past the Udo Kier phase."

50. POPE KIERUS I, PART II

"It was in 1972. At Neuschwanstein Castle, you, the young and exceedingly pert Helmut Berger, were shooting a scene with Romy Schneider. There is rare *Behind the Scenes footage* of the shooting, which I was able to analyze. On the set of Luchino Visconti's masterpiece *Ludwig II,* presumably aided by alcohol, drugs and sex with the whole world, you went completely nuts at one point and never fully came out of character. Visconti cut short a scene in which Ludwig II was supposed to kiss his wife, and cried out in horror: *No, no, no, Helmut! Dovresti baciarla e non toccarla!* Then you went totally berserk and shouted at the director in Kinski style: *Luchino, stupido maiale! Ti abbiamo spesso detto che io sono il vero Ludwig, interpretato da Udo Kier. L'unico attore con un genio uguale a quello del monarca!* Thereupon you stomped off the set, while your co-star Romy would have liked to have had one more take, because she was already all wet in her panties. Since that shoot, your persona has oscillated between Udo Kier, King Ludwig II and your role of Vitali in the Italian giallo classic *Ferocious: Beast with a Gun,* which is featured in clips in Quentin Tarantino's film *Jackie Brown.* In the flick, Samuel L. Jackson asks

Bridgette Fonda if that's Rutger Hauer on screen. She replies that it's Helmut Berger. And that's you!"

In the gym of the mental hospital, Udo shrugs his shoulders, tilts his head and starts to explain his point of view: "Well, that's complete nonsense. In true reality, of course, I am not Helmut Berger, but still Pope Kierus the First, formerly known as Udo Kier. Let me tell you how it really was: It all started when Werner Herzog cast me as his Nosferatu. My manager at the time, Andy Warhol, and I were really just expecting a standard gay casting orgy—an audition, like any other movie. But after some pretty disturbing sex practices, which included being tied to the bed with a bone in my mouth, I was finally exorcised by Herzog and his dwarf. After that, I couldn't manage a single decent performance. Instead, I stammered and stumbled whenever a camera was pointed at me. For example, I played a waiter in *Berlin Alexanderplatz* by Reiner Werner Fassbinder. It was a disaster. The director shouted action, the camera ran, the sound went rolling, the clapperboard was struck. At that moment I tripped and jerked the camera to the floor, Michael Ballhaus fell off the dolly and got his right eye caught on a grease nipple. Blood splattered on Fassbinder, who completely lost his composure and screamed: *Fucking shit, you dirty amateur. And YOU are no good either, Udo!* Then I tried my hand as Adolf Hitler in the film *100 Years of Hitler* by Christoph Schlingensief (the German John Waters). The director shouted action, the camera ran, the sound went rolling, the clapperboard was struck. At that moment I tripped and jerked the camera to the floor, Voxi Bärenklau fell off the dolly and got his left eye caught on a grease nipple. Blood splattered onto Schlingensief, who completely lost his composure and roared: "*Such awesome shit, that's genius! Keep rollin'!*" That was the end of my career in film. For this reason, but also because of the many fantastic orgies, I ended up in the Vatican.

I was studying various files one night in the Apostolic Palace when Pope Benedict XVI, aka. Cardinal Ratzinger, entered the palace. With heavy steps, he approached me. All the other clergy in the hall fell silent and looked over at the two of us, spellbound. Ratzinger placed one hand on the book in front of me and looked down at me with a stern eye. The air was electrified with tension. Then the pope nodded. From under his robe he took out a bottle of Fanta, shook it with all the strength he had left and said in Bavarian *'etz is Bartyzeid!' (Now it's party time)*. He opened the soda and splashed me with it. What must have looked like a bizarre ritual of an even more bizarre old man to outsiders, meant the greatest honor to me: the current pontiff had appointed me as his successor. I was completely gobsmacked and couldn't get a single word out of my dry throat. But then he stuffed the Fanta bottle into my mouth like a phallus and I drank a huge gulp of the yellow nectar made from dairy waste products. The sugar immediately went into my blood, and the carbonation electrified me from the inside out. As if in a rehearsed dance, large loudspeakers were driven into the palace, disco balls were dropped from the ceiling, and the clergy tore off their robes. Beneath them, studded Bavarian lederhosen were revealed. To the music of a classic Schuhplattler, we indulged in a Bavarian folk dance, greedily slapping each other's asses until they glowed red. But I continued to be driven by the obsession to find out what Werner Herzog had done to me back then, and brooded over and over again on old, legendary books that were actually on the index in the Vatican. When I finally became Benedict's successor, however, I had unrestricted access to all the files for the first time and was able to find out the tremendous truth about the super-villain Werner Herzog.

You remember, don't you? You and Guido were standing in my office when I presented you with some secret and yellowed file folders. You, Dr. Plump, leafed through them and paused at one page. On it was a Renaissance drawing of a saint whom you thought looked exactly like Herzog. But I explained to you that Werner Herzog was only his temporary working title, behind which a millennium artist was hiding. Not a man, but a force! A force beyond good and evil. On the occasion of the celebrations of the first Easter festival orgy of my term of office, I gave you and your divine Jewish lover Guido Gusion the order to put a stop to the goings-on of Herzog and to restore order."

Helmut Berger, who thinks he is Udo Kier, who in turn thinks he is Pope Kierus, crosses himself. Dr. Plump, however, can hardly believe the nonsense she has just heard and runs both hands through her hair. Then she looks up from the notepad in her lap: "None of you seem to realize that everything you're telling me here is congruent with the play by Christoph Gräve."

As if on cue, Gräve enters the gym at that moment. "Wrong, Dr. Plump! *You* don't realize that my play, with all its monumental expressiveness, has bridged the gap between theater, TV series, blockbuster movies, novel and reality. We have not only broken the fifth wall, we have blown it up and atomized it."

Dr. Plump turns to Gräve, who approaches the illustrious round with the look of a cocaine addict.

"Mr Gräve. You know that only two patients at a time are allowed to use the Ralf Moeller Memorial Gym."

Gräve acknowledges with a slight shake of his head. "Infidel! I can prove it to you!"

"What?" Dr. Plump wants to know.

"*I* created you, doctor."

"Yes, I know you think your play is reality, but..."

Gräve interrupts her immediately: "You were born in 1978 in the West Berlin district of Zehlendorf, the third daughter of an industrialist family. But while your sisters set about working together to bring the family latex import and export business into the twenty-first century, the nestling Vary Plump was more interested in psychology and religion."

Dr. Plump is perplexed. "How do you know that?" But now Gräve is really turning up the heat.

51. DR VARY PLUMP

"Since the Berlin Senate, due to cost-cutting measures, has given you not only sole charge of the psychological practice at the Bonhoeffer Mental Hospital, but also responsibility for the pastoral care of the comprehensive school adjacent to the institution and the asylum seekers' home housed in this comprehensive school, you have been completely overworked. While seemingly taking notes on your iPad in meetings, you pass the time by operating an app called *Remote G-Spot*, which is wirelessly connected to a small Bluetooth vibrator in your panties. Just recently, a patient jumped up from the couch as if stung by a tarantula and chased wildly around the treatment room swatting at an imaginary insect because he thought the soft buzzing under your skirt was an Ebola mosquito. And while you clung fiercely to your chair as you orgasmed, your patient reduced the room to rubble.—A few weeks ago, you were standing at your locker pulling out various books by Nikos Kazantzakis when several students from the August Engelhardt Comprehensive School knocked them out of your hand and ran off down the hall. Half in a trance, you picked the works up again from the floor. You wondered what you had done to deserve this treatment and looked for the culprits to reprimand them.

In the midst of the educational institution, whose pastoral care you direct and which also houses the home for asylum seekers from southern Germany, a weekly market had formed between blackboards, chairs and tables: Hundreds of merchants and shoppers negotiated the prices of goods there every day with schoolchildren in all kinds of dialects. In one corner, used electric cars were on sale; in another, several solar-powered motorcycles and pedelecs stood. A little further back, tofu skewers were being grilled over an open flame. You were wandering through the maze of stalls in search of the impertinent youths when a merchant addressed you in Low Alemannic dialect: *Se seha so ausch, alsch könnda an Bauschbarverdrag g'braucha, gel? (You look as if you need a building loan contract, yes?)* The man presented you with a paper of several pages, which you signed without reading, because you were no longer capable of any resistance. You were so consumed by the numerous tasks that the Senate had imposed on you. For this reason, my play, which I wanted to stage with other inmates of the sanatorium, came just at the right time: despite the extra workload, you could let yourself go for a while and think about other things. You wanted to be artistically active and find yourself —just like all of us here."

Dr. Plump is speechless. She can't believe that Gräve knows all these details about her and her experiences of the past weeks. The broken woman is close to tears and doubts her sanity.

Director Gräve looks down at her with a somewhat arrogant look. Then he takes another swing, "But all this is only your illusory identity in this reality that you think is true. In real reality, you are a demon hunter. And just like Verne Zog, you are also on a quest to find Klaus Kinski's demon, which will lead you to the wanted criminal of the century, Werner Herzog."

Dr. Plump is gasping for breath, her pulse racing. Gräve takes the clipboard away from her and tears off the written note. The still shocked woman can think of nothing more to say in response, and she feels close to fainting. Gräve begins to sketch a scene on the blank sheet of paper. He writes like a man possessed and reads aloud. Meanwhile, Udo Kier is lifting a few dumbbells in a corner, and Guido is looking at his fingers in a borderline depressive manner. Dr. Plump has to scratch her head and Gräve reads what he just wrote down: "Scene 332a, inside, mental hospital: Everyone is waiting spellbound for what the manic-looking Gräve puts down on paper. On a projector, he runs a film showing a best-of compilation of Dr. Plump's life as a demon hunter."

"We don't even have a projector here at the Gym," says Dr. Plump, who is at her wits' end.

That's when the head of the asylum, Magnus Max, enters the gym. "Of course we have a projector."

Everyone looks down at Magnus. But on the ceiling now hangs, in fact, a film projection device. A screen operated by an electric motor is extended just at this moment. Dr. Plump is now even more confused than before. "How does that work?"

"Wasn't the projector always there?!" Magnus Max points out.

Gräve, however, celebrates. "Yeah, ever since I wrote it into that scene!—Roll the film!"

To the musical theme of *Buffy the Vampire Slayer*, a grindhouse trailer appears on the screen, showing Dr. Plump as a fearless and exceedingly sexy demon slayer. An off-screen announcer with the typical trailer voice comments: "From the makers of *They will claim that I was dead...* comes the latest in demon terror! She is deadly—deadly sexy! The ultimate succubus! She is Dr. Plump! Vary Plump!"

On the screen appears Dr. Plump, fighting an invasion of demons in black SS uniforms in front of the Reichstag, clearing the ranks with a double-edged halberd. The blood of decapitated

Nazi demons soaks her white shirt, and her nipples become visible as if she were in a wet T-shirt contest run on blood. Then she runs toward the camera shooting from two handguns, and her name appears in blood-red letters. Finally, the short trailer fades out, and the screen goes black.

Udo and Guido applaud frenetically. Even Magnus Max whistles on his fingers with enthusiasm. Gräve bows his head in satisfaction, while silent tears run down Dr. Plump's cheeks. "How do you get such recordings of me?"

Now even Magnus Max's joy at the video sticks in his throat. "Yes, wait a minute! Absolutely right: How could you film that at all while you're here in the locked ward?" Gräve turns to Magnus Max by means of the Kinskian screw, grabs the dwarf by the scruff of the neck and takes him to task:

"Magnus Max—that's what you call yourself because of your imaginary omnipotence due to half a Napoleon complex. Your real stage name is in fact—Parvus Klein!"

Magnus Max's face is paralyzed from shock. Superhuman rage rises in him, and he in turn goes for Gräve's throat. "The devil told you that! No one dares speak that name."

Udo Kier and Guido Gusion intervene and tear Magnus away from Gräve. The little man flies like a doll into the opposite corner of the gym and remains dazed on his side.

"Now don't get so excited," Gräve turns to him again. "Because in the really true reality, you are, of course, Verne Zog's unreservedly devoted servant, lackey, hitman, and personal assistant."

52. MAGNUS MAX

"Every day you train body and mind with your glorious, noble master Verne Zog in the Alpine Fortress. In doing so, you handle swords and weapons like a true samurai: impressively and smoothly. Just like Zog, you have almost unlimited knowledge, especially in handling weapons of all kinds. In addition, despite your microsomia, you have great physical and, above all, psychological strength, with which you'll be able to eliminate Zog's numerous opponents that seek his life or expect a favor from him, without much difficulty. For example, with a 360-degree airspin and an ancient Japanese sword, you cut off the head of German filmmaker and dope king Fatih Akin when he tried to enter the Alpine fortress to pitch Zog a feminist stoner comedy. A few weeks earlier, you had riddled the bodies of Tom Tykwer and Wim Wenders for training purposes—with two Uzis in each hand —and emptied all the magazines. When their destroyed bodies hit the ground dead, you did a triple air roll and stepped with the pointed heels of your boots into the faces of the opponents, in whose heads you sank up to the ankles. Quick as a flash, you reloaded both Uzis and fired one magazine each into the already completely destroyed corpses. The flesh of the two directors whirled through the area as in a chopper and you were splattered all over with blood. Then you breathed a sigh of relief for a moment—only to reload immediately afterwards and fire two more magazines, so that the particles of the two Berlinale darlings mixed with the air, rose into the clouds and soon descended as red snow over the Alpine fortress. You wore the severed heads as slippers for a few more weeks before flushing the decomposing remains down the toilet."

———

Change of scene: in a wooden hut in Weimar, a manic-looking man in his late forties was pacing up and down, philosophizing. He had an impressive mustache and smiled to himself. "I know my lot. One day the memory of something monstrous will be attached to my name—a crisis such as there was none on earth! To the deepest collision of conscience! To a decision, conjured up against everything what had been believed, demanded, sanctified until then. I am not a man, I am dynamite!"

His sister Elizabeth entered the scene. She was completely aroused by her brother's words. "Yes, Friedrich! Yes!"

She dropped her robe and now stood naked before him. "Take me, Friedrich. Take me now! Make me the superman!"

The philosopher thought about it for a moment. Did he have many more opportunities to reproduce? Or *up*produce, as he called it. How long would his seed be capable of procreation, when his brain was already badly decomposed by syphilis?

"Elisabeth, you are a terrible anti-Semite—and my sister at that.—All right, then."

Friedrich threw Elisabeth onto the bed and jumped on top of her.

Ten months later, Elisabeth Nietzsche, still plenty worn out from the birth of her first and only child, was lying in a hospital bed in a Weimar clinic. The doctor came in and handed her a bundle of cloth, but there seemed to be nothing in it. The new mother rummaged and rummaged—then she found something between the cloths. Her eyes widened in horror: a baby about twelve centimeters small!

"This is supposed to be the superman?" she asked, horrified.

The disheveled and now completely confused Friedrich Nietzsche walked over to her. His syphilitic imbecility had apparently continued to gnaw away at his cognitive as well as intellectual faculties. "One must still have chaos in oneself to be able to give birth to a dancing star."

The doctor and Elisabeth looked over at Friedrich in a synchronized head movement.

———

"Magnus Max is the incestuous child of Friedrich Nietzsche and his sister Elisabeth," Gräve continued his narrative. "He was given a few months after birth to an orphanage run by Winifred Wagner (Richard's daughter in law). The orphanage was to serve the education of an artist-heroine race. The year was 1917, and in the orphanage in Bavaria, the parentless children were trained by Winifred herself to become fanatical anti-Semites. She stood at a blackboard and lectured about peoples and race, while the bored pupils were forced to listen. One of them was the diminutive Magnus, who was just seventeen years old. The teacher at the blackboard talked herself into such a frenzy that she seemed to have an orgasm, and declared, *We now know with 34 percent certainty that there is a Zionist soy-milk conspiracy to suck the calcium out of the bones of the Germanic master race. This is how we are to be literally decomposed from the inside out. But someone will save us. A Führer will come...and he comes in me!*

A small puddle had already formed under her skirt, and each

of her movements drew a smacking sound. Then the classroom door opened, and the dean entered. He walked up to Winifred, slipped on the slime puddle, and in best slapstick fashion, banged his head against the blackboard. The students laughed out loud, but after the man straightened up, he whispered something in Winifred's ear, and her eyes widened with excitement. *He's here?* she exclaimed. The dean nodded and hurriedly left the classroom. Winifred turned back to her class: *Children! What can I say? One of the great men of our time is coming to visit us today.*

Just then another man stepped into the doorway. His face was hidden by a floppy hat pulled low on his face. He explained that he was looking for extras for his opera *Even Dwarves started small*, which was to premiere in Bayreuth in November 1918. Then he raised his head, and his face came into view. It was Verne Zog, whom Wagner called the *greatest acting führer of all time.* Zog wordlessly let his gaze wander over the students until he finally spotted little Magnus and smiled. He walked up to him, extended his hand and took him to his alpine fortress where he continued to train him. He taught him the art of war, acting and exorcism. As Zog's right-hand man, Magnus was soon responsible for all business inside and outside Zog's bunker world. Time and again, however, he and his noble master went out into the field to harvest the demons of various creators in order to supply themselves with fresh powers. Among his most spectacular captures were certainly Gustav Gründgens and Bertolt Brecht, because they carried the most creative and thus strongest demons of the first half of the twentieth century.

Gulliver among the dwarfs, cried the horrified Mephistopheles actor Gründgens when Magnus sought him out in Manila in 1963 and absorbed his powers. Bertolt Brecht, on the other hand, sang Kurtweillian when Magnus waylaid him in the back of his EMW convertible in East Berlin in 1956: *a race of inventive dwarfs for hire for anything.*

Unfortunately, the quality of German artists' wares increasingly declined after the war, which is why Magnus and Zog had to exorcise artists more and more frequently, while the cans of creativity became steadily smaller. Matthias Schweighöfer, for example, got involved in his demon exorcism, slightly annoyed but without any significant resistance, and immediately afterwards shot an extremely successful comedy quadrilogy dealing with flatus vaginalis (i.e. vaginal air excretions) in women over thirty and under fifty. With this he (posthumously) won 6 German Film Awards, 7 Golden Bears at the Berlinale and the award for best sound design at the Venus Porn Film Festival. As punishment, Magnus decapitated Matthias with his katana at the premiere of the concoction, whereupon the head, separated from the corpus, still gave an emotional monologue of its own, which, however, no one could really understand; *Nnnmmmsmmmjjeemm-mmjjemmmshhhh.*

The reward for serving the noble Master Zog is that Magnus Max's life as a normal mortal dwarf is repeatedly prolonged by the supply of artist demons. Among others, Heinz Rühmann and Hans Albers already reside in him."

———

In the gym of the Bonhoeffer mental hospital, Magnus Max can only shake his head. "I don't know what else to say to that. In any case, you are in very good hands here with us in the asylum, Mr Gräve. I've never heard such bullshit in my life."

There is the voice of Verne Zog, who now also enters the gym. Dr. Plump, Guido, Udo, Gräve and Magnus turn their heads towards the entrance door, through which the noble master is striding at this moment. He wears a mustache like Werner Herzog.

"*They will claim that I was dead…* is without any doubt quite bullshit, I agree with you, honored Magnus. But therein lies the very reality-creating energy and genius. The concept contains the normative power of the factual."

Magnus buries his face in his hands at the sight of Zog. "Not *him,* too!"

Dr. Plump, however, is taken aback. "We had you sedated, didn't we!"

Gräve gives his friend a hug. "Do you feel better now, Verne?"

Zog now speaks exactly like Werner Herzog: "That is completely irrelevant. But it is of great importance for the credibility of this chapter that someone tells my story who is really and truly capable of doing so, and that this is not left to some third-rate dilettante."

"Spare us, please!" Magnus yells angrily. "If anyone here is going to tell your story, it's me."

"Magnus, faithful servant," Zog turns to the head of the asylum. "I'm afraid you can't yet. Your persona of this reality level has no access to that at all."

Magnus ignores him. "You are an inmate of the Karl Bonhoeffer mental hospital. And you are a failed screenwriter whose ideas were too radical for German television."

53. VERNE ZOG

"YOU ENTERED A HIDEOUS RED CONCRETE BUILDING WITH TALL GLASS windows right on the Spree River in Berlin. Emblazoned on the facade of the top floor were the intimidatingly bright blue letters of the First German Television. Gray rain clouds drifted across the sky, and on the roof were several snipers guarding the central administrative office of German information. In a gray conference room in the building, forty-five gray-haired men and women in gray suits sat at a gigantic gray table under gray lights. Verne Zog had just written the serial concept entitled *They Will Claim that I was Dead...* that would later become the basis for Gräve's play here at the institution. At a blackboard, you, Mr Zog, literally pitched your heart out. Full of enthusiasm, you presented your mood boards and a detailed story breakdown for the story of a man who thought he was Klaus Kinski after a car accident. But the broadcasting council ostentatiously shook their heads in feigned indignation at the immoral idea. Even more: you were arrested and brought before the holy Television Council of the German Nation, which condemned you to death by Bavarian folk music on the very same day. The editor in chief himself rose from the pulpit with a morally sour face and nodded, barely visible. Immediately his henchmen jumped up to carry out the execution. For this purpose, they initially shipped you off to Tegel prison. At the last second, however, you were spared due to extenuating circumstances and transferred to our institution. You were admitted to be mentally inferior, since such a highly harmful and shameful serial idea could only have sprung from a brain with physical damage. A normal punishment for popular decomposition by means of film or television ideas according to Paragraph thirty-three, Section forty-five of the German Reich Broadcasting Act, was therefore to be suspended. Instead, you will be incarcerated here with us at Bonnie's Ranch for the rest of your life, so that society is protected from you and your dangerous creative ideas."

Udo, Guido and Gräve look tensely over at Zog in the gym. But he just smiles and explains in full Werner Herzog dialect: "As someone who is beyond good and evil and therefore necessarily above things, I can freely overlook your distorted view of things without any moral prejudice. With this, I join the pacifist way of thinking and acting of the indigenous population of the Puntiaki archipelago in the Southwest Pacific, who always solve conflicts by taking mushrooms and other organic substances from local-regional cultivation, thus avoiding the violence-promoting spiral of argument and counter-argument. I would therefore like the only one here in the room who truly understands my thinking and thus my suffering to give us at this point the actual history of my person: my friend Christoph Gräve."

Gräve rises with tears in his eyes and looks firmly at Zog. His voice almost fails him: "Thank you, Werner.—It was in the year 1520 on a dark and rainy evening in autumn. A wide field opened up in front of a large castle in the land of the ancestors, on whose towers were numerous guards with lances and swords. The design of the banners, which hung down from the walls in long strips, was reminiscent of the logo of *Werner Herzog Filmproduktion-*

GmbH. Inside the castle, an expectant mother lay in labor while the nervous king paced back and forth in the bower. Several midwives helped the birthing queen, and at last the cries of a healthy and splendid boy could be heard. Mother, father and subjects were overjoyed. Verne Zog was born as the only child of the popular, but also feared King Aguir of Fitzgerald and his wife Nosferatete. However, the old blind seer Woyzeka came to the child's bedside and ran her hand over the newborn's head. *Holy shit! The child has no soul!* she exclaimed.

The bystanders looked at the medium with concern. Unfortunately, the old woman was right: Mother Nature had endowed Verne Zog with a serious defect. He is the only person in the world who does not have a demon inside him. In his search for answers, young Verne found out about one of the Vatican's best-kept secrets—and very soon began to use it for his own benefit. At the tender age of just twenty, he sneaked across St. Peter's Square in Rome armed with a saber, ripping apart the bodies of various guards in one short but swift motion, and piercing the guards of the secret papal library with arrows from his crossbow. He set about clearing some old volumes from the shelves. Finally, he held a particularly antique-looking, leather-bound work in his hands and began to leaf through it. The cover was emblazoned with the title in golden letters: *They will claim that I was dead....* On the yellowed pages, ancient, rune-like characters and drawings of demons were lined up. One of them clearly resembled Klaus Kinski.

In an alchemist's kitchen, the stolen book lay open in front of Verne Zog, who felt an unconditional urge to be creative, but was unable to do so. Again and again, in long sessions, he deciphered entire passages of the ancient texts. What he found out in this way is still known to hardly anyone on our globe, but it is nevertheless a law of nature: In some people the wild, orgiastic and uncontrollable demon is stronger and more powerful than its moderate, cooperative, predictable counterpart. These same people become artists, jugglers, and creatives. Such a juggler with a jester's cap on his head was the first artist soul that young Zog harnessed and consumed at that time. As he soon found out, this procedure had two welcome side effects: a slowed aging process and a tremendous output of creativity. For this reason, Zog also invented his alternate persona: the director Werner Herzog, the most creative human since the dawn of time. Soon he was staging plays, painting pictures, and covering the entire range of creative output. When the medium of film was invented, he initially became a fanatical opponent of this art form because it seemed too trivial and mindless to him. However, after seeing the German mime Conrad Veidt in an enlightenment film by Richard Oswald, he decided to work on his own first smaller film projects with which he could lure this most demonic of actors into his trap. Unfortunately, World War II prevented Conrad Veidt from being harvested, and so, after the actor's sudden death in Hollywood in 1943, the demon passed to a young German who, dressed in women's clothing, provided amusement for the soldiers at the front.

Years later, when Zog first encountered Klaus Kinski in his Munich apartment, kicking the kitchen door off its hinges because of poorly starched shirt collars and stabbing the housekeeper with a blunt cake fork, he saw another chance to get hold of this most insane and powerful of creative demons. But despite five films together and hundreds of days of shooting, he never succeeded. The Kinskian power was simply unmanageable, and the actor was always able to elude his director with his eternal screams and violent outbursts. On the set of *Woyzek,* for example, the much smaller Kinski climbed onto a chair to yell at Herzog at the top of his lungs five centimeters from his face:

You're insane, man! No one can live on pea gruel alone. Send Bruno

Ganz out to get something from Burger King! And I'll take care of Eva Mattes in the meantime.

On the set of *Fitzcarraldo*, Kinski fired a rifle at Herzog, but hit the hand of an extra, whose thumb was severed and left on the dusty ground. *Get your fucking hand out of my line of fire, you dirty amateur!* was Kinski's only comment.

Finally, on the set of *Cobra Verde*, Kinski stood triumphantly in his slave trader costume with a high leather boot on Herzog's head, who in turn was lying with his face in the sand. *Level only looks like arrogance from below,* he professed.

For a long time, Zog believed the Kinskian demons were extinct and lost forever after the latter's unexpected death in Lagunitas, California. But he saw a renewed opportunity to finally usurp those powers after they apparently drove into the still young and inexperienced Nico Pacinsky."

At the mention of Nico's name, Dr. Plump and Magnus Max exchange a look. They both have to swallow; after all, they just cremated their patient's dead body, and Magnus sniffed some of the ashes with coke.

"I know this is hard for you to accept, Mr Gräve," Dr. Plump says in a calm tone. "But your friend Nico is dead. He died as a result of your stage play here at the institution."

Out of the blue, Zog, Gräve, Udo and Guido start laughing maniacally, literally rolling on the floor.

"You really haven't read my script to the end!" shouts the grinning Gräve. "Then I'll just read to you from the novel." With that, he pulls a 400-page paperback out of his jacket and begins to read Chapter seven, Section eight, from it. It bears the title:

54. CHRISTOPH GRÄVE

"Even if Christoph Gräve considers himself a genius and a madman in one person, the director, who was born in the small town of Goslar in Lower Saxony, was always a jack of all trades, shimmying from job to job in order to survive. At eighteen, after dropping out of high school, he came to West Berlin to avoid the military draft. Since then, he has been in constant conflict with himself, but even more so with the Berlin authorities. In particular with the ladies of the cultural promotion department, who decide whether his plays are subsidized or not. When he once had to pay back €485.75 in subsidies because a production at the Ballhaus-Ost had been miscalculated, Gräve refused to pay until the authorities sent a debt collector after him. The enforcement officer had already seized Gräve's account at the *Berliner Sparkasse*, which contained about €46.37. To establish justice, Gräve forged a library card in the name of Chris P. Bacon, borrowed all the atlases and the leather-bound complete edition of Max Frisch's works, and threw them into the nearest paper trash can. That was small consolation, but at least he had done damage to the hated state. Gräve had been madly in love with the lead actress of the multi-award-winning historical flick *Emma*.

Gwyneth Paltrow's discreet yet expressive acting, her graceful yet life-affirming demeanor, her obvious intelligence, and the fact that she was Jewish made her his absolute dream girl. Several times he had contacted her agent at CAA in L.A. under the pretext of casting her in a play, but to his dismay, they preferred to put her in the next *Marvel* superhero movie. He argued that such mass-market garbage, which lacked any connection to reality, not to mention logic, was completely unworthy of a grande dame like Mrs. Paltrow—in contrast to his reinterpretation of the play *The Persecution and Murder of Jean Paul Marat, performed by the acting group of the Charenton Hospice under the guidance of Herr de Sade* by Peter Weiss'—but all the arguing, pleading and begging did not help.

When Gräve then also learned that the adored actress had published a candle under her name with the title *This Candle Smells like my Vagina* at a price of $75 U.S. dollars, the director finally burst his collar. He wrote her an angry letter criticizing *mainstream vaginal capitalism*, which, in his view, disavowed the very purpose of feminism, degrading women's genitals to a value-added material commodity while putting on the guise of a political stance. In addition, he continued, he considered the whole thing to be a brazen labeling fraud, because there were reasonable doubts as to whether Ms. Paltrow's cave actually smelled of geranium, bergamot, cedarwood and roses, as the description on the packaging suggested. He qualified that he would, of course, be happy to personally convince himself of the opposite—but until that could happen, he was considering a lawsuit for misleading advertising. But since Gräve was an artist, he could not leave it at that. So he had a replica of his erect penis made out of highly flammable compressed cow dung, with a wick tied into it for lighting, and titled the object *This Torch Smells Like Your Ass*. He included it in the package to the actress. Never would Gräve have expected to get a response to such an action. But Ms.

Paltrow was so inspired by Gräve's idea that she gave him ten percent of the proceeds of her follow-up product *This Candle Smells like my Orgasm* (grapefruit, neroli and Turkish rose) and eventually even agreed to appear in his play in a guest role. However, she had to cancel again for important reasons, as several candle buyers had various limbs severed by the explosion of the orgasmic light source, which earned the product the somewhat tasteless nickname *This Candle Smells like Napalm in the Morning* on the net. Sales then plummeted dramatically, and Ms. Paltrow had to switch to a less dangerous product to save her company. But of course, *This Toothpaste Tastes like my Snot* toothpaste and the single from the duet with Robert Downey Jr. *This Music Sounds like my Flatulences* became even bigger successes, which the *This Tampon Feels like my Intellect* pussy plug could not match.

A few weeks later, however, Gräve made a momentous mistake. During the Berlinale Party of the Filmboard Berlin-Brandenburg, which can be described as the most terrible gathering of ass-hamstering, free buffet-looting self-promoters, he criticized the festival management. In public he declared that the selection of films caused brain edema and that no one wanted to see such machinations of pseudo-intellectual wannabe artists. Gräve was then arrested by jury president Tilda Swinton by means of Everyman's Right and taken in her old Mercedes W124 station wagon to the Karl Bonhoeffer mental hospital. There he soon made friends with the other inmates, especially Nico Pacinsky, who thought he was Klaus Kinski, and Verne Zog, who believed he was Werner Herzog. Gräve wanted to channel the patients' schizophrenic insanity for his own purposes and, with the other inmates, put on the best play ever: *They will claim that I was dead...*"

Silence fills the institution's gym.

"And what does that have to do with anything now?" asks Dr. Plump, horrified. Gräve grins at her and folds the novel shut. As he does so, however, he holds his index finger between the pages as a kind of bookmark. In the meantime, head nurse Erna Rosetzki and her daughter Claudia have joined the illustrious group in the gym and are listening to the words coming out of Gräve's mouth. He notices the two women, greets them with a nod of the head and opens the book again. Then he euphorically reads the next chapter.

55. ERNA AND CLAUDIA
ROSETZKI

"CLAUDIA ROSETZKI IS A REAL BABE. SHE IS CLEARLY TOO NICE FOR her exceedingly good looks and is accordingly often taken advantage of by lecherous perverts whom she thinks are her friends. She believes she is from Berlin-Marzahn and is a trainee in the sisterhood of the Bonhoeffer mental hospital. Her mother Erna, who is the head nurse here, supposedly got her daughter the job after she dropped out of high school by scaring away all the other interns with horror stories about the asylum and its inmates. Claudia is secretly in love with the inmate Nico Pacinsky and has only allowed herself to be involved in the play in order to be close to her beloved.

In reality, however, Claudia has long been Nico's girlfriend. The Romanian ethnic German from Transylvania came to Berlin as a seven-year-old with her mother Erna, where she quickly settled in and made many new friends. She met Nico—still seventeen years old—in the queue outside *Berghain*. But while the extremely attractive, black-haired minor with the blue eyes and the perfectly shaped C-cups, whose pierced nipples always stood out through the lasciviously unbuttoned vintage FDJ shirt (east German youth organization), was let into the hip club without any problems, Nico was self-evidently turned away because he didn't think he was Klaus Kinski at the time and thus couldn't be granted entry. Somehow Claudia felt sorry for the sad dog-eyed Nico, though, and so they exchanged numbers.

Claudia was a regular at *Berghain*. After all, it was not only Berlin's hardest club, but it was also admired, feared and idolized worldwide for its inhumanly tough entrance policy. The bouncers were so übercool that coolness was the absolute criterion for exclusion in the queue in front of them. Anyone who wanted to enter the sacred halls of the anal fisting elite was not allowed to want to do just that in order to be let in. However, anyone as depraved as Claudia no longer needed to undergo the humiliation of having to be interviewed by Sven Marquardt. Going to *Berghain* was like a colonic irrigation; you knew before you entered that you were going to get something shoved up your ass. And just like a colonic, the place wasn't completely empty even after the last piece of shit had been taken out. Due to the growing influence on the scene, the club eventually became so antihyperübercool that at some point it semi-officially became an enclave of hedonism, drug consumption and rosette licking detached from the law of the Federal Republic of Germany, and was no longer subject to the sphere of influence of the Berlin authorities. Thus, at some point, a separate kind of Berghain population also formed, which never left the club. No one knew exactly who or how many people belonged to the Bergvolk. But as it would turn out only a few years later, a completely new kind of cannibalism emerged in the microcosm of a darkroom in the basement, in which the flesh of the victims did not take the usual route through the mouth into the stomach, but through the rectum into the intestine. The followers of this cult very prosaically called themselves *Ass-Eaters* and eventually also learned to excrete their prey orally. Claudia, however, did not get a permanent permit to stay at the club because the coefficient of elasticity of her anus, also called the elongation modulus, was less than $E=1.25$. The value, which in linear-elastic behavior describes the proportional relationship between stress and strain when a solid body is deformed, was the first admission criterion in the Berghain state.

Claudia herself, however, was much more than just a wicked Lolita who liked to go to fetish parties. She also had deep insight into philosophy and sociology through her extracurricular studies of Adorno and Kierkegaard. Unlike her mother, who blamed everything that happened on the merciful God, Claudia held the view that it was a person's task and destiny to find oneself. Of course, this also includes the possibility that one is in disproportion to oneself and unconsciously or consciously misses oneself. Claudia could have graduated from high school at the age of sixteen, but her profound knowledge was exploited and used by Erna to lure customers into her secretly operated fetish studio.

Claudia's mother, for her part, believes herself to be a head nurse at the Bonhoeffer mental hospital. The incredibly attractive, provocative woman, who gave birth to her daughter at the tender age of eighteen, is surrounded by an almost mysterious, metaphysical aura. Just like Claudia, she has pitch-black hair and bright blue eyes, coupled with a distinctly southeastern European profile and a shapely body. The stern but occasionally good-natured woman was punitively transferred to Bonnie's Ranch after publicly admitting to once posing for a TV magazine at a state-owned clinic in Friedrichshain-Kreuzberg dressed only in a pant-skirt and dress shirt. The outrageous news had quickly made the rounds, and soon an angry crowd of lefty eco-olkies, tofu-Trotskis and autonomist asswipes had gathered in front of the clinic, armed with torches and pitchforks, to demand the immediate dismissal of the woman who, because of her obscene behavior, had not only insulted fellow citizens of a different religious background, but also trampled on the emancipation of women. After all, the female sex could only free itself from the shackles of patriarchal tyranny if women no longer decided for themselves how they wanted to dress and appear, but this was determined by a collective of like-minded women instead.

In the reality of the play, however, Erna Rosetzki was always in need of money and addicted to gambling. She had numerous love affairs from which she extorted money, and she often liked to hang out in Berlin bars. It was here that she got the idea of running an S&M studio with her daughter; after all, there were an enormous number of freaks and oddballs in Berlin who also had capital at their disposal. Nevertheless, the passionate Catholic was a deeply sad and offended woman."

At this moment, Gräve's assistant Gwyneth enters the gym. A bit disoriented, she is looking for her ex-boyfriend Nico Pacinsky, whom she actually wanted to visit today. A cold shiver instantly runs through Magnus. "How did you get in here? Didn't you see the sign on the door? The institution is closed for inventory!"

Gwyneth, however, seems all the more confused by the fact that she is in the facility.

"I...I don't know."

Gräve's seven-act insane asylum stage play had a total running time of just under fourteen hours. However, not wanting to overload the inmates in front of and behind the stage, as well as the audience, the individual acts were spread out over a period of seven days. Although Gwyneth herself was involved in the play with several guest appearances, since she no longer played a major role in Acts six and seven, she was only doubled by another inmate during the last big orgy scene. She had therefore not noticed that there had been several deaths in the dramatic finale, and that among them was her ex-boyfriend Nico, with whom she has maintained a friendly relationship to this day.

Gräve, however, was electrified by Gwyneth's arrival and, ignoring the general confusion, read aloud the next chapter from his novel.

56. GWYNETH Q. BRICK

"GWYNETH BELIEVES SHE AGREED TO TAKE A SMALL ROLE IN MY PLAY to help Nico recover from his neuroses. Supposedly, her father was an African-American GI stationed in Berlin-Zehlendorf, where he had met her mother, an automotive mechanic. Before she was born, however, her father had been transferred back to the U.S., and so Gwyneth had never met the man his colleagues always called *Anaconda*. Gwyneth grew up extremely sheltered in a patchwork family in Tegel, as her mother married a French occupation soldier who brought three boys into the family. She graduated from high school with mediocre grades and then began a sociology degree, which she interrupted to take a year-long road trip through Eastern Europe with her boyfriend, Nico Pacinsky. Because Nico saw so much human misery on that trip, he checked himself into Bonnie's Ranch after they returned to Berlin because of post-traumatic stress disorder, and it was there that he first developed the idea that he could be the actor Klaus Kinski.

In order to gain more regular access to the institution and to Nico, Gwyneth blackmailed the facility's director Magnus Max with a video she had taken of him at the *Kit-Kat club*, showing the diminutive man in an eloquent tirade full of expletives against other people with microsomia. Gwyneth liked the *Kit-Kat* because, in her opinion, it was something of the antithesis of *Berghain* in Berlin's club scene. It was essentially frequented by people who would have liked to go to *Berghain* but didn't dare. The *Kit-Kat* did try to copy the strict entrance policy of the Übervater club and chose the motto: *If you let people in wearing normal clothes, only the normal will happen.* But the bouncers didn't understand that *Berghain* didn't bother with such mundane things as clothes, but rather offered something like a religious-metaphysical experience plus fistfucking. At some point, however, Gwyneth stopped visiting because, in her opinion, the transcendent feeling of being part of one's own movement was disavowed by the audience present, which consisted almost without exception of bank clerks, car dealers, and insurance brokers who were looking for nothing more than an opportunity to cheat on their spouses.

In real reality, however, Gwyneth has been my loyal and extremely competent assistant for years and I have grown to love her like a daughter. She is a true suicide girl and has a total of thirty-seven piercings, sixteen tattoos and various other body modifications spread over her body. She changes her hair color at least as often as her underwear—never, because she doesn't wear any. The always good-humored and extremely attractive woman in her early thirties is something like the good soul of the theater I run. Whenever problems arise, she takes care of them immediately and always finds solutions that are agreeable to everyone. She is bisexual and fell in love with Nico the moment he met her in the Ballhaus-Ost.

Gwyneth is from London, where she was born and raised. However, she is a German citizen, as she has a German tennis legend for a father. Her mother is a British model with a black African background. We met when Gwyneth was still a tattoo artist at the *White-Trash* restaurant in Prenzlauer Berg. I wanted to

373

get a mother's heart tattooed on my right butt cheek while intoxicated with absinthe, but I started crying so much after the first stitch that I had to abandon the project. Instead, I hired her as an assistant, since she was looking for a new job anyway. All the hip Prenzlauerberg hipsters with Hitler haircuts who marched into *White Trash* every day to devour the overrated burgers were simply no longer bearable. The restaurant, slash club, slash concert hall, slash tattoo studio, was the pinnacle of nonconformism back in the 2000s, demanding just that as a uniform from its guests. Here, people were proud of shitty food, shitty acoustics and shitty waiters and then transfigured this into the new Berlin lifestyle par excellence. When White Trash went so broke that it had to move out of the former Chinese restaurant on Schönhauser Allee, the restaurant's operators said that they were simply fed up with too many uncool people and therefore had to move the location to Kreuzberg. They were bothered by too much public traffic. Such untrue retrospections were, are and will only be possible in Berlin. After moving to the really hip people on the Spree, the restaurant survived another two full years before the insolvency administrator finally put a stop to the owners' goings-on. Shocked, they argued that they had only accumulated a low million in debts, but in return had created something of cultural significance, a piece of restaurant art, even if the meaning of it was not immediately obvious to everyone. In its demise, however, the White Trash finally became a genuine Berlin institution that perfectly reflected the spirit of the city. Let the others work while we go out and party. That's what we call *culture* in Berlin.

Gwyneth has no idea how she got into the asylum's gym. She thinks she knows who she is and where she came from, but she has no immediate memory of what happened minutes or hours ago. This is because we are now in the reality level of this novel, and as we read it aloud, a parallel universe has manifested itself, into whose reality we have now immediately entered."

Gräve grins again somewhat arrogantly and looks provocatively at the head of the asylum Magnus Max and his chief psychologist Dr. Plump.

Magnus is extremely annoyed by this and wants to snatch the book out of Gräve's hand so that he cannot continue to read from it. "Give me the fucking book!"

But the maniacs are outnumbered. Guido, Zog and Udo seize both the diminutive man and Dr. Plump, who begins to scream. "Hey, let go of me! Help!"

Gräve, however, prances through the gym and maniacally reads out the next section of his novel:

"After the inmates of the asylum had detained Dr. Plump and Magnus Max, something unbelievable happened. In the hallway in front of the gym, two women suddenly appeared, whom Magnus and Dr. Plump assumed had been cremated long ago. Everyone present froze in shock as soon as the two entered the gym."

After the inmates have detained Dr. Plump and Magnus Max, something unbelievable happens. In the hallway in front of the gym, two women suddenly appear, whom Magnus and Dr. Plump assume have long since been cremated. Everyone present freezes in shock as soon as the two enter the gym.

57. IRMGARD AL-HASSANI & WALTRAUD BEERMEYER-STÖPSEL

"IRMGARD AND WALTRAUD ALWAYS APPEAR IN A DOUBLE ACT. THEY think they are a prime example of Berlin officialdom: dishonest, unpunctual, unclean. They believe that they are the dispatched inspectors of the health department of Reinickendorf. That is why they come once a month to inspect the Bonhoeffer mental hospital, to see what is right (or left). Since Magnus Max once offered them only lukewarm instead of freshly brewed coffee, however, he has become their archenemy: they are desperately looking for ways to finally cut him off and revoke the insane asylum license from him and his house according to paragraph 4711 section ß.

For this reason, the two ladies also allowed themselves to be roped in for my play. Under the pretext of actively participating in the patients' recovery, they were able to spend more time in the asylum looking for ways to dismantle the leadership. Unfortunately, their performances on stage were really quite underground. In the epic finale, they were finally killed by an improperly fixed steel beam and subsequently cremated by Magnus Max.

In reality, however, Irmgard and Waltraud reigned in the

Senate Administration for Culture and Good Taste (SAFOCAGT). For decades, the two women in their mid-fifties had single-handedly decided everything that could and could not happen culturally in the German capital. They were the personification of the cultural officials who were always in a bad mood and wanted to prevent anything new at first impulse. Even though they were certainly not bad people per se, the three decades in the public cultural service had left clear traces, both physically and psychologically. As a result, they were on sick leave for about two-thirds of their working hours on average, and were working single-mindedly toward retirement at fifty-nine. The pay for this would have come from the public broadcaster's fee-financed pension funds.

Waltraud, a native of Wiesbaden, was already divorced on her fourth marriage. But since the authorities did not allow her to constantly expand her last name, she always changed only the first part over the years, while her maiden name remained. Thus she had already been Waltraud Ballsberg-Stöpsel, Waltraud Dickhardt-Stöpsel, and Waltraud Hartjerk-Stöpsel. The registrar of her last marriage ceremony already called her *My name hustler* because of the double names, but not least because of the frequent changes of spouses.

Her colleague Irmgard, on the other hand, was hitched only once. In her youth, she married a Syrian exchange student in order to prevent his deportation from Germany. Contrary to all clichés, they remained a couple until the end, even though her husband spent most of the year in Syria coordinating the import of Mercedes limousines for the Assad regime. Why Israel's enemies invariably have a fetish for German luxury cars, and why the dictators of the Middle East, despite all embargoes and import bans, race through the steppes of their homeland, rendered uninhabitable by poison gas, in armor-proof German workmanship, is something that even the cleverest politicians and economists have not yet understood. It must be some kind of natural miracle. *At the next bombed orphanage, please turn right. After that, you have reached your final solution.*

Irmgard and Waltraud both remained childless and were of the opinion that having children should be sanctioned by extra high broadcasting fees in order to create a CO_2 balance and to raise awareness among parents of what reproduction means for our planet. Childless women, on the other hand, should be granted a broadcasting fee reduction of 100 percent for life, starting at menopause. The same should apply to men who undergo a vasectomy.

Moreover, Waltraud and Irmgard saw themselves as entrusted with the task of preventing *bad art* and firmly believed that the state-legitimized filter system was an important instance of excluding entertainment. Such distractions, after all, continued to pose an exorbitant threat to the German national soul and its strength. Among its greatest successes, manifested in exorbitantly low audience numbers, was the support of the play *The Eleventh Temptation in the Cheese Circle* by the Chinese dissident and action artist Ei Di Del Dei, as well as the two-minute short film interpretation of Jules Verne's *Around the World in Eighty Days,* which won the second Audience Award in Karlovy Vary in Czechia and the Best Editing Award at the Pristina Festival in Kosovo, even though the film consisted of only a single take. The masterpiece was directed by the poet Ivana Tinkle and shot with the broken selfie camera of her iPhone 4s. In the film, she is shown scrolling through the world map on Google Maps for two minutes on an iPhone 3G with jailbreak. Immediately, the bravura piece was considered a classic of modern expressionist technology criticism and was screened at over 120 art festivals in front of a total audience of twelve.

I, on the other hand, regularly filled the halls of the city with my plays, which Irmgard and Waltraud considered to be total trash. This circumstance annoyed the two senate ladies to such an extent that they elevated me to the status of their antipode and eternal adversary, whom they wanted to see off at all costs. However, the former Senator for Culture held his protective hand over his *favorite lunatic* for a long time, and success remained with me. However, my last plays *Robocop vs The Golden Girls* and *Better Armageddon than Leg off* received bad reviews by a critic who didn't like the lighting. He considered it a bit too bluish. For this reason, the green party successor senator soon put me on the list of those to be kicked out as I was a pupil of her predecessor. And this despite the fact that the ticket sales of my plays continued to be well above the city average."

———

Magnus Max and Dr. Plump are as white as chalk and can't believe their eyes when the two Senate ladies, who were thought dead, join the others on the floor in the Gym. Magnus becomes dizzy and tries to bring himself to touch Irmgard's shoulder with his finger. "You…they…are dead!"

But since the women materialized in this world only a few seconds ago, they are completely in bondage to their creator Christoph Gräve and await the next command, which he gives them, like all the others, via the various adaptations of *They will claim that I was dead*…. Dr. Plump suffers a nervous breakdown and howls like a wolf. As she does so, tears run from her eyes and snot from her nose. In a wild panic, she runs into the hallway, where the door to the corridor is just opening in slow motion. She slams in front of a six foot five inches high and 290 pounds heavy wall in human form…

58. RALF MOELLER

RALF MOELLER IS THE SECOND BEST MAN IN THE WORLD AND OF ALL time after Arnold Schwarzenegger. The giant is exactly the kind of Homo Sapiens that Friedrich Nietzsche imagined as his superman. Contrary to a widespread philosopher's misconception, the thought-blaster had not imagined his concept as a pampered intellectual with a penchant for life-worldly improvement, but a beast roaming the post-apocalyptic wasteland, clad in a torn and blood-soaked leather cowl, looking for its next victim. Nietzsche was considering ways to prepare humankind's next evolutionary step, a man who should throw off the shackles of morality and God and through his own will to power, fortify body and mind to the extent that prostrating sectarians would be well-advised to judge themselves in his countenance. Ralf Moeller, just like his buddy Arnold, embodies all those qualities. The always euphoric and positive-thinking giant is so open-minded, chummy and jovial that the world can't help but fall at his feet. There is no one on the planet who would not be his buddy or who does not like him. Ralf Moeller is the patron of the organization *Train my brain—shrink my shrink*, which provides mental institutions with free fitness equipment. In gratitude, the institutions name a wing or a hall after the famous sponsor, so that by now there is a section named after Ralf Moeller in an insane asylum in almost every country in the world.

During the celebrations for the naming of the gym at the Bonhoeffer Mental Hospital in Berlin, he met two of his biggest fans in person: Nico Pacinsky and Christoph Gräve. With a great deal of persuasion, the two madmen succeeded in winning him over to participate in their epoch-making play. Ralfi, as the two have since called him, moved into the asylum for the rehearsal and play season. *Mercedes-Benz* was immediately involved as a sponsor, because the gladiator appeared anyway as a brand ambassador for the Stuttgart car company. For the guest appearance, Ralfi demanded €25,000 per day in cash, which was slipped under the door to his dressing room in an envelope every day. Magnus Max was able to secure the financing for this by involving Irmgard and Waltraud in the play, and the two ladies then requested an appropriate budget from their boss in the health department. This was approved without further inquiries, because the appearance of Ralf Moeller could be set off as medical measure. Thus, the AOK health insurance, as the main sponsor of the institution, took over all the costs incurred, including Ralfi's expenses for cigars.

In Gräve's theatrical reality, however, he and Ralfi met at a pumping iron session at *Gold's Gym* in Santa Monica, where the Universal Soldier spontaneously encouraged the weakening director to do a few more sessions. Spurred on by this, Gräve tortured himself with various pull-ups, and after the workout they went together to the *Grand Havana Room* on Canon Drive in Beverly Hills 90210 to smoke a few cigars and eat a delicious Caesar salad. Danny DeVito, Al Pacino and just about every male Hollywood star had their own locker in the *Havana Room's* walk-in humidor, which housed exclusive tobacco treasures. The compartments were identified by the personalized nameplate of the respective owner. As a newcomer who was only allowed to enter the Havana at the invitation of a celebrity, Gräve gazed in amazement and with open mouth at the names of all the legends who exchanged their fees for Cuban gold and stored them here.

From the humidor, they entered the main room, which, like pretty much everything else in LA, consisted of cheap sheetrock walls with plastic appliqués and plastic stucco. Grouped around the too-low glass tables was worn-out seating with rubbed backs and sagging seat cushions. In the dark and smoky room, several producers were currently sitting and puffing away, each of whom fulfilled all the stereotypes of a Hollywood shark. Most of the tables, however, were empty.

Ralfi greeted the cigar pals with an affable smile and a nod of the head, but then headed for the outdoor balcony, where the air was much fresher and the view of the beautiful girls strolling down Canon Drive much better. At *The Havana* only extremely good-looking ladies under twenty-five served as waitresses. Their work uniform consisted of a half-open blouse with a push-up bra visible underneath, a short skirt, and suspenders. Their broad smiles, with which one was literally dazzled by the bleached teeth, and the much too exuberant greeting upon entering the exclusive club were supposed to give the mostly male guests the feeling that the young women were ready for intercourse at any time. In reality, however, this was only intended to encourage drinking and hefty tips. Secretly, most of the ladies also hoped to be discovered by a powerful producer right away. There are a few nice jokes on this subject in LA:

"I'm an actress, by the way."—"Really? What restaurant?"

"I'm a screenwriter, by the way."—"Really? Cab or Uber?"

"I'm a director, by the way."—"Really? Crack or crystal?"

Gräve and Ralfi had just ordered their Caesar salad with chicken breast strips and croutons ($12.50 extra per side dish), when Gräve saw another giant push its way through the door to the terrace in slow motion and in an under-view camera perspective. Gräve imagined he could see the glowing red eye of the T-800 endoskeleton beneath the human flesh grown by *Cyberdyne Systems* and hear the servo motors of the joints. None other than Arnold Schwarzenegger, Model 101, had just entered *The Havana* and was heading straight for Gräves and Ralfi's table. The latter rose and warmly embraced his old buddy before introducing Gräve to the Running Man and the governator finally joined them at the table. Both action heroes had impersonated the barbarian Conan in the past—Arnold in the movies and Ralfi on TV—so the illustrious trio passed the salad waiting time by reciting their favorite quotes to each other in appropriately heavy accents.

"What is best in life?—To grush ze enemy, see zem driven before you and to hear ze lamentation of ze women!"

In no time at all, they were friends. Arnold also introduced Gräve to his nephew, an extremely successful entertainment lawyer, who from then on represented Gräve's interests. After all, every creative in LA needed three things: a good agent, a good manager and a good lawyer. Add up to thirty percent pre-tax dues.

Ever since their salad lunch at *Havana,* the three had wanted to make a film together, with Arnold and Ralf playing themselves. In the action comedy, Ralfi would have been kidnapped by gangsters, and Arnold, along with Sylvester Stallone and other Hollywood heavyweights like Bruce Willis and Jamie Lee Curtis, would have searched all of LA for him, getting caught up in all sorts of amusing situations. All the other actors would have played themselves as well, making for a semi-documentary film. Unfortunately, despite the fact that preliminary contracts had already been signed, the film was never shot because no suitable date could be found and the basic idea was stolen at some point by the makers of the Amazon series *Jean Claude van Johnson* and implemented in a modified version. Nevertheless, Gräve, Arnold and Ralfi never lost sight of each other, and remained on friendly terms. But when they finally met again in Berlin at a charity schnitzel eating contest at *Borchardt*, Gräve immediately pitched Ralfi his new idea for the play *They will claim that I was dead...*, of which he had just won the young, up-and-coming actor Nico Pacinsky for the lead role.

At first Ralfi was still unsure: "Is it all coherent? It seems to me that you switch between philosophical reference systems several times in the piece and that this results in some logic problems on the meta-level.—Come on, Christoph, one more schnitzel!"

But because Gräve then actually won the competition by devouring seven plate-sized schnitzels in under sixty minutes, Ralf Moeller finally agreed to take on a role in the play from the second week of the season. Critics and audiences alike were enthusiastic about his performance skills and were already comparing him to Philip Seymour Hoffman's pool boy. But then, after a performance, he got caught in a hail of bullets from the papal assassins, was badly hit and temporarily killed—until his resurrection.

59. NICO PACINSKY

RALFI LEADS THE DISTURBED PSYCHOLOGIST DR. PLUMP BACK TO THE gym named after him, where his friends are already waiting for him, grinning moronically. Magnus Max is impressed by the sheer size of the colossus and can hardly say anything due to the surreal situation they find themselves in together. In his brain, uncontrollable scraps of thoughts are spinning around, trying to find an assignment in one of the drawers in it. But he doesn't succeed—because the shelf of his mind has already dissolved, and Magnus feels as if he is falling into an infinite hole through space and time. At the same time, he can see himself from the outside, as he staggers from right to left, close to fainting, and finally has to sit down on the floor. Then he too begins to weep bitterly, for he no longer understands the world he has built for himself over the past forty-two years. He knows that he is awake. He knows that what he has experienced is real. He knows that he himself exists —*cogito ergo sum*. But what hellish trip have the lunatics mixed into his drinking water here? Or has what his professor at the university once warned him about actually come true? Have all moral and socio-cultural structures been overturned and reversed without him noticing?

His thoughts turn faster and faster in circles, and it occurs to him that a similar major event is still inevitably in store for mankind: the magnetic field shift, in which the polarization of the north and south poles is reversed, whereby the Earth's magnetic field, which protects us from space radiation, collapses for a few tens of thousands of years, and thus human life as we know it would end in one fell swoop. In the history of the Earth, this event occurs on average about every 250,000 years. Now, however, the last shift is probably already scarcely 800,000 years ago, and the next one is absolutely overdue with it. But this also means that Homo Sapiens has not yet witnessed a magnetic fieldless intermezzo of the Blue Planet in its history and thus goes into this phase of forced migration into the deep underground completely unprepared. Should the play of the inmates perhaps represent a preparation for such an epochal event?

However, while Magnus is getting more and more caught up in his whirlpool of thoughts, Gräve and Zog suddenly stretch out their arms in the direction of the door, completely synchronously. At that moment, an ultra-bright light from the main hall floods the scene, and those present have to cover their eyes to avoid going blind. A few seconds later, the light dims again, and everyone leaves the Gym together to search for the source of the glaring illumination. Gräve and Zog are the last to enter the auditorium. They nod to each other in satisfaction, as naked terror is written on Magnus' and Dr. Plump's faces as they perceive the unbelievable: Standing before them are the director Rainer Werner Fassbinder and the actor Nico Pacinsky, who they believed was dead and cremated!

Dr. Plump wipes the tears from her face and stammers, "But...you're dead, too!"

"They are lying!" Nico shouts at her with wide eyes and trembling body.

386

Nico Pacinsky was born in West Berlin in 1981. His sheltered and happy childhood ended abruptly when he lost his father in a motorcycle accident at the age of ten. The latter was killed on November 23, 1991 in a strip club by a Harley-Davidson mounted on the wall, which fell down in a small earthquake triggered by Klaus Kinski's death. After a trip through Eastern Europe, Nico developed a severe psychosis in which he imagined himself to be Tony Clifton. As a result, he self-admitted himself to the Bonhoeffer Mental Hospital, where he is still an inmate and is coming to terms with his life by staging the play *They Will claim that I was Dead...* with other inmates.

In reality, however, Nico's life had always been sub-par and characterized by boredom. He passed his high school graduation with a grade of 3.4, and continued to prove himself a real loser. For a short time he studied film and theater history at the University of Gdansk, hoping to trace the family roots of his idol. Soon, however, he decided to return to Berlin, where, using clues from Kinski's autobiography *Ich bin so wild nach deinem Erdbeermund (All I need is Love),* he searched out all the places where the mad mime had had sex during his time in Berlin. These were 493 public places, 1091 private apartments, four film studios, three prisons and two sections of the sewage system.

During his lifetime, Kinski was even able to resolve conflicts through the sexual act. For example, when a Berlin resident of an old building, annoyed by the inconvenience of a film shoot, constantly turned up her radio so loudly that it interfered with filming, Kinski kicked in the front door of the structure, snorted with rage and stomped up to the third floor with drool in his mouth, and rang the doorbell until the fifty-four-year-old resident finally opened her door. With a soft voice, pleading vehemence and fatalistic seriousness, he talked at her until the lady invited him in and let him screw her brains out. Three quarters of an hour later, Kinski and the film crew were able to shoot the next take.

Nico always wanted to be like that. But he was not capable of it. It was only after his serious car accident that he finally achieved everything he had always dreamed of in the person of Klaus Kinski...

———

Verne Zog approaches Nico in the asylum and hugs the newcomer. "Klaus, my dear. I am extremely pleased that you, like once Chief Tikka Masala of the Tandoori, with whom I drank several measures of chica, also called spit beer, in the jungle in 1975, have found your way back to us the living."

Rainer Werner Fassbinder and Zog nod coolly at each other, because they obviously see each other as competitors—not only for Nico's favor, but also for that of the audience. Then Fassbinder sits down on the floor without a word, and everyone else does the same. They are completely quiet, but spellbound, hardly daring to breathe. So now Magnus Max, Dr Vary Plump, Guido Gusion, Udo Kier, Christoph Gräve, Irmgard Al-Hassani, Waltraud Beermeyer-Stöpsel, Ralf Moeller and Gwyneth Q. Brick sit in a semicircle on the floor of the sparsely lit auditorium at the Bonhoeffer Mental Hospital. Then Nico steps thoughtfully into their midst. A single spotlight directly above him magically turns on and illuminates him. Nico breathes heavily and wipes his stringy hair from his face. The whole situation is reminiscent of Klaus Kinski's Jesus monologue in the Deutschlandhalle, after he kicked the majority of the ungrateful fucking audience out the door—like Jesus did with the souvenir dealers in the temple. He had recited his entire text only in front of a handful of people worthy of his genius. And so now Nico gets going:

"Wanted is Nico Pacinsky. Charged with seduction, anarchist

tendencies, conspiracy against state power. Special marks: Scars on heart and soul. Alleged profession: actor. Wanted is Klaus Kinski. Charged with insanity, anarchistic tendencies, conspiracy against state power. Special marks: Scars on mind and body. Alleged profession: actor. Wanted is everybody. Accused of everything. Special characteristics: numb of feeling. Alleged profession: modern man."

Nico pulls his pistol out of his pocket and shoots Fassbinder in the head, who is dead on the spot. A pool of blood forms around him, but this does not shock the audience, which continues to hang spellbound on Nico's lips.

In Valhalla, all the gods then dematerialize, for their last hope has turned against them.

"Dead are quite soon all gods—now it is said that man begins to live. But in what kind of world shall we live? In a germ-free and danger-free one, in which imagined security reigns and in which everyone is halfway satisfied with their shitty situation? I call it a world without freedom, in which nothing but mediocrity rules, in which the great number stands against the individual. A world of yes-men who would gladly exchange any personal responsibility and self-determination for the opportunity to own the latest smartphone and languish undisturbed within their own four walls. We, the others, on the other hand, are looking for danger. In uncertainty and in opposition to everything, we seek affirmation. We say yes to the flawed human being. We say yes to the dangerous human being. To the human being in general.

We are ready to bear any risk even for our own body and mind. We reject the society that tries to suppress and kill the individual in favor of the masses. In China, social point systems already exist. The smallest offenses, such as running a red light, are recorded by thousands and thousands of cameras, reported, and then sanctioned with social credit deductions so that, for example, one can no longer go on vacation or to the theater. It seems only a matter of time before such measures are also introduced in Europe. The technical possibilities are there, and the will of politicians in their cross-party prohibition and surveillance frenzy is heading in the same fatal direction.

You can also already hear the voices of the citizens who support any measure, no matter how inhumane, as long as it is only directed against the others. We say no to the surveillance state. No to witch hunts on the Internet. No to denunciation, propaganda and hatred. No to double standards and any attempt to tame the human beast. No to cancel culture and moral fascism.

We, on the other hand, clearly say yes to every human weakness, to danger, to terror, because without these we see not only a flattening of man, but even his own transgression. We will not oppose our opponents. We will bear and endure any opposition, no matter from whom it comes, and even encourage it. For it is precisely in this that we see our greatest possible love of man and find our confirmation. We want to take the next step. Without gods. Without states. Without institutions. Without leaders. Our only rule is the inevitable love of man with all his inherent flaws and weaknesses. The protection of the individual from the masses and the promotion of individualism shall be the supreme goal of our work.

Our yes is an unconditional yes to everything and everyone. To every horror and to everything beautiful that our species is capable of. All gods are soon dead. So are Rainer Werner Fassbinder and Klaus Kinski. Dead was also me, Nico Pacinsky. But in *They will claim that I was dead...* I will perhaps continue to exist until I am understood and my being thus becomes superfluous. But even if that doesn't happen, so be it. At least we'll have had our fun."

All listeners are speechless due to Nico's powerful monumental monologue and await his instruction on how to proceed. Dr. Plump is the first to blurt out, "And what do we do now?"

Without another word, Verne Zog and Christoph Gräve rise. They stand right next to Nico, so that the triumvirate forms a kind of artist phalanx. They smile and nod knowingly at each other. But Dr. Plump and Magnus Max now also seem to understand and rise to begin their work. All the other inmates of the asylum come out of their cells and follow the example of our friends. And only a little later the stage in the auditorium of the asylum is ready again. The performance can begin:

———

Dense and random cloud formations obscure the sunlight over an undulating expanse of land. The wind sighs, ushering in sheets of light drizzle. On a distant hilltop, a group of people has gathered in an apparent state of excitement. Some throw stones and churn up the sand with their feet. All are clad in archaic garb. On either side of the group, two wooden crosses have been rammed into the ground. A person has been nailed to each cross—one black woman, and one white. Both women are dead. Between their crosses gapes a third hole in the ground.

A murmur sweeps through the crowd, as six men in SS-uniforms approach, pushing a seventh man out in front. It is Nico Pacinsky, dressed in nothing but a tattered loin cloth and bleeding from several wounds on his body. Behind, six Japanese soldiers in the Tenno army uniform with silver heatproof Zetex gloves carry a red-hot, glowing crucifix. The drizzle is fast developing into fat raindrops that dissipate with a hiss as they hit the cross. Behind them, six Italian Blackshirts play a military march on their drums. At the sight of the two crucified women up ahead, as well as the hole in the ground between them, a listless and exhausted Nico registers the imminent end of the path. He begins to mutter under his breath:

"Wanted: Jesus Christ. Accused of seduction, anarchic tendencies, conspiring against the state. Distinguishing feature: scars on the hands and feet."

AFTERWORD
BY NIKOLAI KINSKI

"Wow"
- Nikolai Kinski

Milton Keynes UK
Ingram Content Group UK Ltd.
UKHW041723260324
440099UK00004B/79